McAnear, Sharon,
Taste of gold /

Meijer Branch
Jackson District Library   8/11/2017

Y0-ASQ-475

WITHDRAWN

CON_____   HAN_____

PAR_____   SAR_____

Taste of Gold

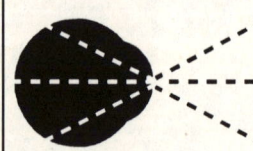
This Large Print Book carries the Seal of Approval of N.A.V.H.

Taste of Gold

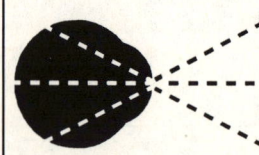
This Large Print Book carries the Seal of Approval of N.A.V.H.

HOMETOWN TEXAS GIRL TRILOGY,
BOOK 3

TASTE OF GOLD

SHARON MCANEAR

THORNDIKE PRESS
A part of Gale, Cengage Learning

GALE
CENGAGE Learning·

Farmington Hills, Mich • San Francisco • New York • Waterville, Maine
Meriden, Conn • Mason, Ohio • Chicago

Copyright © 2008 by Sharon McAnear.
Hometown Texas Girl Trilogy #3.
All scripture quotations are taken from the King James Version of the Bible.
Thorndike Press, a part of Gale, Cengage Learning.

ALL RIGHTS RESERVED
This book is a work of fiction. References to real people, events, establishments, organizations, or locales are intended only to provide a sense of authenticity, and are used fictitiously. All other characters, incidents, and dialogue are drawn from the author's imagination.
Thorndike Press® Large Print Christian Historical Fiction.
The text of this Large Print edition is unabridged.
Other aspects of the book may vary from the original edition.
Set in 16 pt. Plantin.

LIBRARY OF CONGRESS CATALOGING-IN-PUBLICATION DATA

Names: McAnear, Sharon.
Title: Taste of gold / by Sharon McAnear.
Description: Large print edition. | Waterville, Maine : Thorndike Press, 2016. | © 2008 | Series: Thorndike Press large print Christian historical fiction | Series: Hometown Texas girl trilogy ; 3
Identifiers: LCCN 2015041224 | ISBN 9781410485687 (hardcover) | ISBN 1410485684 (hardcover)
Subjects: LCSH: Large type books. | GSAFD: Christian fiction. | Western stories.
Classification: LCC PS3613.C2659 T37 2016 | DDC 813/.6—dc23
LC record available at http://lccn.loc.gov/2015041224

Published in 2016 by arrangement with Barbour Publishing, Inc.

Printed in Mexico
1 2 3 4 5 6 7 20 19 18 17 16

For
Mother and Daddy

Sweet Attitude

Texas wind, like a pack of coyotes,
Not truly evil, only nature's due.
Yet hear it howl as earth is hurled
Toward the humble and those vain few.

Is there no escape for its victims?
Must they endure relentless pain
Like hapless, fenced-in cattle,
Hearts and heads lowered in the rain?

Not me. I'll not cower at the threat
Of giant dusters nor deadly twisters;
No dark sky gloom for me foretold.
I'll kiss, instead, the honeyed dawn
For the bittersweet taste of gold.
— Jemmabeth Chase

The good folks of Chillaton are talking
about newlyweds Jemmabeth and
Spencer Chase
and how crazy in love they are.
But not everybody's happy about it. . . .

Chapter 1
Married Men

Darrell Nelson, class clown of '61, aimed the spotlight at them in the gym bleachers, and Spencer and Jemmabeth Chase squinted into the beam. Spence grinned, then laid a second kiss on his wife, before she had her breath back. This moment would be the hot topic at Nedra's Beauty Parlor & Craft Nook for weeks, so Spencer figured he might as well enjoy himself. Darrell was supposed to be setting up to highlight the homecoming queen, but he couldn't resist exposing the popular newlywed alumni instead, eliciting wolf whistles from their peers, mixed with shocked gasps from the more aged alumni seated below.

On the gym floor, a pair of dark eyes followed the couple's every move, and red lips coiled into a wicked smile. So what if Jemmabeth Forrester had finally become Mrs. Spencer Chase? Nothing was ever set in stone. Things could always change and Melissa Blake was up to any challenge, especially when it came to Spencer.

Melissa, covertly known in high school as The Cleave for her magnificent bosom, edged over to talk with Twila Baker for lack of excitement and an escort.

"You forgot your name tag, Missy. Here, pin this on." Twila shoved a CLASS OF '63 label at her. "I thought you were engaged to a doctor. What happened?"

"I don't use Missy anymore. I'm Melissa now, remember? I've been Melissa for several years." The Cleave threw back her mane of blond hair. "It didn't work out with the med student. He said he was too busy for partying. Twila, you really should get your nails done since you work at a beauty shop." She rolled her eyes toward the bleachers. "What's the deal with those two? Nobody acts like that once they're married."

Twila didn't like The Cleave bossing her around, nor did she care for her tone about the newlyweds. She smiled up at them. "They are the most romantic couple ever. It's like a fairy tale."

"I don't know why I'm asking you, one of Jemmartsybeth's fan club. Anyway, it's more like creepy," Missy said. "It's not like they haven't been boyfriend and girlfriend since birth."

"I wish Buddy and I could say that." Twila patted her generous stomach. "Of course, we have other things to think about now."

"If they keep it up, Jemma's going to be borrowing your tent tops before she planned to. Getting pregnant is the ultimate disaster for people like me. It ruins your figure and you get little stretch marks that don't look good in a bikini." The Cleave turned to check out a young male teacher.

"That guy's married, Missy. How would you know about stretch marks, anyway? I've never looked good in a one-piece, much less a bikini. I bet Jemma does, though. She's got the figure for it."

"She's too tall. I'm about as tall as you can get and still look . . . what's that word . . . to men."

Twila raised her shoulders. "Half naked? No, I reckon that's two words."

"You don't even know what I'm talking about. Vul . . . vul . . ."

"Vulture? Vulgar? How come I know more words than you do? I didn't even get to college."

"*Vunerable*. That's it. I still look vunerable to men," Missy said. "Jemma probably

13

won't even let him dance with anybody else."

"I never heard that word before. You sure you're sayin' it right?" Twila counted the ticket money again, making sure the bills were all facing the same way. She hoped Missy would leave, but she parked herself, instead, on the edge of the table. An elderly attendee dropped her jaw at Missy's miniskirt.

"Everything always goes so perfect for Miss Artsy," Missy said. "It's like she has some special secret or something, and don't throw that religious junk at me either. My mother heard that she and Spence go to the colored church about half the time. She also says that if Brother Hightower had any backbone, he would have them kicked out of his church for praying across the tracks. My family doesn't need church. Daddy says he's just as close to God watching *Goldfinger* as he would be if he were listening to some idiot trying to make him feel guilty. Anyway, where's Jemma's Twinkie? I wish she'd had a baby. It would have totally ruined her figure."

"Sandy's livin' in Idaho. Marty got a job up there on a potato farm, working for his uncle, but I don't think Sandy likes it very much. How about you, Missy? What are you doing now that you've graduated from UT?" Twila paused to take ticket money from a cluster of blue-haired ladies.

"Twila, can you say Mah-liss-ah? You should get a frost job on your hair. It would soften that dishwater-blond look." She fingered her own flaxen tresses. "I work for an accountant in Amarillo, and my boss says that he couldn't make it through the day without me."

"Oh, that's right," Twila said. "I heard your mom say that you were wastin' your education in the copy room. Are those machines hard to run?"

"I may go out to Hollywood and get in the movies. It wouldn't be all that hard since my daddy owns nine movie theaters now — he has the connections." Melissa turned her attention back to the bleachers. "Look at them. Too bad she didn't marry that cowboy from Dallas. I heard he's a wild man."

"Give it up, Missy. You never had a chance with Spencer and you know it. You always were so jealous of Jemma."

"Shut up. I've never been jealous of anybody." Missy curled her lip. "I just remember how good he looked in his football uniform."

"Guys all look alike in those."

"Then you weren't looking very well."

"I only had eyes for Buddy B." Twila squinted toward the stage where her husband's band was setting up. "Anyway, Spencer is married now, so it's too late."

"It's never, ever too late." Missy cut her indigo eyes again at the Chases.

Twila's baby kicked as Melissa Blake, the only girl in their class who could afford braces, eased off the table and slithered away.

Twila rearranged the name tags and smoothed her new maternity top over her middle. She had to be doing something right. The homecoming committee had put her in charge of the registration table for the third year in a row. She moved her chair under her own handmade sign, 1869–1969: ONE HUNDRED YEARS OF CHILLATON HIGH SCHOOL. The sign wasn't easy to make, either, what with her big belly and all. Not to mention she had to do it over after Leon Shafer told her there was no apostrophe in *years*. Smart aleck. No wonder he was still single.

The old gymnasium glistened with twisted maroon and white crepe-paper streamers, gold balloons, and gold confetti that littered the hardwood floor. Early alumni, who would rather not sit on concrete bleachers and endure the chilly autumn football game, had dutifully signed their name tags. They engaged in hushed conversations on folding chairs that lined the gym, waiting for the onslaught of the after-game crowd and the musical gyrations that would follow.

A wayward sparrow had also entered the gym. It repeatedly propelled itself into a closed window, thus stirring some excitement for those with corrective lenses. The janitor and Buddy Baker finally guided it to an open pane. Ladies fresh from Nedra's Beauty Parlor and Craft Nook heaved a collective sigh of relief that their various shades of lavender and blue coiffures would not be soiled from above. This brush with anxiety, however, would be given some verbal attention because nothing much escaped Nedra's Nook. The sign in the window put her gossip mill on the map: HAIR'S WHERE IT ALL BEGINS. Twila waved at Buddy B and grinned so wide that she loosened the spit curl from her cheek that Nedra had plastered with Aqua Net.

Unless they were preoccupied marking off days in the county jail, graduates showed up faithfully to the CHS Homecoming. Legendary reunion stories of selflessness and sacrifice were handed down like family legacies. On one such occasion, the notorious Donnie Pitts, class of '58, snuck out of the county facility by hiding in the jail Dumpster when he was trusted to empty the trash. He rinsed off in the river and showed up at the 1960 CHS homecoming celebration, only to be arrested by Sheriff Ezell during the first dance. Cleta Naylor, class of 1899, claimed she hadn't missed a homecoming in seventy years, but had passed away a month shy of this one. Her parting words were cordial expressions of regret to the homecoming committee. That was how Panhandle people did things. This year would be no exception as far as Twila could tell. She had already collected well over three hundred dollars, and the evenin' was young, as they say in Texas.

Twila kept an eye on Jemma and Spencer, but not so they'd notice. Like she'd said, they were the perfect couple, always had been. Jemmabeth had that long, wavy auburn hair that Twila had always wanted, plus she'd been Miss Everything at CHS. Now she was putting Chillaton on the map with her art but was still a sweet girlfriend. It was only her second month to be Mrs. Spencer Chase, Mr. Everything. He was, in everybody's opinion, the cutest boy to ever graduate from CHS. Besides being the quarterback, he was consistently class favorite, class president, and finally, class valedictorian. Now that he was over twenty-one, he was the richest man in the Panhandle. Sometimes Twila dreamed about being married to him herself. In her dreams they traveled all over the world inspecting the humongous buildings he had designed as an architect, and every night he proposed to her all over again because she was so beautiful and smart.

Spencer and Jemma emerged from the bleachers and visited with some of the older alumni. All heads turned because there was just something about them. They were such good people, Twila thought, but things had not always been perfect for them. Jemma nearly croaked in that wreck, then Spencer went missing in Vietnam. Missy just saw what she wanted to. What most people didn't know was that the couple had made a promise in the eighth grade to not fool around until they were married. That's probably why now they couldn't carry on a decent conversation without looking around the room to find one another. It wasn't pathetic at all; it was their reward for keeping the promise.

Twila scratched her belly. She and Buddy B tried to have a pact like that, but it was too hard to keep. They'd been married now for six years, so surely it was safe to have a baby and not get talked about at Nedra's.

The Buddy Baker Band blasted out their first number, "Try a Little Tenderness." Buddy B had added a little zip by pulling in Toby Watkins to play the saxophone. Leon Shafer, Dwayne Cummins, and Wade Pratt had been in Buddy's band since high school. It wouldn't be homecoming without them.

Jemma and Spencer moved onto the floor, never losing eye contact and moving, as always, like smooth satin. Spencer wore his signature black turtleneck, and Jemma's long legs were tucked into knee boots topped with a leather skirt and a white silk blouse, both purchased by her husband.

"Go home with me, woman," he said over the music.

She gave him The Look. "I keep it in mind," she said, using their private joke from an old Paul Newman movie.

The gym filled quickly after the game. The Cleave followed Spencer to the refreshment table when Jemma finally took a break.

"Hi there, old married man." Missy poked a manicured finger into his chest. She moved in close so that her neckline displayed her namesake. "Wanna dance? Unless, of course, you aren't allowed to do things like that with me anymore." Her eyes roamed around his face.

Spencer smiled, somewhat. "I'm probably allowed, but I think I'll sit this one out."

"C'mon, are you scared of her? There was a time when you weren't."

"Nope. Not scared, just don't want to, Melissa. Thanks, anyway." Spencer walked away to have a few words with Darrell, the spotlight man.

Missy was ruffled. Spencer had never really dated her, but when he and Jemma broke up for a year in college, she had gone out with him a few times. She should have seized the moment then and hooked him somehow, but he never had had eyes for anybody except her old archrival, the ever-present Jemmabeth Forrester. He could have at least danced one little song with her. It wouldn't have killed him.

"Jemmabeth Chase, come on up here," Buddy B schmoozed into the microphone. "Until recently, Jemma has been singing in our band. Let's give her a round of applause and maybe she'll help us out one more time." The band played the intro to "Chain of Fools."

Jemma stepped up to the mike. The saxophone sounded good. She took a deep breath and let loose her husky alto voice. Spencer didn't think he would ever get over being her husband. He was practically in a trance when she finished.

He led her outside and pinned her against the bricks. "That's it. We're going home or to the river. Take your pick. Did you sing like that when I was in Vietnam?"

"Sure. It was your big idea, mister," she said. "You wanted me to sing with the band so you could think about me being happy."

"I didn't know you would be belting out soul music and making every guy in the gym grin like Gomer Pyle."

"I looked right at you the whole time."

"I know, but the gym's not exactly empty. You are too much for me to handle." He ran his finger under her chin. "Now let's go home. I'll warm up the 'Vette."

"Nope. Buddy's gonna play 'Candy Man' in a minute, and I've been looking forward to it."

"We can dance at the apartment. Mr. Orbison sings it better anyway." He knew the pout she was giving him. "Okay, just 'Candy Man,' then we're gone." The wind kicked up and flapped a homecoming banner against the building. Jemma's hair swirled around her like an open umbrella. He kissed her again.

"Cut that out and let's go back inside," she said and dragged him away just in time for their special version of the Chillaton Stomp.

Melissa Blake left when Spencer curled his finger at Jemma as she danced around him. He never even took his eyes off his bride to check out Missy's new red miniskirt. She'd bought it just in the hope that he would.

Meanwhile, the frazzled sparrow blinked and shook his head again. The world remained somewhat out of focus since his collision with the window. He hopped along the telephone line a few feet, then darted off, away from the loud gymnasium and its tricky windows. The sparrow's path was aligned for a few blocks with that of a silver Corvette. They parted ways at the flashing red light where Main Street met the state highway to Amarillo. The little bird rested on the line again as the Corvette's tires squealed into action below, headed for home.

Lizbeth Forrester and Lester Timms were an hour early, as planned. Now they had plenty of extra time to spend in the waiting room of the Amarillo airport. On top of that, the loudspeaker blasted out the news that the flight was going to be late.

Lizbeth had chosen to wear her best Sunday dress. She would be wearing the same outfit to church the next day, and was relieved to see nobody else from Chillaton was at the airport. She paced around with her Sunday purse dangling securely from her folded arms.

Lester adjusted his wedding/funeral tie and double-checked that his new white shirt was tucked into his khakis. He'd been yakking nonstop. "Like I've said before, Miz Liz, when I worked for the Burlington Line there weren't near as many late runs with the railroad like there are with the airplane business. No, sir, we kept things goin'." He squinted and checked his gold watch for the tenth time.

"We've been over this before, Lester. The trains were not always punctual. That's just your convenient memory at work. Besides, you were the stationmaster. How could you keep the trains on time? Wouldn't that be the engineer's job?" Lizbeth touched her hair to see if Nedra had sprayed it well enough to withstand the steady surge of Panhandle wind predicted through the weekend.

"Well, sir, you'd be surprised. There was

the ticketin' of the passengers. That's a whole other story. I took care of the mail — comin' and goin'. Now, that was a job and a half, and I was the signalman to boot. When them trains come through, I was one busy feller, and if I was the least bit behind, they could get even behinder."

"I suppose you were rebuilding the track when there wasn't a train coming."

"No, sir, that was somebody else's job. I had to do the bookwork, you know, keepin' account of folks and packages, plus there was the telegraph to run. Did I ever tell you about the time that I caught Shorty Knox rummagin' through the parcel post cart? We like to have scared each other to death."

The arrival of the flight interrupted him.

"I think I missed that story," Lizbeth said, watching the attendants open the double doors for emerging passengers.

Lester felt his silver moustache again for crumbs. It wasn't often that a man his age got to shine in the presence of two fine-looking widow women.

Helene Neblitt, dressed in a royal blue linen suit with her white hair impeccably tucked into a bun, was one of the last passengers to appear. She adjusted her hearing aid, then smiled.

"Hello, my dear ones," she said, coming

toward them with outstretched arms. "Lester, you are looking quite dapper today," she added in her Cambridge-educated accent.

Lester blushed. She always made him feel like he was Errol Flynn.

"Helene, you never look like you have been traveling. How do you manage that?" Lizbeth asked.

"It's my English upbringing, I suppose. We were so proper that neither a wrinkle nor a wisp of hair would dare appear, unbidden. I am quite grateful to be away from the bustle of Dallas."

"I'll fetch your bags, Miz Helene; you two ladies just relax." Lester strode off, carrying himself upright as best he could. He admired Helene's perfect posture and didn't want to look any older than he was.

An hour later, they sat around Lizbeth's shiny chrome and yellow kitchenette in Chillaton, drinking coffee and catching up on things.

"So, tell me, how are Jemmabeth and Spencer?" Helene asked.

Lizbeth smiled. "They are the happiest pair you'll ever see. It'll make you feel good just to be around them."

"Married life sure does agree with them

two, and it don't look like it's about to wear thin, neither." Lester tapped his foot on the uneven black-and-white-checkered linoleum. "I never had that kind of lovey-dovey feelin' last this long with any of my women folk, exceptin' maybe Pretty Paulette." He shifted in his chair and blushed at that memory.

"Jemma and Spencer could have one of those romantic marriages that one reads about now and again," Helene said. "When may I expect to see them?" The way she said *Zhemma* instead of Jemmer enchanted Lester.

"They'll drive down from Amarillo tomorrow. She's anxious to tell you about their honeymoon in Scotland. I think she has more than a few painting ideas from the trip. My Cameron always wanted to see Scotland. It was his parents' homeland. I think Jemmabeth wanted to go there because of that. She's just like her grandfather, I suppose." Lizbeth smiled at the thought of Cam in his father's kilt on every holiday, worn sometimes just so she could pretend to be irritated with him for showing his legs.

Across the tracks, Joe Cross put the last of the dishes away and changed into his Sunday-go-to-meetin' shirt. His wife sang in the bathroom as she finished up her primping. He smiled. He didn't know how good things could be in this world. The Lord had heaped blessings on him, but letting him marry Willa Johnson in his early middle years was the best one of all. Willa made him laugh, cooked better than he ever did in the Coast Guard, danced like a Methodist woman, and best of all, she had a heart for the Lord.

"What are you thinkin' about, Joe?" she asked, peeking around the door.

"You. I was countin' my blessings, and you're all of 'em rolled into one."

"Come here and let me kiss you for that."

He went. He'd be a fool not to take her up on that offer.

"You are lookin' mighty fine tonight, Mrs. Cross. Maybe we should just stay home, lovey."

"We'll be home early. I gotta go see Miz Helene and find out how my baby's doin' at that fancy school. Ain't nobody nicer than them two white women. They're my travelin' buddies, too. Both of 'em got college degrees. Did you know that?"

Joe nodded and helped her down the steps, then tucked the cobbler she'd baked under his arm. It was still warm.

"You sure you don't want to ride over?"

he asked.

"No, sir, I'm walkin'. The doctor said I needed to work this old leg, and I'm gonna do it. Now, you see if you can keep up with me." She took off at a slow but steady pace across the road and up toward the tracks. They might as well have been teenagers the way they carried on, but she loved it.

"I thought I could hear somethin' besides Texas being spoke," Willa shouted through Lizbeth's back porch screen. She came inside and spread her arms like an eagle, then lifted Helene's petite frame off the floor.

"You are maneuvering much better," Helene said. "What has become of your cane?"

Willa laughed. "Don't need that old stick now that I had me some work done on my hip. It pays to marry a rich man," she whispered.

"Drivin' a semi don't exactly make me a rich man, lovey." Joe set his cowboy hat on the foldout kitchen stool and smiled at the women, wondering if they'd seen him carrying on with Willa on the tracks. The floor creaked as he moved to stand beside her.

"Here, you two have a seat," Lizbeth said. "Joe, would you like some coffee?"

"Thank you, ma'am, I'd be obliged.

Willa's been spoilin' me with her cookin'. My mouth was waterin' the whole time I was carrying that cobbler. How are you doin', Miz Helene?"

"Everything is lovely, thank you. Marriage seems to be the rage around here. I guess I'll have to find me a companion," she said.

Lester cleared his throat. "I hear lots of hammerin' across the tracks. How's your project comin' along, Joe?"

"We're movin' ahead right smart with the remodelin'. 'Course I'm not here all the time, so it's been a slow deal."

"Folks are gonna start callin' it the Cross castle," Willa said. "It'll be the finest thing ever built in colored town, that's for sure. Exceptin' Spencer's chapel at our church, of course."

"How's Latrina doin', Miz Helene?" Joe asked.

"She's doing well and sends her love. She's very involved with a project of her own right now or she would have come with me."

"It's sure good of you to let my baby girl live with you like this. She's gonna be all cultured up by the time she graduates from that clothes designin' school. I just hope she can find a job," Willa said. "She may have to start cleanin' houses again."

"Quite the contrary, Willa. Trina is very talented. There must be something about your little village that nurtures artistic giftedness to have three outstanding young people emerge from it."

"Panhandle wind," Lester said. "It starts whippin' Chillaton's young folks into shape as soon as they draw breath, sorta like one of them sculptor fellers."

Lizbeth excused herself and went to check the extra bedroom one more time. She wanted everything to be perfect for Helene's stay. She fluffed the pillows again, then walked through the "good" bedroom — hers and Cam's. It was the nicest one, but there was no privacy for a guest since it connected the living room to the kitchen.

Cam liked to tease her about their quirky little house, but she loved it for that very reason. She touched his photograph on the dresser. He would have enjoyed Helene's company, but he really would have gotten a kick out of Willa and Joe, if only he'd taken that first step across the tracks. Lizbeth often wondered if she would've ever made their acquaintance herself, if it weren't for Jemmabeth's example. Lizbeth sighed and returned to the kitchen. She uncovered Willa's cobbler and passed out generous helpings, then scooped out some for herself.

Willa's was always better than hers, and she couldn't figure out her secret. Maybe she could get Joe to tell her.

"Willa, you should enter your cobbler in the fair this year," Lizbeth said. "It's by far the best I've ever tasted. I don't suppose you are willing to share your secret, are you?"

Willa laughed. "Ain't no secret, Miz Liz, just habit. Mercy, them fussy ladies don't want no colored woman stickin' her cobbler on the same shelf as theirs. Joe and me went to the Cotton Festival last month. It was all they could do to let us look at them pies and whatnot. I don't want to stir up no trouble."

"Fiddlesticks," Lizbeth said. "I know all the womenfolk who enter that contest and they are all good, Christian people. You should give it a try."

"Sometimes the Christian folks are the last ones to come around to things, Miz Liz. You know that," Willa said. "That's exceptin' Jemma. Them two girls was brought together by the good Lord Himself."

"All I know for sure is that you are supposed to be calling me Lizbeth on a regular basis. It's taking you a good while to come around to that. I'm going to start calling you Miz Willa if you don't watch out."

Lester raised his brow at Lizbeth. He knew that tone. Funny that she never gave him trouble for calling her Miz Liz. It had to be something about him being a man and her still loving Cameron. He wondered, too, if Cam Forrester ever knew what a lucky old boy he was.

Jemma couldn't wait for Spencer to wake up. Being with him as his wife was more than she could stand. It sometimes made her feel guilty. She wrote her new name on his back, waking him up.

He turned over and smiled. "Mornin', my love," he mumbled.

"I'm going to cook breakfast for you. Do you want cereal or toast?" she asked.

"Hmmm . . . they both sound so delicious, but way too hard for my baby to cook. How about we just snuggle? We can pick up some doughnuts on the way to Chillaton."

Jemma stood up on the bed and hit him with her pillow. "I can cook toast! You take that back." She whacked him again. He grabbed her ankles and threatened to yank her off her feet if she didn't stop.

An hour later, they had forgotten all about breakfast and had to hustle just to arrive at Lizbeth's in time for lunch.

Helene could see what everyone was saying about the newlyweds. They stopped in the hollyhock patch behind the house, laughing and kissing, before they came in. She knew that feeling but hadn't felt it in decades.

Jemma shared her honeymoon photo album and her sketchbook with the group. "I'm working on some portraits that you will like," she said. "Time seems to have stopped in some of the Scottish villages. Our favorite, of course, was Kilton. That's where Papa's family came from. There's even a little castle right on the shore."

"It's not ancient, but it's old enough," Spencer said, rubbing Jemma's shoulders. "It's for sale, too, in case you're interested, Lester."

"How do you like living so close to home?" Helene asked.

"It's great," Spencer said. "Of course we don't really care where we live right now. We're just happy to be together, finally." He refrained from kissing her in front of the silver-haired group, but he considered it.

"Spence just took the architectural job in Amarillo because they were so good to him during his internship there. We won't stay there long."

"They're too conservative for my style, but it's good experience for an upstart like me." Spencer winked at Lester, who liked to call him that.

"Are you thinking of starting a family anytime soon?" Helene asked.

"No." Jemma's inflection made Lizbeth flinch. "We are going to enjoy one another's company without any distractions for a long time."

"I see," Helene said. "Well, don't wait too long, my dears. Nebs and I regretted our decision to postpone that part of our lives."

"I haven't seen Vincent around today," Jemma said, making sure that the baby topic didn't continue.

"Oh, that cat roams all over the neighborhood. He'll show up." Lizbeth opened the door to the walk-in pantry and brought out a three-layered, coconut crème cake, Spencer's favorite. He whistled and made room on the table for it.

"Jemmerbeth, have you made your Gram's coconut cake yet for your mister?" Lester asked, accepting a fat piece for himself.

"No, sir. I haven't learned how to make much of anything yet. Do you think he looks thinner?" She squeezed Spencer's biceps.

"You were learning culinary skills quite well when you were in Wicklow," Helene said. "As I recall, you prepared a whole meal in the continental style, with a little help, of course." Helene savored her first bite of cake, eyes closed in appreciation. She couldn't see Jemma giving her the signal to hush about that summer.

"Jemma's getting ready for her next show right now. She'll take on cooking skills when she has the time," Spencer said.

"Nice one," Jemma whispered.

Spencer looked up with a mouthful and grinned. Jemma touched his chin where a stray shred of coconut rested and put it in her mouth. Spence widened his eyes and raised his brow. She wrinkled her nose at him.

Lizbeth watched their antics with a sudden longing for the early days of her own marriage when she and her Cameron had teased and flirted. She understood Jemma's impassioned reply to the question of starting a family. As much as Lizbeth loved her babies, she would have enjoyed another few years of foolishness with Cam.

"Vincent caught two mice today, both at the same time, Jemma," Helene said, as the great hunter himself took a seat on the windowsill outside. "I saw him carrying them around."

"How did he accomplish that?" Jemma asked.

"I'm not quite sure, but my Chelsea could

take a lesson from him. She does nothing all day but sleep."

"Well, sir, you've got your mousers and your moochers. I had me a time once with some cats," Lester said. "I was between womenfolk when it happened. Must've been between Bertie and Mae Ella. No, sir, I take that back. It was after Zippy run off and, after a few years, The Judge give me the go-ahead to look around for a fourth one."

Lizbeth cleared her throat.

Lester hooked his thumbs under his suspenders that he had only recently begun wearing to hold up his sagging pants. "I took a notion to join the ladies' bridge club, and they seemed real pleased to have me. When it come my turn to be the host, I had the house cleaned up good, and plenty of vittles on the sideboard. All was well until out of nowheres a field mouse come hence to waltzin' across the floor. It sat up on its haunches and grinned right at us. Now you can imagine how embarrassin' that would be in a refined social situation like a bridge club gatherin'. All my prospects for a missus lifted their feet and squealed. That mouse just kept on grinnin' like old Beelzebub himself. I chased him off, but the damage was done." Lester shook his head and tapped his foot on the linoleum.

"Where's the cat in that story?" Lizbeth asked.

"It's comin'. I had me a bigger problem than just the one mouse critter. Seems like word got out that old Lester's place was a rodent hotel. So I come hence to lettin' folks around town know that I was in need of a cat. Well, sir, in one day's time I had me a dozen. I never saw another mouse, but then I had me a cat situation. I took a notion to use 'em to my advantage. I went down to the five-and-dime and bought a sack full of ribbons and tied a bow around every one of them cats, which wasn't easy. I loaded up three at a time in my truck and drove from one bridge-playin' prospect to another and give each one of them ladies a purrin' pet for a present. It was a big hit."

Spencer smiled at Jemma. "Does this mean that the way to a woman's heart is through a cat?"

"I wouldn't go that far, son. Them ladies must have talked amongst themselves because not a single one of 'em would give me the time of day after a week or so. I got kicked out of the bridge club, too, but at least I got rid of the mice. I know how you hate the varmints, Miz Liz."

"I had no idea that you enjoyed bridge, Lester. I'm a founding member of the Wicklow Bridge Club," Helene said. "Find us two more players and we're set. But not to worry, dear, I already have a fat feline at home."

Paul Turner pulled the baby blue pickup into his driveway. He set his briefcase on the kitchen table, hung his Stetson on his great-grandmother's hall tree, then sank on the couch to pull off his new boots. They were killing him. He should've broken them in around the house instead of the courtroom. He leaned back against the cushions and stared at the painting of the girl holding the firefly. She remained his heart's only desire. She made him laugh and feel good about himself until she found out that he was a married man. Actually, he was a separated man, not that such a detail mattered to a good Christian girl like her. It was over with before he could get his mother's ring out of the safety deposit box at the bank. He hadn't lied to her, but he hadn't exactly told her the truth, either. That was his everlasting shame and that's how he had lost his Jemma.

The phone rang, but he let it go. It was probably one of his sisters checking up on him. They would have loved her, too, but he could never risk introducing them. They might have let it slip about his pending divorce. He stretched and looked around his house. No amount of substitutes could fill the void she'd left and he had tried, too. She had made the place come alive with her joy that summer, and she never even stepped foot in it.

Paul unfolded the *Dallas Morning News* while his TV dinner cooled off. He flipped through the sports pages, then, as usual, scanned the arts and entertainment section. There it was on the first page: JEMMABETH CHASE SET TO SHOW AT THE GALLERY AT HIGHLAND PARK. His heart jumped, and he spread the newspaper on the coffee table.

He read it twice, then cut it out and put it on his fridge. It didn't matter to him that she was a married woman now. He couldn't wait to see her.

Jemma knocked on the bathroom door. "Spence, I found some photos of soldiers in Vietnam. Could I use them for the French magazine thing? I need to give them several to choose from. Is that okay?"

Spencer emerged, drying his hair with a towel. "Sure, I haven't had the heart to look at them since I got back. Use whatever you need, baby."

Jemma grinned. "I'm counting to two and

you'd better be back in that bathroom with the door locked, or you're going to be in trouble. One, one and a half."

"Two," Spencer said and was almost late to work.

The extra bedroom was becoming a canvas jungle. She wanted to save space for Spencer to have a desk in the corner. It was her plan to fix up a little office for him, but she had spent all her time on the landscapes and portraits for the Dallas show. The French magazine, *Nouvelle Liberte,* had given her a deadline for the Vietnam pieces. It had only taken her two weeks to paint the five photos she had selected. Three were action scenes, showing Spencer's Medevac team working on the wounded. One showed a member of the team resting on the ground, holding the hand of a young man on a stretcher, and she was just finishing up a group portrait of Spencer's crew celebrating Christmas around a little wire and fabric tree that Jemma had mailed to him.

He came in late. Jemma hadn't even noticed the time, nor had she stopped, even for lunch. "What do you think, babe?" she asked and moved away from the easel for his response.

Spencer sank to the floor and leaned his

head against the wall. He started to speak, but instead, covered his face with his hands.

She dropped her brush. "What have I done? Oh Spence, I'm so sorry."

He tried to say something about being okay, but a fiendish moan shifted around in his throat and then unleashed itself with a fury. He sobbed and Jemma cradled him until it was over. The apartment was totally dark when they stopped talking. It was the first time he had really shared his grief over the horrendous attack on his helicopter and crew in Vietnam. He had confided the details of his own rescue before but always avoided the deaths of his Medevac team members. Jemma had never pressed the topic on the advice of her daddy, Jim. It came out just as he had said it would, when least expected.

They went out for hamburgers and got home late. He was staring at the painting when it was time for their nightly prayer. "Those poor guys. They worked their hearts out." He exhaled and took her hand, then read Psalm 4:8 aloud: " 'I will both lay me down in peace, and sleep: for thou, Lord, only makest me dwell in safety.' "

Jemma bowed her head. "Heavenly Father, we thank You for delivering Spencer from certain death in a time of war. We thank You for the men and women who worked so hard to rescue soldiers despite the dangers, and we pray for the families of those who didn't make it home, that they might find peace in their hearts. Amen."

Chapter 2
English Leather

Jemma took her paintings to Lester's house so he could build shipping crates for them and Lizbeth watched. "Which one do you like best, Gram?" Jemma yelled over Lester's pounding. "Help my life, honey, do I have to choose?" She moved around the room, studying them again. "I like the whole lot. This one is really nice, but I just don't understand how you can paint yourself so well."

Jemma put her arm around her grandmother. "That was easy. Spencer took a hundred photos of me on our honeymoon. I liked the old guy who is showing me the dance step in this painting. He was full of the dickens."

"All of them old fellers look like they're getting a kick out of watchin' you dance, Jemmer. Did Spencer get kindly jealous?" Lester asked.

"Everybody in that pub was three times

our age. It was fun, though."

"A pub?" Lizbeth arched her brow. "Isn't that what they call a bar over there?"

"Yes ma'am, but sometimes it's the only place you can get a meal. At night they had great fiddle music, too. Gram, we didn't drink."

Lizbeth sniffed. "Well, back to my choice. The lady hanging her wash while the children play in the basket reminds me of your daddy. Jimmy loved to get in my laundry basket when he was a baby. I like these, too." She pointed to the four pieces of village children.

Lester stopped hammering. "Nobody asked me yet, but I prefer the boat captain, myself. I helped out on a boat one time. I'll have to tell you about that job. It didn't work out too well, seein' as how I'm not a sailin' man. That castle is mighty good, too. It's like we could just walk in them big doors."

"Thanks. I already sent the watercolors for the magazine to choose from. They are all of soldiers in Vietnam. Mom just told us that my cousin, Trent, will be getting out in January."

"That's wonderful, sugar. I know his father will be glad of that. Isn't he an engineer?" Lizbeth asked.

"Yes ma'am, but they had him calculating formulas to blow up roads and bridges while he was in Vietnam. He didn't get to build anything. Uncle Ted is throwing a big welcome home celebration at his beach house in California. He wants y'all to come, too."

"We'll have to see about that. Lester and I are getting on in years, aren't we?" Lizbeth shouted.

"You bet; these crates will last for years. You'll be fat and sassy with ten young'uns before these wear out, Jemmerbeth," Lester shouted back, banging away.

Lizbeth snickered, then motioned for Jemma to follow her to the car house, Cam's name for their garage, where Jemma had created so many of her masterpieces before she and Spencer married.

"Look at this," Lizbeth said and placed a Mason jar in her hand. "I found it on one of the chairs in the hollyhock patch."

Jemma unscrewed the lid and took out two folded sheets of Big Chief notebook paper. "Oh Gram, these are drawings that Shorty Knox has done. How sweet. He's trying to draw flowers, see?"

Lizbeth frowned at the scribbles. "Hmmm. If you say so. I hope he's not snooping around here again."

"Don't worry, Gram. With his TV and now his drawing hobby, he's too busy to take up the peeping Tom business."

Lizbeth pursed her lips.

Jemma smiled. "Besides, I owe Shorty a lot. I'll draw him something and put the jar back on the chair. He'll like that."

Jemma met Spencer at the airport. It was like they'd been apart for a month rather than all day.

"Mother's coming home the week before Christmas," Spencer said as they drove home. "She looked better than I've ever seen her, but who knows? She's been living in that halfway house for six months, but once she gets home, she may fall back into her old drinking routine."

Jemma thought back to the time at the country club's New Year's dance when Rebecca Chase, not totally drunk, gave her a verbal lambasting for breaking up with her son. "She could surprise you," she managed at last. "How's your dad doing?"

"Surprisingly well. He's going to bring her home himself and he's taking off a week from work to help her adjust. He really turned on the charm in Waco, but it makes me nervous — like he's up to something."

"I think your dad has changed his ways,

Spence. He and I had some good talks when you were in Vietnam and I like him."

Spencer frowned at her. "Are you sure he wasn't trying to hit on you? I wouldn't put it past him."

"Spencer! He was really sweet and remorseful. He was afraid that you would be punished for his skirt-chasing sins and never come home."

"Yeah, well, he *has* been decent to me since I got home, but I bet it won't last. It'll be a contest to see what happens first — Mother gets drunk or Dad gets a new lady friend." He threw the Corvette into another gear and they flew down the highway. Jemma looked over her shoulder to see if there were any police cars trying to keep up.

"Rats. I don't want to go alone," Jemma said, throwing toiletries in her makeup bag. "It's not fair for them to make you change your plans. It's our first time apart."

"I agree, baby, but I'm the low man on the totem pole. It'll be exciting when you get back. Just think about that. You call me as soon as you get there and every morning and night."

Spencer insisted that she fly and rent a car in Dallas for her show. He also wanted her to stay in a hotel and not go to Helene's. Cowboy lawyer Paul lived too close to Helene. Paul was the only competition that Spencer had ever worried about. Those feelings were history now, but it crept around in Spencer's mind, especially when she went anywhere near Dallas.

They compromised on her accommodations. She stayed Friday night with Helene and Trina, then Saturday, the opening day of the show, she booked a hotel room near the airport so she'd be ready to get home Sunday evening.

A persistent drizzle seemed to bring out the art patrons. Jemma visited with the last few attendees on the soggy evening and looked around for Anne, the gallery manager, to say good-bye. She spotted a reporter from the *Dallas Morning News* and ducked behind a group of patrons. She did not enjoy being interviewed nor did she like being photographed by anyone but family. Someone else, however, touched her arm.

"Hello, darlin'," Paul said. "Are you trying to hide from me again?"

Jemma caught her breath. He was every bit as good-looking as the last time she saw him. His six-foot-five frame was leaner, too. His hair was a little longer, and those devil eyes were even greener. He had on his usual cowboy formal attire — white Western shirt, bolo tie, boots, and black felt hat. English Leather remained his aftershave of choice. She couldn't help it; her scalp tingled and her tongue twisted. "Paul, I'm just about to leave."

He grinned at her. "I like your work, but I like the real thing even better. You are one breathtaking woman, Jemmabeth." He moved a lock of her hair away from her forehead. She felt his hand touch her waist. A slight movement at her elbow caught her attention, and the flash of a reporter's camera brought her out of her daze.

"Miss Forrester," the reporter began.

"Mrs. Chase," Jemma corrected him.

Ignoring the correction, the reporter carried on with his questions. Jemma was polite but gave no details in her responses. She was aware that Paul had remained by her side and continued to keep his hand on her waist. She moved it away with her elbow, but it went right back and stayed there until the reporter left.

"I know you're glad that's over. At least he didn't ask who your favorite artists are," Paul whispered, implying a former awareness.

Jemma turned on him, her golden eyes

narrowed squarely on his. "Move your hand, Paul." He complied, displaying his hands innocently. "Thank you," she said and hurried toward the exit.

He walked alongside her. "I just like to check on you, darlin'. I'm not breaking any laws. I keep up with that, you know. Besides, I'm one of your best customers."

"Then as a lawyer, you should know you walk a fine line between friendliness and harassment toward me." Jemma picked up her pace.

Paul moved in front of her as they reached the foyer. "Look, Jem, I did what you said. I tried hard to find somebody to love. I even went to church once. There is nobody else I want. I know you love your husband, so what would it hurt for you to spend one evening with me? We could go to the Best Burger Stop. You'd be in control, I promise."

"No. I don't have anything to say to you. I don't love you, so get on with your life. Good-bye." She shoved the revolving door and stepped into the blowing rain.

"Jemmabeth, wait." A jet screamed above them in the night sky. "You don't know what it's like for me. Okay, I messed up by not telling you that I wasn't quite divorced, but you were so innocent. I was afraid I'd lose you. Now I've lost you anyway."

"It wasn't in God's plan, Paul," Jemma shouted over her shoulder. "I never stopped loving Spencer. You just stole my attention for a while. Now, please, leave me alone."

"C'mon, Jem, I've made a wild ride of this life. The women I've had meant nothing to me, but it was different with you. I loved you, darlin'. You wouldn't let me try anything, and I liked that. I need that feeling again. I loved being with you and just talking. What's the harm in that now?"

Lightning flashed, silhouetting the buildings, and raindrops freckled her face. He wiped them off her nose.

Jemma recoiled at his touch. "Go back to church, Paul. Maybe you'll find God. At the least, you might find a good woman there, but don't try your tricks with her."

"She won't be you. I can't help it that you put a spell on me. I can't shake it even after all this time. Besides, I have to tell you something," he said, touching her chin. "I need to explain more about that night of no mercy."

"Yeah, right. You mean the night of big truth? Why don't you write it on a business card and mail it to me? No, mail it to my husband. I bet he'd be interested in what you have to say, but I'm not."

"You hold that against me, too, don't you?

I did everything wrong."

"Look, I've tried to be patient with this obsessive behavior of yours, but it's getting old. Now move; you're blocking my car."

"I love you, Jem," he said as she unlocked the door and slid in.

He bent down and pressed his hands against the window like a little boy looking in a candy store.

She rolled it down a little. "Paul, please, I have the life I want with Spencer. I adore him. We've been through this before, and it's time to let it go. You can't spend your whole life chasing after me. Remember the fireflies? You can't keep me bottled up like this in your head. You need to give me my freedom."

Paul squatted beside the car, head down. Rain dripped off the brim of his hat. "I know." He raised tear-filled eyes to hers. "Even though I was drunk, those last kisses I took from you have lasted me a long time. Could I have one while I'm sober?"

"No! What kind of wife do you think I am? I'm sorry that you can't find somebody to love, but I won't feed your fire. Good-bye, Paul."

She took her foot off the brake and let the car roll. He stood up. She backed out and left him standing in the parking lot.

Spencer met her at the airport with a rose. His arms felt so good around her. "I missed you, baby. Are you tired? I don't think I've ever seen you like this, not even after the Lido game when you scored thirty points."

"Yeah, I guess I might be tired, but I'm glad to see you, too." She rested her head on his shoulder so he couldn't see her eyes. "I think I need some sleep."

"I can't believe I'm hearing this after our first full weekend apart." He felt her forehead. "You really must be getting sick or something. Get thee to bed, woman," he said as they pulled into the apartment complex.

Jemma crawled under the covers. She decided not to tell Spence about the encounter. She didn't want Paul interfering with their bliss, as though she weren't worrying about it already.

Spencer lay beside her, stroking her cheek. "I hope you have sweet dreams and feel better tomorrow."

Rats on her worries; she couldn't resist him. Jemma reached for his face and kissed him. Big-time.

■ ■ ■ ■

The apartment was quiet when she got up the next morning. Spencer had said something about an early appointment. She put on his robe and went downstairs, yawning. She got out the cereal and dumped some in her bowl, spilling a little of it on the counter. Popping the spilled bits in her mouth, she turned to get the milk and choked.

Taped to the refrigerator was a clipping from the *Dallas Morning News.* The photo was very clear. *Jemmabeth Forrester,* the caption read, *and an unnamed companion at The Gallery at Highland Park.* Paul was right beside her, his hand on her waist.

She ran to the phone with her heart pounding in her ears. Spencer's number rang, but he didn't answer — probably on purpose. She threw on some jeans and a paint shirt and raced to the bus stop, barefooted, just as it pulled away. She went home and called a taxi.

The smartly dressed secretaries looked up as she burst into the office. "I have to see Spencer."

"May I say who wishes to see him?" the older one asked, like they didn't recognize her.

Jemma was in no mood for games. "His wife."

There was an exchange of smug glances that she didn't miss.

"He's in a meeting right now, but I'll show you to his office." The younger of the two led the way to Spencer's corner of a vacant conference room. Jemma walked the floor for half an hour. She touched the things on his desk. Right by his phone was their wedding picture and next to it was a photo of her in the first grade wearing her red cowboy boots and a frilly dress. All she could think about was that telegram saying he was MIA. This was going to spoil their joy and change things. Tears, long overdue, poured out. She sat in his chair and tried to quell the urge to throw up.

The door opened and closed.

"Jemmabeth. I suppose we are going to talk about something," Spencer said with the same chilly voice that he had when he left for Italy three years ago, when he had found out the truth about Paul.

Jemma jumped up and rattled off her side of the story, replete with wild gestures. "Spence, I swear to you that nothing happened in Dallas for me to be ashamed of, I promise. He showed up just as that photo was taken and put his hand on my waist.

Babe, you have to believe me. He followed me to the parking lot and wanted to talk. I told him to go to church and to forget about me. It's the newspapers. They always assume things and get mixed up. I am so sorry. You know that I love you. Please forgive me for not telling you. I just wanted the whole thing to go away."

Spencer didn't move. Jemma wanted to hold him, but the iceberg that sank the *Titanic* loomed up between them. His phone rang, but his glare never wavered.

"I thought we were going to be honest in our marriage, Jem. I'm curious to know why you decided not to tell me about this. If I'd known, it wouldn't have been such a shock to see it in the newspaper. Can you imagine how that photo made me feel?"

Jemma clamped her hand over her mouth and nodded. She had messed up again. They were perfect until now, and it had to be her that ruined it. She was back to her Miss Scarlett days. She wanted to throw herself out the window. Instead, she got on her knees, like the beggar that she was. "I told you a long time ago that I don't deserve you. I'm just a fool. I tried to protect your feelings and instead I hurt you. I didn't want to spoil how we are, were. I am bad, Spence. I am a mean woman, just like you've said before."

Spencer sat on the floor next to her, keeping an arm's length between them. "You can't protect my feelings by hiding something like this from me. I'm a big boy, and it's not like I'm going to shoot the guy or something. We could've handled this together, like adults."

"I forgot about the photographer," she sobbed.

"Jem, that picture isn't the worst of this. It's that you kept the whole thing from me. I trusted you to take care of him, but Paul is obsessed with you and you don't seem to understand the danger of that. Besides, I don't think you know how I feel about him. I think he's a sorry jerk, but you obviously still have feelings for him or you would let me get a restraining order against him."

The crying came to an abrupt halt. "Excuse me? I do *not* have feelings for him! That is absolutely untrue." They both stood, and she looked him in the eye. "I didn't want him butting into this beautiful life we have, so I didn't tell you, and now look what's happened. You are my life. Paul came along back when what I really needed was you. I feel sorry for him now and that's it. I can't believe that you would even say such a thing! Don't you know me?"

Jemma turned toward the door and didn't stop. She was careful not to slam it, though, as she had been known to do when steaming mad. She even forced a smile at the secretaries as she left to prevent further looks between them. She bawled in the cab home, then tried to paint.

It was almost nine o'clock when she heard him. She'd gone to bed at eight to avoid another scene and had cried herself into a red-eyed mess.

Spencer turned on the television and watched mindlessly as shapes and colors flashed by on the screen. It was their first real fight since he had gone to Florence and left her to choose between him and Paul. When he opened the newspaper and saw the photograph, he was shot straight through the heart. He knew she loved him and he believed her story about the picture, but he didn't understand why she hadn't warned him. A friend of Jemma's told him once that artists don't think like other people do. He knew that. It was with her heart that she painted and that was the same way she lived her life. He had let Paul get to him. He wasn't mad at Jemma because he knew her too well. He didn't need anybody to tell him that she functioned on emotion.

He was angry with Paul.

He went upstairs to their room and could tell that she was breathing through her mouth. He knew she had been crying all day until her nose was clogged. Their apartment normally smelled like paint and brush cleaner. He liked that smell because it meant she was working. He hadn't seen much progress on the easel today. She'd taken a bath, though. The tub still had a puddle of water left over, and he smelled her floral shampoo.

He'd spent the day thinking about how close to death she'd been after that wreck and what his life would've been like without her. Now, to be in their bed without holding one another was a first. He had wanted her when she was his girlfriend and desired her while she was his fiancée, but they had denied themselves that privilege and reserved it for their married life. It had intensified their emotions and their physical relationship beyond his expectations. For the first time since their wedding night, he wasn't sure that she would want him to touch her. She had left the office madder than he was.

Jemma had turned her back toward the door when she heard him coming up the stairs, and she held her breath as he came into the room. He didn't call out to her, but he did ease into his side of the bed. She listened to each breath he took and closed her eyes to hold back the tears. She hadn't felt this anxious since he was in Vietnam. He was hurting now and it was all her fault. Triple rats. Would she ever use her brain just once?

She didn't know how long she could lie there and not turn to him and beg again for his forgiveness. Sandy had accused her once of being born just to hurt him. That wasn't true, but he might never again look at her in public like he was ready to go home and love her. She sniffed and wiped her eyes.

He laid his hand on her arm, giving her goose bumps. She touched his fingertips. Spencer moved her hair and kissed her cheek, wet with tears.

She grabbed his neck and held him like a drowning woman. "I'm sorry again, Spence. I didn't mean to hurt you. I'm so stupid."

He put his finger on her lips, then moved it away and kissed her. It was the sweet, tender kiss of atonement.

Chapter 3
No Trouble at All

It was almost daybreak, and Jemma knew that she must look horrid after crying most of the day before. She tried not to wake her husband as she slipped out of bed and into the bathroom to check. Good grief. She appeared to have run into another truck. She put a wet washcloth over her face, hoping it would help, but it didn't. Spencer knocked on the door.

"You okay, Jem?"

"Yeah. I just look like I got beat up, that's all."

"Come back to bed, baby. I love you no matter what you look like."

"If you see me, you might kick me out of the house." She opened the door and stood there, looking pathetic.

He grinned. She did look bad.

She went back in the bathroom and shut the door, holding the washcloth under the faucet. Her head hurt, too. She squeezed out the cloth and opened the medicine cabinet to get some aspirin. Her birth control pill packet fell out on the countertop. A chill ran from her scalp to her toes. She raced to the bed and stood beside it with the dripping washcloth in her hand.

"I meant for you to get *in* the bed," he said, pulling her down.

"Spence, I think I'm in big trouble."

"What?" He sat up, wondering what she was going to tell him now.

"I forgot to take my b.c. pills for three nights."

"That's it? Well, what's the worst thing that can happen? We'll have a cute little baby. It was no trouble at all as far as I'm concerned." He snickered into the pillow.

"No! I want us to have a long time together before we have a baby." She threw the washcloth at the bathroom door. "Rats!"

Spencer got out of bed and held her. "Don't worry about this, Jem. Whatever the Lord gives us, we'll be grateful. It won't affect our feelings."

"I know, but once you have children, you can't focus totally on each other. You won't be able to change my mind about this."

"I understand what you are saying, but there's nothing we can do about it now. We can't take back last night."

"I've caused this trouble, though. I've done it again."

"Jemmabeth. This is not trouble. This might be a change of plans, but to have a baby with you would be fantastic. You may not even be pregnant. Now hush and come back to bed."

She blew her red nose. "How did I ever get so lucky to have you love me?"

"It's not luck that brought us together, Jem. It was God's plan that you talk about."

"Maybe you're right. I'm probably not pregnant." She slid under the covers.

"I know one thing. You'd better go take that pill, woman," Spencer mumbled.

Over the next few days, the secretaries became used to Jemmabeth's unannounced entrances. "Hi," she'd say and point to his door. One of them would indicate if he was busy or not. She got the go-ahead this trip.

Jemma knocked on his door. "Mr. Chase," she said in a secretarial voice from the door. "Would you run away with me? I think I love you."

"Sure. I've been thinking the same thing about you. Just don't tell my wife. She has a terrible temper," he said. "Come here, you."

She sank into his lap. "I have to show you my letter." She waved it in front of his nose.

"A show in New York? How did this happen?"

"Anne, the gallery owner in Dallas, has connections with the Sabine Gallery in Manhattan. Can you believe it?"

"What are the dates again?" Spencer flipped through his desk calendar.

"It's your birthday weekend. If you can't go, it could be another year that we won't be together to celebrate."

"That's so far down the road. I'll talk to Mr. Chapman today and see what he thinks. Congratulations, Jem. I'm proud of you."

"Maybe I won't do it if you can't go."

There was a knock on the door as one of the secretaries stuck her head in with a patronizing smile. She had interrupted them on purpose. Probably wanted something to talk about at her coffee break.

"Mr. Chase, there's a call for you. I didn't want to disturb you, but it's important." She shrugged at Jemma. "Business."

Jemma cooked everything exactly the way her new cookbook said and was quite pleased with herself. It was ready way too early, though.

She called him anyway. "Babe, could you come home early? I cooked supper."

"It's only four thirty. Is this a special occasion and I forgot?"

"Nothing special. I guess I miscalculated the time and cooked all this stuff too soon. Maybe I can reheat it or you can eat it cold. Which do you want?"

He laughed. "I'll come home as soon as I can. You paint until I get there."

He managed to get home early, and she watched every bite he took. "Well?"

"It's good, really. I'm very impressed. I think you have raised ham to a higher standard." Spencer took a big swig of sweet tea.

"You're implying that ham is lowly food to start with." She jumped up and got the cookbook, propping it up in front of his plate. "See," she said, reading the title to him: "*Elegant Meals for the Newlywed Chef.* I thought you would like it."

Spencer tried to hide a burp. "I don't know how you did all this and had time to paint, too. I really appreciate such a delicious meal." He burped again.

"Why do you keep burping? Is something wrong with the ham?"

"Maybe it's just the end piece. It has a little kick to it."

She looked at her recipe book again. "I did just what it says. See — 'wash ham thoroughly.' I used plenty of Ivory liquid on it, too. Then I —"

"Wait. You put soap on the ham?"

"Of course. I just read you that part. 'Wash ham thoroughly.' I do know how to wash things." Their eyes met, then she burst into a fit of laughter. "Good grief! How dumb of me. Can you believe I did that? I must not have rinsed all the soap off. I did notice some big bubbles around the ham while it cooked."

Spencer finished off his tea and refilled it. They both laughed so hard that they wound up on the kitchen floor, propped against the cabinets. Spencer had developed a strong case of hiccups, too.

"There's dessert," she said and took out a mixing bowl filled to the brim with tapioca pudding from the fridge. "Ta da. I doubled the recipe so we could have it several nights. It's kind of runny, though."

"Did you wash the tapioca first?"

She set the bowl on the table and punched his arm. "I did not! You'd better not ever tell anybody that I put soap on that ham. Promise?"

"What's it worth to you?" he said with a loud hiccup.

She dumped the ham in the trash and turned to him.

"How about I take you out to eat tonight?"

she said and parked herself in his lap. He tried to kiss her, but the hiccups got in the way.

"Maybe the tapioca would help get rid of those."

"Sure. It looks great. Dish me up some of it." Spencer eyed the contents.

They sat on the couch and ate.

"I hope we never have another day like when I got back from Dallas," she said. "I was afraid that you weren't going to look at me ever again the same way. I thought I had ruined our perfect marriage."

"Jem, there is no perfect marriage. If humans get married, it won't be perfect. It might seem so, but it's not. If they never fight or disagree, one of them is always giving in and not saying what they really think. They hold it in for fifty years. We're not going to have a perfect marriage, but we will always have perfect love for one another."

"What wasn't perfect about us until I messed up?"

"We were still on our honeymoon. The marriage hadn't kicked in yet. I don't mean that ours can't be closer to perfection than all the rest."

"Good," she said.

Spencer put the dishes in the sink and stood in the doorway. "Jemma, we need to make a promise."

"Whatever you say."

"We will tell each other everything. Even if the telling is going to cause pain or words between us. Can you agree to that?"

Jemma slipped her arms around him. "The problem is that I don't want to hurt you. I've caused you enough pain to last our whole lives. I don't like keeping secrets from you, but I feel like some things are better off stopping with me. Does that make any sense?"

"You know that secrets have a way of creeping out and causing more trouble than the telling would've. Most of your secrets have revolved around Paul anyway."

"He's really not a worthless person. I have a lot of sympathy for someone whose love is not returned because that's what I almost did to you. Paul goes around trying to get women to go home with him, looking for love. There's no reason for you to be jealous, but I may run into him again sometime. I think we should just count on it. That way, it won't be a major ordeal."

Spencer swallowed and rested his chin on her head. "Do you promise that you will tell me when that happens?"

"I promise."

"You will tell me everything? No more

secrets?"

Jemma looked up at him and offered her hand to shake on it. "I will if you will, but does that mean I have to go back and tell all the old ones now?"

"There are more?"

"There are details. I don't think you are going to like them, but I'll tell you if you have to know," Jemma said, dreading it.

"Let me think about that. Maybe last weekend was enough for now."

"Good." She pulled him over to the couch. "We're still in the making-up stage anyway."

Spencer awoke before sunrise to an odd scratching noise, followed by a low moan. He shot up in the bed, thinking something else had happened.

"Jem?" He could see the light coming from under their closet door. He opened it to find her wearing the gold silk gown he had given her for their wedding night and standing in a pile of discarded clothing. "What's going on, baby?" he asked.

She exhaled and gestured at a heap of clothes at her feet. "I can't find anything to wear that will make me look like a sweet little wife to your mother. I don't have a single thing." She turned to the rack of dresses still left and scraped them across to the reject side. "Nope, nope, nope, see what I mean?" She groaned. "I need Mom here to figure this out."

"Jemma, what you wear is not going to make any difference to my mother. I always thought it was the liquor talking, but I think she's jealous of you. Wear whatever you want, or we'll stop on the way out of town and get you a new outfit. How does that sound?"

"It sounds hopeless, because we both know she's never going to like me."

"Well, you're perfect to me." He kissed her until the hanger in her hand dropped to the floor just prior to their own descent.

The Chase castle, as it was known around Chillaton, loomed on the horizon just outside town, near Citizen's Cemetery. Spencer's grandfather had built the Texas Gothic mansion to cheer up his wife. The Chase patriarch, being long on money and very short on design experience, had created a bitter architectural pill for Spencer to swallow. The interior, redone by a former lady friend of Max's from Atlanta, was of such elegance as to be featured in *Southern Comfort* magazine the year before. Max had added a swimming pool off the back of the house for Spencer's eighteenth birthday. It was the only one in Connelly County, except for the old one at the Chillaton Country Club.

Harriet, Spencer's Irish nanny who had raised him according to the cowboy code of honor, opened the door. "Ah, my favorite couple," she said. "Come into the den, my dearies. Your folks are waiting."

"Then why didn't they come to the door?" Spencer whispered in Jemma's ear. She took a deep breath.

"Ya'll come on in." Max Chase greeted them with his Cadillac dealer's smile. He was tall, like Spencer, and nice-looking, too, but not exactly handsome. "You sure smell good, young lady. What's that you're wearing?"

"It's something Spence gave me," Jemma said, glancing toward the leather throne.

Rebecca made no effort to get up from her big wing chair. Spencer went to her instead. She didn't let go until Jemma boldly came up beside him.

"Hello, Mrs. Chase. It's good to see you." Jemma said, leery of saying much else.

Rebecca shifted in her chair and looked away. Jemma retreated to the couch and kept her eyes on Spencer as he joined her.

"So how are things in honeymoon haven?" Max asked with a big grin.

"Fantastic." Spencer squeezed Jemma's hand. "How are things here?"

Rebecca trained her dark eyes on her new daughter-in-law. They were not the beautiful gray eyes of her son; hers were blue, but she did appear more together than Jemma had ever seen her. Her makeup was on straight and her blond hair was whipped up in a rich lady's style. She must have had it done in Amarillo because Nedra's Beauty Parlor & Craft Nook only churned out two hairdos, both guaranteed to last a week, and this was neither of them. Maybe Nedra's was only good enough for the drunken Rebecca, Jemma thought, almost smiling. Her mother-in-law held her glare.

Even Max, not known for his social intuitiveness, must have sensed the tension. "We're doing good, good. We were just discussing taking a little second honeymoon cruise ourselves, weren't we, hon?" Max stood behind Rebecca and massaged her shoulders. She reached for his hand and he took it, both flashing major diamond rings.

"Supper is ready whenever you folks are," Harriet said, giving Jemma a smile.

"That's what we needed to hear. Thanks, Harriet," Max replied.

Spencer led the way to the dining room with his arm around his wife. He pulled her chair out for her and whispered in her ear, "Hang in there."

Jemma decided that Rebecca's evil eye was even worse when she was sober.

"Are you getting used to Chillaton again, Mother?" Spencer asked.

Rebecca sneered at Jemma. "I understand you had a creek wedding. I don't think I've ever been to a farm ceremony like that. I wonder, did you kneel at a feed trough, and am I to assume there were cows and other barnyard animals loitering about?"

Jemma traced around the edge of her plate. Spencer put his hand on her leg under the table. A mischievous thought came to her.

"Well, there was the mule I rode in on." She giggled.

Max got a big laugh out of it. Spencer grinned at Jemma's valiant attempt, but Rebecca found no humor in it at all.

"How clever. You probably used some homemade lasso to rope my son and drag him to your little ambush since we all know that you nearly married an elderly cowboy."

Jemma was ready to crawl under the table.

Max cleared his throat. "Actually, Becky, it was a beautiful wedding. Jemma was a real lovely bride."

Spencer looked straight at his mother with

a tolerant smile and took Jemma's hand. "I'm sorry you couldn't have been there, Mother," he said, his voice calm but chilly. "I'm sure you remember that Jemmabeth and I have been in love for a long time. We've been through a lot and feel blessed to be married now. I know you'll want to share our happiness, so that you can be a part of our lives." The last bit was very clearly stated.

"No need to bristle, son," Rebecca said. "I was only making conversation."

Harriet appeared with the main course. The men dug in like orphans in *Oliver Twist,* but Jemma wasn't sure she could eat under the resolute eyes of a condor. She was just glad that she'd remembered to throw on extra deodorant.

They had talked about their first Christmas together since the eighth grade, and their apartment glowed from two blocks away. Inside, Jemma strung popcorn and cranberries across all the windows and made a wreath of cedar boughs, cranberries, and gold velvet ribbon for their door. Spencer's idea was to hang mistletoe from every overhang, and to make certain none of it went to waste, either. It was a newlywed Christmas, for sure. *Nouvelle Liberte* had sent her a few copies of its holiday issue with her watercolor on the cover. It was the painting of Spence's Medevac team gathered around the tree. She hid it from him. He didn't need any more reminders for a while.

"I don't want to go to Twila and Buddy's party this year," Jemma said on their way to Lizbeth's for the annual family gathering.

"Why not? I thought you liked seeing everybody." Spencer slowed down as a state trooper car came toward them on the highway.

"I don't want you dancing with The Cleave." Jemma watched the patrol car over her shoulder.

"Oh, come on, Jem. I won't dance with her. I learned my lesson."

"That's no answer. It sounds like you like dancing with her but you won't, just to keep me happy."

"That's not what I meant, baby."

"That's what you said."

"Let me rephrase that. I don't want to dance with Missy. I learned my lesson about letting her drag me into it. How's that?" He grinned and tickled her pouty lips. "She really gets to you, doesn't she?"

Jemma turned up the radio and sang along with Joni Mitchell. Spencer turned his at-

76

tention to the road. He knew when to let her stew.

"Mom!" Jemma yelled, opening the door before the car stopped.

"Sweet pea!" Alexandra Forrester yelled back as they embraced in the driveway. "You look so happy."

"We are," Jemma said.

Spencer figured he was out of the doghouse and could concentrate on his young brother-in-law clinging to his leg and his father-in-law shaking his hand. They joined the happy crowd inside and opened presents and stuffed themselves with food.

"I sure do like this fancy art book. Thank you, Jemmerbeth." Lester ran his fingers over the slick pages. "I ain't never been to a art museum before, exceptin' the railroad museum over to Dallas when you graduated from college. I need to see these up close, I reckon."

"Most of those are in Italy and France, but New York has a good museum. How'd you like to take a trip up there?"

"No ma'am. I ain't gonna go where folks talk too fast. I'll just enjoy this book for all it's worth. You know, Jemmer, if you'd lived at the same time as all them old I-talian painters, you would've been even more famous than them because your paintings look more like real people. The way them boys painted, the heads didn't fit with the size of the rest of 'em. See what I mean, like this one right here."

"Why, thank you, Lester. Some art historians believe that because the Church was so powerful during that era, art couldn't be too perfect or else the general public might worship it like a graven image. At least that might have been the Church's fear, and that kind of worship would be breaking the second commandment."

"Well, don't that beat all. I'll have to set on that thought for a spell. You're talkin' about the Catholics, I figger. In other words, they come hence to sayin' 'Paint like a young'un or we'll be comin' to get you.'"

"I'm not so sure they said it like that. Now, don't hold this old theory against the Catholics, Lester. There are good people in all churches."

"All churches don't have just one feller tellin' how things is gonna be. Your Lillygrace grandparents over there ain't Catholic, are they?"

Jemma turned and smiled at her hoity-toity grandmother and grandfather. They smiled and nodded.

"No, Lester, they are Episcopalian," she said.

"Close enough. I sure get some pig-eye looks from 'em." Lester shook his head and wandered off with his book. Her little brother, Robby, joined him and listened to Lester's quaint explanation about each piece. Mercifully, he left the pope out of the conversation.

"Baby girl." Jim motioned for his daughter. "Let's go for a walk." They bundled up and walked to the Ruby Store and bought a couple of bags of marshmallows for the hot cocoa that would appear in the evening.

"I miss you, Daddy," Jemma said.

"I know the feeling. Maybe when I retire, we'll move back here. I need to take better care of Mama. How's she doing?" Jim asked.

"Gram seems fine to me. She stays busy with church work and quilting."

"Good. The holidays always get me wondering what things would have been like if Matt and Luke had lived. I think about how they might have turned out, who they would have married — that kind of stuff. Maybe you and Robby could have had some Forrester cousins." He exhaled. "The Lord's been really good to your mom and me. We have two wonderful children. Papa would be so proud of your work, honey. We all are."

"Y'all did a good job of raising me. You always encouraged my interest in art."

"Papa and Gram half raised you. I'm just grateful that you have Spencer to raise your own kids with. As for me, I couldn't have found a better woman than your mother. She's everything to me. The older you get, the more you look just like her. Listen, do you hear a fiddle? That gives me a shiver because it sounds like Papa's warming up."

"It's Joe. He's pretty good, too." Jemma stopped at the front gate. "You were right about Spence and the helicopter crash, Daddy. All his pain came pouring out one night."

"That happened to me when you were a baby. I was rocking you and all of a sudden it hit me about Luke and Matt. Your mother had to put you in your crib for me because I fell apart. We talked the rest of the night on the floor beside your bed. It never really leaves, though. Your head clears up somewhat, but your heart, well, it can't forget." His voice broke. "Let's get inside and enjoy some music."

She put her arms around him. Jim wiped his eyes and held her. She kept her daddy's words tucked in her heart.

"Old Lady Chase, telephone," Robby yelled

over the music. Rats. Jemma knew who it was — Twila. She didn't want Spence to think she couldn't handle Missy, so they went.

It was the same old crowd with the usual chips and dip, but instead of dancing, everybody was fussing about babies. They seemed to be all over the house, like puppies. Jemma smiled politely every time somebody plopped one in her lap so they could have a free minute. Even Twila's walk resembled that of the ducks at the cemetery pond.

Spencer grinned at her. "You do look good with those little ones, Jem."

"Somebody else's, if you don't mind. This is a boring party. I'm ready to go whenever you are."

"Well, if it isn't the lovebirds." Melissa Blake's micro-miniskirt rode up even higher as she leaned across Spencer to plant a kiss in the air near his quite rosy cheek. He jerked his head back to avoid a near-collision with her cleavage, but she brushed against his neck anyway.

Missy smiled as her Chanel rose up like steam off a waffle iron. "Oh Spence. That turtleneck is the same color as your eyes," she said and gave him a real peck right on his earlobe.

Jemma's stomach did a flip.

The Cleave placed a well-manicured finger on the corner of her own mouth. "You've got some food right there on your lip, Jemma." She winked at Spencer. "Some party, huh? I've been to car washes more exciting than this."

Spencer choked out a laugh, and Jemma gritted her teeth.

"Remember when we washed your Corvette at my house and you sprayed me with the hose?" Missy shook back her hair. "My T-shirt was totally drenched. I'll never forget what you said. Are you still a bad boy even though you're married?"

For one evil second, Jemmabeth considered throwing up on The Cleave's boots. Jemma had been on the all-state basketball team a few years back, and she still had good aim.

They left within five minutes. Jemma stomped to the car way ahead of him.

Spencer grabbed her arm. "Okay, before you start. You were dating Paul when I went out with Missy. Keep that in mind, Jem, and yes, we washed my car, but I wouldn't have said anything to her that was memorable. Now, let me have it."

Jemma pried his hand off her. "Did you spray her with water until her shirt was drenched? How dumb. You can see what she has without going to all that trouble." She got in the Corvette and slammed the door. The windows frosted over immediately.

Spencer walked around the car and took a deep breath before getting in.

From the kitchen window of the Bakers' trailer, The Cleave pulled the curtain back just a smidge and blew a kiss as the silver Corvette peeled out.

Jemma was as far on her side of the bed as she could get. She hadn't said a word in the last two hours. Spencer scooted up against her, and she had no place to go but the floor. "Jemmabeth Alexandra," he said, "please don't be mad about this. It's old stuff. I was hurting and she was around. Even if I did squirt her with a hose, at least I didn't consider marrying her like you did Paul. Do you really think that I would make some suggestive remark to Missy? Give me some credit, Jem. Why would I do that when who I really wanted to see in a wet shirt was you? I've told you before — The Cleave was just a distraction from my misery. We never even went parking. C'mon, turn around and wish me a Merry Christmas Eve." He moved her hair and kissed her neck.

"What precisely did you say when you sprayed her?"

"I probably said 'bombs away' like we used to say when I was a little kid and we threw water balloons at the park. That's all I can figure out."

"Did you open the packages she sent you in Vietnam?"

"I did not. I threw them in the trash, along with the letters."

She looked over her shoulder at him. "Why did you need to put water on her at all?"

Spencer kissed her shoulder. "You want the real truth? I wanted to see what she would look like if that famous hair of hers was soaked."

"Promise?" Jemma asked, half smiling.

"Cowboy's Code of Honor promise."

Jemma turned over and leaned on her elbow. "What did she look like? Bad?"

"Like a wet Pekingese."

"Smooth talker."

"Heartbreaker," he said and kissed her pouty lips.

"Wait. I've come up with a new wrestling move." She stood up on the bed.

"I assume that you are about to demonstrate it."

"Yup. It's where I'd like to put her if she

ever touches your face again."

"Where's that? On the floor?"

"Nope. Between the jaws of . . . The Waffle Iron!" she said as she fell on him. She jabbed him with her elbows and knees like a maniacal typewriter.

He couldn't stop laughing long enough to defend himself.

CHAPTER 4
PLAN B

"So, is this going to be the trip where I get to see you in a bikini?" Spencer yelled from the bathroom as Jemma dug through her summer clothes to find something suitable for a warm beach weekend in California.

"Nope. I would just as soon wear my underwear as a bikini," she said, throwing things in her suitcase. "We are going for a welcome home celebration for Trent — not a swimsuit style show."

Spencer stuck his head out the door. "Would you really wear your underwear on the beach? I'll need a private showing of that first."

She threw a sneaker at him, hitting the door as it closed.

Jemma's hair swirled in the breeze off the Pacific the same as it did in the wake of the Zephyr passenger train when it used to stream down the tracks. The waves lapped against her ankles and shifted the sand beneath her. She had hoped to see moonlight reflected on the water, but the moon was shrouded by a thin blanket of clouds. She wrote their names in the sand, encircled with a heart, then put her hand on her belly. She would make an appointment as soon as they got home. The tide erased their names, and Jemma blew out her breath. There wasn't room in that heart now for another name. Someday, but not yet.

"Hello, beautiful." Spencer eased his arms around her waist. "What are you thinking?" The tide enveloped them and they stood ankle-deep in salt water.

"I love you," she said. "That's what I'm always thinking."

"Sorry Trent and I went on for so long. He's really a great guy; but after all, he's your cousin. You'll be glad to know that he looks you in the eye when he's talking business, too, even though he's not a Forrester. His philosophy and mine are a match, Jem. We're talking about getting together and forming a company. Architecture and engineering would be an exciting combination. We both have the financial resources to stay afloat through the lean times. What do you think?"

His enthusiasm made her answer easy. "I

can't imagine two nicer guys getting together to design and build things. It's a super idea."

"There's something in your voice, though. Are you okay?"

"Everything is fine." She turned back to the ocean and chewed on her lip.

"I bet I can beat you to that next dune, Jem," Robby said. "Loser buys ice cream, okay?"

"Robby, you don't have enough money to keep that bet." Jemma laughed.

"I do, too. I brought some money. I've been working hard to buy a new bike." Robby's blue eyes shone like Papa's.

"I'll take you up on that bet," Jim said. "See if you can beat an old man with a bad leg."

They took off. Her daddy was no match for a ten-year-old. Jim came back with ice cream for everybody. "Come on, Rob, let's find some crabs." The two Forrester men walked ahead of the ladies.

"Sweet pea, what do you think about your cousin and your husband having a business together?" Alex asked. "They are spending a lot of time planning things, that's for sure."

"I think it's great. There was a time when I didn't like Trent, but I didn't really know him. I love him now."

"He is so much like Ted. My brother is a gentle, smart, big-hearted man. Thank goodness Trent is nothing like his absentee mother. Now tell me what's the matter with you. I've seen that faraway look in those pretty eyes."

"I may be pregnant, Mom."

Alex stopped. "So soon? You always said you wanted to wait a few years. What happened? Did you forget to take your birth control pills?"

Jemma nodded. "I'm trying not to think about it, but it's driving me nuts. I want to be alone with Spence and stay crazy. We waited and were good all those years. That's what I want right now."

"Things don't always go as planned." Alex wiped a cone crumb from her daughter's chin.

"Spence already gave me this lecture. Just because I know the facts of the matter, it doesn't change my heart."

"Your heart will melt when you see what you and Spence have created. Trust me. Besides, you may not be pregnant. Now tell me about your art. What are you working on?"

Robby ran up to them, giggling over some sea creature that he held out for his mother's reaction. Jemma again turned her face toward the ocean breeze to dry her eyes.

"I've spent so much time with Trent, I feel like I have neglected you." Spence laid the blanket on the sand, and they cuddled up to watch the stars.

"Yeah, well, maybe you'd better start making up for it, mister."

"Any suggestions?" He kissed her palms, for starters.

"Hmm. I'm not the one in trouble here. You'll have to come up with something on your own." Jemma resumed her stargazing.

Spencer nuzzled up to her ear and whispered in it, sending her into a giggle. He loved the way she closed her eyes and threw back her head when she laughed. She had done that since he first knew her. Things like that lingered from her childhood and had endeared her to many, probably even Paul.

Spencer turned her chin toward him and kissed her. "You are precious to me, Mrs. Chase," he said, pulling the blanket over them as a ship out on the Pacific blew its melancholy horn. The sound mingled with the hypnotic pulse of the surf and their conversation.

■ ■ ■ ■

He had an hour's worth of drafting to finish, and, as he was the only one left in the office, he chose to ignore the knocking on the main door. It didn't stop. He exhaled and went to see who could possibly need an architect after office hours. It was Jemma. She leaned against the door as she kept a steady rhythm with her knuckles. Spencer unlocked the door and she fell against him, crying. He helped her to a couch and got her a box of tissues.

"I'm pregnant." She blew her nose, then threw the whole tissue box at the wastebasket. "Rats, rats, rats! I didn't want this to happen. Now we'll be like all the other old married couples who have a kid to take care of and we won't be crazy newlyweds anymore. I'm not ready for a baby. I still want to be wild and free with you. It's all my fault for being irresponsible with the stupid pill. I do *not* want to be pregnant!"

"Whoa. Well, we knew it was a possibility." He chose his words carefully. "It'll be okay, Jem. I know we didn't plan it this way, but think about the little life growing inside you. We made it together. It's our very own baby, and we want it to be loved from the very beginning, don't we?"

"I know all that stuff and I want to have babies. I just didn't want to start so soon. I'm still celebrating us."

"We'll still be us. We'll love each other like we do now."

"No, we won't love each other the same way. We can't be free. Our focus will be on the baby, not us. We'll be a trio. I know the baby will be cute and an extension of our love. I'm not arguing with you. It's just . . . I never stop messing things up." She retrieved the tissues and went to his office, flopping in a chair.

Spencer drew her limp body toward him. "Jemmabeth, I agree with you that this is not Plan A, but it is not the end of the world as we know it. It's just Plan B. We will make it a new part of our joy, though. If we've created life, then we are going to celebrate that. You get a smile on your face and we are going out for dinner and dancing. C'mon, let me see that beautiful smile."

Jemma stared at the carpet. He waited. She looked out the window while he wiped the tears off her cheeks. Without warning, she jerked away from him and bolted out of the room. Spencer followed her to the restroom and leaned against the wall as the joy of morning sickness in the evening took its toll. He had a feeling that maybe she was right; things were going to change.

Chapter 5
Sealing the Deal

Another month passed and they didn't tell anyone the news. "I hope you aren't going to be like this the whole nine months," Spencer commented over dinner.

"What? You mean the throwing up?" She slammed down a milk carton, causing little droplets of milk to spray up on her face. Without so much as a giggle, she wiped them off.

Spencer raised his brow. "Nope, I'm talking about the big pout that has taken over our lives. I think it's been long enough."

Jemma poked at her baked potato, then stabbed it with her fork and flew upstairs. Spencer exhaled and trudged up after her. Their bedroom door was shut. At least she hadn't slammed it.

He knocked and found her sitting on the side of the bed. "Jem, I want us to be happy about this. You are carrying our firstborn. We don't want to create any bad memories of this special event. Our baby can't change the timing. I'm ready to tell everybody and start making plans. Besides, we could be having fun right now while we're still alone."

Jemma was dry-eyed for once. She reached for his hand. "I know you're right, babe. Just tell me what to do and I'll do it."

"How are you feeling?"

"I'm a little better. There are some smells, though, that make me sick to think about them. Like bacon and mayonnaise. Yuck."

He kissed her. "Let's go look at baby furniture."

"How can you be so patient with me, Spence? I don't want to be this way, but we saved ourselves for all those years, waiting until we got married. I wanted to relish this — this golden time, with just you and me. Do you know what I'm talking about?"

"I know that, Jem, and I really do understand. Our schedules and solitude may suffer, but the passion between us is permanent. I think we need a little vacation. Let's go somewhere romantic. I haven't had much time with my wild lady lately. In fact, I haven't even seen her around."

She looked up and gave him a grin. "How much romance can you stand for the next six months?"

"As much as you can dish out, woman,"

he said as they fell back on the bed.

They called Alex and Jim that night. Jim was ecstatic and Robby decided to be called Uncle Rob. Alex was still choosing between Gran and Gramma when they hung up. Lizbeth expressed her excitement and vowed to get started on a quilt, but Jemma detected a certain something in her response. Jemma had voiced her opinion too many times about waiting to have a family, and she knew Lizbeth remembered those remarks.

Spencer wanted to tell his parents in person. "I think it'll be all right. Mother needs to see you anyway. Just remember that I love you, and it won't last long."

"Will you still love me when my belly is hanging over my knees?" she asked, playing with his tie. She looked up and bit her lip.

"Jemmabeth, I would love you even if you gained fifty pounds and never lost it."

"Liar. You might love my personality, but you would get a roving eye."

"Never. Now hush up and get dressed." He gave her a swat on her behind. He watched as she chose what to wear to see his mother. It was a major ordeal and an amusing sight, but he would never tell her that. He just loved to watch her do anything.

The pregnancy had thrown her into a spin, but she was bouncing back. An hour later, he helped her hang up all the rejects and she was ready to go. As he watched her, he hoped that their baby would be a girl — the spirit and image of his golden-eyed love.

Max and Rebecca were late returning from a drive around their ranch. Harriet was the first person that Spencer wanted to tell anyway. She was jubilant.

"I should have known, my girl. You have that special look. Motherhood is written all over you," she said and patted Jemma's hand.

Jemma wanted to hear that particular observation about as much as she wanted to see her mother-in-law. Spencer kissed her as soon as Harriet left them alone in the den. Jemma pulled her black skirt down as far as she could and adjusted the Peter Pan collar on her white blouse.

Spencer smiled. "You look like an English schoolgirl. Stop worrying. You know she is going to say something rude, so just expect it."

Jemma jumped as the back door opened and Max's voice tumbled down the Italian-tiled hallway. She sat up straight and held her breath.

"Spencer, my man." Max gave his son a bear hug. "You look good. Married life is the way to go, huh? I guess that would have something to do with you, young lady."

Jemma smiled at Max as Rebecca embraced her son. "Tell me all about your work, Spencer," she said, taking him to the matching leather armchairs.

Spencer walked instead to the sofa and sat by his wife, grinning. "Before we talk about anything else, Jemma and I have some news." He couldn't hold it any longer. "We're having a baby."

"Well, I'll be." Max laughed and clapped his hands. "So I'm gonna be a granddaddy, huh? I guess I'd better buy myself a how-to book for this deal. Wow! I figured you two would be honeymooning for five or six years."

Jemma cleared her throat to get rid of the lump that was rising in it. Rebecca pursed her lips and stared out the bank of windows that overlooked the swimming pool.

"Becky, what do you have to say about this news? Won't it be great to have a baby around the house?"

Rebecca raised her chin and turned her gaze on Jemma. "So, I guess you've sealed the deal now, as they say in the car business."

Max flashed a shaky smile. "That's not very nice, Becky. The kids are sharing something special with us, and you should be happy for them. I know I am."

Rebecca's face twitched. "I suppose we should be grateful that you waited until you were married to get pregnant; that way we can be relatively certain that it's a Chase."

Jemma was off the couch and out the front door before Spencer could stop her. He came back into the den, his gray eyes set on his mother. "If you don't care for Jemma-beth, Mother, then you don't care for me. She is my love and my life. When you look at her, you're looking at me, and when you speak to her, you're speaking to your son. Until you treat her with respect and honor our marriage, I won't be back to your house. That's a promise. Good-bye, Dad; it was good seeing you."

Spencer caught up with Jemma at the cemetery gates. She could move when she wanted to. He stopped the car and held her. They walked to Papa's grave and sat on the bench.

"I can't go there anymore. Please don't ask me to," she said.

"That's a promise. Mother is acting like a bitter old woman, and she has nothing to be bitter about. She needs to get back into counseling or something. Let's go see Gram. We'll take her to Daddy's Money for dinner."

Jemma said a prayer over her papa's grave. He would have loved having a baby around the house, but he would not have liked Jemma's belated attitude over her impending motherhood.

They pulled into the driveway and sat in the car for a while, talking. Spencer stepped over to Lester's house to invite him to dinner. Lizbeth and Jemma sat in the porch swing. The honeysuckle vine was dry and brittle behind them, waiting for spring. Jemma had avoided her eyes, but Lizbeth put her arm around her granddaughter as they considered the bittersweet twists in life. It had been the same for her and Cameron. God's Great Plan was not always in tune with that of His children, but His was always the perfect way. Lizbeth had known that, too, but it hadn't made the acceptance of motherhood any easier while their hearts were still on fire for each other all those years ago.

Jemmabeth stepped out of the elevator and walked down the shiny hallway to the nurses' station to ask for directions. There was no need to because the window was right there. She approached it much the same as when she entered the room where her mother-in-law sat in her leather throne. When Jemma's eyes fell on the bassinettes filled with pink and blue blankets, she melted. It was the same feeling she had the first time she heard *Praeludium and Allegro.* One of those cribs would hold their own little one with Baby Chase written on a pastel tag. Her hand moved to her heart as the smallest newborn near the window made a sucking motion with its pink lips and turned its mouth toward its own tiny fist. A wave of reconciliation swept through Jemma's body, ripping out her old attitude and leaving behind a sparkling new one. More than anything else in the world, at that very moment, she wanted to be a mother.

"I'm in here, babe," Jemma yelled from the extra bedroom. "Come and see what you think." She wiped her cheek, but the paint was still wet on it. She surveyed her day's work. Spencer, impeccable in his sports coat and turtleneck, walked in the room and whistled. Jemma had on Papa's old overalls and a bandana scarf tied around her head. He kissed her and the paint smudge transferred to him. They were branded as expectant parents.

"What's all this? I thought we were going to paint it together." Spencer looked around the room — stark white when he left for work, but now the color of butter.

"I couldn't help it," she said. "It went really fast, and I think it's perfect for the baby's room. We can buy unfinished furniture and paint it sky blue. I have some ideas for a *trompe l'oeil*."

"I'll bet you do." He grinned at her. "You look fantastic."

"Check this out." She whipped out a book of baby names. "I thought we could look at it after supper. Rats. I forgot to turn on the oven. Do you want dirt pie or water casserole for supper?"

He gave her a sneaky look. "I don't want any supper," he whispered. "I've been a bad boy, and I think you should send me straight to my room."

"Well, now, I'm real sorry to hear that," she said in her Scarlett O'Hara voice. "I'll be up in five minutes to check on you. You'd better be in that bed, too. Or else."

Spencer stopped on the stairs. "Or else what?"

She grinned and wiggled her eyebrows at him. He took the stairs two at a time.

The phone rang while she was finishing up a painting of Max. He had his foot on the front bumper of a Cadillac with a cigarette dangling from the corner of his smile. One hand was on his knee and the other was in a price-haggling gesture. She put her paintbrush behind her ear and answered.

"Stop painting and start packing," Spencer said.

"You're kicking me out?" she asked.

"No, I'm running off to Mexico with you."

"Mexico? You're kidding. What's down there?"

"Puerto Vallarta, that's what. We leave tomorrow morning."

"I'll get the suitcases. Spence, thank you." She kissed the phone.

Jemma took a breath and felt her cheeks. She hadn't been quite right the last couple of weeks. It felt something like the flu coming on, but it never did. That was her big fear, that she would get sick and make the little one sick, too. She put her hands on her belly and closed her eyes. She hoped he looked just like his daddy, right down to the cowlick and those pretty gray eyes. She pulled out the suitcases. The first thing she threw in was the *Big Book of Baby Names*.

Nothing would do but for him to buy her a bikini in Mexico.

"I can't wear this," she said, looking in the mirror in their room by the beach. "I'm starting to show."

Spencer lay on the bed watching her. "I like it. You wouldn't wear one in Hawaii either and you weren't even pregnant then. C'mon, do it just to humor me. You're a knockout in it."

She put it on and stood up on the bed. "Me, Amazon woman, come to take you to my cave. Will you go in peace, or must I drag you?"

He grabbed the ties on the sides of her bikini. "Now what does Amazon woman have to say?"

She couldn't do anything but giggle. He had missed that about her.

They took a boat ride to see the South Shore. It was a romantic tour but endured on rough waters.

"It's a good thing you are over that evening sickness or this could be a disaster," Spencer said, tracing around her lips.

She nodded, wincing. Her head throbbed and the strange tingling sensation that had bothered her both nights they had been in Mexico returned. Maybe it was the drinking water.

Spencer stood between the boat captain and Jemma, easing his hands onto her stomach. "I want you to know, Jem, that this little life growing in you only makes you even more beautiful to me. Don't ever forget that."

"I won't. I'm really excited and happy now, Spence. I want him to be you, all over again."

He kissed her, making her forget about her other chills for a moment.

They were slow dancing in the hotel ballroom after supper when Spencer stopped. "Jem, do you have a fever? You feel really warm to me."

"I'm not doing too well, babe. Maybe we should go back to the room. I'm kind of dizzy," she said as he felt her forehead. She lost her balance and leaned against him.

"You wait here. I'm calling a cab."

"Sorry, Spence. We were having such a good time. I don't want to spoil it," she said as soon as they took the thermometer out of her mouth. The nurse spoke in Spanish but comprehended the couple's anxious looks.

A young doctor read Jemma's chart and gave instructions to the nurse. She wheeled Jemma away, motioning for Spencer to stay put.

The doctor introduced himself in English and offered Spencer a chair. "It is of concern to me that your wife has had these symptoms for almost a month and that she is so far advanced in the pregnancy. We cannot detect a fetal heartbeat, so it is possible that the fetus has died and did not abort naturally. Your wife has all the symptoms of septicemia, which left untreated, can be fatal." He put his hand on Spencer's shoulder. "We will run some lab tests quickly, and I must examine her. She is normally healthy?"

"Yes, very." Spencer couldn't think straight. He rubbed his forehead and stood. Thoughts of death riding in his chopper during Vietnam filled his head and made his stomach turn. How could their baby be dead and threatening Jemma's life?

The doctor left to examine her. Spencer circled the waiting area several times. He needed to touch her fingers like he did when she'd had the wreck and nearly died. Jemma would take this hard, very hard, and he had to be with her.

The doctor returned with confirmation of

his fears. "As I suspected, this is most certainly a missed abortion; that is, the fetus has died, but none of the tissue has been expelled, and it is causing your wife to become ill."

Spencer took a breath and resorted to his Medevac pilot demeanor. "How can you be sure that the baby is dead? Are there other tests?"

"I know the fetus is dead. In Mexico City they could perform tests to be completely certain, but your wife is becoming more seriously ill by the hour. I don't know if you should risk that delay."

"What do you recommend, sir?" Spencer searched the doctor's eyes.

"We have already started her on antibiotics, but it is necessary to evacuate the uterus to assure the septicemia will subside. I will need you to complete some paperwork so that I may perform the procedure."

Spencer nodded. He could not let Jemma die. "Could I see her first?"

"Quickly, please," the doctor said and took him to her.

She turned her tear-streaked face at the sound of his footsteps and raised her head off the pillow to reach for Spencer, pulling the IV stand with her. The doctor stepped out to give them privacy as they grieved before he loosened all that remained of the life they had created.

Chapter 6
A Sharp Blow

Lester and Lizbeth stood outside the apartment door. Their knocks went unanswered, so Lizbeth turned the knob. "Hello, sugar. It's just us," she shouted up the stairs.

"Maybe she's stepped out for a minute," Lester said.

"No, no. Spencer said she won't leave the apartment. She must be asleep." Lizbeth looked up the long steps to their second-story bedroom. "Jemmabeth. It's Gram and Lester."

Jemma appeared at the top of the stairs in her old chenille robe.

"Hi, sugar," Lizbeth said, trying to conceal her shock at Jemma's appearance. "We thought we would drop by for a little visit. I brought you a couple of casseroles, too."

Lester backed away into the living room, twisting the brim of his hat.

"I'll come down in a minute," Jemma mumbled. She turned and closed the door behind her.

"Oh my." Lizbeth shook her head. "Oh my."

Lester headed for the door. "Miz Liz, I'm thinkin' this is a time for woman talk. I just can't see clear to me bein' around for it. I'll wait in the car. No offense."

"That's fine, Lester. Here, take Spencer's newspaper with you. I'll be out directly." Lizbeth took off her hat and set to work washing dishes. She did not expect her precious girl to be in this shape. Spencer said things were bad, but she had no idea it would be to such an extent.

She was about to go up and check on her when she heard the door open and footsteps on the stairs. Jemma's bare feet stuck out from the bottom step. Lizbeth put the broom away and joined her granddaughter on the stairs. Her beautiful hair seemed to have barely survived an eggbeater attack, and she still had on the robe. Her arms hung at her side and her glassy eyes remained fixed on the carpet. Lizbeth put her arms around her. She held her until her arms trembled with her own sense of grief for Jemma's pain.

They were still there when Spencer came in the door with Lester.

■ ■ ■

"Hi, Gram," Spencer said, but his attention was on his wife. He rubbed her back. "Lester and I were saying that we would like a hamburger. I'm going to change clothes and get us some food." He bit his lip and squatted in front of Jemma, brushing her hair out of her face. "Hey, baby," he whispered. "I'll be right back. Would you eat something, just for me?"

Lizbeth pulled herself up by the handrail and disappeared into the living room.

"Y'all go on," Jemma mumbled. "I'm not hungry." She turned and went up the stairs.

Spencer walked with her. "Gram and Lester are here to see us. I know you don't feel good, but maybe you could come back down and visit for a while. We don't want them to worry."

"Do you think they're talking about me?" she asked.

Spencer frowned. "It would only be words of love. We all want you to get well."

"Everybody knows it's my fault that our baby died. That can change the way people feel about you," she said.

"Jem, nobody thinks that but you. Remember the doctor said that one out of four pregnancies ends in miscarriage. It happens to a lot of people. It just happened to be our first."

"No. It's me. I didn't want to be pregnant. I didn't want to have the baby, so look what happened. It's no different than everything else that I've done. I'm so sorry, Spence. You should have married Michelle Taylor. I don't deserve to have your babies. I should have died instead of that little precious child. Everybody is thinking that."

Spencer massaged the bridge of his nose. "I'll see if they can come back another time. I don't think we're ready for company."

Jemma got in bed and pulled the covers over her head so she couldn't hear them talking. She did hear the front door close and his footsteps on the stairs again. She folded the pillow over her face and held it there until he left the room.

Lizbeth kept her thoughts to herself on the trip home. Her head was full of Cameron and her heart fluttered, still, at the thought of him topping the little rise by the home place at day's end. At the windmill, he would remove his hat and beat it against his leg to get rid of the dust of his labors. Those tiny particles, caught in the golden light of dusk, majestically floated back to the earth.

It was on a rainy afternoon when she'd told him they were going to be parents. Thunder rolled as they had snuggled in the storm dugout warmed by the glow of the kerosene lamp. He was quiet at first, then his smile crinkled up his sparkling blue eyes. "Thank you, Lizbeth, for giving me the pleasure of your company these months," he said. "I didn't know such joy was to be had. Now we'll start the business that the good Lord has given us, that of raising Christian children."

She had cried, not wanting their time alone together to be over and not sure she was ready for this new business of raising children. She wanted the unexpected pleasure and fun of just being Cam's wife to last forever. Then, before she understood what it really meant, motherhood had enveloped her with its strong, sensible, and loving arms.

Lester's words invaded her thoughts. "Jemmerbeth's had a real sharp blow to her heart, hasn't she, Miz Liz? I feel right sorry for her, but she'll come out of it okay. There ain't no shame in grief."

Lizbeth stirred in her seat and watched as a tractor made a turn at the end of a cotton row and lowered the contraption behind it into the earth. "Yes, she'll be all right, but it may take some time. She'll need our prayers."

"Yes ma'am. I've already started," Lester said and cleared his throat.

Alex was about to take a cab to the apartment when she saw him in the airport crowd. He forced a smile, but it didn't last long. At the apartment parking lot, they sat in the Corvette even though Spencer saw Jemma looking out the window of their place.

"What did the doctor say?" Alex said, blowing her nose.

"She's been going to the best psychiatrist in Amarillo. He says that Jem is dealing with guilt coupled with depression."

"Guilt? Whatever for?"

Spencer watched as Jemma moved away from the window. "She didn't want to be pregnant. She was mad when she found out because she had a hard time with the idea of us giving up our romantic lifestyle. That lasted the whole first trimester. She did come around and was happy about it, but then, well, you know the rest. At first I thought she was just sad, but that's not all of it." His voice broke. "Now she is convinced that the baby didn't live as a punishment for her attitude."

Alex took his hand. "Spence, this will pass. The Lord will use this to His glory, somehow. Don't let Jemma's misery make you lose sight of who she really is, son. She loves you and probably thinks you're disappointed in her. You know that Jim and I love you like you were our own. We will work through this. I'll never forget your patience when she was in that coma. She's still that same precious Jemmabeth; don't hold this against her."

"I could never hold anything against her. She's in my every thought. I just can't help her through this one. I don't know how. It hurts too much for both of us when she keeps feeling the same, day after day."

"That's why I'm here, honey. I will take up the slack now. You need some rest and probably some food. Let's go see our girl."

"I'd better warn you," Spencer said as they got her luggage out of the trunk. "She never sleeps."

He unlocked the apartment door, but Jemma was nowhere to be seen. Alex was shocked when they found her in the closet, cornered, like a wild kitten.

"Sweet pea." Alex dropped to her knees and held her. "Jem, I haven't seen you hide in your closet since you were a little girl in need of a spanking."

"I'm tired, Mom. I'm so tired and I can't sleep because when I do, I see my baby. I've been bad and I can't make it good," she said and glanced up at her with sunken eyes.

Alex blinked back her tears. "Put your head in my lap, Jemmabeth. Let's talk about when you were a little girl."

Spencer sat on the bed, listening in the dark. He wiped his eyes. Alex had done what he was unable to do. She could speak to Jemma without the memory of conception, the pain of their private loss, and his constant fear that Jemma was slipping away from him altogether.

Alex brought them fresh hope. She took up residence on the sofa bed, and Jemma began to sleep and eat again. Spencer wrote his wife love notes and words of encouragement and left them on their bathroom mirror. They were always gone by evening. She sat with him and let him hold her hand but never looked him in the eye. He had put the baby furniture in storage before Alex came and had carefully returned Jemma's art supplies to the butter-colored bedroom. Jemma had not touched her paints since Mexico, nor had she really touched him.

Jemmabeth let Alex drive the Corvette and

Alex took his hand. "Spence, this will pass. The Lord will use this to His glory, somehow. Don't let Jemma's misery make you lose sight of who she really is, son. She loves you and probably thinks you're disappointed in her. You know that Jim and I love you like you were our own. We will work through this. I'll never forget your patience when she was in that coma. She's still that same precious Jemmabeth; don't hold this against her."

"I could never hold anything against her. She's in my every thought. I just can't help her through this one. I don't know how. It hurts too much for both of us when she keeps feeling the same, day after day."

"That's why I'm here, honey. I will take up the slack now. You need some rest and probably some food. Let's go see our girl."

"I'd better warn you," Spencer said as they got her luggage out of the trunk. "She never sleeps."

He unlocked the apartment door, but Jemma was nowhere to be seen. Alex was shocked when they found her in the closet, cornered, like a wild kitten.

"Sweet pea." Alex dropped to her knees and held her. "Jem, I haven't seen you hide in your closet since you were a little girl in need of a spanking."

"I'm tired, Mom. I'm so tired and I can't sleep because when I do, I see my baby. I've been bad and I can't make it good," she said and glanced up at her with sunken eyes.

Alex blinked back her tears. "Put your head in my lap, Jemmabeth. Let's talk about when you were a little girl."

Spencer sat on the bed, listening in the dark. He wiped his eyes. Alex had done what he was unable to do. She could speak to Jemma without the memory of conception, the pain of their private loss, and his constant fear that Jemma was slipping away from him altogether.

Alex brought them fresh hope. She took up residence on the sofa bed, and Jemma began to sleep and eat again. Spencer wrote his wife love notes and words of encouragement and left them on their bathroom mirror. They were always gone by evening. She sat with him and let him hold her hand but never looked him in the eye. He had put the baby furniture in storage before Alex came and had carefully returned Jemma's art supplies to the butter-colored bedroom. Jemma had not touched her paints since Mexico, nor had she really touched him.

Jemmabeth let Alex drive the Corvette and

played with her hair all the way to Chillaton.

"You haven't been to Gram's house for a while," Alex said as they passed the city limits sign.

"I'm nervous," Jemma said, "and I can't think straight." She knew that she was getting on everybody's nerves, but they just didn't understand; she had let them all down, especially Spence. Now strange ideas had sprung up in her head lately, corners of thinking that frightened her, so she tried not to use her brain too much — but her heart was hurting from all the extra effort.

"Goodness, Jemmabeth, you have lived with Gram for the last few years. It should be like home to you."

Jemma didn't answer. She stared out the window. It wasn't only that she had caused the miscarriage of their baby. What she could never make anybody else understand was that, by doing so, she was responsible for literally losing a part of Spencer. The last time she was in Gram's house, she had life growing inside her. Looking Gram in the eye now would be further admission that she was guilty of wishing away that little life.

Lizbeth had lunch all ready for them. Lester didn't come. He had gone to the barbershop instead.

"Sugar, you look so pretty today. Is that a new dress?" Lizbeth said as they sat around the kitchenette.

"Yes ma'am. Spencer bought it for me." Jemma kept her eyes on her plate.

"How is that boy? Is he still keeping long hours?" Lizbeth asked, exchanging glances with Alex.

Jemma blurted it out. "I'm so sorry about the baby, Gram. I should have rejoiced that God blessed us and instead I acted like a brat." She relaxed into a heavy sigh.

Lizbeth reached for her hand, letting the words come softly, in all tenderness. "You know, Jemmabeth, when I found out that I was expecting Matthew, I threw a wall-eyed fit the first time I was alone. When he died in the war, I considered those feelings I had way back then, but I wanted to be with your papa in our golden time, and that was all. It wasn't the idea of motherhood that made me angry . . . it was that it snuck up and invaded our honeymoon. I think you had the same feelings, too. I saw it in your eyes. Those were honest feelings, but they didn't kill your baby, sugar. It is the never-ending, hard row to hoe in life that did it, not you. I'm sure you've been on your knees about this. Now it's your husband that you must consider. You know, Spencer came to see me last week. He is struggling hard with this guilt you have, honey, and he feels sort of shut off by it. Don't make holes in your marriage over this."

Lizbeth raised Jemma's chin. "Nobody would ever consider blaming you for this, least of all that sweet boy." Lizbeth pushed her chair back and bent down to rest her cheek on Jemma's, leaving a trace of her Moonlight Over Paris perfume on her skin.

The day brightened. Jemma even smiled at Lester when he brought the mail, then she drew some cats and dogs for Shorty and put them in the Mason jar in the hollyhock patch. She remained quiet on the way back to Amarillo but asked Alex to stop at a plant center near the apartment. She bought a small rosebush called "Tiffany" and set it on their balcony. Alex didn't ask why; she was just glad of the little spark returning to her girl.

They waited at the airport.

"Thank you for coming," Spencer said as Jemma paced around the waiting area.

"She's so nervous," Alex said. "I guess that's better than depressed and stressed. I have never seen her like this."

"Jem's gone through a combination of just

about every emotion there is lately. I just pray that she'll come back to me. It's almost like she's angry." Spencer craned his neck to see where she was.

"No, Spencer. She isn't angry with you. She has to get past this guilt. Jemma's embarrassed and ashamed about things only she understands, but she's going to be all right. You start praying with her again. She is still the girl you've always loved," Alex said as the first boarding call came for her flight.

Spencer looked at her much the same as he did when he came to pick Jemma up for their first real date.

Alex hugged him. "I love you, son. You call us any time, okay? There's my girl." She waved Jemma over. "Good-bye, sweet pea. We'll be back before school starts. You get going on your paintings."

Alex had to pull away from Jemma's embrace.

"Bye, Mom. Hug Daddy and Robby for me. Thank you for everything," Jemma whispered.

Neither said anything on the way back to their apartment. Spencer was getting used to it. He missed her in every way that one soul mate misses another, and in every way that a husband misses his adored wife. Most of all, he missed her joy; it was the source of his own.

Jemma stood on the balcony and looked up at the nighttime city sky. Life hadn't been right in such a long time. It couldn't be good again until she and Spence were happy. She could try dancing on the tracks behind Gram's house like she used to, but in her heart, she knew the only lasting peace would have to come from the Lord. She had to know that Spencer didn't regret loving her. She had never once set out to hurt her hero, her Candy Man, but she always did. She reached for the creamy pink bloom of the Tiffany rose, still in its planting bucket. The petals fell to the floor like miniature butterflies escaping her touch. Nothing she did now turned out right.

Chapter 7
A Gracious Spark

Brother Cleo came to see them the day after Alex left. Spencer knew that it was Alex who had summoned him. He filled the armchair. Spencer and Jemma sat on the sofa about a foot apart.

"I always feel a bond with the folks that I marry, like they're my own children," Brother Cleo said in his rich bass voice. "I know you two have been through a troublesome time. Jemma, the last time I saw you, there was a deep pain in your eyes, and I still see it. Your mama told me that this pain is covering the joy in your marriage."

Jemma raised her head a little. Spencer bit his lip and looked at the floor.

"You told me once that it was a family trait to always look folks in the eye when you mean something," Brother Cleo said, leaning to one side so as to make eye contact with her. "Now, I'm not denying that you are suffering, but we've got to make sure that the devil hasn't picked you up as a pet project and is hoping to mark you and your marriage for life. I don't want that to happen to you two. This sadness that has caught you is not through any fault of your own. It is just life and that's all. It needs a place to go."

Jemma looked at Spencer out of the corner of her eye.

"It's been my practice to have my 'children' repeat their wedding vows during troubled times. Some folks scoff at such, but it's something I put a lot of faith in. So I want us to kneel right now like we did that morning at Plum Creek and pray. Then, if you remember any of your vows, I want you to look each other in the eye and say them again, just like it was the first time. Now hold hands." Brother Cleo's voice left no margin for hesitation between them.

Spencer reached for her hands. Jemma offered one, but he took the other, too. She closed her eyes and felt the warmth of him.

Brother Cleo prayed and when he finished, Spencer spoke as though they were alone. "Jemmabeth Alexandra Forrester, you have always been my adored one, and I take you now to be my beloved wife. Before God, I give you my heart and my life. I will cherish and honor you above all women as long as we live on this earth."

Jemma's mouth was dry and tears had trickled to her neck. She glanced at him several times until she could steady her eyes on his, but she could only manage a whisper.

"In the presence of our dear Lord, I promise you, Spencer Morgan Chase, that I will love you and adore you as my husband from this moment until I breathe my last. No one but you will ever fill my heart and my life." Even her whisper broke and she took another breath. "I promise to cherish and honor you above all men, as my only and dearest love."

"Amen," Brother Cleo said.

The three of them stayed like that for a while. The only sound was Brother Cleo's heavy breathing. Jemma looked away first.

Brother Cleo laid his hand on theirs. "May the Holy Spirit move in your hearts to give you hope and restore your joy and, may 'the Lord bless thee and keep thee; and make his face shine upon thee, and be gracious unto thee.' You'll find that verse in the book of Numbers, chapter 6, verses 24 and 25." He stood, leaving them still on their knees and holding hands. "I know my way out. I'll check on y'all next week."

She meant to take her hands away from Spencer's grasp, but he held tight. "Jem, I miss you so much. Don't you miss me?"

She nodded. He reached for her and, for once, she didn't draw back. He inhaled the sweet fragrance of her hair.

Jemma focused on his chin, thinking how the little scar there used to feel against her fingers. "Spence, all I ever do is apologize. You're probably sorry that you've loved me all this time. I'm plain worthless." Jemma stood, and he let her go. She went up the stairs and closed the door to their room.

She waited for the sunset on the balcony. He hadn't mentioned the rosebush, but they didn't talk much anyways these days.

A helicopter flew overhead, sending shivers over her. He flew all those rescue missions in Vietnam, only to crash within days of his discharge. God's Plan was to give him back to her then. That glorious evening when he ran down the tracks against a sparkling sunset was etched in her brain.

The sunset on this night was not much to speak of, though. She went to their bed and fell across it, too weary to cry. Her eyes fell on their wedding picture. That was the most perfect day of her life. She had become a woman with him. Now she was his misery. Her old copy of Emily Dickinson's poems lay on the dresser. She picked it up and it fell open to the lines about a sparrow to whom God had given bread, but the little bird couldn't eat it because he was too struck with just having it.

It struck her that she owned this particular crumb, this guilty grief. It had become her *poignant luxury,* as the poetess had said. Maybe Miss Dickinson had meant something else, but Jemma took that thought away with her. She closed the book and stared at the rosebush. Brother Cleo's scripture about graciousness stuck in her head, waking up her brain again. She could use a whole truckload of God's face shining down on her right now.

Jemma got on her knees beside the bed and asked God one more time to forgive her and to help her find her sparkle for life. Maybe He would be gracious and sprinkle some out on her right then and there.

She lay her head on the bed, Spencer's side, pondering the word *gracious.* That adjective had never occurred to her when she thought of the Lord. It seemed to fit in better with Emily Post.

She wound the Starry Night music box that he had given her on her twenty-first birthday and lifted the lid to read the inscription, *I think of thee.* Spence always had thought of her. Since they were six years old, he had put her first and there she had remained. Rats. She had to get over this and make it up to him, somehow, and then maybe the Lord would shine on her. He had already been more than gracious by giving her Spencer's love and she knew it.

She drew herself up and looked in the mirror. "No more silence, no more darkness, as of this very minute," she said aloud.

Guitar music wafted up the stairs and she put her ear to the door, but almost immediately, it stopped. She heard, instead, his approaching footsteps and moved away, afraid of what he might say to her. The door didn't open, but she heard him playing and singing "I Will Wait for You," the song from the music box, on the other side.

Jemma closed her eyes. The same feeling swept over her that she had when they saw each other after a year — during their big breakup in college — only she was too nervous to open the door this time. She grabbed a scrap of paper and wrote on it, then slid it under the door when the song was over. She stuck the pen under the door, too.

Spencer picked up the paper and read her words. *Do you see now that I don't deserve you?* He took the pen and wrote quickly, *I see now that you deserve all my love and my life,* then pushed it under the door.

A few seconds later it was returned. *I'm scared that I have lost my sparkle.* He wrote back. *We'll find it together.*

There was no response. He heard a shuffling, then quiet. He sat by the door for a long time before picking up his guitar to start downstairs. The door opened behind him. He turned to look right into her golden eyes. He took a few steps toward her and she didn't move away. They stood close enough to give each other goose bumps.

Jemma took his hands in hers. She kissed them, palms up, and put her head on his chest. "I'm so sorry about our baby, Spence. I will love you forever and always. Thank you for sticking with me, despite everything."

His eyes welled up. "I will love you until I become the stars for you, Jem. Please believe me."

"I keep it in mind, babe," she whispered and kissed him.

The ring of love he had given her sparkled in the moonlight as they began their gentle journey toward hope, healing, and joy.

He heard her downstairs when he woke up. She hadn't been in the kitchen in six weeks. "Everything okay?" he yelled.

"I'm bringing you breakfast. Stay in bed." She sounded good to him. Five minutes later she came up the stairs with a tray and a big smile. "Hi. I made you a real breakfast, see? No cereal. There's a flower, too. Smell it."

Spencer inhaled the fruity scent of the rose. "Very, very nice."

"That's all you can say about it?" she asked, sounding like her sassy self.

"I wasn't talking about the breakfast or the rose."

She gave him The Look that he had been dying to see. "Eat, and I'll tell you my plan." She climbed on the bed, settling next to him.

"What plan?" he said, folding a whole slice of bacon into his mouth.

"I want to take the rosebush that's on the balcony to Chillaton and plant it at Papa's grave."

"I wondered why you bought it."

"It will be to remember our first child — the one that I, that we, lost."

Spencer put his arm around her. "I think that's a beautiful idea, Jem. Sometimes I think that I don't deserve you."

She smiled and put her finger to his lips. "Everything good that I do, I learned from you, my husband. Everything."

■ ■ ■ ■

The sun was shining, and there was not a cloud to be seen. They drove through the arched gates at the Chillaton Citizens' Cemetery and waved at Scotty Logan, the caretaker. Spencer stopped and chatted with him. Jemma watched Spencer talk. He was such a good listener and genuinely cared about people. He would be a sweet daddy someday.

Scotty gave Spence a shovel, and they stopped at Papa's grave. Spencer dug a hole in the hard-packed ground. Jemma cut the plastic away from the plant and together they set it in the earth. On their hands and knees they filled it in, patted the soil, and poured four jugs of water on it.

Spencer put his arm around her and prayed, "Lord, we thank You for our blessings, for those we can keep and those that slip away. Help us to cope with the loss of our unborn child. Amen."

They sat in the bench by Papa's grave and held hands. A yellow butterfly landed on the smallest rosebud and rested. Its wings opened and closed for a long moment before it moved away.

Spencer leaned his head against hers.

"Jem, you accused me last night of being sorry that I've loved you all these years. I'll tell you what I regret. I regret that I kept my promise to you and didn't try to see you when we broke up in college. I'm sorry that I went fishing the day you had the wreck, and I regret that I couldn't save my crew when our chopper went down in Vietnam."

"Oh Spence, I'm sorry that I ever made you promise such a thing that year. It was so stupid. As far as the wreck is concerned, there is no way you could have known that I was going to run head-on into Joe's truck. Daddy wanted to spend time with you that day anyway, and the helicopter crash, babe, there was nothing you could have done to prevent it. It wasn't your fault they died." Her voice trailed off with a sense of understanding.

"You're never alone again in this or any grief, Jem. I will always be beside you. Please promise me something, though. Say that you will never question my love for you. No matter the circumstances, that will always remain constant. The idea that you're not worthy of my love and devotion will never cross my mind. Promise that you'll never doubt that again." He held out his hand to shake on it. "Look me in the eye."

She squeezed his hand. "I promise that I

will never again question your love for me."

"Now, c'mon, let's go see some people and have some Chillaton fun for the rest of the day."

"We aren't going to the castle, are we?" Jemma peered over her shoulder at his parents' house.

He opened the car door for her. "Nope. I'll stop by the dealership and see if Dad's there, but apparently, Mom has some thinking left to do."

They went to Plum Creek and played in the stream. The old cottonwood tree creaked and swayed above them as they relaxed in its shade. They got burger baskets with milk shakes at Son's Drive In, then surprised Lizbeth, Lester, Willa, and Joe with the feast. They visited until dark, then parked at the Salt Fork of the Red River to watch the stars. After spreading the quilt on the hood, they kissed and reclined on their arms to enjoy the sparkling night.

"I miss this, don't you, Spence?"

"There's nothing like it." He took a deep breath and reached for her.

"Unless it's this," she said, snuggling against him.

A shooting star made its way across the heavens. "Make a wish," Spencer said.

Jemma closed her eyes and crossed her fingers.

"Okay, now tell," he said.

"Nope. Then it won't come true. You always do that to me, but you never tell me yours."

They waltzed in the moonlight. Jemma closed her eyes and inhaled the familiar scent of his skin. "I wished for me to go to heaven before you because I cannot bear for you to become the stars for me."

"Sorry; that wish is already taken, only with a different outcome."

She grinned at him. "Maybe when we're one hundred and ten, we'll just take a nap on the tracks, okay?"

"I'll keep it in mind," he said.

Jemma was now running a tight schedule to be ready for the New York show. They created a drafting corner for Spencer in her painting room. She was usually quiet, and he could get lots of work done, but not always.

"Remember when you got your driver's license and we started going to the drive-in movies?" she asked. "We decided to do everything they did on the screen. I guess we couldn't do that if we were dating now, huh? We would have to break our eighth-grade promise of no fooling around until the wedding night. Movies are going to be the ruin of promises like that. Can you imagine trying to be good kids and seeing all the sex that is in movies now?" She waited for a comeback, but he was absorbed in his work. "Anyway, I want to watch *Saturday Night Wrestling* and do everything they do on that show, okay?" No response. She stared at his back. "Spencer!"

He jerked around in his chair. "What?"

"I said I want to watch *Saturday Night Wrestling,* okay?"

"Sure, baby. That'll be fun."

She narrowed her eyes at him, and her mouth formed a crooked little smile.

"Jem, I've decided that I don't want to build a chapel at the nursing home like we planned," he announced after supper.

Her jaw dropped. "That was supposed to be in memory of Kenneth Rippetoe." Spencer left the room while she was talking so she followed him, dish soap dripping from her hands. "Spence, we have to build the chapel. Kenneth was so sweet and wanted to do something to change nursing homes. Remember his granny?"

Spencer unrolled a set of blueprints on his drafting table. He pulled her in front of the table and she put her soapy hand over her mouth. "A new building? Whoa." She clapped and jumped around the room. "You are too much, Mr. Chase."

He grinned at her old cheerleading moves. "We'll have to find the right person to run it, though. Somebody with Kenneth's tender heart for the elderly. I'm excited to get started on it. I've bought the old nursing home and the land out by the drive-in theater. It's a great spot. We'll phase out the old one and move the residents into the new one."

Jemma watched him talk about the plans. He showed her every door and window. She put her arms around his waist and leaned her head against his chest, hearing his words through his heart.

By Saturday night, the portrait of Harriet was finished and she had the background done for the next one of her feisty, generous Great-Aunt Julia. She kept her eye on the clock and when it was five minutes until nine, she cleaned her brushes and dragged Spencer in front of the television. He didn't mind. Only Jemmabeth could get by with watching such a goofy thing, yet be so serious about her art. He actually enjoyed watching her more than she liked the silly program. It was so very good to have her back.

"Now, remember what we talked about. Be ready," she said with a cocked eyebrow.

Spencer frowned at her. "What's that?"

She was ready. Jock, The Spider, Snyder was pitted against the local favorite, Mory, The Snake, Watts. The Snake came out with his first move a little too slow and The Spider bounced off the ropes and flattened him with his full weight. Jemma forthwith stood up on the couch and landed on an unsuspecting Spencer. He couldn't move. Jemma giggled and rolled off him.

"Have you gone crazy?" he asked, coughing.

"I told you that I wanted to do everything they do on the show tonight. You weren't listening to me, were you? Oops, now you aren't watching." She moved like lightning and was on him with The Claw. Spencer flipped her over and caught her with a leg lock. She was helpless. "No fair," she moaned. "They haven't even done this one yet, you dog."

"All's fair in love and wrestling, baby." Spencer shook his legs unmercifully.

"I can't breathe," she said, her voice vibrating.

"Yes, you can. I'll let you up if you promise

to use your skills for good and not for evil."

"I can't do that. I don't know what else may come up on the show."

"Then you can just stay there, young lady," Spencer said and changed the channel.

Jemma curled up in a ball, bit his leg, and escaped up the stairs while he yelped in pain and chased after her.

"Trent is coming this weekend, but he says he'll stay in a hotel," Spencer announced.

"Why? He could sleep on the sofa bed for free," Jemma said, then stuck a thin paintbrush behind her ear as she analyzed Do Dah's left eye.

"I don't think money is an issue with your cousin, Jem."

"Two rich guys, huh? So are you going to form a partnership?"

"If all goes as planned. You're for it, right?"

"You'll be a great team. Whose name goes first?"

"I think 'Lillygrace and Chase' sounds good, don't you?"

"I knew you'd put yourself last. I was just checking."

They celebrated their new corporation with dinner at Cattlemen's, the Golden Globe penthouse restaurant. Jemma took an official photograph of the partners signing a napkin. They decided to begin with an office in Chillaton, just to get their feet wet.

"I can't believe we're going to end up there," Jemma said during dessert. "Actually, I think we used to joke about that."

Trent folded his arms on the table, his dark brown eyes dancing. "It's my idea. I've never lived in a small town. It's kind of exciting to me."

Spencer and Jemma exchanged looks and laughed.

"You're in for some big cultural changes, man," Spencer said, "but at least you can drive an hour and fly wherever you want, if it starts to get to you."

"Are there any more girls like you left in Chillaton?" Trent asked, his question directed at his cousin, but his eyes on a female diner next to them.

"If you mean smart aleck and stubborn, yeah, I guess." Jemma laughed.

"I mean beautiful and funny."

Spencer pulled her to him. "I got the beautiful one, but there are plenty of funny ones left."

"You'll find somebody. Not to worry. Where are you going to live?" Jemma asked.

Trent shrugged. "I have no idea. Maybe

Lester would let me stay with him for a while."

"That'll be something to go from a Park Avenue town house to Lester's place."

Trent leaned back in his chair. "I decided in Vietnam that I wanted to live where life is peaceful. So I changed my goals over there, and I'm learning to appreciate family and friends more every day. You guys are an inspiration to me."

Jemma smiled at that. "Well, we can't promise you that it will be peaceful in Chillaton, but I guarantee it'll be different."

As they left the restaurant, Trent watched his cousin and his new business partner; they had what he really wanted — crazy love. He took a taxi to his hotel.

They drove home with the top down. "By the way, where do you plan for us to live?" Jemma asked, watching the speedometer.

"I think we'd better take a trip and see what we can find tomorrow," Spencer said as the Corvette zipped along the highway.

The flashing red and blue lights behind them made her scalp tingle. Spencer pulled over and knew he was doomed. Nobody gets a warning ticket in a Sting Ray convertible with a fabulous-looking girl in the car, and he was right. The state trooper walked away, and Spencer pulled back onto the highway much like Lizbeth did when she took her driver's test.

Jemma exhaled. "How many of those can you get? I don't want to be the only driver in the family, but I guess it's kind of a relief to know that you aren't completely perfect."

Spencer chewed on his lip and adjusted his rearview mirror.

The next day they drove around Chillaton, looking at the small selection of rentals and homes for sale. "Let's take a break and head out to Plum Creek," Spencer said, driving like an old man.

The creek was still. It needed rain just like the cotton crops. This was one of those summers when Papa would have quoted his Scottish gran when she'd say, *"The coos need a wooshing."* The cows definitely needed a washing around Chillaton. Even the coyotes were restless and thirsty. Everybody was talking about packs of them yipping and slinking around the countryside, coming close to the city limits. There was a threatening bank of dark clouds to the north, and Jemma was well aware of them. She had been through one tornado and didn't relish trying it again. The rusty windmill by the road groaned as it moved momentarily — against its will. Papa had built it decades ago and it marked the entrance to his and Gram's land on Plum Creek.

Jemma wrote their names in the sandy bank near where they had exchanged their marriage vows while Spencer got something out of the trunk. He was gone for a few minutes, then snuck up behind her and put a gold box in her lap.

"Happy early anniversary," he said and sat next to her.

Jemma untied the ribbon and looked inside. A piece of twine protruded through a hole in the bottom. She pulled the box off and followed the twine down the sandy shoreline to an old stand of cottonwoods, each one a giant. There, the twine was attached to survey stakes in a geometrical shape with one prominent pole in the middle. Attached to the pole was the piece of driftwood that Robby had carved for her hope chest when he could barely spell. JEMMA'S PLACE, it said.

She covered her mouth with her hands and turned to Spencer in realization of it all. She jumped on him, squealing in delight. He whirled her around in a circle like they did when they played "sling the statue" in the second grade. They fell, landing in the soft sand. This spot on the banks of Plum

Creek would be their home.

Lizbeth waited in the doorway with her arms stretched wide. Jemma and Spencer nestled right into them. "Thank you, Gram," Jemma said. "I love it."

"It was nothing but right for you two to have that spot of land. Your papa would have wanted it this way. I'll make sure Robby has a special place, too. Have you already made the plans for your house?"

"Well, just in the dirt." Spencer laughed. "It'll be something else, though. An artist and an architect should be able to come up with a sensational home. Thanks for letting us stay here until it's ready."

Jemma grabbed his arm. "Come with me, Spence, hurry."

They ran out to the tracks just in time for the freight train. Jemma took a deep breath as it clamored past, then turned to Spencer. "Now touch the rails," she said, putting his hand on the steel. "That's the way I feel about you even when you leave my sight. You warm my heart, Spencer Chase."

"It has to cool off sometime." He tucked her hair behind her ears.

"Yeah, but it's made of metal, and I'm not." She kissed him like they were still in high school.

■ ■ ■ ■

Lizbeth watched Jemmabeth and Spencer as they walked back to the house. Life shouldn't be so hard toward the end. Cam was her greatest blessing, and she had hoped he would be there with her to make the last of it as sweet as the beginning.

Nobody else had enjoyed Plum Creek as much as Jemmabeth. It was only natural that she and Spencer would inherit that land. When she'd signed the papers, though, Lizbeth's thoughts had wandered to Matthew and Luke. Had they survived the war, perhaps they, too, would have walked their daughters to an altar on its sandy shore. She sighed and set out Spencer's favorite cake along with her nicest dishes and was ready with a smile when they came back in the door.

Jemma had everything packed for New York. Spencer got off early and came home. He presented her with a business card.

"I thought it was going to be Lillygrace & Chase," she said, taping the card to the refrigerator.

"Trent pointed out that if we put my name first, we would show up closer to the front of the listings in the Amarillo phone book," he explained, taking off his shoes.

Jemma snapped her fingers and went into the bathroom.

"Almost forgot something?" Spencer asked.

"I remembered, though," she said and climbed on his back. He stood, and she flopped back on the bed. "Come here." She puckered her lips at him.

"No time for that. We need to be at the airport in thirty minutes."

"Then we have ten minutes to kill, the way you drive." She grabbed him around his waist and pulled him down beside her. "I love you, Mr. Chase of Chase & Lillygrace. We are going to have fun in the big city."

He gave her the once-over. "You look like a New York model. Let me see if you kiss like one."

"Are you going to compare me to Michelle?"

"Nope. Don't even remember ever kissing her. You have erased every memory of every woman I ever dated."

"Nice answer," she said, "because if you had said yes, there would have been big trouble coming down your road, mister."

"You're big trouble anyway. Now let's get out of here. Save this for Manhattan."

∎ ∎ ∎ ∎

Jemma stepped out of the cab and drew a deep breath. Since forever, she had wanted to have a show in New York City. Spencer offered his arm like a true gentleman. "You are stunning, Mrs. Chase," he said in the elevator. "That's the dress you wore for your second exhibition in Paris."

"My, my, what a memory, and don't you look good in that tux."

They were mid-kiss when the elevator door opened directly into the Sabine Gallery. It was very chic and urban and made for an interesting contrast with her work. She had twenty pieces of varying sizes and mediums for a two-week show that was a part of the "young artists" series at the gallery. It was bizarre to see people she had known most of her life hanging on the walls of a gallery like this, complete with designer lighting. She had painted Leon, from the Buddy Baker Band, rocking out on his guitar, hanging next to Son Shepherd, owner of Son's Drive In, whose cigar was clinging to his lip as he flipped a burger.

Jemma pointed out the painting of Trent and Spencer huddled around the kitchen table in California as they discussed their prospective business venture. The overhead light lent a glow to Spencer's blond hair.

"Oh man, I didn't know you were going to use that one," he said as they waited for the gallery manager to arrive.

"I like it. It's priced way, way high so nobody will buy it, and we can hang it in your waiting room someday," she said.

"I just hope there will be somebody to wait in the waiting room. Actually, I doubt we'll have one. Maybe just a comfortable seating area." Jemma could see the plans already forming in his head.

"Did you get the tickets for *Promises, Promises*?" she asked.

"The matinee was all I could get. Let's go dancing tomorrow night. Trent told me about a place that has a great band."

Jemma raised an eyebrow. "Trent goes dancing? I can't believe that."

"I think he is looking for a woman like the one I have."

"You think he'll find one?"

"There aren't any others," Spencer whispered as the gallery manager, a tall woman with hair like Cleopatra, approached them.

If she met one more celebrity, Jemma would have to sit down. To shake hands with people she used to read about in movie magazines was too much to handle. Now what she really wanted was to dive in to the fancy food table with several luscious-looking items she'd never even seen Helene make. She had her eye on a nice meringue dessert with caramelized fruit around the edges. It looked like an edible sunset.

"Mrs. Chase, I'd like to introduce you to someone," the gallery manager said, just as Jemma was about to take a bite.

Rats. She dusted off her hands and left Spencer talking with the mayor of New York. The manager took her to a cluster of people who were admiring the painting of Harriet.

"Sir, I'd like you to meet the artist. This is Jemmabeth Chase. Mrs. Chase, this is Governor Ronald Reagan."

Jemma swallowed and shook his hand. He was even more handsome in person than he was on the screen, big or little. "It's a pleasure to meet you, sir," she said. "I hope you enjoy my work." He grinned and introduced her to his entourage. The twinkle in his eye reminded her of Papa's. Jemma answered some of the group's generic questions about her art, but the governor was interested in several pieces and wanted to know more about the people she had painted.

Spencer watched her from across the room, as he enjoyed doing in public places. She could converse with kings and queens about her art, but Spencer got a chill when he saw her talking with Ronald Reagan. Lester would get goose bumps, too, when he found out because they shared a secret about the governor. Spencer couldn't wait to tell him that Mr. Reagan had bought the painting of Harriet. He had especially liked it that Harriet was Irish, like him.

"Happy birthday, babe," Jemma said at midnight as they waited for a cab. "We could stay up all night and celebrate if you want to. I'm on a roll."

"Nope. Staying up all night is what we did before we got married." He whispered something in her ear, then gave their hotel address to the cab driver.

"Well, since you *are* the birthday boy." She giggled. "You realize I haven't been with you on your birthday in four years." She gave him a package from her bag. "Here, open this. I can't wait."

Spencer unwrapped the tissue and held up a midnight blue frame with tiny gold stars painted on it.

"It's to frame the four-leaf clover that you took to Vietnam. I painted a star for every night that we missed being together while you were there."

"You have a way about you, Jem," he said. "This is perfect."

"No, you are perfect," she said. "Did Papa ever tell you about his dream that Ronald Reagan became the president and invited you to the White House to paint his portrait?"

She nodded. "I didn't think about it until the governor left. That's kind of weird."

"We shall see just how weird it is; his dream could come true. You are blessed."

"I'm blessed, all right. I am blessed that you have held me in your heart for all this time and never wavered."

Spencer whispered in her ear again, making her giggle. He tipped the cab driver and they ran inside their hotel.

Lester dusted the bedroom for the third time. If Trent didn't hurry up and move in, Lester would have to sacrifice another undershirt for a dust rag. "I never had me a boarder," Lester said as he watched Lizbeth punch down a fat ball of bread dough. "I ain't countin' that mail-order bride. She didn't give me nothin' but grief. Trent's payin' me a right smart amount of money to lay his head down at my house."

"Are you going to cook for Trent?"

"No ma'am, he told me that he's gonna cook for the both of us. Says it's his hobby. I'm hopin' he ain't fond of Chinese or something. I don't cotton to vittles that a feller's not sure whether he's eatin' plant or critter."

"I'm sure Trent will try to cater to your tastes, Lester. If not, you can come over for leftovers. Have you seen their office?"

"Yes ma'am. You won't recognize that old post office. Them boys have good heads on their shoulders, for rich kids. I reckon I'll just go down there now and see how things are comin' along. I don't suppose you'd like to accompany me, Miz Liz?"

"I can't stay long. I'll have to get back and tend to this bread." Lizbeth got her purse and followed Lester out the door.

Spencer had their house plans tacked on their home office wall so that whenever one of them got an idea, it was easy to make notes, but it was going to be a long time before any ground would be turned at Plum Creek. They were both too busy.

Jemma was getting better in the kitchen.

She was using the rose-patterned dishes from her hope chest, and she had discovered casseroles and salads.

"This is good, Jem. What do you call it?" he asked.

"Friday night," she said. "I just make this stuff up. You can put anything in a casserole."

Spencer grinned at her. "You put it in there, baby, and I'll eat it. What a team."

"Have you decided on the paintings you want for the office?" Jemma asked.

"Trent picked the one of Lester in his stationmaster uniform, and I want the one of the little kids sitting on the bench in Scotland."

"You need a landscape, too. It soothes the savage beast."

"Are you calling me a savage beast?" Spencer raised his brow at her.

"Maybe. Want to play King Kong again?" She giggled.

"I don't think I can carry you up the stairs," he said, pulling on her braids.

"So now I'm fat?" Jemma put her hands on her hips.

"No, I'm the one out of shape. How about we play some basketball tomorrow?"

"You're on," she said, begrudgingly leaving the rest of her casserole on her plate.

■ ■ ■ ■

Trent met them at the office. They let Jemma decide where to hang the paintings. It bore no resemblance to the old post office where she used to go with Papa to mail Christmas packages to Gram's old maid sisters in Houston. The new owners had stripped the hardwood and refinished them with a light varnish. A skylight filled the room with Texas sunshine. The old wallboard had been removed, exposing the original brick construction, and the oak and leather furniture lent a Panhandle flair to the office. Jemma bought a half-dozen giant potted plants, and the place couldn't have looked finer.

Trent and Spencer sat in the comfy armchairs talking about advertising while Jemma put the final touches on things. "I almost forgot," Trent said. "I hired a secretary since you turned that task over to me. She's a friend of yours, so I figured that was a solid reference. She's quite the looker, too, but I'm sure you already know that."

"What's her name?" Jemma asked, holding the last potted plant at such an angle that water spilled out on the polished wood floor.

Trent pulled out a file folder and read from it. "Melissa. Melissa Blake. She'll start next week."

Chapter 8
Hardtack

They sat in the corner booth at Daddy's Money. Spencer puffed out his cheeks and exhaled slowly. "Okay, Jem, what do you want me to do?"

Jemma took a sip of her sweet tea. "All she wants is to have you for her own. That's her goal. It always has been. Now she'll be able to spend more time with you every day than I can."

"Baby, it's the first decision that Trent has made in our partnership. I can't very well tell him to rescind it. I could, I guess, let him know that you are paranoid about Missy and we need to rethink it, and I'll do that if you want me to."

She narrowed her eyes at him, then folded and unfolded her napkin. "Why does The Cleave have to come along and make me miserable? You have to admit that she throws herself at you and she has a lot to throw."

"Everybody in Chillaton has seen enough of Missy to last a lifetime. You know that I'm not interested in her. I've never been attracted to her. Besides all that, Mrs. Chase, you are my wife and you made me a promise, remember?"

"I know that you love me, Spence, but you took her out more times than necessary when we broke up. You sprayed her with water and kissed her."

"You've never caught on to my plan, baby. I only had three dates with her, and I did it hoping that you would hear about it. I was using her to win you back. Did you ever consider that? If not, it was a lousy plan because it has caused me much more grief than it was worth."

Jemma's eyes darted up. "Really. That was it? Why did you have to kiss her to accomplish that?"

"Jemmabeth, you dated half of Dallas for almost a year, plus Paul Turner for about four months. Am I to believe that you never kissed anybody?"

"Truce."

"I am curious to know what you think Missy has that could possibly steal my heart."

"She is assertive and very self-confident. She has a perfect figure — beyond perfect.

She hates me. She has all that blond hair, and she is the queen of flirts."

Spencer sighed. "Jem, if you don't remember all the reasons that I love you, I'll tell you again. I love your heart, your laugh, the way you walk and dance. I love your talent, your temper, and your kisses. I love your spirituality, your sense of humor, the way you wear your hair, and those pouty lips. I think *you* are the one with the perfect figure. I love the scar on your head, the way you say my name, the way you sing, and the way you love me. There is no room for Melissa Blake in my heart or my head." He kissed her right smack on the lips even though there were elderly diners nearby.

He wasn't playing fair. "The fact remains that she'll be with you all day and she'll flaunt herself the whole time," she said. "How can you not watch her?"

Spencer raised his hands like an evangelist. "Baby, I'm not going to watch her. I can't help but see her, but watching is something I only do with you. Besides, I want to work at home all that I can. If we get busy enough, Trent can use her, and I'll hire some old lady. It could very well be that Missy is not secretarial material anyway."

Jemmabeth took some consolation in that thought, but not much.

■ ■ ■ ■

Lizbeth went to the grocery store and loaded up. Spencer had given her more than enough money to feed the three of them for a year. She put the groceries away and checked their room again. It needed fresh flowers; her granddaughter had to have them.

Lester knocked, then let himself in the back door. "I've got the car house ready for our little artist. These young'uns are goin' to give us a boost. I feel it in the air."

"I do too, Lester. How is your new chef working out?"

"No offense, Miz Liz, but he's as good as you are. Well, not quite, but comin' along." Lester thought again. "He can do some things good, but he's still got a lot to learn. He ain't tried bread and cobbler and such yet."

"That's nice," she said, surprising him. Either she was in a rare mood or wasn't listening.

"Did I ever tell you about my pa and the biscuits?" Lester asked.

"No, I don't recall that one," Lizbeth said, humming.

"Well, sir, my pa fancied himself a sharpshooter. He was kindly boastful about it, too. Claimed he could hit a day-old hardtack biscuit thirty foot up in the air, then catch the crumbs from it in his mouth."

"You don't say," Lizbeth muttered, going through her recipe box.

"My uncle lived just down the hill from us. He and Pa were always playin' pranks on each other. So, one Sunday, Uncle Ketch and Pa were going on about who was the best shot, and they come hence to makin' a wager about it. Pa grabbed his bucket of stale hardtacks — we kept 'em for the hogs — and his Winchester. He was all set up in the pasture, ready to prove himself. Uncle Ketch said Pa couldn't shoot three in a row and trap a single crumb in his mouth. Pa did, though. When Uncle Ketch got ready to throw up the third one, I seen him grab somethin' off the ground instead of out of the hardtack bucket. He let 'er fly. Pa nailed it and run around until he got himself a chunk of it in his mouth. Uncle Ketch come hence to laughin' his head off while Pa upchucked all over creation. Seems Pa had swallowed himself a crumb off a cow chip. Uncle Ketch took off down the road as fast as his old paint horse could trot. I'll never forget the look on Pa's face when he come back up to the house."

"What did you say, Lester?" Lizbeth asked. "Were you talking about biscuits?"

"Miz Liz, are you feelin' all right?" Lester looked at her over his bifocals.

"I'm feeling fine. I think I must have missed part of your story, but now I have my recipes written down and organized for Jemmabeth. She wants to learn how to cook from me. Would you like some biscuits and dewberry jam, Lester?" Lizbeth poured him another cup of coffee. "Shooting food seems like a waste of everybody's time to me. I hope you don't take up with such nonsense."

"Good-bye, honeymoon house," Jemma said, sniffing into a tissue. Her voice echoed around the empty apartment. "We had some rough times here, huh?"

"Oh, but we had some really, really good times here, too. Let's have one last dance. May I?" he asked, taking her hand.

They danced around the living room where their first Christmas tree had been and into the spare bedroom where Jemma had painted her way to Manhattan and where the baby furniture had waited. Spencer carried her out the door. "I carried you over the threshold the first time, so I should do the same for the last, right?" He locked it up. "Now, come on, we have a new chapter in our life to unfold," he said and kissed her.

They had borrowed Lizbeth's car for this last part of the move. The Corvette just wouldn't hold enough stuff. Spencer turned on the radio for a distraction. Lizbeth had it set on the Cotton John Show. "Welcome to the best part of a Golden Spread day," Cotton John said in his nasal tone before Jemma switched him off.

"Spence, would you show me where I had the wreck? I've never really seen it."

He was a little surprised because she had never mentioned it before. "Sure, if that's what you want. I'm not all that fond of the spot." He pulled off the road.

They walked around the nondescript ditch. A few sunflowers sprouted among the Johnson grass. Jemma held on to his arm as though the wind could carry her away from him. "Why do you think God didn't want us to get married then?"

"I have no idea, Jem. It's like Gram says, His ways are not our ways."

"The only good I can see from it was that Willa married Joe. Could that have been worth — well, never mind," she said and looked out over the pasture adjacent to the highway. A cluster of Hereford cattle gawked back at her, chewing their cuds. "Let's go."

"Don't you think this is weird to live next door to Trent and see him at the office every day, too?" Jemma asked as they pulled into the driveway. She had not mentioned The Cleave in a week.

"Yeah, but it's only temporary. I'm sure Trent will find someplace else to live. Look at Gram. She's beaming because we're moving in." Spencer got out of the car and gave Lizbeth a hug.

Jemma watched them. She might never have a hugging relationship with his mother. She had hoped that the baby might make a difference, but the Lord had other ideas. She took a deep breath as Spencer opened her door. Maybe he was right. This was a new chapter.

They wanted to see the sunset from their old necking spot at the river after supper. As the Corvette topped the last hill before the turnoff, Spencer slowed up. "Good grief. Somebody hit a deer. We don't have that many around here to spare, either."

"Oh Spence, look!" Jemma pointed to the ditch beside the dead doe. "It's her fawn. It can't even be a day old. Look how tiny it is."

Spencer pulled off the road. "Its leg is

caught in the fence."

"We have to do something." She was out of the car before Spencer could think straight.

He jumped out and caught her elbow as she approached the little animal.

"Wait, Jem. We don't want to frighten it any more than it already is," Spencer said. "Let me think."

The fawn made a pitiful noise and jerked its leg. Jemma froze by the front bumper. It turned its brown eyes on her and shuddered. "Hurry, Spence," she whispered.

Spencer grabbed their old stargazing quilt. He motioned for Jemma to follow him. They inched their way toward the fawn. A car sped by on the road, causing the baby to resort to another spasmodic attempt to free itself. Spencer took advantage of the distraction and eased the quilt over its little body. Jemma held the quilt in place while Spencer worked its leg free of the fence wire. They both held tight to the animal, binding it as best they could with the quilt. "Get in the car and I'll hand him to you." Spencer struggled with the fawn as Jemma let go. She ran to the car. Spence laid it in her lap and shut the door.

She covered its head with the quilt, but its sharp hooves dug into Jemma's legs until it stopped wiggling. "Where can we take it?" she asked, holding it against her.

"We'll take it by Doc Evans. Maybe he could keep it overnight in one of his big kennels. He'll know who to call in the morning. Are you okay?"

Jemma nodded, her pulse racing. She could feel the fawn's heartbeat even through the folds of the quilt, and its little body was warm and helpless in her arms. She turned to look out the window so Spencer couldn't see the tears in her eyes.

Chapter 9
Mr. Universe

Lizbeth had her work cut out for her. Jemmabeth was never interested in cooking before, but now it was time to learn. She knew how to plan a menu, but had no clue what to do about it after that. Lizbeth worked side-by-side with her every evening for a month so that supper was on the table at six. The rest of the day Jemma was in the car house doing what she did best, creating masterpieces on canvas.

"Cooking is divided up into science, math, and art," Lizbeth said. "You should like the last of those three."

"It's so time-consuming, though." Jemma frowned at the piecrust she was about to bake. "I just need to hire you to do it for us. Wouldn't that work?"

"Even so, honey, everybody needs to learn the basics so you can pass them on to your children," Lizbeth said, then wished she hadn't. She recanted. "When the time is right. Now remember to watch the clock, or this crust will get too brown."

Jemma put it in the oven and set the timer. She plopped down in one of the yellow and chrome chairs.

"How's Trina these days?" Lizbeth asked.

"She's fine. Nick told Spencer that he's going to propose at Christmas because he'll be finishing up his internship this spring." Jemma moved to the window as a freight train went by. "She'll be Mrs. Fields by next summer."

"What's wrong, sugar?" Lizbeth asked. "You can't seem to sit still these days."

"I miss Spencer."

"Why don't you walk down there and see him? Surely he's not that busy yet," Lizbeth said.

"I don't want to look like I'm spying on him. He's working on plans for the nursing home and our house. The firm in Amarillo is sending some business this way, too."

Lizbeth lowered her coffee cup. "It's the Blake girl."

"Missy is such a flirt, Gram. I know she wants Spence even though we are married. She spends eight hours a day with him and I don't."

"Jemmabeth, you surely aren't suggesting that Spencer could, for one minute, be distracted by that silly girl."

"He dated her when I broke up with him. She's beautiful. I know he loves me, but he's only human," Jemma said, sketching a passenger train for Shorty's jar.

"Spencer is not that kind of man, honey. If anybody should have his eyes peeled, it would be Trent. He's a willing target in my mind. You have every right to go see your husband. I'll watch this crust for you."

The phone rang. Jemma sprang up, hoping it was her man.

"Jem? It's Sandy. Can you talk a minute?"

"Sandy! I haven't heard from you in so long. How are you?" Jemma asked. Sandy broke down. Jemma hadn't heard her cry since the tenth grade when Marty broke up with her for a week. "What's wrong?"

"I'm leaving Marty. It's horrible. Everything has gone to pot. I can't do this anymore," she moaned.

"What happened?"

"Marty is messed up. He is moody and ticked off most of the time. I'm afraid that he's going to explode."

"Has he been to a doctor?"

"Yeah, right. He won't go anywhere except to a bar."

"Well, he'll come around. It'll be all right." Rats. That sounded pathetic.

"No. There's more." Sandy took a deep breath. "He has a girlfriend."

Jemma gasped. "He wouldn't. He's too crazy about you."

"He's crazy all right, but not about me. I've gotta go. I'll be home this weekend. Don't tell anybody but Spence, okay? Jem, never take anything for granted."

Jemma hung up the phone and went back into the kitchen. "Gram, I'll be back in an hour." She took off running toward the tracks and the Chase & Lillygrace office.

The office reeked of Chanel No. 5. The Cleave opened Spencer's office door holding some papers and laughing. Jemma's face prickled.

"Well, look who it is." Missy bent over her desk to write a note.

Jemma looked away, knowing the scoop-necked dress would reveal more than she cared to see.

"I assume you're checking up on Spence. We'll be finished with this in about an hour," Missy said, her miniskirt barely covering her thighs. "We've had our heads together over this all day."

Spencer came out of his office. "Hey, Jem, come in. Melissa, you can finish that up yourself sometime."

Jemma glared at her. She even wanted to stick her tongue out, too, but didn't. Spencer closed the door behind them and gave her a good kiss as they sank into his chair.

"What was so funny to make Missy laugh?" she asked.

"Oh. I told her that miniskirts and low-cut tops are not allowed, as in the dress code, and she said that she hadn't read the code. I reminded her that she had signed it, but she claimed that her dress shrunk in the laundry. She thought that was hilarious. I wasn't laughing because I included that dress code just for this very reason." Spencer studied Jemma's face. "What's up? You have a look that worries me."

"Sandy is leaving Marty."

"No way. What happened?"

"She said he's mean, drinking, and has a girlfriend."

"He's been known to be a hothead, but man, this really shocks me. They were always so tight." He lifted her chin. "What happens to other people has nothing to do with our relationship. Remember the promise."

Missy opened the door. "Sorry. I thought you might want to look these over. It's the bid from the contractor in Lubbock." She flashed her perfect smile at Spencer.

"Melissa, always knock before you come in my office, and if my wife is with me, don't disturb us at all. Got it?" Spencer said, his voice low and direct.

"Sure. You're the boss." She turned to leave, then came back. "Listen, Jemmabeth, this is so weird, but one of my closest sorority sisters went out a few times last Christmas with your old boyfriend, Paul Turner. Isn't that just too wild? She said he's the sexiest hunk ever, and he confer . . . confron . . . *told* her a few things about you. I thought you'd like to know that." Her lips puckered up, delighted in her own revelation.

"Why don't you leave a little early today, Missy?" Spencer said, his tone now chilly. "Remember the dress code tomorrow. This is your third warning. When Trent gets back from New York, we will all sit down and review a few things. Are we clear on that?"

Missy left with a triumphant toss of her mane.

Jemma was still in his lap but dry-mouthed and wilted. Spencer's arms were around her, and they had not loosened during Missy's little scene. "Don't let it get to you, Jem. I'm the one who has to deal with those memories now."

Jemma nodded. She closed her eyes and

moved her fingers over his hand. He was the most patient person on the planet, but there was a healthy portion of melancholy in his voice. She exhaled and slid off his lap. "I'm making you a pie for supper. I'd better go home and finish it."

He smiled. "Go home and paint. I'm not worried about your cooking like Gram is. I'll see you in a couple of hours or you can stay here with me. Forget the pie."

"No. I'd better get home. I miss you, babe. I hope you can work at home someday. I love you."

When Jemma stepped out of his office, The Cleave was pretending to tidy up her desk.

Jemma paused, then moved right up next to Missy, so close that her nostrils were filled with Chanel. "You know, *Missy,* I read the other day that when men see a large, exposed bosom like yours, it only reminds them of their lactating mothers. In other words, it makes them want to go eat pizza or a burger. You might think about that if you are hoping to hook a man with cleavage. You could be transporting them mentally to Son's or Daddy's Money with that very dress. Sometimes less is more, if you catch my drift. If you are thinking large, maybe you should invest in a really big dictionary for your desk; the word you couldn't think of was *confided*."

Spencer, listening from his chair, grinned broadly at Jemma's spunky rebuke. He laid the papers on his desk and leaned back, thinking of the afternoon of their wedding — the first time he ever saw his sweet wife's body. That moment was something he would never forget. He put the papers in his drawer and turned off the lights in his office. If he hurried, he could still catch Jemmabeth and give her a ride home.

Jemma and Sandy sat in the Corvette at Son's Drive In. Sandy's hazel eyes held none of their old fire and her makeup was not exactly perfection, which was even more shocking. Her frosted blond flip was droopy, and she had not touched her favorite food, French fries.

"It got so that I couldn't figure out what to say to him," Sandy said. "You know me; I'm sarcastic, but it's just for fun. He always liked that about me. I even tried to tone it down, thinking that might help. If I said it was a rainy day, he would take it personally and jump all over me, then sulk about it. If I asked him to take out the trash, he growled at me and gave me the evil eye the rest of the day. He made sure I had gone to bed before he came home at night, but if I mentioned it, he would leave the house and slam the door behind him."

"What about the drinking?" Jemma remembered the time Marty got suspended from CHS for drinking and fighting under the bleachers during a pep rally.

"I think the heavy drinking started in Vietnam. The MPs arrested him one night. He drank when we first got married but never alone at a bar. He met his girlfriend at one."

"I'm sorry, Sandy. Y'all always seemed so much in love. I never thought this could happen. Do you think it was the war that changed him?"

"All I know is that I am not one to stay around if somebody hits me. I don't care even if he is Mr. Universe. I could work through the girlfriend business, but not his temper. I would have come home sooner, but my daddy would have killed him if he'd seen what Marty did to my face one night."

"Good grief." Jemma squeezed Sandy's hand. "You should've had him arrested."

"He would've gotten out and done it again."

Jemma couldn't shake the idea of Martin qualifying as Mr. Universe — not if she were one of the judges. "Has he called yet?"

"Nope. He doesn't care. Besides, I'm sure she's moved in with him."

"What's she like?"

"She's kind of mousy with narrow eyes and a big bust," Sandy said.

"Like The Cleave?"

"Kinda, but The Cleave has those long legs and all that hair. This one gets by on just being loosey goosey. The girlfriend business doesn't bother me that much anymore. Isn't that weird? I think he may have fooled around in the army, too."

"Good grief, Sandy. I can't believe this is happening. Life changes so fast."

"Believe it, Jem. It can happen to anybody. Marty's on a path of self-destruction, and he can go straight there with his girlfriend for all I care."

"Do you still love him?"

Sandy sniffed and stared at the flashing neon sparks above Son's sign. "The well is dried up in that department. He used it up with his surly temper and his fist. I can take a lot, but he dished out too much. It wasn't fun anymore, and now it's over."

"Just like that? You don't even want to try and work it out?"

"No. Once he started the punching and kicking, I looked at him with new eyes. I don't care how long we've been together.

The last time I saw him, he came home drunk and slapped me for scratching an old 45 record he had. Get this: The name of the song was 'If Jesus Came to Your House.' I accidentally scraped it when we were packing to move to Idaho, and he knew that. Some of the things he said to me will hang in my ears for the rest of my life, even if he apologizes on his knees." She drew herself up. "But I will never be mistreated. You know me better than that."

"Good grief, Sandy, nobody expects you to put up with getting hit, but surely you feel something for him. Maybe you're being too hasty. Let your heart rest awhile. Remember me and my stupid decisions."

"You had to be there, Jemma. I'm not sentimental like you. I don't hold on to things like you did with that cowboy of yours. You're not still carrying a torch for him in the back of your mind, are you?"

"I am not!"

"Just curious. My mom sent me your picture with some guy in the Dallas paper right after Christmas. If that was Paul, it's no wonder you fell so hard. He was something else. He'd win Mr. Universe even over Marty."

"Yeah. That picture was a bad deal. I guess he's obsessed with me or something."

Much to Jemma's relief, Sandy changed the subject. "Do you know of any jobs around town? I need money."

"You could have been Spencer and Trent's secretary, but The Cleave got that job."

"You're kidding me. Spence hired her? No, wait, I bet your cousin hired her. His tongue was probably hanging out as soon as she walked in the door," Sandy said. "I bet that's driving you nuts."

"I'm trying to be cool, but you know she only wants to flirt with Spence."

"Maybe she wants to be your cousin-in-law. Don't worry, though. You have Spencer all to yourself."

Jemma laughed at the *cousin-in-law* part. "What's next for you?"

"I don't know. You and Spence don't know what it's like to be married and broke. If things had been different, I could have put up with living on a potato farm in the middle of nowhere. Listen, I need to get home. My mom is worried sick about all this."

"Here, take this." Jemma slipped a hundred-dollar bill into Sandy's hand. "You can pay me back sometime."

Sandy looked at the money for a second, then burst into tears.

Jemma dropped her off at the Bakers'

house. She sighed and watched as her best friend since nursery school trudged up to the steps and waved. How could love be so easily whipped around in the wind? Jemma had doubted her love for Spencer when she met Paul. Were it not for the good Lord's Plan, she might have been Mrs. Turner now. She had a sudden urge to see Spencer, so she dropped by his office. The Cleave was typing but stopped when Jemma slipped past her. She probably didn't want her to see how many mistakes she was making.

"Nice skirt." Missy eyed Jemma's hand-me-down silk that sported a couple of holes. "Still working on the bohemian thing, huh? Ever think you could be embarrassing your husband? He's such a professional."

"It's amazing that you consistently remember the word *bohemian,* when so many others escape your brain, Missy. Anyway, I don't really care about fashion," Jemma said. "I wear what feels good. I like cotton and silk."

"You should get that colored friend of yours to help you. It's weird how she's making something of herself, going against the nature of the coloreds. Maybe she'll save the government some money and won't be having a bunch of babies to get more money in her welfare check like the rest of them."

Missy returned to her typing.

Jemma's throat tightened. "Your comments about Trina are unfounded and unappreciated, Missy. What would you know about welfare? Your daddy owns every dinky movie theater in the Panhandle." She lowered her voice. "It's not the natural order of things, Missy. It's not *nature's due* or something. I'd like to see how you would have turned out if you were born black in a white world."

"Me? Black?" She laughed. "It's nothing but right for some to be born less than equal to us. Deal with it. Hey, I bet Spencer has never sprayed your T-shirt with water and said, 'bottoms next' to you."

Jemma took a step toward Missy's desk with the full intention to slap her just as Trent emerged from his office. "Hi there, Jem. Spence and I thought it would be fun to catch dinner and a movie tomorrow in Amarillo. How does that sound to you?"

"Sounds great," Jemma said. The Cleave had been spared a slap or The Claw once again.

Spencer appeared and put a folder on Missy's desk, then turned his attention on his wife. "Just the woman I'm looking for. Come into my office."

Jemma took a breath to regroup.

"See you tomorrow night then," Trent said.

"How do you like your new house?" Jemma asked over her shoulder. "Lester misses you."

"It'll work for now. I'll have you two over soon. The painters are finishing up today," Trent added as Spencer guided Jemma into his office and shut the door.

"We are not leaving this office until we finish these house plans." Spencer unrolled their dream home. "We need to be alone again."

"You design it and surprise me." She reached to straighten a big painting of Plum Creek that hung over his drafting table. "I'll like anything you come up with, except your obnoxious, ignorant, big-mouthed secretary who thinks you said 'bottoms next' when you sprayed her with water."

He laughed. "Missy has a problem with words. She makes typos all the time. Now come on; I'm not doing this by myself. We are designing it together. What do you say if we push the deck out just a little more here." He pointed to the spot on the plans, then took off his tie, unbuttoned his shirt, and rolled up his sleeves. "We need to break ground this month."

Jemma picked up his tie and looped it

around his neck, pulling him to her. "First things first, mister."

Trent picked them up in his new convertible. Jemma and Spencer sat in the back. "You aren't going to put the top down, are you?" Jemma asked.

"No. Melissa probably wouldn't like it if the wind messed up her hair." Trent laughed.

Jemma's googly eyes bored a hole in the back of Trent's head. "*She's* coming?"

"Yeah. I haven't been out with anybody since I moved here." Trent pulled up in front of the Blakes' colonial, redbrick house. It took up half the block. "I'll be right back," he said and went to the front door.

Spencer held up his hands. "I had no idea he was going to ask her. Just make the best of it."

"There is no 'best of it' with Missy. Why don't you tell him that I can't stand her?"

"I know she's always acted witchy toward you, but don't let this ruin the evening, baby. Trent deserves some fun."

"Well, The Cleave knows how to dish that out. Ask any boy in our class."

"Except me," Spencer said. "Remember, I was only gambling for your attention."

"Are you two necking already back there?"

179

Missy asked as she burst into the car, bringing her Chanel with her. "Jemma, that color sort of washes your skin out." She smiled over the back of the seat at Spencer. "Anything looks yummy on you, though, Spence."

The evening was ruined as soon as Jemma saw her. *Witchy* was putting it mildly. Missy overwhelmed Trent. If Jemma caught her ogling Spencer one more time, though, she was ready with The Claw, The Sleeper, and a full Cinderblock. The Cleave would be a good name for a wrestling move. She could clamp one hand around Missy's mouth while the other applied a thick coat of mayonnaise to her hair, just to settle an old score.

"Do you have your house plans ready?" Trent asked as they waited for their sundaes after the movie. Missy rested her chin on his shoulder while he talked. Not exactly first date behavior, in Jemma's opinion. How could they go back to an office relationship after that?

"Yeah, almost. The excavation starts next week. I want to get rolling on it before Thanksgiving," Spencer said.

"How exciting," Missy gushed. "Let's go see the building site. Maybe we could have a picnic there tomorrow. That would be kind of . . . homespun. We could splash around in the water. I have a crazy new bikini, or I could wear a T-shirt and cutoffs." The T-shirt part was directed straight at Spencer.

Jemma's mouth twitched.

"We're busy tomorrow," Spencer said quickly, squeezing Jemma's hand under the table.

"Well, then we could go, huh, boss?" Missy breathed in Trent's ear. Trent gulped.

"There's a lock on the gate," Spencer said.

"There must be a key then." Missy took the cherry off Trent's sundae and held it by the stem as she ate it with her perfect teeth. *Fangs,* Jemma thought.

Spencer changed the subject by discussing the movie they'd just seen while Missy laughed way too loud and traced around Trent's ear with her long, red fingernails. *Witch Claws.*

It was a painfully long ride home. Jemma watched helplessly as The Cleave tried every move she had on poor Trent. Probably 99 percent of it was for the benefit of those in the backseat. Jemma spent the last half hour of the trip with her eyes closed but her ears wide open.

Jemma could not let it go. "That was totally

unethical. I think Missy should always call y'all Mr. Chase and Mr. Lillygrace."

"I don't know what Trent is thinking, but we'll talk," Spencer said with an audible yawn.

"He doesn't have a chance and you know it. The Cleave has a plan. If she can't get you, she's going for him and wants you to watch." Jemma turned over. "Remember, I'm the only show you watch."

He turned over. "Are you about to put on a show for me?"

"Maybe. Is Gram asleep?"

"She's snoring. What are you doing?"

"Shhh. I need to work out my frustrations with some wrestling moves. You are going to get what The Cleave deserved all night long. Get ready, mister, and keep your voice down." Jemma assumed a grappling stance on the cool floor. Her husband stifled his laughter as best he could until she hit him with **The Cinderblock**.

Chapter 10
Hauntings

The wind rattled the car house windows and whipped grains of sand against the glass. On days like this, even the birds took shelter. Nedra would use up several cans of Aqua Net on her patrons today. Jemma, however, stood on the tracks and surveyed the houses on the other side. Her ponytail flew at her side like a flag in a gale. Missy's comments and insinuations about welfare haunted her heart. Rats on Missy's ignorance, but her own indignant words were worthless unless she took some action. Lecturing The Cleave about inequality was one thing, but Jemma hadn't done anything, really, to help the situation, either. Maybe the Holy Spirit had laid this burden on her heart for a reason. How long would it take for things to change if left to the natural order of life in Chillaton? There was no pride for anyone picking up welfare checks. Pride came from working hard and doing the job well.

Jemmabeth walked with her head down, against the wind, along the rails to further survey the neighborhood. She waved at Joe as he hustled into his house with the mail. Jemma smiled. He and Willa were so happy that nobody saw much of them these days. She had invited them over for supper several times so she could show off her new cooking skills, but they always gave some excuse to stay home. Jemma knew that feeling. She hoped that she and Spencer would always have it. It was fun living at Gram's, but it was not the unabashed freedom they had enjoyed at their own apartment.

She plodded down the tracks for a while until she saw a FOR SALE sign stuck in the middle of the cow pasture across from Shorty Knox's dugout. Her scalp tingled at the thought, and the sign quivered in the wind. She memorized the number, then ran down the tracks to Main Street. She burst into Spencer's office without asking Missy, but he was on the phone. Jemma paced around his office until he hung up. She landed on his lap.

"This is a pleasant surprise," he mumbled before he kissed her.

She jumped off and resumed her pacing. She took the rubber band out of her hair and played with it as she talked. "You know that things are far from equal in Chillaton, and nobody wants to change anything. They just sit around and gripe about it, as though it's part of our destiny — like enduring the wind or something. I think we have the resources to make a difference. So, I want to buy a little land across the tracks and start some kind of business to help that neighborhood become independent of welfare. There's a for sale sign in a pasture there right now, and I think it's a sign from God. What do you think?"

Spencer blinked. "Now tell me this again."

Jemma started over, adding bits of heartfelt philosophy here and there. Spencer nodded, jotted a few notes, including the number of the Realtor, then smiled. "I understand what you are saying and I agree, but something like this would take a lot of planning, Jem. What kind of business are you thinking about?"

"That part I don't know. I suppose I need to do some research to see what skills are floating around over there, but we have to do something, babe. I mean it's not right for some of us to be so content while others are hurting, you know? I just can't accept that nothing can be done. I want everybody to feel good inside about living here," she said, then got distracted by his eyes. "I love you, Spence." She kissed him like they hadn't seen one another in a month.

"Let's go out to the river, my little thinker," he said.

"Tonight?"

"No, right now."

Willa's old 'tunia path was no longer the dirt lane with perennial petunias planted in old boots. Jemma and Trina had rescued all the boot planters they could carry when a tornado ripped through town. Joe had changed that when he laid out flat, smooth rocks in a curved design. On both sides he had created flower beds lined with bricks. The porch was graced with a railing, as were the steps leading up to the front door. The roof that had been damaged by the tornado was new, as was the addition Joe had begun on the back and side of the old house.

Willa stood at the ironing board. The old sign that had advertised her business from her porch post for years — DOES IRONING AND GUARANTEE HER WORK — was now hung nonchalantly above her rocking chair.

She threw up her arms when she saw who was knocking. "Come in this house, child."

"Your place is looking so good," Jemma said.

"It's been way too long since I seen you, sugar," Willa exclaimed. "Set yourself down. You know this ain't gonna be my kitchen when Joe finishes his project. This'll be the laundry room, he says. I'm gonna have me a whole room to do the wash and my ironin' jobs. Don't that beat all?"

"Where is Joe?" Jemma asked.

"He had to run to the lumber yard for somethin'. That man is the hardest-workin' human I ever saw." Willa laughed. "He can't sit still, except for lovin' on me." She covered her mouth and giggled.

Jemma smiled at her own knowledge of that kind of man. "I need your help, Willa. Is there one thing that folks in your neighborhood know how to do better than anything else?"

"Law, child. What kind of a question is that to start off with?"

"I have to know. Let's say that just the women were all in business together. What is a skill that they would have, other than cooking?" Jemma leaned forward for the answer.

"Are you workin' for some TV game show? My ol' noggin ain't even been turned on yet today." Willa puckered her lips and considered the question. "I can see you're set on a quick answer. Hmm . . . folks over here makes nearly everything they wear. I reckon that's what you'd call a skill. 'Course we been workin' the land ever since folks needed help, too."

Jemma wrote it down. "Hand sewing. Does anybody know how to run a sewing machine?"

"Gweny Matthews and, of course, my Latrina. What you got cookin' in that pretty head of yours?"

"I want to start a business over here to help families get off welfare."

"Oh, for land's sake, sugar, that ain't gonna happen. It would take a miracle."

"I believe in miracles, Willa. I'll see you later and we'll talk more."

Jemma dashed out of the house, down the path, and across the train tracks.

Willa shook her head and turned back to her ironing. "That child's headin' for nothin' but disappointment, but Lord love her for tryin'."

"Maybe what you should do next, Jemma, is have a meeting and see if the neighborhood is interested in such a venture. It would have a better chance at success if you have their support," Trent said as the three of them sat in the conference room.

Spencer nodded. "I agree. If this is going

to get off the ground, it'll need the whole community behind it. At the earliest stages, maybe we could use the basement of the Bethel Church and, of course, pay rent and all utilities for it."

Jemma had written everything they said on her notepad. "Want to come over for supper tonight, Trent? I'm cooking Gram's Cornish pasties. It's an old family recipe with meat and potatoes that are folded up in pastry," she said in culinary triumph.

"Thanks, but I'm cooking for Melissa tonight at my place. I'll take a raincheck. You guys should come over later, if you want." Trent yawned.

Jemma nudged Spencer's leg. "You two are really mixing business and pleasure," he said.

Trent drew in his chin. "Oh. I hope that's not a problem."

Jemma turned to Spencer. He grimaced and stammered. "I trust your judgment, man. But I do think we should keep things as professional as possible in the office." He avoided Jemma's evil eye. "You know, Missy and Jemma were . . . rivals in high school."

"Yeah, Melissa told me there was some intense jealousy coming at her, but I assumed you've worked through it by now." He grinned patronizingly at his cousin.

Jemma stood, pushing in her chair. "I'm going home and get started on supper. Thanks for the suggestions. See ya'll later."

She flew through the door and past Missy, who was watering the plants as the sun cast a glow through her cascading, Breck Girl hair.

"Sugar, you look like you are about to pop." Lizbeth wiped flour off her granddaughter's chin.

"I need the Lord to forgive me, Gram. I think I hate someone." Jemma stirred the potatoes, then sat down at the kitchenette. She twisted her fingers through her hair and gazed out the window.

"The Blake girl again." Lizbeth clicked her tongue. "Nobody is all bad. That girl must have something to like about her."

Jemma looked up at Lizbeth. "Not to my knowledge. Now she is dating Trent and she told him that I used to be jealous of her. I know she is a tramp, Gram. Do you know what that means?"

"Well, I think I can come up with an idea or two. Didn't Spencer take her out a few times? I find it hard to believe that he would have had a date with that sort of girl."

"Spencer is naïve about Missy, but not half as naïve as Trent is. I can't let this happen to my only cousin, but I don't know how to stop her."

"I assume you've prayed about this."

Jemma nodded. "I don't know what to do. I think I want to hate her. I know that's an awful thing to say."

"Then pray to love her." Lizbeth saw the twinge run through Jemma. "It's in the Scriptures. The fifth chapter of Matthew, verse 44. Loving your enemies is never easy, but you must do it or you are never going to mature in your Christian walk. The Scriptures also tell us to praise God in all things. We are quick to ask Him for things, but often we neglect to praise Him. Praising Him in a bad situation can be even harder than loving your enemies. I don't mean to preach, Jemmabeth, but when things seem at their worst, remember that verse."

"Would you watch these potatoes for me, Gram? I'll be right back." Jemma left the house and went outside, sketchbook in hand.

Lizbeth opened the screen door. "You keep an eye on those clouds, Jemmabeth. They look like trouble brewing to me. Could be a twister or a duster heading our way," she yelled.

Jemma waved back and stepped up on the rails in the bitter wind. Lizbeth went back to the kitchen and watched her through the window. She was not a child anymore. She was a woman with a loving husband and the loss of an unborn child still haunting her. Dealing with this jealousy and anger could possibly make her life easier and increase her testimony for the Lord. Lizbeth herself had never known jealousy with Cameron, but she had known anger at his passing. It lingered over her like a swarm of locusts. She had scriptures of her own — committed to memory but not yet fully realized in her heart.

Spencer's car pulled in the driveway. Lizbeth met him at the back door.

"Where's the chef?" he asked.

Lizbeth nodded toward the tracks. "She's doing some thinking, son. Just let her be. She'll come in directly."

Spencer turned to the tall windows and saw her. The wind swirled her hair around her as she clutched her arms against her chest. "She's upset about Missy," he said, "and probably with me, too."

"For all her beauty and talent, Jemmabeth still has some doubts about herself, honey, and she's not over that miscarriage. She needs more time and your love." Lizbeth patted his back and tended to the supper.

Spencer stayed at the window watching her as she sat on the rails, now writing in her sketchbook. A half hour later, she was still there. He went outside and sat next to her, putting his coat over her shoulders.

"How's my girl?" he asked. "Are you composing a poem?"

"Maybe."

"Am I in the doghouse for saying that you and Missy were rivals in high school?"

"Maybe."

He sat next to her. "Bad choice of words on my part. I know that Missy is a royal pain and a big flirt. Are you writing a poem about her?"

"Not exactly." She closed her sketchbook and smiled up at him. "I'm not Emily Dickinson, but it makes me feel better." She grabbed his hand. "Let's go in. We have some Cornish pasties to eat."

Chapter 11
Revelation

Jemma burst into his office again. "They want me to teach a two-week seminar in Paris!"

Spencer was on the phone but gave her a thumbs-up. She danced around until he hung up, then grabbed his neck.

"I like what good news does to you," he said. "I have some of my own. That was your uncle Arthur on the phone and he wants us to come down and discuss two expansions of Billington's. One will be in Austin and the other will be their second one in Houston."

"Congratulations! We can see Carrie while we're there. I miss her."

"I've missed you all day long." He pulled her to him. "When's Paris?"

"The last two weeks of November. I guess that's the bad part."

"I think that's when we will be wrapping up the nursing home. I don't know if I can go with you or not. I'm sure there will be plenty of loose ends to tie up and everybody will be wanting their money. It's kind of my project."

"Trent can handle it."

"If he's back from California. The day before Thanksgiving is when we are making our presentation for the mini-mall in Sacramento. It's a big deal for us."

"It's okay. I can go alone. I'll just hook up with some Frenchman and he'll take care of me. *C'est la vie.*" She shrugged.

"Oh yeah? Well, *such is life* for me to be in love with a famous artist. C'mon — let's go celebrate at Plum Creek. They should have some walls up by now."

"Where are you two going?" Missy scanned Jemma's painting jeans and old sweatshirt.

"Personal information," Spencer said, much to Jemma's amusement.

"It's weird to see it coming to life, isn't it?" Jemma asked as they walked under the cottonwoods. "I guess that's the way all your projects are, though."

Spencer ran his hand across a piece of lumber. "Yeah, I love it."

He took her for a tour of the house and she stopped in a corner of the kitchen.

"Wait, what's this? I don't remember this on the plans." She took two steps up a narrow stairwell.

He grinned. "This is my little surprise. I thought we might accidentally need a pouting room like Gram's. I threw it into the plans, just in case. What do you think?"

"I think I love it, you sneak. It looks like the hidden steps up to the Sainte-Chapelle."

"I'm putting in some stained glass so whoever needs to pout can cheer up quicker."

"Well, I wonder who that will be?" Jemma kissed him. "I love you, Mr. Architect. Maybe I'll pout even more since you made me a special room for the purpose."

"C'mon, let's finish the tour," he said and led the way up another stairway to their shared studio. "This is the room where the renowned Jemmabeth Alexandra Chase paints her masterpieces. Notice how the light changes from dawn to high noon then to the setting sun by the perfect placement of windows."

"Ah, but over in this corner of her studio is where the prominent architect, Spencer Morgan Chase, envisions timeless structures."

They left the studio and went downstairs to a large room that curved along the creek.

"Here, ladies and gentlemen, is the happiest room of all. It is within these walls that Mr. Chase tells Mrs. Chase how much he loves her every night." He curled his finger at her.

Jemma backed up in mock defense. "What if somebody is still around?"

"They will be trespassing. Come here, woman."

A flock of geese floated across the sky, paying no attention at all to the giggling activity directly below them on the banks of Plum Creek.

"Mother has invited us to supper," Spencer announced as he stood in the car house admiring her latest work, a piece showing the town postmistress, Paralee Batson, leaning over the counter in the old post office checking the weight of a package. "This is great, Jem. I like it that her tongue is sticking out just a bit and that her cat is staring at those scales."

Jemma cleaned her brushes. "It's sort of *Saturday Evening Post.* Now what's this invitation all about? I'm not sure I'm ready for your mother yet."

"I'll be there to protect you. She called the office and told me that she's doing the cooking herself for the first time in fifteen years." Spencer looked around at some of the other pieces. "Wow. You've been churning out the work, haven't you? Who's this pianist?"

"That's Melanie Glazer's fiancé. I wanted to thank her for playing that sweet violin music at our wedding." Jemma turned off the light. "When do we eat?"

"Six thirty. So that guy is the reason that you double-dated while we were still going steady. Melanie needed your help to catch him."

"You know I'll regret that until the day I croak. C'mon, there's not much time for me to find something to wear. Rats."

Spencer waited while she dragged out one dress after another to hold up in front of the mirror. "Jem, it's already six o'clock. You take a quick bath, and I'll pick something out."

She pouted into the bathroom. Spencer picked up all the discards and hung them up. He slid a few dresses around on the rack, then pulled out a black dress her mother had given her and laid it on the bed.

"Not that!" she shrieked when she came back. "Your mother will think I'm a floozy."

"I love that dress on you. It's very sophisticated and she will be impressed," he said, kissing the back of her damp neck.

"Maybe you should start choosing all my clothes. The Cleave always says that I'm stuck in a bohemian rut." Jemma slipped into the dress and dabbed on some lipstick. She shook her hair and ran her fingers through it.

Spencer watched, mesmerized by such beauty carrying his name. "Missy is jealous of you and that's that. She's harmless."

"The chimes of doom," Jemma whispered as Spencer rang the Chase castle doorbell. "Nobody rings the doorbell at their own house."

"This is not a normal house."

Max Chase came to the door. "Vah-vah-voom, daughter-in-law, you look spectacular." He grinned at Jemma.

Jemma jabbed Spencer with her elbow. "See, *floozy*."

"Son, it's so good to see you, sweetheart." Rebecca rearranged the centerpiece flowers on the dining room table. She embraced him, then turned to Jemma, exhaling. "You look nice this evening, Jemmabeth." The words came out of her mouth like lukewarm breath on an icy morning, but they came out.

"Thank you." Jemma turned to Spencer, wide-eyed.

"Let's eat." Max pulled out a chair for Rebecca. "Your mother's been in the kitchen all afternoon."

It was a gourmet meal. Rebecca was very talkative, and Max was his usual jovial self.

"I've been going to church," he whispered as he and Jemma cleared the table.

"Good for you. Does Mrs. Chase go with you?"

"Oh no, hon. She's not much on religion. I think her family belonged to the church of the firstborn atheist or something like that. She's being good tonight, huh? No catty remarks."

Jemma nodded as Spencer came into the kitchen. "Mother wants us to have dessert by the fireplace. She says you can serve it. I'll help."

They had lemon tarts and coffee. Jemma stuck close to Spence's side.

"Have you seen my new Caddy?" Max asked.

"No, but it probably looks just like last year's model," Spencer said.

"Take a look for yourself." Max and Spencer headed to the garage to view the Cadillac, leaving Jemma and Rebecca alone.

"The meal was delicious, Mrs. Chase. Thank you for inviting us," Jemma said, her eyes on the coffee table.

"I've been thinking about your miscarriage, Jemmabeth," Mrs. Chase said, taking Jemma off guard. "You may not be aware that I lost three babies before my Spencer was born."

A chill ran over Jemma. She looked right at Rebecca, tears gleaming in her eyes. "I didn't know that. I am so sorry."

"People underestimate the fracture it leaves in a woman's heart. I understand that you struggled with some of that yourself." Rebecca stirred her coffee.

"Yes ma'am. I wanted more time to be alone with Spencer when I found out I was pregnant, and I wasn't excited at all. When the baby died, well, I blamed myself." Jemmabeth glanced at Mrs. Chase, surprised by her kindness.

"Nonsense. Miscarriages just happen sometimes. I'm sure you will be one of the lucky ones who turns right around and carries the next baby full term." Rebecca set her cup on the table. "I realize that Spencer has always loved you. He is a rare person who gives his love for a lifetime. I know that I have been rather cold toward you, and I want to change that about myself. I don't want to lose my baby after all these years of being a useless mother to him. I trust you will bear with me." She paused. "My therapist says that I'm jealous of you, of your relationship with my son. Maybe there's some truth in that, and if you are of the same opinion, forgive me, please."

Jemma placed her hand lightly on Rebecca's shoulder until Spencer and Max's laughter trickled down the hallway. She moved back to the couch and exchanged unsteady smiles with Rebecca. Jemma considered how extraordinary it must be to suddenly wake up and realize that your child has grown from a toddler to a fine man without your assistance.

Julia met them at the Houston airport. "Look at you two. The honeymoon is still going, isn't it?" she asked in her straightforward style. Her hair, as always, was a little too red.

"You are always right, aren't you, Do Dah?" Jemma slid her arm around her great-aunt's naturally well-padded shoulders.

"Here's the deal. I don't want to hear the name Do Dah mentioned the whole time you are in Houston. I'm going to break you of that habit if it's my final act on this old earth," she proclaimed.

"Do Dah!" Spencer said, arriving with their luggage, "I'm so glad to see you."

"*Julia.* Call me Julia for three days in a row and I'll buy you supper at the best restaurant in Texas."

"I don't know." Spencer grinned. "Do Dah is a cute name."

"It was cute coming from my nephew's mouth when he couldn't do any better, but not from two fully grown adults. Now let's get moving. Arthur wants you delivered by ten o'clock sharp, and he's a man bent on punctuality."

Spencer was right on time. He and Arthur met behind closed doors until noon. Jemma and Julia went shopping at Billington's. "Let me pay for it, sugar. I get everything at cost. You can reimburse me when I'm old and dotty."

"You'll never be like that, Do — Julia."

They drove back to Julia's mansion in the classy River Oaks area of Houston.

"Now tell me about this business you are trying to get started across the tracks. Are you sure you'll have enough workers?" Julia wagged her finger at a driver who cut her off on the freeway.

"I hope so. I can't sit around and wait for change in Willa's neighborhood. Things are so pitiful over there. They need some pride, and I think pride comes from working hard and doing your job well, don't you?" Jemma said as they entered the gate to Julia's home.

"That's true, but folks may be scared off by a white girl coming in and changing things. You'll have to take it slow and easy. Get it going, then fade out. Do you have enough funds to get it off the ground and take a loss for a while?" Julia parked the car and unloaded their packages. "Art and I would be happy to help. He's a believer in projects like this."

"Spencer says we'll be fine, but I have no clue about business. I hope he's going to talk to Uncle Art about it while we're here." Jemma surveyed the lavish home. "Your home is even swankier than my Lillygrace grandparents' home in St. Louis."

Julia laughed. "That's good to hear. Come look at this." She led Jemma down the shiny marble hallway and pointed at her portrait on the wall, now encased in an ornate frame. "We get so many compliments on it, sugar, you could make a fortune in Houston. Everybody likes to see themselves captured in oil, no pun intended, and hanging in their own foyer."

"I want to paint Uncle Art, too. I just need about an hour's worth of sketches when he has the time."

"We'll make the time. I was going to ask you when you could do just that. It looks egotistical for an old hen to have her portrait up without her rooster. My old sweetie needs to slow down. We both could stand to shed a few pounds, but we love to eat. Speaking of which, let's go see what's for supper."

"I'd forgotten how pretty this part of Houston is," Jemma said, looking out the bay windows. "Doesn't somebody famous live in this neighborhood?"

"You must be thinking of old Ima Hogg. She's the daughter of Jim Hogg, the governor during Texas's Wild West days. Ima's done a lot for the state, and her gardens are something else. I doubt she got much dirt under her fingernails, though. Anybody can have a gorgeous garden if you hire enough people to work on it. I know that firsthand." Julia was never one to pass out compliments lightly.

"I need to paint my other great-aunts, too. Would they like that? I feel funny coming here and not visiting them. I don't know them at all."

Julia snorted. "Those old maids wouldn't waste their time on portraits. All they do is watch TV and fuss about housework. Let them be, sugar. I know them."

After supper, Jemma sketched Arthur in the study that night while he advised them on their project, and she got more than her hour's worth of sketches. "What you need for a cottage industry is enthusiasm and commitment over time. Of course, this may not be a typical cottage industry, but you should treat it like one, initially. If the products are appealing, it could take off. We will certainly be interested in giving the goods a go," Arthur said, puffing on his pipe. Jemma put down her work and gave him a good bear hug of appreciation.

Carrie came to the door using her walker. Her blond hair was cut in a pageboy, and her twinkling blue eyes were still full of mischief. "They're here, Phil," she yelled. "I'm so glad to see y'all."

Spencer picked her up for a hug and Jemma waited her turn. "You look so good, Carrie. It must be the Houston climate."

Spencer and Philip shook hands and the foursome settled into the living room of their modest home. Jemma sat on the arm of Carrie's chair.

"Phil and I would like to get out of Houston, actually. It's too big. You know what I'm used to, and Chillaton is the size we want. Now that I have my own built-in therapist, I can live anywhere. I'm up to three hours a day with my walker. What do you think of that?"

"I think that's fantastic," Jemma said. "Are you looking for a job in rehabilitation therapy, Phil?"

"Maybe," he said, looking at his wife.

Jemma put her arm around Carrie. "You've done wonders for this little twerp, that's for sure. The first time I ever saw her I thought she would be tethered forever to her circus cannon, that iron lung. Now look at her — Mrs. Suburbia."

"That's all because of you, Jem. If you hadn't made my dad angry with your crazy ideas and that portrait, I never would've met Mr. Philip Bryce, and I definitely wouldn't be using a walker, even if it is only for part of the day. Plus, I never would have danced with your husband," Carrie added, grinning at Spencer.

"I can't imagine why such a beautiful piece of art would make anybody angry," Spencer said, studying the portrait of Carrie striking a pose in a tutu. "I remember he thought Jem was mocking her, as if that could ever happen."

"I think The Judge felt like she was giving Carrie wild ideas." Philip laughed.

"I was painting her spirit," Jemma said. "She told me once that she could do whatever came into her head. She could even fly, if she thought it up. Of course, there was also the little matter of me arranging for Carrie to go to church as well as play with Buddy's band at a dance. Actually, the dance infuriated him, right, Carrie?"

"None of that matters now. I have Phil, and I'm able to take care of myself! Let's eat. I'm starving." Carrie struggled upright with her walker, refusing all offers of assistance.

"Phil, do you have any background in management?" Spencer asked while the girls were away from the table.

"I'm the supervisor for the hospital's rehab unit, why?"

"Do you have a certain age group that you like to work with?" Spencer added, evaluating Philip's interest.

"I like them all." Philip leaned toward Spencer. "Do you know of a job opening somewhere?"

"Maybe. Jemma and I are looking for a manager for our nursing home. It's almost complete, but the person we're looking for has to have the same compassion for the elderly that the building's namesake had. He was this kid in high school that was a good guy, but he was always on the fringes of the teenage social scene. His family struggled to make ends meet, then his dad died. Kenneth delivered groceries even before he had his driver's license. He became an Eagle Scout and hoped someday to run a nursing home, but he and his mother were killed in a tornado that ripped through Chillaton a few years ago. Jemma had a real soft spot in her heart for him. Now we're about to open this home in his name, and I think you could be just who we're looking for."

Philip nodded. "My mom died in a nursing home. She's the reason I went into rehab therapy. She had several little strokes and eventually lost control over her life." He tapped his fingers on the table. "Let me talk this over with Carrie. I don't know how she'd feel about going back to Chillaton and her father."

"Oh sure, but let me know as soon as you can."

Jemma and Carrie came back laughing. "So what have you two been talking about? You look suspicious to me," Carrie said. "It's so good to be with y'all. I'd love to be back home in Chillaton with my husband. You two are lucky."

Jemma smiled at Carrie's declaration, but Philip and Spencer grinned at each other, big-time.

Jemma waited until 7:30 to begin, but there were still only five women present for her first meeting, including Willa. "I could've told you this, child, but you didn't ask me," Willa said, behind one of the handouts that Jemma had passed around. "People are plumb scared of change. They'd rather be worse off than a skunk with their liver draggin' than to figger out a new way to do things. It's just the way life is, at least on this side of them tracks."

"Be that as it may, we're going to try." Jemma stepped in front of the pews. "Ladies, thank you for coming tonight. As you know, I'm here to share a business idea with you. I need your input to see if it could work, though."

A large woman with white streaks in her hair spoke up. "What kind of business? Me and my man, Terrill, is already takin' care of things at the Dew." Jemma had seen her before when she went with Trina to the Dew Drop Inn — a combination grocery store, dime store, and social center for the neighborhood. Bernie Miller, Chillaton's one-eyed town barber on the other side of the tracks, owned it.

"I was thinking of a small business that creates handmade items, like quilts and rag rugs, those kinds of things," Jemma said with a sparkling smile.

A pencil-thin, white-haired woman shifted in her seat and spat something into a can. "Ain't nobody gonna pay for no rag rug. Have to be crazy to do that."

"Maybe we should introduce ourselves," Jemma said. "I'm Jemmabeth Chase. I know a few of you from church."

"They call me Grandma Hardy, and that's all you need to know," the white-haired woman said.

Willa cleared her throat.

"You know me, I'm Bertie Shanks, Shiloh's sister." She pointed to Terrill's woman. "I'm real interested in this idea of yours if it'll pay off in the long run . . . that's what I want to know." Bertie's voice was high-pitched and kept going in a soft whirring sound, connecting her words like a remote control car.

The last one to speak was a young woman with coal black eyes that had not left Jemma's face since the meeting began. "My name's Gweny Matthews. What's in this for you?"

"Nothing," Jemma said. "I want to make sure it gets off the ground, but the idea is to turn the profits back into the community, back to you."

"You mean we won't get paid?" Gweny asked.

"Oh no. Of course you'll get paid. That's how the community will benefit. You can be more independent," Jemma looked at the group for any encouragement.

Willa spoke up. "What the child is sayin', girls, is that the gov'ment might not have to buy your groceries and whatnot. Now, I know Jemmabeth. She's sweet and for the most part, smart. Her and my Trina have been friends for a good while now. I think we should at least see what she's got to say."

Jemma held nothing back. She told them just what Uncle Art said and explained how she and Spencer would be involved. When she finished, she asked who would like to give it a try.

Willa spoke up. "Sugar, you know old Willa here can't sew nothin' for nothin'. I can iron what gets sewed, but I can't help you none with a needle and thread."

Bertie and Shiloh both volunteered. Gweny and Grandma Hardy said nothing.

Jemma sighed. "Surely there are more ladies who can sew in the neighborhood. We'll need a bigger crew to get much done."

"They's all busy," Grandma Hardy said.

"We'll let 'em know what you got in mind."

"Thank you; that would be great. Please see what everybody thinks. Maybe you could encourage more people to come," Jemma said. "We could brainstorm."

"I ain't gettin' out in no kind of storm," Grandma Hardy said with a solid hit in her can.

Gweny eyed her like a guard dog. "How much would we get paid?"

"Minimum wages, I suppose, until we see what the profits are, then everybody would share in that," Jemma said. "Unless we have more interest than we do tonight, though, we couldn't really fill an order for my uncle's stores."

"Just how much will you be sharin' in the profits?" Gweny asked.

"Not at all."

"What kind of orders are you talkin' about?" Bertie asked.

Jemma brightened at the interest. "My uncle said that he would like to try a dozen quilts in one store, and if they sell within a certain period of time, he would double the order and expand the quilts to another one of his stores, too."

"Her uncle's got four real fancy stores," Willa added.

Gweny left with the others but not before

she gave Jemma one hard, last look.

"Whoa. That was a tough crowd," Jemma said as she and Willa cleaned up the juice and cookies.

"I told you, honey, folks don't like change. If they see a white girl tellin' it to 'em, that's even worse."

"That Gweny looks so familiar to me. I must have seen her before."

"She's been around for a few months. She's Weese's little sister. You gotta remember him."

"Really. Well, I'll never forget Weese. I was afraid of him when I first met y'all."

"That's the one and only. Shot off his mouth more times than not. He's out of the military now and brought his little sister with him to Chillaton. Appears he got his high school diploma and is tryin' to go to junior college. Don't that beat all? I figgered he'd get himself killed in Vietnam, but I think he's too pigheaded or ornery for even the devil to take him. Anyway, Gweny looks out at folks just like him. Kinda scary, ain't it?" Willa brushed the crumbs off her dress. "I gotta get home to Joe, sugar, but I need to lock up. Joe and me are in charge of the church key this year."

"I think Weese hated me, the way he

talked," Jemma said, gathering up her things.

"Aw, he hated white folks in general. He's drivin' back and forth to the power plant now. Got a good job over there. Don't worry about him, sugar. He's come home like a three-legged dog. I think he got the pee-widdles scared out of him in that war. Let's go, honey. I miss my man." Willa held the door open for Jemma, motioning her through.

"Isn't Trina coming home this weekend?" Jemma asked.

"She ain't comin' home until she graduates. She sent me a dress for the ceremony. Come over tomorrow and I'll show you. That girl's good. I don't know where she got it, but she can dream up Sunday-go-to-meetin' clothes even for a big old barn like me."

"I know she's busy, but I really need to call her."

"You ain't keepin' secrets from old Willa now, are you?" Willa locked the door, then gave it a good tug.

"No secrets, just in need of sewing machine advice."

"Then you're headin' down the right track for that. Sleep tight, Jemma. Say hello to Miz Liz for me." Willa headed toward her house and Jemma, lost in thought, waved good-bye as she crossed the tracks.

Lizbeth met her at the door. "How did it go?"

Jemma hung her coat on the hall tree. "It was a pitiful turnout. I hope this all works out. Did Spence call?"

"Not yet. He probably had a late meeting or something, but Buddy B called. Twila had a little girl or maybe I should say a big girl. She weighed over ten pounds. Buddy said they named her after his mother, Twila's maiden name, and you."

Jemma grinned. "That's great! I'll have to go see her. What's the baby's name?"

Lizbeth was about to burst. "You know how everybody calls Mrs. Baker 'Sweety' and Trout was Twila's maiden name, and, well, I suppose you can tack 'beth' on to just about anything. They named her Sweetybeth Trout Baker."

"Can you imagine her name being called out at graduation?" Jemma giggled. "Do people ever bake trout?"

They howled until their sides ached.

"I made hot cocoa. Would you like some?" Lizbeth produced a bag of marshmallows.

"That sounds good. I should have served cocoa at the meeting. Maybe it would have warmed them up. How long does it take to make a quilt, Gram?"

"Oh my. Let's see."

"Wait." Jemma jumped up from the table. "I'll be right back. I need to call Trina."

Lizbeth wrapped her hands around her cup. Lester came in the back door.

"Don't you knock anymore, Mr. Timms?"

Lester went back outside and knocked. She had to laugh. "Come on in and have some cocoa with us."

"I don't mind if I do." He draped his coat on the back of his chair. "I think a storm's comin' in. It's downright cold tonight. I don't see Spencer's car. Where is that boy?"

"Los Angeles. It just amazes me how young folk take an airplane everywhere they go these days." Lizbeth offered him the cookie jar. "Help yourself, Lester. Jemma made them today, but she took most of them to her meeting."

"Well, sir, I've been thinkin' about this business across the tracks. If it's a quiltin' business they're considerin', don't it make sense to get your quiltin' club in on it?"

"I don't think that's the idea, Lester. Not that I wouldn't help if asked, but it's supposed be a neighborhood venture." Lizbeth lowered her voice. "Something special to take pride in."

"You think it'll fly?"

"Anything's possible with the Lord."

"Here are my flight numbers, the Academie's number, and my hotel number. Call me whenever you can. It doesn't matter if I'm asleep," Jemma told Spencer, tucking a piece of paper in his pocket.

"I'll put this in my desk and I'll keep another copy in my wallet. It'll be like you are with me everywhere I go." He put his arms around her, starting the good-bye kisses a little early.

The Cleave moved away from the door just as they opened it.

"If anybody calls, I'll get back with them tomorrow," Spencer told her.

Missy shook back her hair, like a horse slinging its head at the bit. "I thought you were expecting to hear from Trent this afternoon. Nice suit, Jemma. I had one just like it about three years ago. I gave mine to the Salvation Army. Wait; maybe that's where you got yours. How weird."

Neither Jemma nor Spencer answered and went straight to the Corvette.

"She makes me sick. Aarrgghh!" Jemma shuddered, then inhaled. "Okay. How come you don't have a new Corvette this year, babe? What happened to your dad's perennial gift?" Jemma asked as they turned onto the highway. Spencer tried to hide his grin.

"I told Dad that he needed to stop giving me cars. I'm a big boy now. Maybe we should buy something different." He adjusted his rearview mirror, working hard to look nonchalant. "I was thinking about us buying matching motorcycles."

"Spencer Chase, don't even think about that. You know I have a problem with motorcycles. They are deadly. I will never forget the sight of the Kelseys sprawled across the road when Mom and I came upon them. When those deer ran out, they never had a chance on that machine."

"Okay, okay. I'm sorry I brought it up, but you know I like cycles."

"You should have gotten that out of your system in Europe. Say you won't bring it up anymore. I love you too much."

"I won't bring it up anymore. I'll miss you, baby. You take care of yourself in Paris. Don't go out at night alone and all that. We haven't been apart this long since we got married."

"Say that again and I'll start crying. When we're apart, do you think more about the dumb things I've done or the good things?"

"You've done some good things?" he teased. "C'mon, Jem, I think about holding you again and that's the truth."

An hour later, he raced to the parking lot to watch her plane shrink into the clouds. He'd meant to let her take his four-leaf clover with her, just in case she needed it. It was with him in Vietnam when his chopper got shot out of the sky. He drove home in silence, wishing already he had gone with her.

Chapter 12
Blindsided

Paris coming into view was one of Jemma's favorite sights, but that would not be the case today. Gloomy clouds shrouded the city, and it didn't stop raining until late afternoon. She walked past cafés, whose rain-slick chairs were turned upside down on the tables waiting for the sun. As usual, she had not slept well after her long flight and had talked way too long to Spence on the phone. She drank some coffee, loaded with cream and sugar, to wake her up, then walked to Le Academie Royale D'Art. There was really no need for the coffee; she was invigorated the instant she stepped inside to meet with her old supervisors.

Peter, her onetime liaison when she was the Girard Fellow, met her in the hallway. "Jemma, my dear, you are perhaps even more beautiful. It must be matrimony that has done this to you. Ami and I insist that you come for dinner while you are here, *oui?*"

She gave him a Texas hug. "Of course I'll come. I can't wait to tell y'all about my life." Jemma thought everyone should say her name like the French did — *Zhemma.*

She met her former Girard advisor, Louis, and the Academie Director. "Here is my syllabus, Monsieur Lanier," she said, after they had all exchanged pleasantries. "I've already given a copy to Louis and he approved. I'd like to mingle with the students and see how they approach their work. I want to listen to their thinking today, so that I can address their questions when we begin tomorrow." Jemma waited for his response as he thumbed through the pages.

Monsieur Lanier played with his moustache. "Ah, very nice. The pupils also wish to observe you as you work and exchange ideas about perspective, technique, and the unique voice in your art," he said in his impeccable English.

Louis raised his finger, as was his habit. "What we are seeking, Jemma, is a certain essence of personality that all of your work has — the voice. Is this voice something that can be, how do you say . . . fostered . . . or does it only spring from the heart? We shall explore the answer. I strongly believe that it comes from your heart, my dear."

"However," Monsieur Lanier added, "we can, with your permission, listen to your heart, as you exercise that voice."

She smiled. "I do believe that artists can train their thinking to include something extra in a portrait that adds the spice, the zest. You can get caught up in realism to the point that characters look alive, but boring as all get-out. Of course, some people are just plain boring. Everybody can have a little zing in their personality, even if you have to give it to them. Believe me, I've done my share of zinging."

The men laughed. "Perhaps we should call your seminar 'Zinging with Zhemma,' " Monsieur Lanier quipped. "This will be a fascinating time that will be gone before you know it. Did your husband accompany you?"

"No, he had other responsibilities, but he wanted to, very much." She sighed. "Let's get going with these artists. Who is the Girard Fellow this year?"

"A very talented young man from Russia. I think you will like his work. It has this zing you speak of," Louis said as they left the director's office.

Jemma had the class's eyes at her first brushstroke and ears after her first Texas vowel. Peter interpreted for her and she stayed late every night. After the third night, she knew most of the students' names. Her own piece was taking shape. It was a large portrait of Marie, the Academie's secretary, sitting behind stacks of paper at her desk. Marie was massaging her own neck and watching the leaves outside her window. Jemma spoke intermittently, when she had made a conscious decision related to Marie herself or the inanimate objects in the piece that would enhance the viewer's understanding of Marie's emotions.

Louis and Jemma collaborated until half past eleven with a student who was struggling with a concept in his own piece. "It is so good of you to come, Jemma," Louis said as they descended the steps from the studios to the main entrance. "Your passion will be contagious with our students. Have you been well?"

"*Oui,* I have been very well. Marriage has made me complete," she said as they walked out the massive Academie entry door.

Louis smiled. "Your husband is most fortunate."

"No, it is just the opposite," Jemma said. "I'll see you tomorrow."

Louis frowned as Jemma turned down the sidewalk toward her hotel. "Jemma," he said, coming alongside her, "perhaps I should see you to your accommodations. There have been ah . . . how do you say . . . *agresseurs* nearby in recent weeks."

Jemma laughed. "Aggressive people? Don't worry. I can take care of myself. I know some wrestling moves."

"Are you certain? It is no bother for me. Let me call a taxi for you."

"I'll be fine." She waved. "It's just four blocks from here, and I need the exercise."

Jemma yawned and glanced at some young men playing bongos under a tree just a block from her hotel. She smiled, thinking about Robby and the bongos that he had included in his Christmas list. She decided to write to him as soon as she got to the hotel.

She checked her watch as she passed under the streetlight. It was almost midnight. Suddenly she became aware of heavy footsteps behind her and quickened her pace. It was too late. A wrenching blow to her back lurched her forward, and she fell hard on her face. The agonizing pain in her nose was followed by a choking gush of blood.

There were two of them, pinning her arms down as they dragged her into the alley between darkened buildings. She struggled and screamed as a hand was clamped over her mouth. The men scrambled around her. Jemma landed a solid kick against one, causing him to yelp in pain. The other pressed his knee into her stomach and spoke low, grating French in her face.

Jemma writhed under his weight. She held her breath as a third man appeared in the dark. She coughed, gagging on blood that oozed down her throat. The new arrival grunted and yanked the men off her, simultaneously slamming each against the wall.

Jemma rolled on her side and tried to stand. Her ankle gave way. She wobbled up, lost her balance, but managed a few steps, spewing blood that flowed from her nose. The third man shouted something in English, and they all ran past her as she stumbled into the street.

The lights down the block swirled in front of her. Her nose throbbed and her back hurt like fire. She hobbled toward the lights, shaking uncontrollably.

"Wait, darlin'," a voice thundered behind her.

She froze.

Paul moved in front of her and gathered her up in his arms just as she fainted.

Jemma woke up in a fog. She didn't know

which hurt worse — her nose, her back, or her ankle wrapped in tight bandages. Muffled conversations drifted in and out of her aching head. She heard French and a thick Texas accent, engaged in a discussion over her condition.

"She had a serious concussion a couple of years ago. Wouldn't that make her more susceptible to another one?" a familiar voice asked.

"Ah, she is awake. Let me speak with her," the Frenchman said.

Jemma responded to a series of questions and an eye exam to his satisfaction. The doctor explained that she had been given pain medication and she would remain in the hospital overnight for observation, then left her in the room with Paul.

Jemma blinked at the ceiling as he came over to the bed. Rats, rats, rats.

"Hello, my darlin'," he whispered and took her hand. "Sorry you had such a scare. If I see those cowards again, I'll kill 'em. Guaranteed."

Tears rolled down Jemma's cheeks. She tensed at his touch and withdrew her hand from his. She coughed up a gross blood clot and glanced at her unlikely nurse. "I have no idea why you are here, Paul, but thanks for whatever you did," she whispered. "I think you saved my life."

"No thanks ever needed," he murmured, dabbing at her chin with a damp cloth. "The police came by earlier and I told them all they needed to know. I just hope they catch those scumbags before I do," he said through clenched teeth. "How are you feeling?"

"Like I've been in another wreck. Is my nose broken?"

"The doc says no broken bones, only deep bruises and swollen tissue. You are going to be black and blue by tomorrow."

"What about my ankle?"

"Sprain." Paul pulled a stool over beside her.

"I need to call Spencer."

"Wait until morning."

"No. I want to call him now. I'm getting up." She grunted to her elbows and fell back on the pillow.

Paul patted her arm. "I'll find a phone. You don't move."

The effects of the pain medication took hold as she sat on the side of the bed. Paul returned and she squinted up at him. She had forgotten how tall he was. "You have blood on your shirt. Are you hurt, too?" she asked.

"No, darlin', it's from your cute little nose.

I thought we'd struck oil there for a while. I pinched it all the way to the hospital. Come on, I found you a phone down the hall, but there are lots of nurses lurking around out there." He helped her off the bed. "I think the doc ordered bed rest, so we'll have to sneak out."

Jemma had not realized she was wearing a hospital gown until the cool hallway air hit her bare back. She gasped and clutched the gown around her. She hadn't forgotten about Paul's wandering hands.

The Cleave answered Jemma's call in her usual velvety tone. "Chase and Lillygrace. May I help you?"

The operator asked if she would accept the charges. The Cleave paused, then lost her kitteny voice. "Yeah, I guess."

"Missy," Jemma began.

"Melissa."

"I need to talk to Spencer, Missy. It's an emergency."

"Spence is not here. They've gone to a meeting in Amarillo. By the way, I'm cooking for both of them at Trent's place tonight."

Jemma could see her smirk clear across the Atlantic. The drugs were taking over or else she would have had a pertinent comeback.

"Then interrupt the meeting. Spencer needs to call me in Paris immediately." Jemma read the number on the pay phone. "Read it back to me, please." She was drifting off by the second, but held on until Missy repeated the number. She handed the phone to Paul, who hung it up for her. That was the last thing she remembered.

Jemma awoke to another foggy French conversation between a different physician and Paul. She could not focus long enough to see the men clearly.

The doctor checked her pupils and asked her a series of questions. "You are her husband?" he asked Paul.

"No." Paul struggled with the words. "We're . . . old friends."

"You are feeling better, yes?" the doctor asked Jemma.

She nodded.

"Eat some food, then perhaps we will dismiss you. You will rest today, of course."

"I'll see to it that she does," Paul said.

Jemma rose up to protest, but went down again. "Did Spence call?" she mumbled. "I need to call the Academie, too; they will be worried."

"I've already called the school, Jem. Everything is taken care of. They were very concerned about you, though." Paul moved the bed up for her and adjusted the pillows.

"How did you know to call them?" Jemma touched the tip of her sore nose and ran her hands through her hair. "I must look like a witch."

"On the contrary." Paul sat on the stool beside her. "You look like an angel." He hadn't changed the bloodstained shirt.

"Paul, why on earth are you in Paris and how did you, of all people, show up to rescue me from who-knows-what?" She tried to look him in the eye, but her swollen nose was in the way.

He smoothed his overnight stubble. "I came to see you. I'm not ashamed that I was . . . well, watching you from afar, as they say."

"You're good at that, aren't you?" Her breakfast was set up in front of her on a tray. She picked at the food and drank the juice. "Stop looking at me. You're giving me the creeps. There's a name for people like you."

He grinned. "Oh yeah. What's that, Guardian Angel?"

"*Obsessed*. Did you stay in here all night?"

He nodded.

"Oh great. Spencer is going to blow his stack. Can't you see how wrong it is for you to keep this up? Have you seriously considered your behavior?"

"Darlin', I told you; I'm under your spell."

"Arrgghh! Paul! There is no spell. Listen to me. I love my husband, and I always have. This obsession is hopeless."

A nurse interrupted and took her blood pressure, which was up, and her temperature, then gave her a form to fill out, in French. Jemma hoped that she hadn't agreed to a lobotomy.

"I bought you some clothes since your others were ruined," Paul said, setting a bag and her own purse on the bed. He left the room as Jemma opened the bag and took out a blouse and a miniskirt. Leave it to him to pick out a miniskirt. The tags were still on them. She dressed and did what she could to her hair. Her nose was skinned up and its size rivaled W.C. Field's. She had bruises all over her, and everything that had a nerve ached.

She limped to the door and opened it. "Did Spencer call? You never said."

Paul was leaning against the wall, his black cowboy hat pushed back. He looked her over and sighed. Two nurses walked by and gave him admiring, giggling glances. He tipped his hat, then turned to Jemma. "No calls, ma'am. I asked at the nurses' station. Let's get out of here. I hate hospitals." He held her arm as they entered the elevator.

"That's not like Spence." Jemma bit her sore lip. She had a sudden urge to phone him again, then recalled vaguely that The Cleave said she was cooking supper for Trent and Spencer. Spence wouldn't eat with Missy. She must have been dreaming.

"Do you want some real food, darlin'?" Paul asked as he flagged down a taxi.

"Paul, stop calling me *darlin'*. I am not your darling. You shouldn't even be in Paris," she said, holding the miniskirt down as she got in the cab.

He raised his brow. "Do you know what might have happened to you last night if I hadn't been here?"

Jemma exhaled and looked out the window. "I know. It's weird that you were in the right place at the right time, but my husband is not going to understand this at all. He wants to have a restraining order put on you."

"I'd do the same thing if I were him, but we're in Europe, darlin'. I don't think a restraining order would hold up over here."

"Paul, you and I are not going to have a

rendezvous or something just because you saved my life . . . or at least my virtue."

He turned his beautiful, green-eyed gaze on her. "Preserving your virtue is something I would give my life for, Jem. Watching you sleep last night will be one of my life's sweetest memories."

Jemma held on to the door handle in case he tried something. Paul told the driver an address in French, and they were dropped off at a café.

Jemma looked at her wrist. "Rats, my watch is gone! It must have fallen off in that alley last night." Her nose stung at this added insult. "Spence gave me that watch before he went to Vietnam."

"I'll look for it," Paul said. "I bet those creeps stole it. You can't be walking around alone in a big city at midnight, Jemma. It's dangerous. I seem to remember you doing the same thing when I first met you, but Paris isn't exactly Wicklow, my darlin'."

"I can't believe they took my watch. What happened to my clothes, anyway?"

"The police took them. They were ruined," Paul said, his hand in the small of her back.

Jemma moved it away. "Just order me some tea and toast. I've got to talk to my husband." She inched her way to a pay phone and called Lizbeth's number.

"Hi, Gram. Sorry to wake you up," she said, holding her voice steady. "Is Spencer there?"

"No, sugar, he spent the night with his folks. Are you all right?" Lizbeth asked.

"I'm okay now, but there's been a little trouble. Could you have Spence call me at my room, please? I'll be there in an hour," she added.

"What's wrong, Jemmabeth?" Lizbeth's voice crackled over the phone.

"I'm all right. Spencer can tell you, but I have to go now. I love you." She hated not telling her everything, but she had to tell Spence first.

"I love you, too, honey. You take care."

"Wait. Gram, did Spencer eat out last night?"

"Why, yes, I believe he planned to eat with Trent."

A large lump crept up her throat. She said good-bye and turned toward the café. It was all she could do to walk.

"Maybe we should take you back to the hospital. I'm not so sure you're ready for the outside world," Paul steered her to her chair.

"I'm okay. I just need to sit down."

Paul's eyes were on her every move. She

knew it but didn't care. She only wanted to know if The Cleave had cooked up something more than dinner for her husband.

"I don't need you to babysit me, Paul," she said, even though he had practically carried her from the café to the taxi. "I appreciate all you've done, really, but now you have to go home," Jemma said as they stood in front of her hotel room. "I'm not going to invite you in." She narrowed her eyes at him. "It really wasn't wise for you to follow me across the ocean like this."

"I'd follow you anywhere if I thought it would change things." He reached for her, but she caught his hand to push it away. He took her off guard and kissed her fingers, looking at her with his eyes half-closed under those lashes black as night. "Even if I find somebody to settle down with, Jem, it'll be you that I'll be lovin' the whole time. That's a solemn promise."

She wriggled her hand out of his grasp. "How did you know that I was in Paris?"

"Apparently you have some competition yourself, back in that little one-horse town."

Her scalp prickled. "What do you mean?"

"All I know is that I got a phone call from a breathy sorority sister of some old girl I took out. She said if I'd like to be alone with you, I should whip over here to France. She gave me all the details, right down to the school, your flight number, and hotel. Sounds serious, darlin'."

Jemma's face burned. "Good-bye, Paul," she said, controlling her voice. "I'll pray for you. I have to tell Spence about what happened, and I don't know what he'll say or do. Now go home." She turned her attention to getting her key in the door. The Cleave was all she could think about.

Paul seized the opportunity. He pulled her to him and kissed her, full on the lips.

Jemma panicked and dropped her keys. She pushed hard on his chest, but he had her face firmly in his big hand and she had nowhere to go. Her nose still ached from the attack and now her mouth hurt from this.

After the longest time, he backed away and smiled, not with a smirk, but in a sweet way. "I love you, Jemmabeth Alexandra, and I'll see you whenever and wherever I can. Stay safe for me." He walked down the hallway and paused before taking the stairs. "You'll always be the only one," he said, "my darlin' Jemma."

Jemma wiped her mouth and cried. This was the worst twenty-four hours she had endured since Spence was reported as MIA in Vietnam. She leaned her forehead against the door to let a wave of nausea pass. The phone was ringing in her room as her trembling hands struggled to get the key in the lock again.

"Spence!" she yelled into the receiver.

"Jem, what's happened?"

His voice unleashed a torrent of emotion.

Spencer's temples throbbed as he pulled up to Trent's house. He blew out his breath, then rang the doorbell.

Trent answered. "Hey, Spence, what's up?"

"I need to talk to Missy." Spencer's voice resembled a pilot's when he gives the warning just before upcoming turbulence. Heavy turbulence.

"Sure, come in," Trent said, big-eyed.

The Cleave was curled up on the couch, barefooted, watching television. She ran her tongue around her lips at the sound of Spencer's voice and fluffed out her hair. "Hi, Spence. I thought old married men weren't allowed on the streets this late." She flashed her perfect smile.

Spencer's jaw twitched. "Did Jemma call me yesterday morning and ask you to get in touch with me immediately?"

Missy puckered her lips and peered up at

the ceiling. "Let's see . . . oh yeah, I guess she did. I totally forgot about it. I just got busy, plus y'all were in Amarillo all morning," she said with a follow-up smile and indigo eyes that shifted from steely-eyed Spencer to big-eyed Trent.

"Did you call Paul Turner and tell him Jemma's flight number and the address of her school and hotel in Paris?" Spencer asked.

Missy turned to Trent, who stood with his arms folded and his gaze now stuck on the floor. She shrugged. "Of course not. I don't even know those things."

"Mr. Turner told Jemma that a sorority sister of one of his old girlfriends called him and gave him all of that information. You have a sorority sister who dated Paul Turner, but you had to go through my desk to get those other details." Spencer's breath whistled through his teeth. "As far as I'm concerned, you are fired, *Missy*," he hissed. "Trent, Jemma was assaulted in Paris and called me from a hospital yesterday. I just got off the phone with her, and she told me the rest of the story. I trust you'll do the right thing." He shot one last look at The Cleave, then left.

Jemma sat in her room all morning, afraid

that Paul would be waiting for her somewhere outside. She felt stronger, physically. Her heart was hurting, though. She needed to have Spencer's arms around her, but it would be ten more days before that could happen. Her head reeled with questions. How could so many things she touched wind up hurting people she loved? The Bible said that things work together for the good of those who love God or something like that. Why would it be good for her to be attacked and for Paul to be the one to come to her rescue? Now she would have to tell Spence everything because she promised not to keep secrets from him. That would only serve to hurt him more. Maybe she should break that promise and not tell him everything. It couldn't make things easier for Spence to know that Paul had sat up with her all night in a hospital room. Who knew what went on in Paul's head while she slept in that hospital gown? There was nothing to do but to paint. Paul surely had to be on his way home by now.

Jemma said a prayer, took two aspirin, and changed clothes. She peeked into the hallway, locked her room, and gingerly made her way to Le Academie. She stayed on the other side of the street, away from that awful spot. She could have taken a cab, but

Papa had always taught her to face her fears.

Spencer hadn't slept since her call. Twice now he had stayed home while she went away, and twice there had been trouble with the cowboy. What kind of man was Paul? Spencer didn't have to give that question much thought. Jemmabeth Alexandra was, to both of them, like fresh air. They needed her, but he couldn't share her with another man, even if she were only shared in Paul's mind. He wasn't sure if he could bear periodic visitations from an obsessive old boyfriend as though he were no more than a wayward uncle. At the same time, he couldn't very well get angry with a man who saved Jemma from some terrible fate. Now didn't seem like a good time to ruin the guy's reputation with a restraining order, either.

Why did the good Lord let Missy contact Paul? Maybe this was a warning from Him that this big-shot architect husband was a little too busy. He should have been the one to rescue his own wife, but Mr. Busy Architect was in Texas. If he had gone with her, like she wanted, she wouldn't have been attacked in the first place. Mr. Selfish Architect Husband. He couldn't wait to hold her and know that she was really all right. He closed his eyes and tried to pass the time with sleep.

Jemma stood at her window and sipped hot tea. She caught a glimpse of herself in the mirror. Both eyes were black, and her nose was still like a sausage. Spencer had said he would call, but the phone hadn't rung. She set the cup on a small table and took out the letterhead stationery from the desk drawer.

Dear Robby,
 I hope you are having a good time. I am in Paris teaching a class for two weeks. Are you sure you want bongos for Christmas? They can be very annoying. When you get in high school, take French. There are important words that you might need to know when you travel to Paris.

She was interrupted by a knock on the door. Her pulse shot up, thinking it could be Paul. Rats! She decided not to answer and instead sat motionless on the couch.
 A movement by the door caught her eye. She crossed the room and reached for the envelope that had suddenly appeared on the floor. *You need this more than I do now* was

scrawled on the envelope. Puzzled, she opened it. Inside was the four-leafed clover that she had found for Spencer just before he left for Vietnam. He had taken it from the starry frame.

"Spence!" she yelled and flung open the door. They were like two trains appearing out of the fog and smashing into one another. She didn't even care if the collision hurt like the dickens. He held on while she sobbed into his shirt.

They sat on the couch for hours. Jemma told him everything that she thought he could stand. "I can't believe you are here. I wanted to come home, but I didn't want to disappoint the Academie."

"You have to be in a lot of pain, baby." Spencer scrutinized her face.

"My nose doesn't look too good, huh? I'm taking aspirin for my back and ankle, but I'll be okay now that you are here."

"I should have been here all along. I can't believe Missy pulled such a stunt. I guess she did us a bittersweet favor."

"I think when we get home you should teach me more French," she said. "Louis warned me that there were *agresseurs* in the neighborhood, but I thought that meant aggressive people."

Spencer hung his head. "Oh Jem, I'm so

sorry. You're learning French the hard way." He exhaled. "What makes Paul think that he can follow you around, anyway? He can't keep this up. I'm grateful that he was here and all that, but, it's not right. It's sick."

"I don't know, and I don't get why the Lord used him to help me this time. Now it's like we are indebted to him in some twisted way."

"That's a scary thought." Spencer smoothed her hair. "I fired Missy, then drove straight to the airport. My clothes probably stink," he said, smelling under his arms.

"You are the best thing I've seen since I left home."

When he kissed her gently, she only hoped he couldn't taste the last kiss that had been on her lips. For a while, they forgot their woes.

Chapter 13
Details

Spencer, always keeping busy, spent the next few days visiting architectural firms in Paris and working from the hotel room. "I like walking you to the Academie every day," he told Jemma. "It's like we are in grade school again."

"In grade school, we couldn't do this," Jemma said and kissed him as they stood on the Academie steps.

Monsieur Lanier passed by and smiled. "*Bonjour,* Jemma and Spencer."

Jemma waved without stopping her business with her husband.

"There is a concert at Sainte-Chapelle tonight. Want to go?" Spencer asked as she wiped the lipstick off him.

"You bet, mister. I'll try to finish early. I love you." She grinned and disappeared inside.

Spencer headed back to the hotel to call Trent.

Trent answered the phone himself. "How are things in Paris? How's Jemma?"

"Better. I see you are taking calls yourself. What happened with Missy?"

"Hey, I like to have fun as much as the next guy, but not at the expense of my cousin's welfare and our firm's security."

"Good riddance. She's always walked a thin line, but I was hoping she had grown out of it by now."

Trent cleared his throat. "Did that old boyfriend of Jemma's assault her?"

"No, no. It was a couple of French thugs. The cowboy sort of saved her life." Spencer toyed with his pen, not ready to share the details. "Listen, I've made some great contacts in Paris. I figure since I'm here, I might as well see what's going on. I think I may have sparked some interest for our business."

"No kidding? Well, I have nothing keeping me home at night. If there's traveling to be done, I'm your man." Trent laughed.

"Are you and Missy still seeing each other? It's really none of my business; I'm just curious."

"No way, not after this fiasco. She was beginning to get on my nerves, to tell the truth, and this episode was just evil. I get the feeling that she's spent some serious time making dumb guys like me happy. We're going to have to find us another secretary, though. I've pecked out a couple of letters, but my typing skills are about like Robby's. Any suggestions?"

Spencer sat back on the couch and rubbed the bridge of his nose. "You know what? Call out to my dad's car dealership and ask for Buddy Baker. See if his sister, Sandy, has found a job yet. She won some kind of typing contest when we were in high school. She's good friends with Jem, and is going through some hard times right now."

"I'll do it. I think I met her at your wedding. I'd better go now. The other line is ringing. Keep up the good work. We'll see you soon. Give my love and apologies to Jem."

Spencer got the phone book out and made his list for the day.

The orchestra was warming up as they found their seats. "This has to be the most incredible setting for a concert," Jemma whispered.

"There's nothing like perfect Gothic architecture to put you in your place as a mere mortal," Spencer said. The evening light filtered through the ornate stained glass, reducing the two of them to tiny glass jewels like those inside a kaleidoscope.

She touched his hand. "Spence, how much detail do you want to know about this whole incident?"

"There's more? About the assault or about Paul?"

"Paul," Jemma whispered.

He looked away, his jaw tight. "For you to ask if I want to know about the details means there are some things you don't want to tell me."

"I don't want to hurt you, babe. It's nothing horrible, but it would be hard for me to tell it. I will if you want me to, since we made our promise."

"Why would I want to get hurt? I should take comfort that God is going to handle things, but it's tough being a mere mortal. More details that you'd rather not share, huh? I guess I'll have to give that some thought."

Jemma tried to enjoy the concert and forget about those details, but she couldn't. She watched him, her sweet Candy Man, the whole time. If he chose to know, she would have to think of the gentlest way to tell him. They didn't talk much during intermission, but he finally looked her in the eye and nodded. She squeezed his hand and took a deep breath. They might as well have left at that point.

At the hotel, Jemma asked Spencer for the key to their room in the hallway. She put it in the lock and turned to him. "This is what happened right here at the door. I said, 'Good-bye, Paul. I pray that you won't keep this up. I'll tell Spencer everything and I don't know what he'll say or do. Go home. You can't follow me around even though you are the hero this time.' Now you grab my shoulders, Spence, and pull me to you no matter what I do, okay?"

Spencer yanked her to him with more force than she expected.

"Now kiss me," she said.

She felt him shudder at the word. She pushed on his chest with all the power she could muster. She had expected a tentatively executed response, given her recovering condition. Instead, he kissed her hard, much harder than Paul had a week earlier. She didn't wipe her mouth as she had with Paul but looked away from Spencer's blistering stare.

"That's it," she said, "except the key fell out of the door."

"I'm not sure I like your little melodrama," he said at long last. "So your hero collected his reward, did he? Would you like it if I was on the receiving end of that kind of passion from, say, Michelle Taylor?"

"Her name came up really fast, didn't it?" Jemma fired back, disappointed that he didn't get the point of her reenactment. "I wanted you to see that I couldn't help what happened."

"Did you like it?" Spencer's voice had an unfamiliar tone.

"His kiss?" She glared at him, shoved open the door, and flung her purse on the bed.

Spencer was right behind her. "It's my worst fear, baby, that you did like it and you will miss it someday." He touched her face.

Jemma pulled back from him, sniffing. "Never, Spence. I wiped my heart clean of him a long time ago even if he keeps popping up. You are my precious husband. I tried the rest but you won, remember, babe? I love you, and I want nothing more, ever."

Her golden eyes were on him. He had called them tiger-eyes in the third grade and made her mad. Every time her temper flared they glowed. Now they were brimming with pain, and he was fast becoming the source of it. He buried his face in her hair and inhaled. She smelled of paint and flowers. He tucked her hair behind her ear, and made a trail of warm kisses down her neck.

"Remember our first time, at the That'll Do Motel after our wedding?" he whispered in her ear.

"Of course," she said.

His chest rose and fell against hers. "Let's reenact that event because I remember all of those details," he said, "and those I liked."

Jemma smiled. "Me, too." Then she kissed him, long and sweet, ignoring all pain.

Their flight was delayed out of Paris. Spencer watched as she sketched passengers in the waiting area. He would never tire of seeing her brain work. She could take just a few pencil marks and re-create a complete stranger from fifty feet away. In ten minutes, the stranger would come alive with personality and have facial details that most people wouldn't have noticed for days.

Jemma looked up and smiled. "Where did you and Trent eat dinner before you left?" she asked, remaining quite serene, considering the question.

"What?" Spencer wasn't ready for quizzes. "Oh, Dad took us to Amarillo. He wants to get to know Trent better."

"Just the three of you?"

"Yeah. Why?"

"When I called you the night of the attack, Missy told me that she was cooking supper for y'all," Jemma said and held her breath.

Spencer put his arm around her. "Jem, she knows just what to say to you, and you fall for it every time. We do have to find a new secretary, though. I told Trent to check with Sandy."

"Great idea. That would be nice for her." She gave him The Look, then whispered something in his ear. He took a deep breath and got in a little more necking time while they were still in the City of Love.

"Where did they come up with a name like this for a restaurant?" Philip asked.

Spencer laughed. "Our local burger joint, Son's, is owned by a character who sent alimony to his ex-wife for years. When his daughters grew up, they came to Chillaton and started this place with the proceeds, out of spite. Thus the name — Daddy's Money."

"It used to be a feed store, but now it's Son's biggest competitor. His daughters don't even live here," Jemma added.

"All we need now is for Trina to move back and the circle will be complete." Carrie surveyed the plastic flower arrangements in empty gallon pickle jars.

"I can't wait to see her wedding dress,"

Jemma said as Spencer and Philip talked business. "Not to mention our gowns."

"You have no idea how happy we are to get out of the city. We've been praying about it. Phil is a strong believer in prayer," Carrie whispered.

Jemma nodded and reached for her hand. "Me, too. Sometimes that's all we have."

"Are you getting over your miscarriage, Jem?"

Jemma bit her lip. "Mom says that time heals pain, but that hasn't happened yet."

"Phil and I want to start a family, but not for a while. Of course, I don't know if I can even get pregnant. If not, we're going to adopt."

Jemma nodded and watched Spencer talk. His wedding ring, a gold band engraved with Scottish thistles, glinted in the restaurant light. He was to her like the beat of her own heart. He turned briefly toward her and smiled, warming her inside and out. Someday they would have babies, too; then maybe her guilt would fade away. She didn't want to ever again bring him pain.

"Call me every night, okay?" Jemma asked as they sat in the boarding area. "I'm nervous about Paul. The Cleave may tell him every time I'm alone, simply out of spite."

Spencer held her hands. "Jem, you told me he would never harm you. Is that not true?"

She looked away. "He wouldn't do me any harm, but he is desperate for me to love him. You know that I don't, right?"

"I'm not worried about your love. It's just him and this is his last chance. If there is one single problem, no matter how much you protest, I'm going to a lawyer. Don't look at me like that, either." He reached for his briefcase. "That's my flight. I'll call you when I get there. Give Trina a hug for me and smile. I'll see you next weekend."

Her lips were made for the perfect pout. "I'll miss you, Spence." She looked up at him like a sick puppy.

"Aw, baby, don't do this to me just as I'm leaving. You know I have to go. I'll be back before you know it." He whispered in her ear, making her smile, then was gone.

Jemma went through the skirt sale rack at Kidwell's Department Store in Amarillo. Trina probably wouldn't approve of some of the styles she was considering. She pushed apart two bohemian skirts to have a better look and revealed another customer on the opposite side of the rack.

"Missy."

"Jemmartsybeth."

Their eyes locked for an instant, and without giving it a thought, Jemma stepped between the skirts and stood squarely in The Cleave's face. "How dare you try to undermine my marriage," she said, the words swarming out of her mouth.

Missy looked as though she might throw up, but it was actually the beginnings of a smile. "I don't know what you're talking about."

"I'm talking about you and your constant flirting with Spencer, and now you've tried to stir up trouble with Paul Turner."

"Oh sorry. Did you ever consider that Spencer might like my attention? I know he did at one time."

Jemma's mouth twitched. The Claw would work, but she'd seen Bull Von Tersch wrap his opponent's long hair around his neck in a new move called the "The Calf Roper" last weekend. It would be a satisfying way to drag The Cleave around Kidwell's.

"How about this, Missy? You leave my husband alone, and I won't run for cheerleader anymore, and, let's see, I'll decline the football and prom queen elections. Would you like to step into my little time machine and get rid of some of your pent-up jealousy?"

"Ouch. The pain. Like I ever cared about your popularity. But it would be only fair if I could have had my turn with Spence. You have no idea what I'm capable of doing for his happiness."

"News alert, Missy. Spencer is completely happy."

"That's not what I heard. It's all around town that he wants a baby and you can't give him one."

Jemma swallowed hard. She had no comeback, and The Cleave gave a soft snort, knowing she'd struck gold.

"I could give him all he wants. That's a proven fact, twice over," Missy said.

"Really. A proven fact." Jemma's eyes lit up like bonfires. "If you ever try another stunt like you did by contacting Paul, I will call the Women's Prayer Circle at your parents' church and tell them exactly what you just told me. I'll picket your father's movie theaters with big signs telling just exactly what a flirtatious tramp you are."

The Cleave took a step toward Jemma until their perfume mingled. "You loser. Leave my parents out of this. They've never done anything to you."

"They gave birth to you, Missy."

She slung back her hair. "I'm Melissa now. Get that through your thick skull. I suppose it's all clogged up with unused baby names, though. Too bad."

"You know what, Missy? The real reason I can't remember to call you Melissa is that I don't care about your real name; all I can remember is what we all called you in high school."

"Still in high school. What a constituted toad you are. So, what little nickname did you think up for me?"

"The Cleave, short for 'cleavage,' which you threw in everybody's face until it became boring. People were laughing at you, and they still are. Even the guys call you that. I hear them. Respect is something you've never had, and it's something you can't steal, either. The only way you could get it now is by turning to the Lord."

"Ding, dong, missionary time. Don't give me your bull. I'm not interested. You just sit back, Miss CHS, and watch me get what I want. I'm not down and out yet, and your little threats don't scare me. Here, why don't you buy all these hippie skirts; then people can laugh at *you* even more." With that, she hoisted an armful of skirts off the rack, dumped them on the floor, then twisted off like she was leading the CHS band off the field at halftime. Jemma replaced the skirts and left.

She sat in the parking lot while her body buzzed with emotion. She had lost her temper and tried to feel better about it by bringing in the Lord. All her Bible verses and prayers hadn't done her a lick of good when confronted with Missy. She bounced her head against the steering wheel. The Cleave was a clever liar. Those hateful things she had said about Spencer being unhappy were lies. How dare Missy mention their lost baby. If she brought all this up to Spence, it would give power to the lie. She knew her husband, and he was anything but unhappy.

Jemma started the car . . . and turned it off. She winced, then prayed out loud, "Please, please, forgive me, Lord, for losing my temper. Help me learn to control it better. . . ."

She blew her nose, then burst into a giggle. *Constituted* toad. Missy herself was the embodiment of a *conceited* toad.

Rats. That wasn't exactly a Christian thought and right after a heartfelt prayer, too.

Chapter 14
Clever Mrs. Baldwin

Trina's class threw their hats in the air, then she scrambled to find hers for the refund. Her family and friends had yelled louder than anybody's, digging her dimples even deeper as she clutched her diploma. She made her way through a sea of purple graduation gowns until she found Nick. Jemma caught the moment with Spencer's fancy camera.

"I hope I did that right," Jemma said. "He showed me how to use it, but I was packing."

"Jemmabeth!" Professor Rossi, always Jemma's most vocal fan, embraced her. "Where is your husband? I was hoping to see both of you."

"He's in California. He has a project there, and he couldn't come on this trip. How are you? You look happy, as usual."

"My wife and I are leaving next week for Italy. Come, I have someone you must meet.

I trust you have been working hard."

"You know me. I paint every day, all day. I have thirty pieces that are just sitting around, waiting to be loved by someone other than me."

"Not to worry," the professor said. "I have the solution." He escorted her to a cluster of people talking with the dean. One member of the group was a distinguished, slender man, impeccably dressed with a rosebud in his lapel and a moustache that appeared painted on. He smelled like sandalwood, but his face bore a slight resemblance to that of a mustachioed rat.

"Don't tell me," he said in an accent similar to Helene's, "you must be the young American artist that everyone is talking about — Forrester-Chase, is it?" He bowed slightly and held her hand by the fingertips, his eyes on her lips.

Professor Rossi laughed. "Ah, the English, always hyphenating names. Jemma, this is Mr. Howard-Finch, owner of the Finchgate Gallery in London."

"It's a pleasure to meet you, Mr. Finch. I visited your gallery on my honeymoon." She released his hand, but he tugged her to him.

"Call me Thornton, please," he said in a glib tone. "Rossi, here, has been extolling your praises, madam." He lowered his voice and spoke in her ear. "He assures me that you are exactly what we need for our next one-man, pardon, one-woman show." His hand slid to her waist. "How may I see your portfolio?"

"Jemmabeth lives in a small village in the far reaches of Texas," the professor explained. "Perhaps you could meet her somewhere. Jemma, what is the nearest airport?"

Jemma's words stumbled out. "Uh, Amarillo."

"Of course, Spanish for yellow. See what arrangements you can make, Thor. I have her telephone number. You will not be disappointed; you have my word," the professor said just as the dean called him back to the group.

Thornton scanned Jemma's face and came to rest on her eyes. "Such unusual eyes. You must have some hot French blood in you. I knew a girl in Paris with eyes like that." He smiled. "She was a dancer." He raised an eyebrow. "Do you like to dance?"

Jemma turned to Professor Rossi for help, but he was still laughing with the dean. "My husband and I like to dance." She forced a smile. "Do you really want to see my portfolio?"

His brow arched. "Indeed. I know you

have shown in New York and studied in Paris. What harm could there be in it? You may surprise me, and I like surprises." He winked. "Though, I must warn you, our gallery is very discriminating. Our shows attract collectors and buyers from all over Europe. We pride ourselves on featuring only those established and emerging artists whose work is preeminent and thoroughly dynamic. I have business this week here in Dallas and then on to Houston. Rossi says that he has one of your pieces. I shall see it later at dinner. If I like it, I'll be in touch." He lifted her hand but kept eye contact as he pecked it. "I surely like what I see before me now. I assume you have been told before that you are a stunning woman."

Jemma looked away from his shifty little eyes and back, exhaling. "Thank you. I'll look forward to hearing from you."

His mouth curved into a smirk. "We shall see." When he pursed his lips, his scrawny moustache folded up like bat wings.

Jemma walked away, feeling his eyes still on her. She wished she had worn a different dress, but Trina had made this one just for her. It was too short, too tight, and too purple at the moment.

The Fields, Nick's family, threw a party for Trina. Lots of laughter came from the corner where Willa sat with Nick's parents. They had big things to discuss about the wedding. Nick and Trina were both only children in their families, so their parents wanted everything to be special all around.

Lizbeth and Willa took the Trailways bus home. Jemma stayed to help Trina move her belongings back to Chillaton. Jemma cleaned out some of her own things that she had left in her old studio. She looked around at the place. There weren't nearly enough memories there with Spence, and that was all her fault. If she hadn't gotten it in her head to see if there was somebody else that she was destined to love rather than him, her life would have been simpler now. Most of her Wicklow memories revolved around Paul, and they weren't all good, especially the thought of him pinning her to the daybed, hungry for kisses and reeking of hot beer breath. She gathered up her things and locked the door behind her. She missed her husband, especially with the memory of Paul Turner ferreting into her brain.

"I'll never be able to thank you enough for Le Claire," Trina said as Jemma helped her pack. "Do you know what I'd be doing right now if you hadn't paid my tuition?"

Jemma feigned concentration. "You would

have stopped being so stubborn and gotten a scholarship?"

"I wasn't being stubborn. I just didn't want some rich person giving me money and knowing nothing about me. I guess you and Spencer are rich, though, huh?" Trina packed each of her design sketchbooks as though they were fine china. She glanced at Jemma. "Jem, did I make you feel like you had to help me go to school?"

Jemma wrinkled her nose as though a skunk had sprayed the room. "What are you talking about? You are my talented, sweet friend, and I wanted you to get the training you deserve. You always think I operate on guilt, but I don't. I'm not sure what drives my decisions. I'd like to think that the Lord uses me sometimes to do His will. I know He uses Spence."

"Yeah, but it was you, girl, who gave me the money. You've got a fine heart that drives you, and you don't even realize it. I'm the one who should feel guilty about whining over my situation back then. Right now all I can offer you is my talent, so from now on, I'm designing your clothes with my Le Claire School of Fine Arts degree. I think you need a fresh style."

Jemma laughed. "What's the deal with everybody talking about my clothes? I'm happy with what I have."

"Oh. Is that why you keep griping about that Blake girl calling you a bohemian, and that you don't have anything to wear except what your mom hands you down or what your snobby grandmother or Spence buys for you?" Trina grinned, her dimples set. "It doesn't take your Nancy Drew to figure out that you need help."

Jemma sighed. "You're right, as usual. When we get to Chillaton, you can go through my clothes and get rid of everything that doesn't meet your designer standards. There. Does that make you happy?"

Trina taped a box shut. "It would make me happy if I knew where Nick and I will end up after his residency. I want to live in a place where I can think. I don't want to be in a crazy city full of pressure and ego. You know what I mean?"

"I know that Spence felt the same way and look where we ended up. It amazes me that he and Trent have so much business with an office in Chillaton. They do spend a lot of time flying around the country, though. Did I tell you that they now have a client in Paris? Maybe y'all can move back home like everybody else is doing. It works for us."

Trina pooh-poohed that. "You think all those blue hairs would let Nick even check their blood pressure? That would be a miracle."

"Don't say it like that."

"I know, you believe in miracles and so do I." Trina went back to packing. "So you think I can make a difference with your neighborhood business idea? Sorry nobody showed up for the first meeting."

"A few came. I'm taking it slow. I don't want to scare anybody off."

"Speaking of scary, I suppose you know that Weese is back, and he brought his sister. She looks just like him and has the attitude. Mama said he got his high school diploma and somehow got into a junior college. Maybe he'll be a wiser Weese. Have you seen him yet?"

"I saw his sister. Her name's Gweny. She came to the little get-together I had. I wonder if Weese still hates me."

"He was all talk. Don't worry about it."

"Ladies," Helene called up the stairs, "lunch is served."

"I'm going to have to start running laps." Trina patted her stomach. "Helene is a good cook. I'm going to miss her and this beautiful place. I've been so lucky."

"Just like me," Jemma said, putting her arm around her as they went downstairs.

"Now let's talk more about my new wardrobe."

They discussed all the aspects of outfitting a portrait artist in colors to suit her mood and fabrics that felt good to her. Helene set her hearing aid a little higher and listened with delight. She, who had never had children of her own, had come to love these two young people, their families, and their circle of friends. It had been a panacea for her the last few years, and she did not want it to end. "Trina," Helene asked, "how did you meet Nicholas?"

Trina giggled. "*Nicholas* sounds so funny. Sorry, Helene." She cleared her throat. "I got a basketball scholarship to a junior college when I got out of high school."

"A scholarship?" Jemma said.

"Yeah. I know what you're thinking, but it was only a dinky one. I had to pay most of the tuition and expenses myself. Anyway, Nick and I worked at a burger place in Dallas. Nick had been in the army and was starting medical school. We just hit it off."

Jemma narrowed her eyes. "You never told me he was that much older than you."

"Hey, girl, he still wasn't as old as *Paul.*" Trina whispered his name.

"I challenge you to a duel for that. Outside in an hour. Bring your basketball."

"You're on." Trina grinned and had a second helping of Helene's broccoli quiche.

Helene tapped her teacup with a spoon. "A toast." The girls raised their glasses of cold sweet tea, which Helene had begrudgingly made for them. "To the three of us as we begin — or continue, in Jemma's case — new chapters in our lives." She clinked her cup against their glasses, then took a sip of hot tea and returned to her seat, her expression quite serene. Jemma and Trina still held their glasses aloft.

"Wait a minute, Helene. What's all this 'new chapter' business?" Jemma asked.

"Are you getting married or something?" Trina asked.

Helene dabbed at her mouth with her napkin and chuckled. "No, dear, I am not getting married, although I have not dismissed the idea."

"What, then?"

"I am moving to Chillaton. Lizbeth has invited me, and I have accepted. We are going to be flatmates. I will get to hear all the Lester stories that I want, and I can play Nana to all Lizbeth's great-grandchildren, when they arrive."

Jemmabeth and Latrina embraced her at once.

"Moving to Chillaton is a brave move for

an Englishwoman," Trina said. "You know who your neighbors will be across the tracks. Wait 'til Mama hears about this."

"Lizbeth and Willa have known for the past year. They were sworn to secrecy. Now that you have both moved on, I want to keep you in my sight, so I'm carrying on as well."

"What about your home?" Jemma asked. "How can you stand to leave it?"

"That's the sad part. Perhaps if anyone needs a place to stay, it can serve as the That'll Do Motel for Wicklow. Nebs would be amused at such nonsense."

Jemma and Trina played basketball in the driveway. Helene had installed a goal just for her boarder's amusement. They worked out until Trina quit.

"Ha!" Jemma announced. "I'm finally in better shape than you are."

"You and Spencer have been chasing each other around the house for over a year. I've been slaving away in school and eating Helene's rich food. What are you looking at?"

Jemma's attention was on the road. A baby blue pickup had stopped near Helene's driveway — *Paul.*

"Inside, quick," Jemma said. "Don't look at him."

They went in and locked the door, giving Helene specific instructions to not answer if he knocked. The three women huddled around the conservatory windows peeking through the panes. After several minutes, he drove away.

Trina shivered. "That was so creepy."

Jemma flopped in an armchair. "If he does one more thing, it will put Spence over the edge. Paul has to back off."

"Do you think it would help if I talked with him, dear?" Helene asked. "I know his father, slightly, from Neb's legal dealings."

"That old boy could step on you like a sugar ant, Helene," Trina declared.

Jemma was still watching out the window.

"Of course," Trina added, "you might die happy, lookin' at him."

"I don't know what will ever help." Jemma sighed and slumped back into the chair.

"You should introduce him to that Blake girl. They would be the perfect couple," Trina suggested.

"Y'all don't leave me alone, okay?" Jemma paced around the room.

Trina and Helene exchanged glances, and Helene put her mind in Clever English-woman Mode.

The next morning, the girls went for a run

around the Wicklow High School track. When they got home, Helene and her red MG were nowhere to be seen.

"She must be at the supermarket. There's a new one down by the highway," Trina said.

Jemma wasn't too sure about that, but kept her ideas to herself.

Helene sat in the law office. She was not as calm as she thought she would be. The secretary was pleasant enough and had even offered her tea. She didn't drink it, though. It was that awful brand Americans buy just to be on the safe side with the odd hot tea-drinking guest. She adjusted her pearls.

"Mrs. Baldwin? Mr. Turner will see you now." The secretary smiled as she picked up Helene's teacup. "Wouldn't you like to take your tea with you?"

"No thank you, dear," Helene said, concentrating on the task at hand.

Paul was on the phone with his back to the door. Helene seated herself and surveyed the room. It was impressive, but with a somewhat melancholy, perfunctory air. Her eyes came to rest on a watercolor self-portrait of Jemma laughing. It hung directly behind his desk next to a large, vibrant painting of a river flanked by rolling meadows of bluebonnets. She remembered that piece, too. It had been a gift from Jemma to Paul before his secret was found out. Helene knew also that he had paid a thousand dollars for the watercolor and another two thousand for others she didn't see in the office. She took a deep breath. This was not going to be easy.

He did the same double take that Helene had enjoyed watching in silent movies as a child. In her younger days, her heart would have quaked at the sight of such a splendidly handsome man, but not now, and especially not after all she knew about him.

She extended her hand. "Hello, Paul. Your office is quite nice."

He pressed his hand to hers. "Helene. Are you using an alias these days?" he asked, recovering, and turning on the charm.

"Baldwin is my maiden name. I use it sometimes for legal documents and such." Helene sat forward in her chair, straight as a hatpin. She concentrated her attention on a small watercolor of flowers on his desk, another of Jemma's works. "I'm here, Paul, out of concern for Jemmabeth. As you know, she is very dear to me."

"She is to me, as well." He leaned back in his leather chair, watching her.

She knew those eyes of his could mesmerize even an old sort like her, so she returned to the watercolor and weighed each word. "I'm not sure that you comprehend what has happened. Jemma has committed her life to Spencer and that will not change, dear. She is not a woman to be twisted about like a university girl anymore."

"What's your point, Helene? I've heard speeches like this before."

"My point is that all of us who love Jemma want her life to be full of joy and as peaceful as possible. If we impede that joy, we become a negative influence on her life, and also on her art, since I see that you enjoy her work. Unfortunately, you have managed to jeopardize her happiness. I don't mean to become threatening, Paul, but I do know your father, and I have made an appointment with him as well, as soon as we are finished here. I truly hope that you will be able to convince me that our Jemmabeth is not in any further danger of your harassment. Perhaps you have already confided this troublesome behavior to your father, but I am prepared to help you in that revelation, should you need such assistance."

Paul drummed his fingertips on the desk, his face solemn and his voice low. "Coercion doesn't become you, darlin'. My father has a heart condition, and it could kill him to hear this. Regardless of what you think, I have never harmed Jemmabeth. I love her. Just because she chose the kid over me doesn't change that fact. Remember, I saved her life in Paris."

"I am well aware of that situation, and nobody denies that you kept her from a ghastly fate. That incident, however, was coincidental to your obsessive nature. Harassing her does not send a message of affection. I have, myself, witnessed her fear and anxiety over your actions. You have infringed on Jemma's pursuit of happiness, and I believe that is assured us in the *Declaration of Independence.* I have dual citizenship, you know."

Paul leaned back in his chair and stared at her. His green eyes matched her emerald earrings. "Don't talk to Dad, Helene. Like I said, he's had two heart attacks in the last three years." His voice quavered, and the room became quiet.

He finally stood and moved to sit on the corner of his desk. Trina was right; he truly was a large chap, and he could quite possibly squash her like an ant.

"I am not ashamed to say that I adore Jemma," he said. "She's as close to perfection as a woman could ever be. If I've frightened her, as you say, I'm sorry. Ironically, nobody understands my feelings for her except the husband kid. To be frank with you, ma'am, she's the only woman, besides my mother, that I've ever respected. I just want to be near her whenever I can, to see those golden eyes and to hear her laugh. I like the way her hair . . ." He ran his hand through his own.

Helene spoke quietly and with unforeseen tenderness. "I understand your affection for her, dear. She is an extraordinary person, but you mustn't put your desires above hers. It is not fair to her, Paul. Surely, as a lawyer, you can see that. What do you say, then? If you can assure me that this nonsense will stop, I shan't keep my appointment with your father." She kept her breath steady and her eyes on the watercolor flowers.

"You are asking me to give up all hope, Helene. What is a man without hope?"

"Hope is always inside us, Paul, but such hope must abide only in your heart and not infringe on this dear girl's joy. She is worth more than that to you, is she not?"

He brushed his cheek with his thumb. "I need to always know, somehow, that she is safe and lacks for absolutely nothing."

Helene put her hand on his. "I can write to you now and then, if it would be of any consolation to you."

He nodded. "The first time I ever saw her,

she was dancing in this very room with a vacuum cleaner. She stole my heart that night, and it's never ticked right since. I've handled things all wrong, but I do know that she cared for me, once. My miserable past caught up with me at every turn. It was the chance of a lifetime, and I blew it."

"Nevertheless," Helene said, "Jemma believes the Almighty has His own plans for us all. It would appear, then, that you are meant to find another woman to love and let her be. Do carry on, dear boy." She looked directly at him, ill-prepared to find this beguiling man in tears.

"I will let her be, if possible," he said, "but I will never love anyone the way that I love Jem. How could I? You know her. She is the rose in a garden of daisies."

Helene could not disagree. There was nothing more to be said. She reached for one of his business cards. "Good day, Paul. I wish you well," she said, and meant it.

"Helene, you've got a lot of guts, pardon my French, to come here and talk to me about this. Jemma brings out something in people, and they do things for her that normally they might not. Promise me that you really will keep in touch."

"I shall. I am a steadfast woman, and you are quite right; I would do anything for her."

She offered her hand. He took it in his and held it for a moment.

"By the way, darlin', our rights are guaranteed by the *Constitution,* not the *Declaration of Independence.* Just for future reference," he clarified with a feeble smile.

"I did say that I have dual citizenship. At my age it's difficult to keep historical things from two countries straight." She closed the door on his vacant stare, then dabbed her eyes with her lace hanky after tucking his card into her purse.

Jemma waited in the garden by the fragrant Tiffany rose. She closed her eyes and inhaled. The rosebush they had planted by Papa's grave would duplicate that scent this summer. Such a heavenly creation stirred hope in her. Their merciful Lord might bless them again with a baby.

Her eyes popped open when she heard the MG rolling down the lane. Helene waved and pulled it into the garage. She emerged, dressed in the same aqua blue linen suit she had worn to Trina's graduation.

"Such a lovely morning," Helene called from the gate.

"Yes," Jemma said. "What business took you out so early in your new suit?"

"Personal business, much like a mission

trip. You wouldn't interrogate a missionary, now would you?" She gave Chelsea, the cat, a quick pet and went inside.

"So does this mean that you're ready to join a church?" Jemma asked, following her down the hallway.

Helene removed her suit coat and set her handbag on the hallway telephone table. "Perhaps that will be one of my endeavors when I move to Chillaton, but for now, dearest, we need to make plans for dinner. Remember, Nicholas and his family are our guests. Where is Trina?"

"She's upstairs sketching some dresses for my new wardrobe." Jemma watched Helene scamper up the steps like a twenty-year-old. Jemma peered after her for a second, then turned to find Chelsea sniffing at Helene's handbag. It tumbled to the floor with a thump, spilling the contents and sending Chelsea into a speedy exit down the hall. Jemma collected the scattered things: keys, wallet, coin purse, and a damp handkerchief.

That's when she saw it. She read it to be sure, but there was no need. It was just like the other one hundred or so cards that he had sent her in hopes she would call him after he'd played with her heart. Jemma placed it back in the bag and returned to the garden. Chelsea jumped in her lap as she sat again by the Tiffany, pondering the significance of it all.

Trina's car was so loaded that they thought the tires might go flat.

"Now, Jemma," Helene said, "you must come back to help me move when the time arrives. You will do that for me, won't you?"

"I will. Just call out my name and I'll come running, like the Carole King song says."

Helene twisted her hearing aid. "What's that, dear?"

Trina shook her head. "Jemma just needs to see Spencer, that's all. Thank you for so many things. Someday, when I'm famous, I'm gonna make it up to you two ladies for everything y'all have done for me."

"How about a burger on the road for now?" Jemma asked as she readjusted a couple of boxes in the front seat. "Bye, Helene and Chelsea. Chillaton, here we come." Jemma squeezed behind the wheel and honked the horn.

Trina shouted out the window as they rolled down the lane, "See you at the wedding!"

Helene stroked fat Chelsea and sighed. Were it not for her own plans to move to their village, the moment would have been too heavy for her to bear.

Chapter 15
Coming Attractions

Lizbeth was at Nedra's Nook for her weekly appointment, and Jemma was trying out a new home hair dryer for the first time. Her long, wavy locks flared out en masse and the bathroom emitted an odor of singed fur. She heard him at the back door.

"Jem?" he yelled.

"She's not here," Jemma answered and appeared in the bathroom door. "It's only me, wild woman." She ran around the kitchenette to land on him.

"Now," he said, catching his breath, "who are you, and what have you done with my wife?"

Jemma giggled. "You, sir, are early. See what you get when you arrive ahead of schedule? This mess is the result of something called a blow-dryer. It's more like a blowtorch if you ask me. I bought it at Kidwell's."

Spencer closed the back door. "You sure

make my old shirt look good, but I don't think Lester needs to see you in it."

Jemma perched herself on the kitchenette table, grinning. "Guess what? Trina is going to make me a whole new wardrobe. She says I need a 'fresher look,' whatever that means."

Spencer stood close to her with dreamy eyes.

Jemma giggled. "Now, Mr. Chase, before *you* get fresh, remember, Gram could walk in at any moment."

"Well, come on, then, help me unpack, but we are going straight out to the house. I have paint choices for us. Are you ready for that?" Spencer offered his hand, and she jumped off the table and followed him through the good bedroom to theirs.

"The question is, are you ready for this?" She pushed him on the bed and held him down with a sleeper hold. Spencer overpowered her and got her in a tremulous leg lock. Even her teeth chattered. She couldn't stop laughing.

"Give up?" he asked.

"Yes!" she rattled.

Spencer stopped, his legs weak, and Jemma sat up. Her hair was even wilder than before.

"Remember," she said, "I have to practice

my moves for Thor, The Lech. *If* he calls, I have to meet him with my portfolio, and *if* you aren't with me, I'll have to fend for myself."

"Oh, I'll be there all right. I'll knock that boutonnière right out of his lapel for him." Spencer took off his tie.

"Oooh, tough guy, huh?" Jemma whispered, smoothing the front of his shirt. "I dare you to try that leg lock again because I'm ready for it this time." She looked up at him and bit her lip.

Spencer responded with his own whispered ideas.

"Hello, anybody home?" Lizbeth called from the kitchen.

Jemma dashed into the closet to finish dressing. Spencer, ever the gentleman, went to see the lady of the house.

They sat under the cottonwoods discussing paint colors. She knew it would be an odd time to bring it up, but she had waited as long as she could.

"Tell me something, babe, and don't spare my feelings."

He raised his brow. "I get the feeling that this is not going to be about paint."

"Are you unhappy that we don't have a baby yet?" she asked quietly, looking straight into his eyes.

He put the color strips down. His answer came slowly, as if he were turning over the source of this question in his mind. "This life of ours could not be happier, Jem. Well, maybe if our house was finished and I could chase you around more. That might make me happier. What's going on?"

"I was just wondering."

"Yeah, I believe that one. Look at me. Who has been messing with your brain?"

She should have kept her trap shut. Rats. "I saw Missy in Amarillo. We sort of had a confrontation, and she said a bunch of things."

"Like what?"

"She said that everybody in Chillaton knew that you were unhappy because I couldn't give you a baby, and that she could because she's already had two abortions, and that I can't remember to call her Melissa because my head is full of unused baby names." She threw her arms around him and bawled. "I wanted to take her hair and choke her with it. I am so bad, Spence. Don't chew me out, either. I know that she's a liar and that she gets to me, but it was the first time I'd seen her since Paris and I just—"

"Jemmabeth. If we never have a baby, it

my moves for Thor, The Lech. *If* he calls, I have to meet him with my portfolio, and *if* you aren't with me, I'll have to fend for myself."

"Oh, I'll be there all right. I'll knock that boutonnière right out of his lapel for him." Spencer took off his tie.

"Oooh, tough guy, huh?" Jemma whispered, smoothing the front of his shirt. "I dare you to try that leg lock again because I'm ready for it this time." She looked up at him and bit her lip.

Spencer responded with his own whispered ideas.

"Hello, anybody home?" Lizbeth called from the kitchen.

Jemma dashed into the closet to finish dressing. Spencer, ever the gentleman, went to see the lady of the house.

They sat under the cottonwoods discussing paint colors. She knew it would be an odd time to bring it up, but she had waited as long as she could.

"Tell me something, babe, and don't spare my feelings."

He raised his brow. "I get the feeling that this is not going to be about paint."

"Are you unhappy that we don't have a baby yet?" she asked quietly, looking straight into his eyes.

He put the color strips down. His answer came slowly, as if he were turning over the source of this question in his mind. "This life of ours could not be happier, Jem. Well, maybe if our house was finished and I could chase you around more. That might make me happier. What's going on?"

"I was just wondering."

"Yeah, I believe that one. Look at me. Who has been messing with your brain?"

She should have kept her trap shut. Rats. "I saw Missy in Amarillo. We sort of had a confrontation, and she said a bunch of things."

"Like what?"

"She said that everybody in Chillaton knew that you were unhappy because I couldn't give you a baby, and that she could because she's already had two abortions, and that I can't remember to call her Melissa because my head is full of unused baby names." She threw her arms around him and bawled. "I wanted to take her hair and choke her with it. I am so bad, Spence. Don't chew me out, either. I know that she's a liar and that she gets to me, but it was the first time I'd seen her since Paris and I just—"

"Jemmabeth. If we never have a baby, it

won't be some kind of a blemish on our marriage. The way I feel about you is enough to keep me content for a lifetime. To have a child with you would be a blessing, but I don't have any secret desires to produce an heir or something. I won't give you any lectures about Missy, but I want you to think about this the next time you see her: Pretend she has hooves, horns, and a tail because I do believe that the devil uses her to get to you. Promise me that you will give that a try."

She glanced up at him, wiping her nose on the back of her hand. "Are you mad at me for asking that?"

"Maybe. Let's make up and see if that helps. Do you understand how I feel about us and babies?"

She nodded and hugged him.

He held her tight. Someday, surely Missy Blake would get her comeuppance.

"You look like Doris Day sitting at that desk," Jemma said as Sandy hung up the phone.

"I love this job. If I don't get fired for spouting off about something, I could work here forever." Sandy stood and danced around in her hot pink pantsuit. "Like what I did with part of my first paycheck? I made it myself." Marriage had not packed any extra pounds on her petite figure.

"I like it a lot better than the dance hall stuff The Cleave wore."

"I heard that she got another job in Amarillo. You'd think that they would call here for references." Sandy sharpened pencils for her bosses.

"I doubt she listed this one for that very reason. Have you heard anything from Marty?" Jemma watched Sandy out of the corner of her eye.

Sandy mouthed the words, "I filed for divorce last week."

"No regrets?" Jemma whispered back.

Sandy shook her head without hesitation. "Anybody hits, I quit. Even if it's Mr. Universe." She went back to the electric pencil sharpener, her perfect makeup still looking good in the air-conditioned office.

Jemma watered the plants, something she hadn't done when Missy was the secretary; then again, maybe she should have and denied The Cleave the opportunity to lean over the pots. "How do you like working for Trent?"

"He's so shy." Sandy lowered her voice. "Hard to get to know, but I guess that's okay. He's cute, but that's probably a prerequisite just to be in your family."

"Easy does it; you're still a married woman."

"Hi, cousin," Trent said, emerging with a stack of folders. "Sandy, would you please call these people and ask for their bids for the job numbers listed on the files? Remind them the deadline is Monday."

Jemma sat on the corner of Sandy's desk. "So, Trent, are you back to your lonely days now that Missy is gone?"

Trent blushed. "I'm keeping busy. It's amazing how Spencer and I have so many clients. Nobody even complains about our location. Of course we meet them at their offices. Our travel and phone expenses are going to be off the charts when tax time rolls around. I just made another call to Paris."

"What do you think of your new secretary?" Jemma asked. "You know she won state in typing."

Trent turned red again. "She's great. Goes by the dress code, too," he said, with a quick look at Sandy. "Well, I guess I'd better get back to work. See ya, Jem."

"Did you see how embarrassed he was? Too shy." Sandy got busy on her assignment.

"Hi, baby, are you ready to go?" Spencer turned off the lights in his office, then dipped Jemma back for a kiss. "Sorry I took so long."

"Kissing is not suitable for the office," Sandy replied.

"Your comments are unsuitable for the office." Spencer grinned and kissed his wife again. "We're leaving this joint. If a call comes from New York, be sure to get their mailing address, okay?" Spencer grabbed Jemma's hand and his briefcase.

Jemma waved on their way out the door.

"What's going on in New York?" Jemma asked on the way to Plum Creek.

"We may get a shot at a chapel design for a new hospital. The plans didn't include it, and some lady gave a big chunk of money to add one. She doesn't like the original architects and won't give her money to them. It's a mess."

"Maybe you could specialize in chapels." Jemma braided her hair.

"That would be nice, wouldn't it? Okay, I have to tell you something, and I don't want you to get upset."

"The sooner you tell me, the sooner I can get over it."

"The firm we would be working with in New York City is the firm that Michelle Taylor is with." He said it fast and waited.

Jemma looked out the window. It was her

turn to trust now. Spencer had set a very high standard in that department. They passed two mile markers before she spoke. "I know that you love me even though she is an aggressive, possessive woman. Is she married yet?"

Spencer exhaled. "I can't answer that. All I know is that when Trent and I researched the firm, her name was on the list as Taylor." He reached for her hand. "You are taking this well."

She shrugged. "I'm trying to put faith into action, but let's don't talk about it anymore. Same rules I have with Paul. You call me if anything happens."

"Nothing is going to happen."

"Just don't let her touch you. Remember she called me a shehick, a *shick.*"

"I remember you called her a fool in French. What if she wants to shake hands?" He grinned.

"You may only salute, soldier," she said, giving him The Look that he loved.

This time the pews at the Negro Bethel Church were full. Word had gotten out that Latrina, college graduate and fashion designer, would be there.

"Some of these women are from Red Mule and Pleasant," Trina whispered.

"That's okay with me. If they're interested in making this work," Jemma said.

"How come there ain't no cookies?" Grandma Hardy called out.

"Hold your horses, Grandma," Willa yelled back. "There's sandwiches when the meetin's done."

"Thanks for coming, ladies. I hope that this big turnout means you are all interested in making a go of the project," Jemma said as the crowd quieted down. "I have arranged for you to have ten sewing machines, and Trina has chosen the fabric. She will help with the details of the machines and the actual quilting. I hope everyone signed the sheet at the back table."

Gweny sniffed. "Some can't write. You should've known that." Murmurs of agreement sputtered around the room.

Jemma's face reddened. "Oh, I'm sorry. If you'll tell me your name, that will do. I want to make up a work schedule as a guide, so everybody will have something to do."

"What's your job?" Grandma Hardy asked.

"I'll drop by when I can, but I have my own work. I don't know how to quilt. I'm an artist," Jemma said almost apologetically.

Bertie Shanks raised her hand. "Who's gonna be the boss?"

"You're lookin' at her," Willa announced proudly. "I don't want no fightin', neither."

The group who knew her laughed and relaxed.

"Me and my husband, Joe, are takin' a real interest in these goin's-on, and Brother Cleo is lettin' us use the basement here at the church during the weekdays. My baby, Trina, is gonna give sewin' machine lessons every day startin' tomorrow at eight in the mornin'. Now if all of us pull our weight, we can make us some grocery money that don't come from the guv'ment. It can't be no harder than pickin' cotton. Now, in the past, I've been thinkin' that Jemmabeth here had fertilizer in her head, but after she told me and Joe the details, I seen the light. I'm ready to go on it, but I ain't no quilter neither. I can iron, so I reckon that means I can iron out problems if any come up."

More laughter.

Trina showed the ladies her original pattern ideas. They voted on their favorites and broke into smaller groups to argue about fabric colors and quilting styles. Most had been quilting since childhood, but never with material like Jemma had purchased. They ran their hands over the bolts and cast their first approving glances her way.

Jemma had done her homework, with

Lizbeth's help. The North & South Chillaton Quilting Club President had even calculated bathroom breaks into the plan. It paid off. Jemma taped the schedule, drawn on Spencer's oversized drafting paper, on the basement wall, as the whole group descended downstairs for sandwiches and sweet tea. They looked over the sewing machines resting on the folding church tables with oohs and aahs. Lester and Joe had made four quilting frames that were suspended overhead like giant spiderwebs. The air was tinged with excitement and high hopes. The women from Pleasant and Red Mule would only be able to work two days a week, when they could all pile into the back of a truck belonging to Teeky Samson's son. He would drive them over and only charge gas money. Jemma said she would pay him for his trouble.

"My Joe's gonna keep the books, so y'all be sure to make your mark on the days you work. We'll all be on the lookout for each other, so keep everybody honest. Now I think we should have ourselves a prayer over this business," Willa said, and the group joined hands, except for Gweny Matthews, who took her sandwiches and left. "Lord Almighty, we give You thanks for this food and the hands that prepared it. We come to

Your holy feet, Lord, and lay down this here plan for a quiltin' business. If You want to bless it, Jesus, we'll know that's what You think we should do. Also, we ask You to bless Jemmabeth, Lord, for comin' to us with this here notion, the machines, and the cloth. Help steady our hands to Your glory and to get off welfare. Amen."

Shiloh Favor approached Jemma and smiled. "I just wanna say that me and my man, Terrill, think this is a fine idea. Lots of folks think it's gonna flop, but if nobody never tries nothin', then nothin' never gets better. That's all I've got to say on it." She lifted her chin and left.

"Thank you, Shiloh," Jemma said to her back. She turned to Trina, blinking back tears. "Let's eat. Are there any sandwiches left?"

"Nope. What wasn't eaten was taken home. Mama wants to get out of here. Joe comes home tonight from a run to L.A."

"Then we'll go to Daddy's Money." Jemma cleared off the refreshment table.

"Let's just go to Son's." Trina shook the tablecloth over the wastebasket. "I still get looks at Daddy's Money. Nobody can see me that well if I'm sitting in the car at Son's."

Jemma was taken aback. Chillaton had

come around faster than this, surely. Still, Trina avoided her eyes. Rats. Double ugly rats. Maybe it hadn't. The momentary silence between them was broken by a freight train clamoring down those tracks that still divided their little town.

"So, what's the plan?" Jemma asked, turning toward Son's. "Are you going to work for a design house?"

Trina laughed. "I doubt it. One of my professors helped me put together a portfolio, though. She sent it to a few places for me. I might as well get used to the idea of living in a ghetto and being Nick's assistant."

"Don't give me that. You're a fantastic designer. Something will come along. A ghetto? Good grief, Trina."

"I have thought of a label for myself, but don't tell anybody. It's my initials, *LJF*, with the *F* coming off the *J;* you know what I mean, like the *J* is a flagpole? I want to keep the Johnson in there to honor my daddy."

"I do like it. You get started on my clothes, and I'll tell everybody they're from the *LJF* label. Thanks for your help on this project, Trina. You made all the difference."

"Mama's the one who made the difference. It's great to see her getting out and having something to do besides ironing. Joe is a real blessing to her. I wish we'd had him twenty years ago."

"Do you think all those women will show up on Monday?"

"Yeah, I do. Out of curiosity, if nothing else. Hey, maybe we could shoot some baskets before we eat. I need to trim off a few inches before my wedding."

"You're on." Jemma did one of her famous U-turns and headed to the high school tennis courts. They both loved the old hoop without a net on the side of the concrete court. It was there that they had first become friends.

Jemma called Do Dah and Uncle Art as soon as she got home. "It should be interesting," she said. "Do you want me to send the first quilt for your approval when it's finished?"

"I trust your judgment, Jemmabeth," Arthur replied. "If you like it, I'll like it."

"Go ahead and send the first one and we'll put it in a window display with a 'Coming Attractions' banner. That'll stir some interest," Julia, ever the thinker, added.

"I defer to my better half." Arthur chuckled. "Good idea."

The women were waiting on the church

steps when Jemma drove up on Monday. Willa arrived about the same time and unlocked the door. After a bit of confusion about chairs and coffee cups, they got started. Jemma left them under Willa's watchful eye. It was up to the Lord now. She didn't know what else to offer.

Chapter 16
Chased Out of Town

"Hey, Mrs. Chase," Sandy said, knocking on the door to Spence's office.

"Yeah." Jemma turned from the color chips spread all over Spencer's desk.

"There's some Englishman on the phone with three first names. He wants to talk to you." Sandy lowered her voice. "Must be Thor."

Jemma bugged her eyes at Spencer, who gave her a thumbs-up. Sandy and Spencer listened as best they could while Jemma made the appointment. She took notes and hung up the phone.

"Well?" Sandy asked. "We're dying here. What did he say?"

Jemma shrugged. "I'm meeting him at his hotel room. I have to bring six pieces, blah, blah, blah. Y'all don't want to hear all of that. I guess I'd better get home and get busy."

"When is this happening?" Spencer asked.

"Today," Jemma said, palms up.

"Baby, we can't go today. We have to meet with the painters this afternoon about our house. Call him back and be assertive."

Sandy snickered. "How about I call him back and be assertive? Jemma has to get fired up to be assertive." She strode back to her desk.

Spencer held Jemma's shoulders. "I don't want you going alone. If you call him back, he'll see that you are not intimidated by his position and power. Just try it."

"He's only going to be in Amarillo for a few hours, Spence. He got this room just to look at my work. I can handle him. You know what my choices are for the house. I'll hurry back. The painters can't even buy the paint today. They'll have to get it in Amarillo." Jemma looked him in the eye. "This is a major opportunity for my career. I can't let it slip away."

Spencer traced around her chin. "Every time I don't go with you, something happens that I could have prevented. I don't want that to be the case today."

"I'll be all right, babe. Right now I need to get out of here and load up the car. I don't think the paintings will fit in the Corvette. What should I do?"

"We're going to have to get another vehicle. Ask Gram if you can borrow hers for today. I'm sorry, Jem. I really wanted to be there with you."

Jemma picked up the phone to call home, then changed her mind. "Rats. Gram's gone to her quilting club meeting for the day. I don't have a clue where. Maybe Lester could take me. At least I would have a man along." She giggled and grabbed her purse. "I'll see you tonight."

He watched her leave before picking up the phone.

Lester was busy in his shop. The paintings were too large for his car, too, and she couldn't risk transporting them in the back of his old pickup.

"That Buddy B feller that works for Spencer's dad has a big truck. He tows folks' cars with it. I'd give him a call," Lester suggested, slapping his overalls to get rid of the sawdust.

Jemma ran to use Gram's phone.

"Sure, you can borrow the truck," Buddy said. "It's kinda beat up, but it will get you there. Just come on down and get it. Are you sure you don't want to talk to Max? He'd let you take something off the lot."

"Oh, I hadn't thought of that. Do you think he would mind? I guess that's his business, huh?"

"Yeah, and you're his daughter-in-law. He's always bragging about your art. Let me put you through to his office. Hang on." Buddy B had a way of talking her into things.

Max came on the line. "Hey, beautiful, how are things? Buddy tells me that you need some transportation to Amarillo, and I've got just the thing."

Within ten minutes, Max was in the alley, ready to load the paintings from the car house. He was driving a new turquoise and white 1969 Suburban. It was perfect. "I don't have anything to do this afternoon. Would you like some company?" he asked with a sheepish grin.

"Spence called you, didn't he?"

"Right before you did. Come on, we haven't talked in a while. Let me go with you."

Max loaded the last big canvas into the Suburban. Jemma climbed in the passenger side. "I may need moral support anyway," she said.

Max drove like Spencer — way too fast. "Now who's this guy we're going to see?"

"He is the owner of a very prestigious art gallery in London. If he likes my work, he could offer me a one-woman show. This is a great car, Max. Thanks for coming to my rescue."

"Anytime. Now, tell me about your new house. I'm trying to talk Rebecca into taking a drive out there to see it."

"Really?" Jemma asked, thinking of her last conversation with her mother-in-law. "Spence is talking with the painters today. I love the house. It is a little of both of us, mostly in the Craftsman style. Of course we wanted to make it as perfect as possible, knowing our professions. It's sort of in the shape of a four-leaf clover — so, not pure Craftsman," she said, sketching it for him in her book. "The center is called a 'great room' with a kitchen, dining room, and living room all rolled into one. It has a really high ceiling, then the bedrooms and bathrooms all branch out from there. There's a spiral staircase leading up to our shared studio loft and a spot for stargazing. Spence added this tiny little room with stained-glass windows for me to pout in — that's a long story. Oh, it's all so fantastic. Coming up out of the deck is a big cottonwood tree that we carved our names on in grade school. Isn't that sweet? We'll have a big party, I'm sure, when we move in."

Max watched her draw the house plans. "You and my boy were just meant to be together, weren't you? You're like some fairy-tale couple," he said, then was quiet for a long minute. "I'll tell you something that I've never told anybody before, not even Spencer. I used to sneak into his room when he was a little boy and kiss him good night. We all know those were the beginnings of my bad days, the times when I chased after every halfway decent-looking female in six counties. It made me feel better about myself to see him lying there, so peaceful and perfect, and know that he was part of me. He was the best of me, if there is any. I'd look around his room and learn about his life. As time went by, I'd go through his homework and see how he was thinking. He was a smart kid. From the time he was little, though, he kept pictures you'd drawn and tacked them up around the room. Isn't that something? He loved you even then."

Jemma smiled. "Max, you need to tell this to Spencer. It would mean a lot to him."

"No, I don't think I could handle that. I might start bawling or something." Max checked his rearview mirror.

"Maybe it would be good for both of you to talk about those years," she said quietly. "It could ease some of the pain. Think about it, okay?"

Max nodded and looked in the mirror again. "I guess I'd better slow up. We've got company."

The state trooper turned on his lights. Jemma looked back and shook her head. She knew what was going to happen next. These Chase men.

"May I see your license and registration, sir?" The trooper tipped his hat.

Max pulled out his wallet and obliged.

"Mr. Chase? The Chevy dealer in Chillaton?" the trooper asked.

"The one and the same, sir." Max perked up at a potential reprieve.

"Well then, you should know better than to drive a vehicle without tags on it." The trooper smiled at Jemma. She looked away.

"Shoot," Max said. "I was in such a hurry to pick up my daughter-in-law here that I forgot to tape this on." Max reached in the backseat and showed the officer the dealer's plate.

"Jemmabeth?" The officer took off his glasses. "I guess you don't recognize me. I'm Jeeber McCleary. You were a couple of grades behind me in school. I married Lorena Hodges."

Jemma raised her brow and leaned in for a better look. "Oh, hi, Jeeber, I do remember you. I thought Lorena was a stewardess working out of Dallas."

"Naw, that didn't happen. Too many rules about her weight. I tell you what, Mr. Chase. I'm gonna give you a warning this time, but you need to get that license stuck up on the back window ASAP." Jeeber tipped his hat and grinned at Jemma. "Tell Spencer hello for me and that I'm glad he got out of 'Nam in one piece. I heard about his close call."

"Tell Lorena hi for me, too," Jemma said as he walked back to his car.

"Whew." Max exhaled. "If there's one thing I don't need, it's another ticket. It's a good thing your pretty face sticks in a fellow's mind. Now if I can get this to stick on that back window."

Jemma took some tape from the wrapped paintings and plastered it onto the license plate. It almost lasted to the city limits before dropping free.

They pulled into the parking lot of the Fairmont Hotel. It was the best that Amarillo had to offer. Jemma went inside and called up to his room. "Mr. Howard-Finch? It's Jemmabeth Chase. I'm downstairs. Would you like for us to bring my pieces to your room now?"

"Us?" he asked. "Please, call me Thornton. Yes, now is fine. Do come up, *alone* preferably."

Max loaded up a luggage cart, and they took it to the room. Jemma set the paintings up while Thornton moved around them. He scrutinized every detail while smoking a cigarette at the end of an ebony holder.

Max called Jemma to the door. "I'll be right back, hon. I have to get something to keep that plate on the window. Won't take but a couple of minutes."

Jemma nodded.

Thornton backed away from a painting of Weese leaning against Willa's porch, holding a bottle. "I would have to say that your work is truly brilliant. It goes beyond mundane portraiture and exudes a 'slice of life.' Articulate for me your objectives, my dear."

Jemma folded her arms. "I want the viewer to experience the subject's life. I want an audience to breathe the same air as the subject, to feel his skin, and to hear his voice — literally and figuratively," Jemma said, her eyes on Weese.

Thor put out his cigarette and moved to the piece showing Sandy, looking out the window of a car, her hazel eyes reflecting disappointment and determination. "Fascinating eye treatment. You tell me everything I need to know through them."

Jemma smiled. "When I was a little girl, Papa, my grandfather, would give me a stack of National Geographic magazines to copy. The eyes in those photographs inspire my brush. I want that one detail to be perfect."

"You have succeeded admirably." He ogled Jemma as she commented on the other pieces, moving nearer as she spoke. Then he touched her arm. "I think I've found my one-woman show," he said, his lips moving curiously. "There are but a few particulars to discuss." He slipped his hand under her hair to stroke the back of her neck.

Jemma jerked her head at his touch. "What are you doing? Cut that out."

Thor made a fist around her hair and pulled her to him until his cigarette breath filled her nostrils. His thin lips skimmed hers just as she raised her right foot and hooked the back of his knee with a walloping blow. Thor's leg buckled, and he stumbled to the floor. Jemma scrambled to nab him and hold him down with The Sleeper hold. She knew how to react to The Calf Roper. Thornton never knew what hit him.

"I shall have you arrested for this, you

wench," he gurgled. "Let me go immediately, or I shall call for the police."

"You'll have a hard time reaching the phone from here, sir," Jemma warned.

They stayed on the floor until Jemma thought he was going to faint, but she knew this man needed to be taught a lesson. She had just the moves to accomplish that.

"Let me up," he whispered. "I'll not press charges if you do as I say now."

"I may press charges myself, Thor," Jemma said, her voice rising. "How do I know that you won't try something else?"

"My word as a gentleman," he whispered.

"Well, that's no good. Any other ideas?"

"I won't touch you." Thor rolled his eyes up to look at her.

Jemma let him go only because he looked like he might throw up. Better him than her.

He coughed and sat up. One of his tasseled, leather loafers had come off in the scuffle. He fumbled around on all fours, then staggered up. He lit a cigarette and sneered at her, blowing smoke. "My, my, my, that was some demonstration of brute strength."

Jemma wasn't listening. She opened the door and set her paintings on the cart in the hall.

Thor reclined on the bed and watched

with interest. "I misspoke earlier. Your work is by no means suitable for my gallery." He flicked ashes in a cup. "I can assure you that it will be unsuitable for any London venue, if you grasp my meaning."

Jemma put her purse on her shoulder. She shut the door and rolled the cart toward the elevator, trembling.

The doors opened and Max stepped out. "Done already? Sorry it took me so long."

Jemma nodded and stared at the carpet.

Max touched her shoulder. "What's wrong, hon? Did things not go well? Is the guy blind or something?"

Jemma put her hands over her face and cried. Max consoled her as best he could all the way to the Suburban. She spilled out the story once they were inside. He lurched open his door and disappeared inside The Fairmont. Jemma yelled after him, but it was of no use.

She sat with her eyes trained on the lobby doors. After about ten minutes, Max-a-Million, as Lester called him, came back to the car, breathing heavy and shaking his hand. Jemma didn't know what to say.

Max grimaced in pain, then started the engine. "Well, I'd have to say that Mr. Thornton or Finch or whatever his name is has been thoroughly *Chased* out of town, and I think we should go celebrate. What do you say, Mrs. Chase?"

Jemma blew her nose and started laughing. Max joined her, and they were still laughing when they pulled up in front of Meyer's Ice Cream Shoppe. They compared tactics and ate their banana splits in mutual admiration.

Back in Chillaton, Spencer did not think it was funny. He was angry. "Do you see what happens when you are stubborn? We're lucky he didn't try something more than kissing. What's the deal with everybody trying to kiss my wife, anyway?" He took a deep breath and looked at her.

She sat head down, playing with the embroidered design on her skirt.

Suddenly he changed his tune and lifted her chin. "Baby, I'm sorry. Here I've been yelling about him and haven't even considered your feelings. Something better than his gallery will come along. He was just bluffing you with those threats. He can't blackball you from every gallery in London. He's an idiot."

Spencer had taken the humor out of the situation and had her thinking about other things.

Jemma sighed. "I'm going home. I'll see

you later."

"Oh no you don't. You are staying right here with me. I'll be finished in a minute. I should have been there instead of Dad. I'm the idiot."

She waited and relived Thor's speech. Her day was clouded with "maybes." Maybe he could keep her work out of London. Maybe she was too stubborn. Maybe she shouldn't have put the Sleeper on him — maybe she should have just stuck with The Claw.

That night Spencer edged up against her back. "Are you mad at me, Jem? I'm sorry about what happened with Thor." He put his chin on her arm and felt around for her lips. "Yup, big pout. I thought so. Is it me or him?"

Jemma faced him. "I did what I thought was best. You made me feel like everything I did was wrong."

He smoothed her hair. "I was just angry with myself for not going. It's kind of funny to think about my dad punching somebody. He's never been in a physical fight in his life."

"Me neither," she said and turned back to the wall.

"That's not true. You've been practicing on me for years. Now Thor knows what it's like to suffer under your power." He made an unsuccessful attempt to tickle her. "The more I think about it, the funnier it gets. A snobby gallery owner being taken down with The Sleeper hold by the most beautiful artist on the planet is actually hilarious. I guess I'm jealous that you would use that hold on anybody but me." He nibbled on her ear.

She smiled, but not so he would notice.

"Is it possible that you could demonstrate what happened now that we're alone?" Spencer asked. "So, he was coming at you like this," he said, moving in front of her and making the old bed squeak, "and then you knocked him flat and put The Sleeper on him?"

Jemma rose up from her side of the bed and flung her body across Spencer, knocking the breath out of him. "This is what I should have done to him." She giggled.

Spencer's voice was rather weak. "Not the Waffle Iron again," he said, shaking with laughter. "This is too special for anybody but me. I deserve it, I guess. Have mercy, O great one."

Jemma got off him and sat up on the bed. "Do you think that if I don't make it as an artist, I could be a professional female wrestler?"

Spencer hung his head and laughed even harder, making Lizbeth's snores change rhythm. Spence lowered his voice. "Well, I don't think there would be any question as to you being a female wrestler as opposed to a male one. What would you call yourself?"

"I'm thinking about The Big Hurt. Do you like it?" She grinned at him in the dark.

"I like it. I think you would have a large fan club, too. Maybe Thor could turn pro, too, and y'all could tour together. I could be your mercy man, the one you practice new stuff on."

"That's all the mercy you get." She kissed him until they fell off the bed and landed on the cool hardwood floor without missing a beat of their activity.

Lizbeth finished blind-stitching her latest quilt, a rose and cream floral pattern. She tied off the knot and spread the quilt on the good bed to check her work. It was one of her best, and made especially for their second anniversary. Jemma and Spencer could use it in their new guest bedroom. The hammering from Lester's shop was more than she could handle for the fifth day in a row. She went out the back door and yelled at him.

He came out, his overalls and hair covered in sawdust. "Morning, Miz Liz." His hands were shoved into his pockets and a hammer hung off the loop at the side of his overalls.

"Lester Timms, what are you doing? I haven't asked you for nearly a week now, hoping that you would volunteer the information. If I know what the secret is, maybe I can tolerate the noise." She held her hairdo down in the wind.

"Well, sir, I'm sure sorry for the aggravation, but I'm on a business adventure," Lester said, not divulging anything.

"What kind of venture?" Lizbeth asked, her mouth pinched to one side.

Lester dropped his head and poked at a stone with his work boot. "No offense, Miz Liz, but you scared me off from sharin' business secrets with you a while back."

"I assume you mean the chinchilla ranching thing."

"Yes ma'am. I was hopin' to get this new adventure up and runnin' before givin' out any details." Lester paused and looked out over the tracks. He took off his glasses and rubbed his eyes. Between sawdust and Panhandle grit, he had a mouthful to spit, but not in front of her.

"You aren't going to tell me, are you?" Lizbeth raised her brow. "What if I promise not to make light of this one?"

Lester folded his arms and gave her a sideways look. "Is that a fact now, Miz Liz? No disrespect, but I know how you get around that kind of promise."

"I'll be gentle. I might even have a suggestion or two. Fiddlesticks, Lester, what's going on in there?"

Lester whipped back the door to his shop. The fresh air scooted inside, then curled back, full of sawdust. His transistor radio blared out the early morning news. He turned it off and picked up a cedar box the size of Jemma's hope chest. It was polished to a fine sheen and the hinged lid was decorated with a sculpted rose.

Lizbeth smiled. "Are you going to sell hope chests?"

Lester set the box down and rubbed his chin. "I hadn't thought of that; maybe I'll give 'er a try. Anyway, these here are gonna be coffins." He gestured to several more of various sizes at the back of the shop.

"Coffins? My stars."

"For critters," he said, avoiding her eyes.

Lizbeth drew in the dusty air and coughed. "Critter coffins? You mean for cats and such?"

He nodded. "Cats, dogs — of course they'd have to be them kind of dogs that folks carries around, but whatever takes an owner's fancy. That's what I'm namin' my company, too. Critter Coffins. You caught on right fast, Miz Liz. It's plain that you're a college girl."

Lizbeth shifted her weight. "Well, now, Lester. I think you've come up with a halfway decent idea this time. I know lots of folks who are silly about their pets and might take you up on this notion."

Lester brightened. "Well, sir, I come upon the notion down to the barbershop. Pud Green was saying how his missus's Siamese up and died on her, but she had to bury it in a plastic cake holder. It had a lid on it, but that just didn't seem right to me. I come home and got me some ideas on paper, then went to the lumberyard. This cedar is top-notch wood. Jemmer drew me some flower designs, and the rest you see before you."

Lizbeth ran her finger across the rose. "Maybe you should put an ad in the Amarillo paper. There are probably a lot more small pet owners up there than in Chillaton. Most farmers don't go for house pets and whatnot. They keep working animals."

"That's a fine idea, Miz Liz. I'll send the paper some money and get that goin'. I sure do appreciate your support. Now that my secret is out, I think I'll put me an ad in the

Chillaton paper, too."

"I wouldn't do that if I were you, Lester. I think I'd wait until the idea catches on in Amarillo, then go ahead with it here." Lizbeth walked to the door. "Now that I know what all the commotion is, I can handle it better. Good luck, Lester. Are you coming over for coffee later?"

He picked up a screwdriver. "We'll see, Miz Liz. I need to finish off what I've started here. You go on without me for now." He eased around the corner and spat.

Lizbeth went home and sat at the kitchenette. She sipped her hot coffee and grinned. She made sure the liquid was all the way down, then laughed for a full minute. When the laugh subsided, she wiped her eyes and drank the rest of her coffee. One last chuckle took her to the window as a tardy freight train rattled past. Vincent, her mouse-catching, snake-killing cat jumped up on the windowsill and settled down for a snooze, but not before looking up at her with loving eyes. Lizbeth cleared her throat and poured out the rest of her coffee.

Chapter 17
Prizes

"Have you heard anything from Thor Hyphen-Hyphen?" Trent asked.

"No." Jemma stabbed her chicken-fried steak at Daddy's Money.

"We're not sure that we care, either." Spencer winked at Jemma.

"Spencer told me about your wrestling match." Trent laughed. "I wish I could have seen that. Can you imagine our grandparents' reaction to that story?"

"I hope they never hear about it, but I'm out of luck for a show in London," Jemma said.

"That's not true," Trent fired back. "I'll bet that you have a show in London before this time next year."

"Really? I'll take that bet. Loser buys burgers at Son's Drive In."

The cousins shook on it.

"Shhh . . . you're not supposed to mention Son's in here," Spencer whispered.

"Did Spence tell you that we may hire an interior designer to consult with us on a few projects?" Trent asked.

"No," she said. "He didn't."

"Not my idea. Talk to your cousin." Spencer pointed at Trent.

"Are you looking for anybody in particular?" Jemma asked, shooting her husband the evil eye.

"I don't know. Why? Do you have somebody in mind?" Trent asked, watching a new waitress with interest.

"Le Claire might have some graduates looking for jobs. Their interior design department is very good," Jemma said.

Trent nodded. "Thanks, I might check that out. I've already talked with someone in Dallas, though. She's coming up to meet us Monday."

"Tomorrow?" Jemma asked.

Spencer held up his hands. "Hey, this is all his deal. I won't even be in the office tomorrow. My flight leaves at nine forty in the morning."

"Hers gets in at nine fifteen. Maybe you'll run into her at the airport," Trent said.

Spencer smiled weakly at Jemma. He could tell this topic would entail further discussion.

∎ ∎ ∎ ∎

"When were you going to tell me about hiring an interior designer?" she asked as soon as they got in the car.

Spencer gave her The Look that she normally gave him. "Jemmabeth Alexandra Chase, do not be jealous of someone that neither you nor I have seen and with whom we are only consulting. I'm telling you, this is all Trent's idea. He thinks we need to jazz up the mall in Sacramento. Personally, I think it looks great."

"I am not jealous. I just like to know about your business, that's all."

"Oookay," Spencer said, starting the Corvette.

Jemma reached over and turned off the engine. "What does *oookay* mean? Do you think I am a jealous wife? Just tell me." Her nostrils flared a bit.

"I think you don't give yourself enough credit for being the only woman on this earth that I could ever love. You also believe that if any women, other than Twila Baker or Eleanor Perkins, come into my line of vision, I check them out with the serious notion of comparing them to you."

"Well?"

"What do you honestly think, Jem?"

"That you can't help but check them out because you are a man."

"I can't help but see them because I have two eyes, but I don't look at them with the eyes of a man seeing a potential lover or something. I'm not Thor. Do you want me to wear a blindfold all the time?"

"Maybe." She turned toward her window.

The Corvette was quiet. An elderly couple came out of Daddy's Money and pulled away in their car, but not before they had a good stare.

"May I start the car now?" Spencer asked.

"Sure," she said, her voice cool, although she was still rather hot.

"You'll have to drive, then."

"Why?" She swiveled toward him.

Spencer sat facing the steering wheel with his tie wrapped around his eyes and in a knot at the back of his head. Jemma laughed so hard that her sides ached. He knew just how to handle a sticky situation.

They drove to the river and got on the hood of the Corvette to watch the stars.

He kissed her, and they lay back on their old stargazing quilt.

"Baby, how do you think I felt the first time I ever saw Paul?" he asked when he had her securely wrapped up in his arms.

"What kind of question is that?" She could barely turn her head, he held her so close against him.

"When I saw that guy, my heart fell. I knew that this big hulk of a cowboy, the best-looking man I'd ever seen, had held you close, tasted your pretty lips, and whispered things in your ear that probably gave you chill bumps. I knew that he had to know that your hair smells like flowers, and he had looked on you with the desires of his heart, body, and mind, just like I do. I knew, too, that you had considered giving me up for him, and, to this day, he still wants you. That's what I still have to contend with. I will always have to share those feelings with Paul because we have you in common. Jem, I want you to remember this for the next one hundred years. Granted, I have kissed lots of women, but only because you broke up with me twice. You will never have to hurt in your heart for any of those other reasons like I did and still do. Whether a bearded lady comes to work for us or a bombshell from Hollywood takes over as secretary and sits across my desk every day, stark naked, you will never have to know the pain I feel sometimes. That's a promise."

She felt like dirt and couldn't speak. When

she did, it came out in a whisper. "I'm so sorry, Spence, as usual. Remember, before Vietnam, you wrote in my sketchbook that I didn't have to carry that guilt around anymore. You said it was like I had just tried all the rest and you won first prize. There was never even a contest, babe." She struggled around to look at him, her voice shaky. "You know if I could erase that time in our lives, I would, but Paul just keeps showing up, doesn't he, twisting the knife? How can I ever make it hurt less?"

"By learning not to be jealous of other women. At least that way I won't feel like you don't trust me or believe my wedding vows to you."

She sniffed. "I try, Spence. I do well sometimes and other times I flop. Don't give up on me. I guess I don't think I'm worthy of you. Maybe I'm just one of those people who always needs reassuring," she said and turned back to the stars.

"I'll reassure you, baby. But give me some credit when it comes to admiring and loving you, and only you, okay?"

"Okay." She kissed him, hoping to lessen the hurt that came with Paul, Mr. Summer Romance Everlasting Pain. To her credit, she succeeded, too.

∎ ∎ ∎ ∎

"Is this the last load?" Buddy B asked, wiping sweat off his forehead.

"That's it." Lizbeth looked around at her house. She was excited for these precious children to have their own home. Her lonely days would return, but not for long. Helene would be moving into Jemma's old bedroom before Christmas. Of course, Helene was not Jemmabeth, but they would keep each other company.

"Gram, come on and ride with me," Jemma yelled from the back door.

Lizbeth grabbed her purse and her headscarf. She moved as fast as she could to catch up with her long-legged granddaughter. "Is Lester coming?" Lizbeth asked.

"He's already gone with Spence," Jemma said as she backed her new Suburban down the driveway. "Lester is going to inspect the house and see if the builders knew what they were doing."

"Honey, do you think we could check the mail? Things have been so busy around here that Lester didn't get to the post office today. I hope they're still open."

Jemma ran back to the car with two letters.

"Paralee says hello. Here's one for you and one for me. Yours is from Do Dah and mine is from Le Claire." She ripped the end of the envelope. "I wonder who . . . oh wow. Oh wow! An art gallery in Florence is offering me a show. I can't believe this. The owners saw my work — oh, how sweet — at the Grassos' house. I had given them a couple of pieces. The Grassos are the ones who got the whole thing put together, through Professor Rossi and the gallery in New York. Professor Rossi wanted to surprise me after the London deal fell through. Do you know what this means?"

"Something wonderful, I'm sure."

Jemma closed her eyes and held the letter to her heart. "It means that I have what it takes to go across the Atlantic and show my work as an artist, not just a student artist. It means that I'm on a roll, maybe." She clapped her hands like she did at her third birthday party when Cam played a Highland tune on his fiddle and she danced for him, whirling around until she fell down, laughing.

"Jemmabeth, you may be a Chase now, you may be a Forrester and a Lillygrace, but underneath all that there remains a Jenkins girl. We are strong and have what it takes to keep standing when all else falls down. I'm proud of you, sugar. Now let's go tell that husband of yours."

On a wet evening with tornado alerts all over the television, they had their housewarming party. The JEMMA'S PLACE sign was officially nailed above the front door and Plum Creek was up to its banks. Alex and Robby surprised them by showing up the night before. They had seen pictures of the progress, but the real thing took them by surprise. "Cool, way cool." Robby scrambled up the spiral staircase.

Lizbeth stood on the deck, keeping an eye on the storm. This was the way Cam would want their Plum Creek to be remembered, as the joyful home of this precious couple. Someday they would bring their own babies home to grow up in this house. Lizbeth didn't choose to wax melancholy at such a happy occasion, but Cameron remained in her head, always, and that fact was bittersweet comfort these days.

"Gram!" Robby burst into her thoughts. "Come on, I want to show you something in the pouting room. You're not too old to climb up there, are you?"

She laughed. "Let's see if I can make it, young man. Maybe a good pout is just what I need."

∎ ∎ ∎ ∎

"I hope you have flood insurance," Sandy said. "You know that all this rain will bring out the snakes."

"What snakes?" Jemma asked. "I told Spence to get rid of every snake out here and he told me he did."

"I'm hopin' y'all got a 'fraidy hole that will hold all of us," Willa said, holding on to Joe as they came up the steps with a cherry cobbler and a shoe box full of petunia plants. "Here you go, sugar. Now you'd better not let these babies of mine die." She kissed Jemma and stood wide-eyed, gawking at their home. "My lands, child, you've gone and built yourself a mansion. Wait 'til Trina sees this."

"I'm glad you approve, Willa. Come in and let me show you around." Spencer took her hand and led her into the sunken Great Room with its double-sided, river-rock fireplace separating the kitchen and dining room from the den.

Rebecca Chase sat on the suede couch, holding a coffee cup. "Mother, have you met Willa Cross? Willa, this is my mother, Rebecca."

Willa put out her hand. Rebecca paused

momentarily, then took it with a stiff smile.

Spencer grinned at the scene. "I'm giving Willa a tour, Mother. Do you want to join us?"

"No, I'll wait for your father. He's showing that old fellow, Lester, something just now." She picked up a magazine and flipped through it.

"Rebecca," Jemma said, bringing Sandy to her, "this is my friend, Sandy. She grew up with Spencer and me."

"Of course I remember you, Sandra," Rebecca replied, suddenly friendly. "Didn't you marry that Skinner boy? What was his name?"

"Martin. We're divorced now — well, almost divorced. It's nice to see you, Mrs. Chase. Spence and Jemma have a fantastic home, don't they?"

Rebecca nodded. "It has Spencer written all over it, and of course, Jemma, too," she said and went back to her magazine.

"What's the deal with her?" Sandy asked. "She acts like she's got hemorrhoids or something."

Jemma giggled. "She's trying to be sweet. I guess it's tough when your reputation precedes you. Don't you just love this house? I think it's incredible."

"It is, Jem. I'm really happy for y'all. I

also think that painting of Spencer is incredible. How come you got him, anyway? Everybody wanted Spence. Look at those eyes." Sandy stared up at the painting that Jemma had titled "I Think of Thee," when she had her first show as a student in Paris. Spencer's guitar lay across his lap, and he was stretched out under a big cottonwood tree at Plum Creek.

"He wasn't in favor of hanging it in here, but I threw a fit."

"I bet you did. Show me this studio you've been bragging about." They climbed the stairs to their shared space. Sandy whistled. "Oh wow. It's nearly all glass. You are going to burn up in here. We'll find a little scorched spot on this pretty hardwood floor and that'll be what's left of the famous artist. You should just go ahead and sign a spot now."

Jemma laughed and pressed a button as window shades covered the glass.

"Nice," Sandy said. "You've thought of everything."

"Look through here." Jemma turned a telescope toward her. "We don't have to get on the hood of his car for our stargazing."

Sandy took a little framed drawing of a flower off Jemma's worktable. "Who did this — Robby?"

"Nope. An old friend of mine who recently got into art."

"Now for the biggie." Sandy lowered her voice. "Show me the bedroom."

They met Willa and Spencer coming out of the master suite. "Mercy, child, that room is somethin' from a movie. I ain't never seen nothin' like that."

Sandy stepped in and looked around, bug-eyed. "Cheezo. Did you two make this up? Don't answer that. So this is what happens when you have a no-fooling-around-until-we're-married rule, huh? I wish I'd done that. Of course we never got past the two-room trailer-house dream." She touched the lighted, stained-glass pillars that flanked the French doors. "So you can just walk out to the deck whenever you want? What a prize y'all have given each other."

Jemma sat on the bed and rubbed her hand across the silk bedspread. She looked out at Plum Creek and the cottonwood tree protruding from the deck where their initials were still visible. "Yeah, I guess you could say that this is one of our prizes, but the best prize is that everything is new every day with Spence."

Sandy sat next to her. "I hope that someday I'll find love again."

"You will. Just remember to be still and

watch for God's blessings. It took me a while to learn that. Now, let's go eat my first attempt at baking Spencer's favorite cake, if it's not already gone."

"Wait." Sandy grabbed her arm. "I have to tell you what I did last night."

"Okay. This is not a confession about messing up the bookkeeping at the office or something, is it?"

"Oh please. This is something I am proud to tell. Remember when you and I were always comparing our hope chest stuff? You had those dishes with the roses on them, and mine had daisies. Well, about eleven o'clock last night I drove out to the river, opened the trunk, took out a box filled with those dumb daisy-patterned dishes and chucked them, one by one, into the Salt Fork of the Red River. It's up to its banks, too, with all this rain. Each time I heard that stuff shattering in the water, I began to feel like a new woman. I never want to see anything Mr. Universe touched ever again."

Jemma frowned. "Whoa. I guess it was worth it if made you feel better."

"It did, trust me."

"They really shattered? Weren't all your hope chest dishes Melmac?"

"What's your point?" Sandy asked. "Plastic was all I could afford."

"Never mind. Coconut crème is calling."

Alex helped give tours, as did Robby. His style was short and to the point. His favorite place was the pouting room with its stained glass and window seats. He didn't have many customers, which was fine with him. As soon as the storm cleared, he went outside to catch frogs.

"Sweet pea, why is there no art in your bedroom? You have several pieces that seem perfect for those walls," Alex asked, after everyone had gone home.

Jemma took off her shoes and propped her feet on the deck railing. "I know, but someone doesn't want to use them." She took a sip of her tea.

"All she wants are giant paintings of me," Spencer said. "I don't want to get up every morning and see myself everywhere." He grabbed Robby and held him upside down. "This is a shakedown, mister. Give up all illegally gotten Plum Creek frogs."

"This is cool." Robby looked around. "Keep doing it."

Spencer dangled him over the deck rail. "How do you like this, then?"

"I love it. Your old man arms are shaking, huh? I can feel it from way down here," Robby teased. "Hey, I think I see a snake."

Alex and Jemma both jumped up. "Spencer!" they yelled in chorus.

Robby was hoisted to safety, then giggled and ran off with Spencer chasing after him.

"You have a lot to be thankful for, Jem," Alex said as they sat listening to the crickets and leftover frogs.

"I know, Mom." Jemma put her arm around her mother. "I am well aware of that. God's Plan just gets better."

CHAPTER 18
A WONDER

Trina and Nick's ceremony would be at her church and the reception at Willa's house, followed by dancing on the deck at Plum Creek. Spencer was cutting it close. His flight was due in from New York just an hour and a half before the ceremony. Jemma paced the adult Sunday school room in her *LJF* designer dress of emerald green brocade. Carrie tried to keep up with her for a while with her walker.

Spencer stuck his head in only seconds before the music began. "Hi, gorgeous, I'm here. Don't trip walking down the aisle," he said and shut the door before she could throw a shoe at him.

Trina's gown was a dress designer's, for sure. The bodice was fitted cream satin with hundreds of tiny seed pearls covering it in the shape of *fleurs de lis* — to remember the postcard her daddy had sent her from Paris when she was a baby. The waistline was a gathering of English netting from the skirt that clasped to form a rose at her side. Her skirt was slender, like Jemma's had been. A veil fluttered behind her with a scalloped hem upon which even more seed pearls had been hand sewn. She wore her hair swept up in a bun, with the veil attached. She was beautiful.

Jemma and Spencer left the reception early to make sure that Buddy B's band was set up on their deck and that all the refreshments were ready.

"You haven't asked if Michelle was in New York City," Spencer said as they necked in the kitchen. "This dress is outstanding, by the way." He held her back for a better look.

"I'm trying to be good, like you said."

"I didn't have to salute her. She came in late to a meeting and left before it was over. Her services were not required, I guess. I think she just wanted to make an appearance," Spencer said, wishing suddenly that there was no party scheduled at their home.

"And? How did she look?" Jemma asked.

"The same, but Michelle is not my big news. The woman next to me on the flight from New York to Dallas is the features editor of *Panache* magazine — you know, the men's magazine that no man buys. Anyway, she wants to do a story about me. She said the magazine is about men's style, but that it's women who buy it."

"You mean the magazine with all the pretty boys striking poses next to their motorcycles and airplanes?"

"I wouldn't say pretty boys. They're just guys who are supposed to have been somewhat successful and dress well. Which of those descriptions do you disagree with about me?"

"Neither." She pulled on his tie and kissed him. "You fit all of those, even the pretty boy part. I'm proud of you, babe. I really am. But no wife in her right mind wants her husband flaunted in a magazine for other women to drool over. When's all of this going to happen?"

"She's supposed to call me. It may not work out. I don't know. It was just kind of flattering, I guess," he said and went to open the door for their first guests.

"Spence." Jemma grabbed his arm and went nose to nose with him. "I'm thrilled for you. I am married to the handsomest, brightest architect in the universe, plus you have impeccable taste."

"Go ahead and say it; you know you want to."

"Okay," she said, wiping lipstick off him,

"you married me, didn't you?"

"Feel better?"

"Yeah." She grinned as she opened the door.

They didn't want to take away from the wedding couple, but they had to dance when Buddy B played their song. Lizbeth was once again embarrassed by their antics, but nobody else seemed to notice. Lester asked Trina for a waltz. Lizbeth smiled, thinking that never would have happened ten years earlier, not in Chillaton, and not with Lester. Jemmabeth had made the difference. She had opened up their hearts and minds to what it is to be a friend and to love like Christ. When the dance was over, Buddy B called Jemma up to the microphone to sing with him, but he tricked her into a solo. Jemma sang some low-throated song about love that would have made Cam blush. Spencer seemed to like it, though. Lizbeth exhaled and had a second cup of fruit punch.

Trina asked Jemma to sing a song that was a favorite of Nick's — "How Sweet It Is to Be Loved by You" — but Jemma wouldn't do it unless Spencer sang with her, which he did, in his sweet way, and the newest newlyweds had the floor to themselves.

Nick's family was a dancing crowd, too, filling up the deck. It was a good thing that Trent was a structural engineer and was involved with all the details of the house.

Lester got up his nerve to dance with Helene. Lizbeth sipped her punch and watched.

Afterward, he came over to her. "Miz Liz, I'll just come right out with it. Would you care to dance?" His silver moustache seemed extra trim in the moonlight.

Lizbeth considered it for a second. "Lester, if we danced, things would never be the same between us, would they?"

Lester scratched behind his ear. "No ma'am, I reckon they wouldn't, but it never hurts for a fella to ask." He walked away.

"Lester," Lizbeth called after him. He came back, his expression hopeful. "I've never danced in my life. I would step all over you," she added in a whisper.

His face relaxed into a grin. "Maybe I'll have to teach you sometime."

Mr. and Mrs. Nicholas Fields went to the microphone. "We want to thank all of y'all for coming tonight to share our happiness," Trina said. "We especially thank our parents and the Chases for the wonderful celebrations."

Nick moved in to speak. "Thanks to Spencer and Jemma for lots of things they've done for us. We'll be leaving in the morning for our honeymoon in Acapulco, thanks to those two, again. We appreciate every last one of y'all. My grandpa must be doing somersaults in his grave to see the beautiful mix of the colors here. Life is good."

Trina tossed her bouquet, and an embarrassed Trent caught it. His red-haired date, a chatty interior designer from Dallas, raised her brow at him.

"That was fun," Jemma said as she picked up the last stray napkin off the deck.

"No, this is fun." Spencer carried her to their bedroom. He pressed a button, and a skylight opened up above their bed, revealing the starry night. "You look great in that dress. You'll have to wear it to Florence for the opening of your show."

"I'm not going if you can't go with me, and I mean it."

"I'm getting tickets tomorrow. I'll go, no matter what."

"There's a shooting star. Did you see it?"

"Nope. I'm looking at my wife."

"This life we have is a wonder," she said.

"Yeah, it's almost scary."

"Ummm. I liked singing with you tonight."

"I liked listening to you sing Aretha. I'm

just glad we're married so that the boys in the band don't whistle at you like they used to."

"Oh, they still do, but not so you can hear it."

"That magazine thing doesn't bother you, does it?"

"No more than the guys' whistling bothers you."

"It bothers me some."

"The magazine bothers me."

"How about you sing something for me now?"

"Like what?"

"Leon said your voice is like Peggy Lee's, so how about 'Fever'?"

"What will you give me if I do?"

"A new pair of cowboy boots."

"Red?"

"Yeah."

Jemma stood up on the bed and sang, silhouetted in the starlight. She didn't even get to make it through the chorus.

The *Panache* magazine editor called the next week. She and a photographer would be arriving on the last flight into Amarillo on Friday night. Jemma didn't want to dwell on it, so she painted from dawn until Spencer came home. Plum Creek was perfect for her work. Jemma walked across the room to analyze the painting. The man's back was all that was visible of him, but the ebony cigarette holder gave his identity away. He stood in the aisle of a wrestling arena, wearing his tasseled loafers. She liked it.

"I thought you were going to work at home when we got married," she said later, setting a masterpiece salad in front of Spencer.

"I know, and I will, too. I just have to get squared away first, kind of get in a rhythm. Maybe next year."

"Maybe never," she said. "Isn't there anything you can do at home? You could do your drafting here, but it's all the phone calls you think you have to take, isn't it? I know it is because Sandy told me."

Spencer looked up from his salad. "You're right, Jem. I just need to commit to working at home. I will surprise you, and you'll be getting sick of me someday."

"Never. I love it out here. It's so peaceful, but it's lonesome without you. All I have are the coyotes."

"There's always motherhood." He grinned.

"Right. That's the solution to every problem, even you working at home." She went to get the steaks and chewed on her lip. She would get an appointment on Monday.

"When's Jem supposed to get home from Amarillo?" Sandy asked.

Spencer checked his watch. "She said by two. It's four thirty now. I've tried the doctor's office, but they're closed."

"Well, I'm heading home, if that's okay. Jemma got a call from Italy. That's gotta be important, so here's the number." Sandy tapped her message pad and pushed her chair in. She turned to Spencer. "Don't worry. She's probably sitting on a rock drawing a cow or something."

Sandy knew, though, that the road to Amarillo held a sore spot for everybody who loved Jemmabeth. "She'll be here any minute now." Sandy waved and left.

By five o'clock Spencer decided to drive to Amarillo. He locked up the office and started the Corvette. Jemma pulled up next to him, and he knew as soon as he saw her face. Something awful had happened. He got in the car with her, and she burst into tears.

"I've been at the hospital having all these tests done. There's something wrong with me. I thought maybe I was pregnant, but instead, it's this scary thing."

Spencer's pulse raced. "Cancer?"

"No. One doctor sent me to another doctor who said that this happens sometimes after a miscarriage like mine. There's scar tissue in my uterus. I have to go back Friday so he can explain it all. I should have told you, but I wanted to surprise you if I was pregnant."

He held her. "We'll face this together, whatever it is. Let's go home."

The week dragged by. Jemma couldn't paint, so Spencer took her to Amarillo and they bought a dozen rosebushes, a dozen honeysuckle vines, and packets of sweet pea and hollyhock seeds. Willa's petunias were already in the ground. She borrowed Lizbeth's cat, Vincent, to keep the snakes away while she worked. From the time Spencer left in the morning until he came home, she created pocket gardens around the perimeter of their home. When the plants ran out, she called Alex.

"They can work wonders nowadays, sweet pea," Alex said. "You mustn't worry so much about things after you turn them over to the Lord. You can't say out of one side of your mouth that you are trusting Him, then whisper out of the other side that you're scared to death."

"I know. I haven't told Gram yet. After we

see the doctor tomorrow, we'll stop by her house." Jemma sat on the deck and listened to the soft ripple of water in Plum Creek. "Mom, surely it's in The Plan for us to have babies."

"Honey, nobody knows what the Lord has in mind. We just have to pray about things and wait to see if our will matches His. There's always adoption. You and Spencer will be parents one way or another. Now you call us as soon as you know something. I'll be home all day tomorrow."

Alex had to hang up quickly so her daughter couldn't hear her cry. Even her own advice was easier in the giving than it was in the taking.

Jemma and Spencer held hands. The doctor was a middle-aged man, polite but straightforward. "When the physician in Mexico found it necessary to remove tissue from you, the procedure left scars. You may have even had an infection afterward, but that's immaterial now. We need to remove the adhesions, and get you back to as normal as possible."

"Is there a name for this?" Spencer asked.
"Asherman's Syndrome."
Jemma cleared her throat. "Will I be able

to have babies?"

"Time will tell. Some women do, and some don't. We'll know more after the surgery." The doctor called the appointment desk at the hospital.

Jemma tightened her hold on Spencer's hand.

"Will next Thursday be all right?" the doctor asked.

Spencer nodded. "Sure. Fine. How long will she be in the hospital?"

"At least two days, barring complications."

"I'll be sleeping in the room with her," Spencer said.

"I would expect that from the looks of you two." He reached across his desk and shook Spencer's hand. "Have you been married long?"

"Not long enough," Spencer said. "Thank you, Doctor."

They went to their favorite Mexican food place. Jemma picked at her food. Spencer tried unsuccessfully to cheer her up. "What happened to the faith in action that you've been talking about? Last night we said we'd give this to the Lord and let Him handle it for us."

She looked at him and shrugged. "I know, but it's different when you hear the words from the doctor."

"Like I said, Jem, it's not the end of the world if we can't have kids. We can stay in this present state of matrimonial bliss forever, or we can adopt, too."

"I wanted to have your baby."

"You think I don't want a wee Jemmabeth?"

"I still feel guilty, I guess, for not wanting to be pregnant when I was. All this just brought it up again. Let's go home. I'm not hungry."

They sat on the deck, talking until after dark. Spencer put on some old records and they danced, all slow ones.

"What did the gallery owner want the other day? I forgot to ask you," Spence said as they moved under the watchful feline eye of Vincent van Gogh.

"He wanted some photos of me. I guess I'll have to dig out those from the New York show."

The phone rang. "Let it go," Spencer said. "It's probably Sandy."

"Or Mom and Daddy. I forgot to call them." Jemma went inside but came right back. "It's for you. The *Panache* people are in Amarillo."

Spencer slapped his forehead. "I totally forgot about them coming." He talked for a few minutes while Jemma played with Vincent's notched ear.

"They'll be here in the morning." Spencer took his seat next to her. "I'm sorry, Jem. This is bad timing, and I know you're not crazy about the whole thing anyway. Maybe something good will come of it. Trent and I might get a great project somewhere."

"Yeah, or maybe you'll get a job as a model."

"If there is anybody around here who could be a model, it's you, woman." He kissed her pouty lips, boring Vincent into sleep.

Chapter 19
Pain with Panache

Jemma followed the two women and her husband all over their house, around the creek, and into the pasture by the road. She couldn't believe they talked him into wearing cowboy stuff. He had only worn that once before, when he'd proposed to her on the train tracks. Now they had him leaning against a barbed-wire fencepost with his hat pushed back on his head.

The photographer got him to unbutton more than the top button on his shirt, too. "Just enough to inspire," she'd said. Spencer snickered and glanced toward Jemma. "Give me that again," the skinny photographer said, taking off her beaded headband. "I like that look."

"I was looking at my wife," Spencer replied. "Why don't we have her in some of the pictures? She is the one with the good looks."

The editor, a willowy woman named

Simone with hair nearly as short as Spencer's, turned to Jemma. "Lucky girl, aren't you? Don't take offense, but we like to keep the marital status of our subjects a mystery. The mystique must be preserved to keep the sales up, you see. Sheer business. By the way, I love your art; it's quite brilliant. We must talk later. Okay. Now, Spence, we need intimacy. Say you just woke up — that's fantastic. Now try giving us a pout. Women like that, don't they, Mrs. Chase?" she added in her stilted British accent.

Spencer laughed and put his thumbs in his pockets. "James Dean, huh?"

"We have to get that old windmill in the next shot. Where's the corral?" Simone asked. "After we get some good ones of you in the office, I want sunset shots of you working with your horse."

He laughed again and shook his head. "I've never been on a horse, ma'am, much less worked with one."

The photographer smiled and touched his arm. "Well, Spence, looks like today will be a first, then."

Jemma dusted the seat of her pants and walked back to the house. She thought it was time for her to paint. Nobody called him *Spence* unless they had known him most of his life. Nobody except these two and Michelle Taylor, that is. She had even called him *Spencey.* Assertive, presumptuous women. Rats on them.

If she didn't have her surgery to worry about, Jemma would have been in a snit. She hadn't seen Spencer much in the two days that the *Panache* crew had been in Chillaton. She needed to know that they were breathing the same air. He came in late on Saturday night and left before she got up Sunday morning. There was a love note in the refrigerator, but a note wasn't the same as him. She went to church with Gram, then painted until the Corvette pulled into the garage. Jemma gave herself a quick speech and put on a smile.

Spencer came up the steps to the studio and plopped in a chair.

Her pasty smile faded. "Oh my gosh, babe, what happened to you?"

"I fell off the horse. Simone Legree and her evil sidekick nearly killed me with their ideas. This had better be worth it." He opened a puffy eye. "I should've been home with you. I'm sorry."

She tried to sulk, but he was too funny looking. Jemma sat on the floor and laughed. Spencer moved onto the floor with her, moaning. "I'm glad that you think this is funny. I'm never doing it again. Who knew it was so hard to be in a magazine?"

"Oh poor baby. You didn't seem too upset with your Stetson and your shirt unbuttoned."

Spencer's face drooped. "I was just going along with the business. I got what I deserved, I'm sure."

"Well, I guess I'd better be the good little wife and take care of your cuts and scrapes. Stay right here."

"Don't worry, ma'am. This cowpoke ain't goin' nowhere but to sleep."

She put the finished canvas on the drying rail. He was going to hate it, but she might hang it above their bed without asking. For him to be leaning against a fencepost was one thing, but for him to have cowboy gear on was something altogether different. He looked like a real buckaroo. She caught him for posterity even if the *Panache* photos didn't turn out. Jemma had painted only one button on his shirt undone. She knew her man. Maybe she should hang it next to the one of him on the train tracks, the morning he proposed to her.

The phone rang, interrupting her daydream about Spencer.

"Jemma, it's Gram. I just talked with Alex,

sugar. I'm so sorry about your female problem. I know everything is going to work out for the best. The good Lord is going to take care of you."

"Oh Gram. I would have said something, but I didn't want to worry you. Are you mad at me?"

"Jemmabeth, have I ever been angry with you? Of course not. I may have disagreed with you on occasion, but never angry. I want y'all to come for supper tonight. I know you have to be up early tomorrow for your hospital stay, so I've got it cooking, and I've already talked to Spencer."

"I guess we're coming then."

"Oh honey, would you do me a favor?" Lizbeth asked. "If you're finished with Vincent, you might bring him along. I hate to admit it, but I miss him."

"Say no more, Gram. He's as good as home." Jemma looked out the studio window to the deck below where the cat was stretched out, snoozing. She would miss him, too. He had been good company since her husband couldn't figure out how to work at home.

The first thing she saw when she woke up in the hospital was a pair of bright red cowboy boots appliquéd with turquoise flowers. She tried to smile.

"You sure do look cute in your hospital gown," Spencer said.

"My mouth is dry," she managed.

"Drink this water, Jem. The nurse said so."

She sipped her fill, then waved it away. "Is it over? What did the doctor say?"

"He said you're not the worst case he's had. He thinks you'll recover and be fine."

"Babies?" she mumbled.

"Time will tell. Those were his words." Spencer kissed her forehead. "Go back to sleep. They gave you some painkillers. I'm finishing some paperwork, but I'll be right here beside you, and I won't leave."

As Jemma fell back to sleep, Spencer smoothed her hair and glimpsed the scar that had brought her to this hospital before. He shuddered at that memory. He traced his fingers along the lifeline of her palm. "I love you," he whispered in her ear.

He moved his chair closer to the bed. Even in that sterile place, there was the faintest scent of flowers about her. He watched the rise and fall of her chest. She had to outlive him in their old age, because he could not bear to be without this precious blessing ever again.

■ ■ ■

"I think I left my passport in my old suitcase. Would you check and bring it when you come?" Spencer asked over the phone, giving orders to Sandy at the office simultaneously.

"Sure," Jemma said, putting on her shoes. "What if it's not there? You are the most organized person I know, so you're scaring me."

"It's there. I just forgot to transfer it to my new bag because my wife was messing with my brain last night."

She giggled. "I thought you would like a preview of the wardrobe that Trina sent me, that's all."

"Yeah. I liked the presentation, too. Stop talking and come to see me. I need some affection."

"Sandy says that we are too affectionate in the office."

"Sandy talks too much. Drive safely. Tell Gram good-bye for me."

"Love you." Jemma hung up the phone and loaded her car.

Lizbeth waited in the porch swing with Vincent for Jemma to arrive. It was too hard to keep up with the passage of time. If she let herself, she could get down about it, but nowadays there seemed to be things to look forward to, like Helene moving in with her in less than a week. Jim's little family would be coming for a visit before school started, and there could be Dr. Huntley's retirement party around there sometime, if he could ever find a replacement.

Lester appeared, holding an orange crate full of cedar chunks. "Miz Liz, would you have any use for these wood scraps?"

"You could make me a doorstop for the pouting room. I'm trying to keep it aired out, but the door hangs so cockeyed that it won't stay open," Lizbeth said. She had never mentioned that she was the one who nearly knocked it off its hinges the morning Cameron died.

"That's a good idea. Maybe I should make several and add them to my newspaper advertisement. You know, I've offered many a time to fix that door for you."

"Just leave it be, Lester. Have you sold many of your critter coffins?"

"Well, sir, I've sold me enough to break even with the advertisin'. I'm hopin' to get ahead of the game and make some profit. I ain't chargin' nearly what I put into 'em."

Lizbeth stroked Vincent's silky black and

white fur. "I suppose you could take comfort in the fact that you don't have much else to do and you might be bringing some peace to folks when their pets pass on."

"That's a good thought, Miz Liz. I suppose you're waitin' for Jemmerbeth?"

The Suburban pulled up as he spoke.

"Lester, would you go with me and drive her big car back to the house?" Lizbeth set Vincent van Gogh on the porch swing. "I don't like sitting up so high in that thing. I feel like I'm driving Joe's semi-truck."

"You're sure you don't mind giving us a ride, Trent?" Jemma asked. "I hate to ruin your Saturday, but the Suburban needs some work done on it while we're gone and the Corvette won't hold all our stuff."

"No, no that's fine. Actually, Sandy's riding up with us, too. She's buying office supplies," he said with a faint blush.

"Oh, I see. Well, you won't get lonesome, that's for sure. She'll keep you laughing."

Spencer came out of his office with his briefcase and a carrier for blueprints. "Yeah, you might want to invest in some earplugs for the trip home," he said, picking up on the conversation.

Jemma elbowed her husband. "Sandy has a good heart, Trent. Don't let her sarcasm fool you."

"I think I can stand a little sarcasm. It's just a business trip, anyway. You two are the ones off to Italy."

Trent went to the Bakers' door to get Sandy. She had on the hot pink pantsuit that she'd made. Her hair was perfect, and her makeup was flawless. She smiled at Trent, who stood at least six inches taller than Sandy's petite frame. She still had the posture and figure she did when she won the Sew It with Wool competition their senior year.

Jemma watched them. Good grief, was she blind? She should have thought of it sooner.

Spencer saw it coming. "I know what you are thinking, baby. Stay out of it. Trent is hungry for love, and Sandy doesn't need anybody who's hungry. I'm getting in the front seat so you two can talk, and Trent and I can go over some things."

Jemma tried to look innocent. She swatted the seat of his pants as he got out. "You'll regret that, young lady," he said, looking back at her.

She pouted and put her finger to her lips. "Promise?"

The first stop they made in Florence was for gelato near the Piazza della Signoria.

Jemma had been dying for some. "If and when I ever get pregnant, I want this every day for nine months," she said, inhaling the first bite.

"Done and done." Spencer watched her take on ice cream much the same way she enjoyed life. "Stay right there." He took a photo of her with her eyes closed and a gelato moustache. "This is the picture they should use at your shows because it's the real you."

She laughed. "I suppose we'd better mosey on down to the gallery."

"How about we drop off this luggage at the hotel first?"

"Details, details," she said and picked up her multitude of bags.

The Galeria Fiorinzi was near their hotel. The owners, Mr. and Mrs. Fiorinzi, greeted them.

"Signora Chase, what a pleasure to meet you in person." Mr. Fiorinzi bowed slightly. "We were not able to contact you yesterday, but we hope you won't mind a slight change of plans."

Jemma and Spencer exchanged glances. "You mean the opening date?" Jemma asked.

Mrs. Fiorinzi laughed. "No, no, nothing like that. We had a request for a private showing."

Jemma's first thought was of Paul; it just flew into her brain and she panicked. "Who made the request? An American?"

"Ah, yes, very American. Come, you must meet him."

Jemma grimaced at Spencer, and they followed the couple to another section of the gallery where men in black suits and sunglasses stepped in front of them, blocking their passage.

Mr. Fiorinzi gestured at Jemma. "This is the artist. We thought he might like to meet her."

"Please, bring her in." A familiar male voice changed the demeanor of the men.

"Mr. President, permit me to introduce Signora Jemmabeth Chase and Signore Chase."

"Ah, the artist from Texas." President Richard Nixon extended his hand to a dumbfounded Jemma.

They sat on a bench in a nearby park. "Good grief," Jemma said for the umpteenth time. "I can't believe that The President of the United States now owns a painting of Lester building critter coffins. I didn't even vote for him."

"Me neither." Spencer shrugged. "It's an

honor, but it took me off guard."

"I think she was the one who loved the piece, though. What did she say, that he reminded her of her grandfather? Lester won't like that comparison at all. Besides, he'll have a cow when he finds out that a Republican has his portrait."

Spencer laughed. "Jemmabeth, you're missing the point," he said, turning her palms up. "These hands that have won basketball games, wrestled men to the ground, and held my heart for nearly twenty years, have created something so beautiful that it caught the eye of the leader of the most powerful nation in the world. Maybe Papa was wrong and it'll be Nixon, rather than Reagan, who wants you to paint his official portrait."

Jemma smiled at that thought.

They visited the Villa Rossa, the Syracuse facility where Spencer spent much of his time as an architecture student. The secretaries fell all over him. He brought that out in people, especially the Italians. At the American Military Cemetery, they laid flowers on her uncle Matthew's grave. Had the war not claimed him, he would be a minister now. Her daddy's other brother, Luke, was killed within months of Matt, in an air raid over Tunisia and buried on the cliffs overlooking the Mediterranean Sea. Someday she wanted to send her parents to both places. For now, Jim claimed he was too busy, but Jemma wouldn't give up because she knew he needed to touch their crosses, just like his mama had done not so long ago.

They celebrated their second anniversary on their last night in Florence, climbing the steps to the Campanile, a beautiful tower next to the Duomo with the best views in town. The last time they had made this climb, they got caught on the third floor right as the big bells tolled. From the fourth floor, the views in every direction were amazing. The Uffizi art gallery, where they had just spent most of the day, and the Tuscany hills called to her. She couldn't wait to get back to her little red boots filled with brushes and paint these memories. Her husband, however, was equally tempting. "Am I the only girl you've ever been up here with?" she asked.

He rested his chin on her head. "You know how you're always saying that you want to protect me from all the facts?"

"It was Michelle, wasn't it?"

"Nope, and don't ask unless you can handle it."

"The Cleave has never been to Florence, has she? Tell me. I won't throw a fit."

"Actually, I've forgotten her name. She was an Italian student and wanted to show me the tower." He glanced at her, briefly, testing the waters.

"Rats. Did you kiss her? You said that you've forgotten about all other women."

Spencer was silent, but with his lips wrestled with a smile.

"Double rats. So this is meaningless. I thought it might qualify as one of those golden moments in our lives."

"Jem, when we are a hundred and one we won't be able to tell the golden moments from all the others. They will all melt into one big, gleaming chunk of gold. We are just getting the taste of it now. Besides, I didn't kiss her like this," he said, then proceeded to melt her pouty lips. "Keep that in mind when you're thinking of golden moments."

"Show me what hers was like," she said.

He gave her a quick peck.

"Promise?"

"Now, Mrs. Chase, do you think I really remember one silly kiss with a girl whose name I don't recall?"

"You shouldn't have been kissing on your first date anyway."

"Who said it was our first date?" He

grinned and dodged her punch. "Hang on, hot stuff, and open your present." Spencer reached into his jacket and gave her a small box. Inside was a gold barrette in the shape of a four-leaf clover. "Now you'll always have one with you."

"Happy anniversary, Spence." She slipped a package into his hand, giggling. "It's the pin-pen anniversary."

He opened it to find a gleaming brass pen engraved with his initials. "Thanks, baby; it's very classy."

"Just like you. Remember when you used to wear those shirts in high school with your initials on them?"

"Yeah. Mother was really into initials. I think it was so she would remember who I was when she was drunk out of her mind."

Jemma was quiet. Rebecca Chase had chosen a nasty way to forget her sadness with her husband and lost babies. The devil's nectar had made her miss out on the time with the sweet child she did have, but there was always tomorrow, like Scarlett O'Hara had said.

The *Panache* photo proofs were waiting for them when they got home, and she was dying for him to open the big envelope. He did, with an uproar of laughter. He spread out the glossy black-and-white pictures on his drafting table and called her over. "Would the real Spencer Chase please stand up?" He snickered.

Jemma didn't snicker. The images were fascinating. The camera and some Western duds had transformed her handsome architect husband into an equally beautiful buckaroo. There was a time when she would've danced all night with such a fine example of Panhandle fare. She slipped her arm around his waist. "I don't want any other women to see these. They'll be calling to ask you out," she said and held a particularly good one up to the light.

"You can screen all my calls."

"Nothing good is going to come of this," she said. "What's worse is that hundreds of girls will tack these up in their dorm rooms and offices."

"Girls don't do stuff like that. Besides, this is not me, Jem. You know that." He put the photos back in the envelope. "I need to get to work."

Her lips assumed the position. "You don't know girls very well. I bet The Cleave alone will buy a dozen copies of this issue."

"When you get your lips all puckered up like that, I assume you're ready for a good smooch. Come here." Spencer leaned back on their leather chaise lounge.

"I thought you needed to work," she said, falling in his lap.

"This was the job I was referring to," he whispered and got started.

Helene didn't want her prized collections tossed around in a moving van, so the Chases placed each boxed item with great care into the big U-Haul and pulled it to Chillaton behind their Suburban. Helene had to put most of her furnishings in storage, but it would be worth it to be in such a happy place. She did not look back at her Tudor-style home that her beloved husband had built for her. Instead, she held Chelsea in her lap and smiled. No more dreary days spent alone. She would have the company of dear ones close at hand. Lester would make her laugh, Willa would keep her on her toes, and she could nurture her friendship with Lizbeth, the most spiritual woman she'd ever known. Perhaps it was time for her to consider her own spiritual life. Their small village might be the right place for her to do so.

More than anything, though, she would be near Jemmabeth and share in her life joys. Jemma, the child she longed to call her own, and Spencer, her sweet husband, would be her delight. At the first stop for gas, Helene checked her purse. The business card was there. She would keep her promise to Paul.

Home again, they invited the silver-haired group out for supper. Jemma knew that she was on trial with every meal she cooked. This one was received quite well, and Lizbeth had brought dessert. They ate in the living room.

"Lester," Jemma began, "I have some good news and some bad news about my show in Florence."

Lester sipped his coffee. "I don't know how it could be nothin' but good news, Jemmer."

"We shall see. I sold that painting of you in your workshop to a *very* famous American," Jemma said, choosing an upbeat tone.

He smiled. "Good for you. Is it one of them movie stars? They don't make 'em any more like Jimmy Stewart or Henry Fonda."

"He's a Republican," she added, not knowing the political affiliation of either of the two actors.

Lester frowned. "Bob Hope? I never could figger out why he joined up with that side. I'm bettin' it was all that golfin' that done it."

"No, bigger than Bob Hope. It was bought by the president of the United States."

A perplexed Lester set his coffee cup on the lamp table. "Well, sir, Ike's passed on." His expression evolved into one of great pain. "Not Nixon."

Jemma nodded, and a silence hung over the room. Helene turned up the volume on her hearing aid.

"Doggone it," he said, rising from his chair. He paced to the door and stood for a moment, looking out at the darkening creek, then returned to his chair and slumped into it. After a few taps of his foot, he drew himself up and took another sip of coffee. "Well, sir, he don't know me from Adam. Did I ever tell you about the time that I snapped a photo of a woman in New Mexico and she come hence to yellin' that I owed her two dollars for it? Maybe I'll have to start chargin' you, Jemmerbeth."

Jemma glanced at him. She would just die if Lester were truly upset about the whole thing. He raised his brow, then chuckled. He was joined at once by the rest of them, all very much relieved.

"Bravo, Jemma, bravo," Helene said and basked in the pleasure of her first outing as a member of this fair company.

■ ■ ■

"How is Spencer ever going to live this magazine thing down?" Sandy whispered at the office, pulling out her own copy. "Twila said that Nedra's Nook is already going crazy with it. Nedra has a copy at every hair dryer. Did you read the part that says your house is 'sophisticated in design, yet warm, bright, and airy in presentation'? What does that mean?" She folded back one of the pages with his photo on it. "Spence really does look fantastic."

Jemma shrugged. "I suppose we might as well go with the flow."

"What?" Sandy dropped her pen in astonishment. "The most possessive wife in Texas is going with the flow?"

"I am not possessive. What am I supposed to do — share him with everyone? So, how was your trip back from Amarillo with my cuz?"

"Not too bad." She clicked her tongue a couple of times.

"Don't say anything to Spence because he doesn't want either of you to get hurt."

Sandy snorted. "Get hurt? My idea of getting hurt is when Mr. Universe knocks me around. I don't think Trent would hurt a fly."

There was the Mr. Universe title again. Jemma tried not to laugh. "I suggest you keep it quiet if you really are interested. I personally like the idea," she said, then changed the subject fast when Trent opened his door.

"Jem, you're just the person I want to see. Come in here for a second," he said.

Jemma grimaced over her shoulder at Sandy, then took a seat in Trent's office. "What's up?" she asked, hopeful he hadn't overheard them.

Trent leaned across his desk and smiled. "I just heard something that I got a big kick out of, and I'm letting you in on the secret."

She couldn't make eye contact with him. *He must have great ears.*

"Missy Blake is going to run for Miss Texas. Isn't that a hoot? Can you imagine her as the epitome of Texas women?" He stretched back in his chair and laughed.

Jemma was wide-eyed. "You're joking me."

"Nope. I saw her mother at the grocery store yesterday. Missy's won all the preliminary rounds. Her mother is delighted that she's doing something *constructive,* as she called it, but wants to let the newspapers break the news. I think they are worried about polishing up her talent, whatever that is. I couldn't wait to tell you because we know the real Melissa."

Jemma flew to Spencer's office.

He looked up from the blueprints on his table. "You look like trouble to me."

"Trouble's where you find it," she said, closing the door. "I think the Miss Texas Pageant Committee is heading down a troubled road very soon."

"You're a married woman now, my little heartbreaker, and I can't allow you to be in any beauty contests. I'm keeping you all to myself."

"The Cleave is running for Miss Texas."

"Good grief." He laughed. "I wonder if they'll check references."

"What do you think her talent will be?"

"Twirling, of course. The problem will be the question and answer section, and that'll be fun to watch." He curled his finger at her. She made herself comfy in his lap.

"Okay, but you're skipping the swimsuit part," she mumbled and concentrated on the moment at hand.

Chapter 20
Missy Texas

Lester sat in the barbershop waiting his turn. He liked waiting so much that he would gladly let other customers go ahead of him. The barbershop and the post office were the best places in town to keep up with the local happenings. The news was usually fresh, and for the most part, accurate — coming from the menfolk of the county.

Today the shop had too many young people to suit him. Their conversations tended to be about girls, sporting events, and girls. His ears did perk up at the mention of Flavil Capp's name. Flavil was Chillaton's contribution to the state penitentiary system a few years back, and everybody knew he was only two days into his parole.

Toady Ballew was having his turn in the chair. He tilted his head so Bernie Miller could finish up his neck with his good eye.

"Your cousin gonna make it to his mama's funeral today?" Bernie asked, squinting.

"Sure hope so." Toady grunted. "My mama's been cookin' like all get out to welcome Flavil home. She figured he ain't had a decent meal since he left."

"I reckon that's true." Bernie rubbed Crown Wax on his hands and then into Toady's flattop. "A man's gotta give up somethin' when he goes to Huntsville. How much was it that he got away with?" Bernie whisked the chair around and dusted the stocky neck before him.

Toady turned his head from side to side, wrinkling his nose at the mirror, then got out his wallet. "It was something like eight thousand dollars that went missing. Flavil claims to be a changed man now, but my daddy says he ain't gonna hold his breath."

Lester couldn't let that go by. "Somebody ought to tell that boy that if his mama hadn't got bad sick when she did, most likely he'd had himself six more months behind bars."

"Yes, sir, we're all well aware of that fact. Flavil does have himself a girlfriend, though. She's a Sunday school teacher. He got her while he was in the pen. She wrote to him ever' day."

"I reckon that makes her a pen pal then," Lester said, creating a ripple of laughter around the customers. He scooted himself into the chair because he needed to get on home and change into his funeral clothes.

Lester tried to attend all graveside services. He hated to see anyone laid to rest without a decent amount of mourners. This wouldn't be a big turnout like the 180-car procession that wound around the cemetery when Spencer's grandfather passed on. No, Lacy Capp had been a surly woman with a sorry mister and a good-for-nothin' son. The only respectable thing about that union was the fact that Leemon Capp, her mister, had run off to join the Merchant Marines and never came back. Lacy had worked at the Chillaton Dry Cleaners for twenty years until female cancer claimed her. She raised her ornery son alone and always smelled of naphtha, which to Lester's way of thinking helped keep her single.

Flavil was there all right. Had on dark glasses, a Hawaiian shirt, and shoes like Pat Boone's. His pen pal was hooked on to his arm like a night crawler, too, and she sure didn't look like any Sunday school teacher Lester had ever seen. They whispered in each other's ears during the graveside services, showing no respect at all.

Flavil was a hot topic at the post office and

the barbershop for a couple of weeks. Then everybody lost interest when Carson Blake offered everybody in town complimentary matinee tickets to a double feature Western at the Parnell to celebrate his daughter being a finalist in the Miss Texas Beauty Pageant. Lester loved shoot-'em-upper movies, and especially a free one.

Connelly County had never been represented in the Miss Texas contest, and every resident would be glued to the TV on the big night. It would be hard to find a better all-around swimsuit contestant than Missy Blake.

Jemma was reluctant to host a gathering to watch the proceedings, but Twila was dying to, and did. Sweetybeth was in the center of the room in her playpen and bowls of chips and bean dip were on the coffee table when Spencer and Jemma arrived. Trent, Sandy, Twila, and Buddy B rounded out the audience. Jemma had been nursing a big pout all day but had successfully hidden it from her husband. The Cleave didn't deserve to win anything in her opinion, but beauty contests weren't about dignity or honor; they were just about looks, so The Cleave actually had a chance.

"She'll win the swimsuit part, but the interview will kill her," Sandy predicted.

After the initial introductions and a silly group song and dance, the contestants began the traditional parade to display their physical blessings. The closer it got to Miss Panhandle, Spencer excused himself to make a phone call to a client.

Sandy nudged Jemma. "Smart boy."

Missy must have been working out because she didn't have a single ounce of baby fat anywhere. She knew how to walk, too. Being the CHS band majorette had served her well. The camera didn't linger on her face for long. Spencer came back just in time for Miss East Texas to strut her stuff.

The announcer called out the runners-up, then blurted, "The winner of the swimsuit competition is: Miss Panhandle, Melissa Blake!"

Big surprise. Rats. Jemma looked briefly at her husband. His eyes were already on her. He leaned over and whispered in her ear, "They don't have the best of the best."

Jemma smiled slightly. "Smooth talker."

Buddy B pushed back in his recliner. "Now the fun begins. I heard that Missy's gonna twirl two batons."

Trent frowned. "While she sings or something?"

"Nope." Sandy sighed. "While she wears something short on both ends."

"I heard that the batons are going to be on fire," Twila added.

"Naw, that's Nedra news," Buddy said. "Carson laid down the big bucks and hired a choreographer from New York to plan the whole thing. He even had the music especially recorded."

Trent shook his head. "You can be Miss Texas and just twirl a baton?"

"Two batons," Twila corrected. "Texans appreciate twirlers."

Her routine was well executed, much to Jemma's disappointment. She had hoped that The Cleave would drop one baton and get hit by the other in the meantime. At least she hoped that her hair would cover her face, but Missy was dressed like a cowgirl whose outfit got washed in hot water and shrunk down to nothing. Her hat was fastened to her head with a drawstring under her chin. She pranced and cavorted to a song from *Oklahoma*. Jemma thought that choice alone should have gotten her disqualified. Instead, she came in third in the talent competition.

"Oh brother." Sandy moaned. "Every little girl in the state will sign up for twirling lessons now."

Twila, ever the faithful employee, defended the notion. "Twirling's a sport.

Nedra's niece got a twirling scholarship to a college in Louisiana."

After a medley of songs by the pageant orchestra, it was time for the finalists to be announced and interviewed. The Cleave was among the chosen few. She made her phony surprised face that Jemma couldn't stand. Her daddy had probably bought off the judges. If Missy Blake became Missy Texas, Jemma would beg Spencer to move to Scotland.

The camera moved in close to scrutinize each contestant as she pondered the question. The master of ceremonies read slowly, as though speaking a foreign language. "What challenge in your life have you overcome?" The camera lingered on The Cleave as she pursed her lips in profound concentration.

"If she says that being a total jerk has been a challenge, she'll be lying," Sandy said. "It comes naturally to her."

Twila spoke up. "She's not a jerk all the time, is she?"

"Whose side are you on, Twila? The Cleave has a personality problem. Plus she went through Spencer's desk for her own benefit," Sandy said. "Cheezo, it's like she's your best friend or something."

"Well, let's see if Melissa's small brain is

working tonight." Trent slipped his arm around Sandy.

The first contestant spoke about her struggle to overcome a learning disorder. The second was studying to become a space scientist despite her meager monetary resources, and the third went for universal peace and how, as Miss Texas, she would strive to overcome world unrest.

Then it was Missy's turn. She slung back her hair and made eye contact with the camera, like a viper. "I've had to deal with jealousy all my life. Ever since I was a little girl, people have hated me because I'm so pretty. Now that I've grown up, it's even worse. Nobody really understands how beautiful people suffer because of jealousy. I've overcome it by learning to just love myself and my God-given beauty. It is only . . . uh . . . native . . . nativity . . . *nature's due* that I be crowned Miss Texas." She arched a brow at the camera and smiled, showing the results of her junior high braces.

Jemma felt like Missy was looking right at her. Twila's guests erupted into laughter.

"There goes the shootin' match." Buddy B spoke for them all.

Jemma exhaled. The Cleave had exposed herself at the Houston Convention Center on tri-state television in more ways than one. No learning disorder, no world peace, no rocket science major — just ego. Even her daddy couldn't fix The Cleave's embarrassing response, and thus Miss San Antonio tearfully wore the crown down the runway. Despite invoking God and using a phrase she had learned from Jemma, Missy came in dead last.

"Uncle Art," Jemma bubbled into the phone, "I just sent you the first quilt, and there are six more almost finished. You're going to be impressed."

"Good," Arthur said. "I'll be looking forward to it. Your aunty has been working with the marketing department to get started as soon as it arrives."

"Love y'all," Jemma said and handed the phone to Spencer. He was to begin the new Billington's in Austin soon and had a list of questions.

Spencer pulled up to the nursing home; it was coming along at a slow pace, unlike their other projects. He probably needed someone else to supervise the construction of it, but he wanted to make sure it was done right. He and Jemma had been praying for a solution. Pinky Simmons and his brother, Skinny Jack, of Jack's Concrete, rolled up next to him in a beat-up '49 pickup.

Pinky stuck his head in the Corvette window. "Hey, Spencer, how's it goin'?"

"This job is taking forever, Pinky. We need to speed things up."

Skinny Jack moved in so as not to miss anything. "I heard you're in one of them girlie magazines. I betcha your pretty wife don't like you gettin' naked for a magazine." He guffawed, hoping to get him going.

Spencer grinned right back at him. "So, do y'all have any ideas for making some quick progress here? I'm open for suggestions."

Pinky took off his straw hat and squatted beside the car. "Money talks, Spencer. Offer Pa a bonus for overtime; maybe that'll light his fire."

"Throw in a copy of that girlie magazine, too," Skinny Jack offered, wheezing with laughter.

Pinky lowered his voice. "You ain't really naked in them pictures, are you, Spence?"

"Of course not," Spencer said. "Now about this project . . ."

Jack Simmons honked his horn and lurched his truck to a stop on the other side of the Corvette. "Nobody said nothin' about a pity party this mornin'. Young Mr. Chase, you best be earnin' some money to pay us with." Jack scratched his enormous belly under his overalls and yawned.

Skinny Jack piped up. "Spencer's gonna give us all raises and nudie magazines if we cut loose on this place. It was Pinky's idea."

Jack guffawed. "Magazines? I ain't sure Skinny Jack here can read, young mister. You might want to change that to something helpful, like cigarettes. I thought you was in some pretty boy's magazine anyway."

Skinny Jack put his arm around his pa. "Don't need to read nothin' to enjoy them kind of pictures. Hold on. Pretty boy's magazine? I ain't wantin' to see no naked bucks like you. You can forget that idea right now." Skinny Jack backed away from the Corvette.

"Jack, we were discussing your slow progress. I might consider a bonus, though, because the target date is already history."

"You boys hightail it on out there and start working before I kick your sorry hides." Jack spat a wad of tobacco into an orange juice can stuck in the front pocket of his bib overalls, then turned to Spencer. "Listen here, sonny boy, you're making me look bad in front of my family when you whine about the way I do things."

"It's not your work quality that I'm concerned about. It's the long lunch breaks, late arrivals, and early quitting times. It's nine o'clock right now, and y'all just got here. The sun has been up for three hours."

"Family comes first with us, young Mr. Chase. My mama's got a rattler holed up in her outhouse foundation. Me 'n' the boys went over there and cemented him in. I ain't gonna have my mama gettin' her hindquarters bit by a rattler, even if it harelips the gov'ner. Besides, your old man's got enough money to hire you some more help so we can get your pretty little place done in time. Nobody's gonna live here anyway, except a bunch of rich old bags." He spat again. "I see no hurry."

Spencer looked him in the eye. "Jack, I have twenty-five elderly men and women who need to move into this building right now. I would appreciate it if you would get your crew over here, on time, tomorrow. Maybe you should spend some of your earnings to get your mother an indoor bathroom."

Spencer backed up the Corvette, and it threw a bucketful of gravel as he left the site.

The bosses and their perky secretary were

having lunch in the conference room at the office, courtesy of Son's Drive In new delivery service.

"This is hilarious." Sandy giggled. "Whoever heard of a hamburger place delivering to your door? There are deadbeats in this town who will never have to leave their houses again."

"I think Son is trying to compete with his daughters' place. Daddy's Money is raking in the supper crowd," Spencer said.

"Is it true that Son invented the spork, and that's why he has them on his neon sign?" Trent asked.

"Yeah," Sandy said between bites. "Supposedly, Son developed sporks when he was one of the cooks for General MacArthur during the Second World War."

"Really." Trent drew in his chin. "The names in this town kill me. For instance, why is Buddy called Buddy B, and what's the deal with the two Jacks who are working on the nursing home?"

"If you could call it work," Spencer muttered.

Sandy took a sip of soda. "We call my brother Buddy B to not confuse him with Buddy Holly. His band used to only play Buddy Holly songs. The Simmons daddy is Jack and he's a tub of lard, but rather than

382

call him Fat Jack, folks thought the best thing to do was to call the son Skinny Jack."

"Why not call him Jack Jr.?" Trent asked.

"That's Pinky's real name."

Trent hung his head and laughed. "What that Simmons bunch needs is some competition."

Spencer exhaled. "I couldn't get anybody else to come until the fall, and Jack was the only crew around. They do know how to pour concrete and lay bricks, especially Pinky." Spencer cleaned up his trash and walked to the door. "This is what I get for trying to act as the contractor on this job. It's not my field."

"Don't look at me." Trent held up his hands.

"You want me to do it?" Sandy asked. "I will, because Jack Simmons is a liar. He and my daddy had a major falling-out about five years ago. I'll call around. The new Amarillo phone book just came out."

"Thanks, Sandy." Trent smiled admiringly.

"Yeah, thanks," Spencer added. "I have to get back to the Billington projects, and I've got a hot date tonight." He turned toward his office, but not before he saw the smile that Sandy gave Trent. They weren't even listening to him.

■ ■ ■

Jemma sat on the edge of the chaise lounge in their study. She smiled at the photograph. She knew that right after they had snapped this shot, her dear husband had been thrown off the borrowed horse that resembled Gene Autry's Champion. She just knew that if the horse had been a Trigger look-alike, it wouldn't have thrown Spence. Roy Rogers remained supreme. She still had his cowboy rules tucked in her wallet.

She eyed the canvas. He would hate it if she did another huge painting of him. She jumped up and got started.

She worked on it all day until she saw the Corvette coming down the county road. Then, tearing off her paint-spattered clothes, she jumped in the shower. She emerged to hear him groaning in the studio.

"Jemmabeth Alexandra, not again. Can't you find something else to paint?" he yelled as he descended the stairs, then came into their bedroom. "Well, hello, good-looking. Are we going out with you dressed like that?"

She grinned. "I paint however my heart leads me, and it led me straight to you today." She went in her closet and began the tedious task of choosing an outfit for their overnight date in Amarillo.

Spencer stood in the doorway. "Let's stay home. We can eat peanut butter and jelly for all I care."

She gave him The Look. "What changed your mind?"

He didn't answer but shut the closet door, leaving them marooned in the dark.

The painting was her new favorite, well, maybe not her favorite, but she really liked it. Cowboy Spencer stood on the banks of Plum Creek holding the sorrel horse's reins. It drank from the stream as Spencer's attention was on the minnows scattering from the commotion. The sun filtered through dust particles, settling behind horse and rider, and the light provided the scene with a regal luminescence. She had just added a dragonfly hovering above the water when the phone rang. It was her cowboy.

"Hey, you, guess what?"

"You're coming home to work, like you promised you would do someday."

"You just watch. I'm going to do it, Jem. But first, here's some news you'll like. Sandy has found somebody from Amarillo to do the brickwork on the nursing home. I've already told Jack, which was very satisfying, I might add."

"Super. How did he take it?"

"He was ticked off and called me an assortment of names. This other crew can be here tomorrow if we need them. Apparently, it's a group of buddies who worked construction in the army and are just getting started. Sandy found them in the Amarillo newspaper."

"It's an answer to our prayers. I hope they'll do a good job," Jemma said, studying the horse's right nostril.

"We'll keep an eye on them, but the guy gave Sandy several numbers back East to call for references. Sorry, baby, I have to take another call. See you tonight."

Jemma took his advice and did find something else to paint. She had been thinking about this idea for a while.

She walked down their lane and turned east on the county road for ten minutes or so. Making her way across the cattle guard, she passed the windmill and horse tank, then rounded the corner and unfastened the gate to the green field of cotton, the cotton field that Papa had called Jemmalou's, meaning he would spend all the profits from it on her art lessons and Christmas presents, if possible.

At the far end of the turn row, a giant,

lone elm tree held many memories for her. In its shade stood a cedar bench that he had crafted himself and placed there for his lunch breaks. Now a hawk was perched on it. Papa would have liked that.

She stopped and sketched the sight, then moved closer until the bird spread its wings and lifted into the branches of the big elm. Jemma peered up into the tree. She caught a movement and there he was, cinnamon feathers ruffling in a sudden cool breeze. His black eyes pierced into hers; then he was off, drifting on the wind until he disappeared in the clouds.

Jemma ran her hand across the wooden bench, then looked out over the field, to see things as Papa might have. She took out her pencil again, making pages of sketches as the wind moved through the cotton patch and moaned in the branches, bringing with it a bank of heavy clouds.

A gust whipped around the bench and peppered her face and arms with sand. She turned her back to it and felt the first drops of rain.

A streak of lightning brought her out of her artistic stupor. She tucked her sketchbook inside her cowboy shirt and walked toward the gate. With every step she took, the storm intensified.

By the time she reached the gate, she was soaked, and the lightning propelled her into an all-out sprint. She knew Spencer would call, she wouldn't be home to answer, and there would be a scolding tonight. She never considered the weather in her plans, so it was always a blessing when things worked out.

She strained to see the county road. All she needed now was to get run over; she'd never hear the end of it, if she lived. Rats. She pushed her hair back from her face and plodded ahead. A horn beeped behind her. She turned to see the smiling, nearly toothless face of Shy Tomlinson. He yelled for her to get in. She ran around to the passenger side to comply, but Shy motioned her to the driver's side.

"Sorry, Jemmerbeth," he said, taking off his hat. "That door ain't worked since 1954. Scoot on across, hon." He ran his hand through his white hair. "This is one miserable storm, but we can sure use the moisture." The smell of old rags and machine oil permeated the pickup. "I suppose you need off at your place. It's sure different-lookin', ain't it? Spencer's a smart feller to come up with such a interestin' house."

Shy was Chillaton's best fix-it man and had done some work for her mom and daddy before they sold their house. She peered out the back window into the bed of the truck. "Your spruce tree looks pretty this year, Shy. This rain will be good for it."

"Sure will. I won't have to water it for a good while. The Lord's blessed me with a special knack for growin' things back there. My melons are coming along, too. Take a look."

Jemma turned again. The cantaloupes made a ring around the tree. The blue spruce was the same size it had been since she was a little girl. Some folks said Shy bought a new one every year and pretended it was the same tree, but she knew he couldn't afford to buy new trees.

They pulled up in front of her house. "Thanks for the ride, Shy. Would you like to see the inside of our home? I have some leftover chocolate cake, and I could make you some coffee." She assumed he could manage those without teeth.

"Oh no, ma'am. I'm way too dirty to go anywhere but to the dump. I'd get mud on your floor, but thanks anyway. I'm sure it's fixed up real pretty in there."

"You can take your shoes off. C'mon. I won't take no for an answer. Besides, I'd like to do a few sketches of you, if you don't mind." She touched her shirt to see if her sketchbook was intact. It was there, and only a little moist.

Shy hesitated, then opened the door into the rain. Jemma skipped up the steps and onto the deck. Shy ambled along behind her. She changed clothes and served him the promised cake and coffee. He wolfed it down, and she gave him seconds.

"Now, you sit right there and let me draw your picture, okay? I'll show you the finished portrait in a few weeks."

He chuckled and rubbed his chin, then sat very still for several minutes. "Last time somebody wanted to make a likeness of me was when I took a notion to grow things in my truck. That was right after them Dust Bowl days. The Amarillo newspaper come down here and wrote a story about me and took pictures. It was plumb embarrassin'."

"This won't be embarrassing, I promise." Jemma flipped the page. The phone rang, and she knew it was Spencer. "Take a look around, Shy. Make yourself at home." She picked up the phone.

"Where have you been?" he asked.

"I'm fine. I just took a little walk over to Jemmalou's."

Spencer sighed. "Do you ever look at the sky?"

"Of course I do, I'm an artist," she said,

playing with the cord. "Shy Tomlinson gave me a ride home. He's here now, and I'm doing some sketches of him."

"Tell him thanks for me, but you haven't heard the last of this."

"I know. Love you. Bye." She hung up the phone and found Shy studying the painting of Papa.

"That's some likeness, hon." He shook his head. "He sure was a good man. I first met your grandpa at the hospital. He come in to pray over the sick and afflicted. I'd got myself pretty beat up in The Great War. I was what you'd call a wild young'un up until then, so I figgered the Lord said, 'Okay, sonny boy, you've been askin' for a whuppin' and here it is.' Your grandpa helped me see the light, and I was much obliged. Anytime I worked for him, I did it for free. He always made me chuckle. He said you might as well laugh about your troubles as cry about 'em, and he was right, you know." Shy shifted in his stocking feet. "It sure made me sad about his boys."

Jemma smiled. "I miss him a lot, and I love hearing stories about him. Thanks, Shy."

"I reckon I'd best be gettin' on home. This is my day for checkin' the roadside for odds and ends. You'd be surprised at what folks throw out or lose along the highway. Last week I was passin' over the Salt Fork bridge and spotted me some real nice dishes washed up on the sand barge. Had little daises painted on 'em. You just never know. Anyways, your place sure is somethin' to brag about. You tell Spencer I said that."

Jemma grinned. It was good to know that Sandy's hope chest dishes had found a deserving home. "Come back anytime." Jemma walked him to the door. The rain had lessened. "I like your pickup garden. It's always fun to see you around town, especially when the lights are on the tree."

"Well, I know folks think I've got a few loose screws, but that's all right by me. I've had me some good tomatoes and melons out of it, except a couple of summers back when somebody messed around with my plants. I figgered it was some kids, out for some mischief."

"Probably. Have you ever been married, Shy?" she asked.

He grinned. "No ma'am. I was kindly sweet on Eleanor Perkins back in the forties, but that woman talks enough to bend a mule's ear for life. No ma'am, never married."

Jemma laughed. She knew he'd spoken the truth about Eleanor. "You take care,

Shy. Thanks for rescuing me. I hope you have good luck on the highway." Jemma closed the door and ran upstairs with her damp sketchbook. She had more ideas than she had canvases, and it was time to get busy.

She got up early to take Spencer and Trent to the airport the next morning. They were to meet with Arthur and iron out the final details for the department stores.

"I'll be thinking about you while I paint," she said as they waited.

Spence leaned his forehead on hers and looked into her eyes. "Really? I thought you got lost in your work when you paint, but I'm flattered that you would even try."

"You are the same way and you know it. Once your brain starts walking around those blueprints, there's no room for any other thoughts."

"Mrs. Chase, you are always in my mind. Always." He kissed her.

Trent peeked over his *Wall Street Journal.* He would like to be doing the same to a special someone, and it was at that moment he really cranked the door wide open to his heart.

Chapter 21
Nancy Takes Charge

Jemma stopped by the office to leave Sandy some notes from Spencer. Sandy was sitting at her desk with an expression of doom.

"What's wrong with you?" Jemma asked.

"I may get fired."

"Is this from your crystal ball, or have you been embezzling funds?"

"I'm serious, Jem. The new masonry crew got here right on time this morning."

"That's good."

"You don't understand. There are six of them, and they are all black. I had no idea."

"So why are you getting fired?"

"Spencer and Trent trusted me to get them a good crew."

"Are you insinuating that these guys aren't?"

"I don't mean that. They may be fantastic at what they do. The problem is that this is Chillaton. We are still living in the fifties here; haven't you noticed, Miss Liberal?"

"Look, Spencer and Trent are certainly not going to fire you because a construction crew is one color or another. They aren't going to fire you even if this crew doesn't work out. Your job is secure, so stop worrying."

"Just wait until word gets around about this, Jemma. Can you imagine what Jack Simmons will say or do, for that matter? This is not Dallas or even Amarillo. People around here think Negroes should still be picking cotton and little else. You know that's true, even though they complain about them being on welfare. Now these guys come in and take a job away from local whites. Cheezo. It could be a disaster."

Jemma thought for a moment. "Well, I do know that we can't live in the past. Who cares if there is a reaction? Let people say what they want. If there is a true Christian spirit in Chillaton, it will all be for the best. Life goes on, and we have to grow up. Prejudice is ignorance, and I think people in this town are smarter than you think."

"You are not a realist, Jem. All I know is that Jack Simmons will stir up trouble. I just hope he doesn't do anybody any harm."

Jemma bit her lip and decided to leave a message for Spencer to call as soon as he got to Do Dah's. Why did trouble always rear its head when they were apart? It had to be the devil. She just hoped the devil didn't wear overalls stretched to the limit over a porker beer belly. If so, she would have to give some thought to a new wrestling move or two or three.

She drove home by way of the building site. The A-1 Concrete and Masonry crew were hard at work. Nobody else was around. At home, she built some canvases and had two completed when he called. She told him the whole story.

He considered it for a minute. "Call Buddy and ask him to get in touch with Leon Shafer. He just got laid off and could use a few extra bucks. Tell him that I need Leon to get the grounds at the nursing home ready for sidewalks and landscaping. It's already been excavated."

"Is he going to be your spy?" Jemma asked, feeling relief already at the decisiveness in his voice.

"Yup. Leon's a good guy, and once he knows the score with Jack, he'll keep a lid on things."

"That's why I love you, because you're so smart."

"You be smart, Jemmabeth. Don't get involved in this. Jack Simmons is not to be trusted."

"I know."

"I mean it. You stay home and paint."

Nancy Drew would not stay home when trouble was afoot.

She had supper with Gram and Helene, then drove to the nursing home site near Blake's Drive In Theater. It was deserted. The A-1 crew had left their mixer and several neatly stacked bags of concrete on the west side of the structure. She parked her Suburban and walked around the site. She had picked the brick color herself. It was a salmon tone with accents of white and black. The A-1 crew had done a good day's work. Leon had been working, too. The front of the building was hand raked and rocks were piled outside the survey stakes. Jemma walked back to her car and was about to get in when she spotted the pickup. Jack and Skinny Jack made one pass before turning in the lot. Their truck idled for a minute, then took off, radio blaring.

So they had heard. Jemma sat in the Suburban and gave some thought to her options. It would be dark soon, and there was nobody to guard the site. Jack Simmons was brazen enough to break the law and do some damage, but Spencer would be calling the house soon to see how the day went. She went home and painted. He called around nine and they talked for an hour.

She sat at his desk, touching his things after they hung up. He had told her again to stay out of the Jack deal. Spencer didn't think Jack would do anything yet, and he would be home soon to handle things. Jemma wasn't so sure. She would just die if Jack pulled a stunt and ruined this crew's chance to do a good job. Rats. She grabbed her pillow, a quilt, and a flashlight, then drove back to town in the Corvette. It would be easier to hide behind the bushes than the Suburban.

Nothing was amiss when she pulled up to the site. She drove the Corvette to the east side of the building and killed the engine behind the stout cedars that separated their property from the Blakes' outdoor theater. She locked the doors, moved the seat back as far as it would go, and tried to sleep. After an hour or so, she dozed off and didn't wake up until just before dawn. She shook her head and opened the door, moving the flashlight around the premises. All was well. She yawned and drove home. There was a light on at Lester's.

She worked on the painting of Jemmalou's until Spencer called. He and Trent had eaten dinner with Carrie and Phil. They would move to Chillaton in the fall, but Phil could come earlier to get things running and screen the staff. Carrie sent her love. They ended the conversation in whispers, speaking of love and longings. She hung up, grabbed her stuff, and headed for town.

The A-1 group had finished one whole side of the building and had turned the corner with the next. Spencer would be pleased. She repeated her routine, and the ticking of her alarm clock lulled her to sleep much quicker this time.

It was just after two that she heard voices. Her heart thumped like she was playing basketball again. She squinted into the moonless night and detected the outline of Jack's truck. Then she heard Skinny Jack's voice, the wheezy, cackling voice of a *good-for-nothin'*, as Lester called the younger Jack. She had a plan, but it was becoming sketchier by the moment.

Jack coughed and spat on the ground. "Can't you do nothin' right? Give me that sledgehammer. You gotta get a good backswing on it."

"What if the head comes off and falls on me?" Skinny Jack asked. "Did you ever think about that? You could have yourself a dead Skinny Jack. Then you'd have to put up with Pinky all by yourself."

"I'm fixin' to beat the soup outta you," Jack snarled.

Jemma went into action. She turned the lights on the Corvette and pushed on the horn without letting up. The headlights weren't directly on them, but they were close enough.

Skinny Jack ran to the truck and Jack shaded his eyes with one hand while still holding the sledgehammer in the other. He walked a few steps toward her, then abruptly jerked around and dropped the sledgehammer, kicking it behind him. He put his hands in the air.

Jemma took her hand off the horn in time to overhear Jack's words.

"I wasn't doin' nothin'. Me and the boy here were just takin' a bathroom break on our way home from Amarillo. Yes, sir, we'll get right on home. Thank you, sir. Are you new in the sheriff's office? No, sir, I didn't mean no disrespect. You have yourself a good night, sir." Jack lumbered to his truck.

Jemma heard the sledgehammer hit the truck bed, then the cab dipped as he got in and drove away. A big beam of light came toward her and she got out of the Corvette, ready to meet Sheriff Ezell.

"Jemma? Is that you?"

"Leon?" she yelled back.

He clicked off his flashlight and came toward her, grinning in the dark. "What on earth are you doing out here? Spencer will have a fit."

"I thought you were the sheriff."

"That was good, huh? I used some of the stuff I've seen on my TV shows. You can learn a lot from them, you know. Actually, Spencer asked me to camp out here at night until the project is done. I'm on a twenty-four-hour stakeout. It's real exciting. Were you here last night, too? I got off to a late start. *Mannix* was on."

"Please don't tell Spence; he'll croak. I'll tell him sometime. I was just afraid that Jack would pull something, and he would've, too, if you hadn't run him off."

Leon lit up a cigarette. "Well, to tell the truth, I didn't hear nothin' until you laid into that horn. I'm a sound sleeper. I guess this was a two-man job. Excuse me for saying so, Jemma, but you've got a lot of guts, and I sure do respect that. You go on home now. I've got my detective adrenaline going."

She laughed. "I doubt Jack will be back, but you'll tell Sheriff Ezell about this, won't you?"

"Sure will. Law enforcement is a real tight circle. Don't worry. Your secret's safe with me. We're old band cronies anyway, huh?"

"We are. Thank you so much, Leon." She gave him a hug and went to the Corvette. He was standing in front of the building as she drove past. She rolled down her window. "Leon, I want you to know that I appreciate your attitude about the A-1 crew. I know this is a first for Chillaton, and you might take some flak."

Leon put out his cigarette and coughed. "In my book, we're all the same under our skin. Them boys fought just like Spencer did in 'Nam. No difference in 'em."

Jemma bit her lip and waved. She had told Sandy that Chillaton people were smart. They also had some good hearts amongst them.

She waited until she had buttered him up with a good meal and sweet nothings. They sat on the deck barefooted, enjoying the sounds of the evening.

"We need a porch swing, Spence. I miss Gram's."

"I'll have to come up with a plan for that, I guess. You look very suspicious tonight, my love."

"You can't read my mind. It's just that I

missed you. I don't sleep well when you are away. I worry about things." The seed was planted.

"What things?"

She watched him out of the corner of her eye. This could turn out badly, and she knew it. "I worried that Jack Simmons might do something evil. So . . ."

Spencer sat up, but it was too late to stop now.

"So, I checked the site both nights you were gone."

"Tell me that again."

"I sort of waited around to make sure he didn't do anything."

There was a very pregnant pause, as in quintuplets.

"Now let me get this straight. I made arrangements with Leon to hang out at the building site twenty-four hours a day, but you went all by yourself to the site in the middle of the night and checked to make sure that a man who weighs twice as much as you, not to mention his crazy son, wasn't committing any crimes there. Is that pretty much it?"

"Well, pretty much," she said, shrinking into the patio furniture. "You should have told me that Leon would be there at night."

Spencer leaned against the railing and

exhaled. "Is there more?"

"I was kind of there when Leon confronted Jack and Skinny Jack." She had done it again, but it was a good thing this time. Maybe not all that safe, but a really good thing.

He paced around, then picked her up, took her in the house, and deposited her on their bed. She looked at him, big-eyed and pouty lipped. He left the room and came back with a legal pad and a pencil. "All right, little Miss Smarty Pants, start writing. When you've filled up the page, I'll let you know what's going to happen next." He plumped up the pillows and lay on the bed, arms folded across his chest.

Jemma looked at the words written so perfectly in block letters, like only a draftsman could do. *I scared the wits out of my husband, and I'm sorry.* She looked at him, but he was not smiling. She copied the words, filling every line, and handed it to him.

"I really am sorry, Spence."

He crawled across the big bed toward her until their noses touched. She couldn't help but notice how pretty his eyes were in the soft light of their bedroom. If he weren't so mad at her, she would have told him, too.

"Jemmabeth Alexandra Chase, promise

me that you will stop acting on every idea that pops into your head, especially if it endangers your life."

"I don't know if I can promise you that. I thought A-1 needed me. Jack could have stolen their equipment."

"Jemma! What if Jack had hurt you? Leon told me that he and Skinny Jack had been drinking. Didn't you consider that I knew what Jack might do and that's why I had Leon there?"

She hung her head. "Okay. I promise I'll try to be more careful. You have really pretty eyes," she said and gave him the puppy dog look.

"I can't leave you alone. Something happens nearly every time, and you know that I'm going to have to be away a lot with all these projects."

"I could come with you, but then I can't paint as well. I'm sorry I scared you. At least it was all over when you found out. Retroactive scares are easier to handle, aren't they?"

"It doesn't change the facts."

"What's going to happen next?"

"This." He grabbed her in a merciless leg lock.

She giggled and tried to curl around to break the lock, but couldn't. He was shaking his legs and jiggling her insides. She settled for a toehold and bent his foot backward. He yelped and let her go. She slammed him with The Pancake and Waffle Iron combined, but he maneuvered his arms out and pinned her to the bed. They stayed like that for a while, both gasping for air.

"Truce?" he asked.

"Truce," she said, and he let her go.

"Sucker!" She grabbed his ankles, pulling him to the floor.

He landed like a cat and chased her out of the room and up the stairs to their studio loft. "You've had it," he said and kissed her like they were still on their honeymoon. All things considered, they were.

The quilts were finished. Jemma brought Lizbeth over to Willa's house to see them after dark. Lizbeth set right to work looking over the quilts.

Willa laughed. "You sneakin' around? You 'fraid them women will think Miz Liz is the inspector?"

"I just don't want to mess up a good relationship. It's been smooth sailing, hasn't it?" Jemma asked.

"If you don't count all the whinin' about who sits where and choosin' radio stations. Then there was Grandma's spit can that spilled."

"Do Dah and Uncle Art are excited. They have gotten lots of interest from the first quilt I sent. So, what's the latest with Trina and Nick?"

"They've about spent all their money sendin' him on wild goose chases for interviews."

"Don't hospitals pay him back?"

"Some do, but there's a chunk of time in between where there ain't no money in the bank. Joe sent 'em what we could afford, and his folks is helpin', too."

"Spencer and I will send them a check," Jemma said. "I wish they would come to Chillaton. Dr. Huntley is about to retire."

Willa laughed. "Sugar, ain't no white folks gonna let a colored man see them in their underbritches. You should know that."

Jemma nodded, but she didn't really agree. Leon had proven that.

"This is fine work." Lizbeth eyed the last quilt. "The bindings are a little stiff, but the rest is very nice."

"I tell you who's been the biggest surprise in all this business," Willa said. "Gweny. She even come over at night and got the keys to the church from us several times so she could work on them quilts. She's been by once this mornin' already to see if they was ready to mail. Beat all I ever saw. Weese didn't do a lick of work the whole time he lived at my house."

"Maybe she wants extra money. I bet she marked down her time."

Willa shrugged. "No ma'am. She just worked. You gonna take these to the post office?"

"I'll have to get some boxes and pack them first. I'll come back in the morning. Maybe we should give Gweny a bonus."

Jemma saw him as she turned the corner toward the railroad crossing. He was thinner. She slammed on her brakes and backed up. He raised his eyes to her like the same old angry Weese.

"Hi," Jemma said. "How are you? I heard that you're going to junior college. That's great."

He gave a slight bob of his head.

"Your sister seems to be excited about the neighborhood quilting business. I hope you like the idea, too."

"I told you a long time ago that I don't care about you or anything you do."

"You don't know me. I'm only trying to help the neighborhood be more financially independent. Surely you can agree with me on that."

Weese turned suspicious eyes on her. "You don't know squat about bein' poor, otherwise you wouldn't be flashin' your fancy Corvette around here. Why don't you sell it and give the money to Gweny and me? That would make you feel better about yourself. That's all you're lookin' for anyway."

Their eyes locked up. It was a pointless conversation. A monster whirlwind passed between them, needling their skin with sand. A tumbleweed fastened itself to Weese's leg, and the aftermath of the gust left Jemma's hair full of dirt. She rubbed her eyes and he was gone, trudging down the street and spitting the encounter out of his mouth along with the dirt. She exhaled and ran her tongue over the grit that stuck to her teeth.

Weese didn't speak for everybody. It could work out for the women and that's what mattered, despite his opinion of her motivation. The Lord knew her heart.

The next morning Jemma went behind Household Supply and flattened three portable television boxes she found in the alley. She bought wrapping tissue at the dime store and took it to Willa's house. They packed the quilts like eggs in the sturdy containers. Jemma taped them shut and wrote the address on each box. It was an exciting moment, tempered only by the fact that the boxes wouldn't fit into the Corvette.

"I'll use the Suburban. I need to buy groceries, anyway, so I'll be back in a couple of hours to pick these up. Thanks for your help, Willa. We're making history today."

"Let's hope it ain't history like Pearl Harbor. I gotta get this ironin' done. Joe wants me to cut back on my work if the quiltin' business takes off. I can't argue with that. It'll give me more time to spend on him, too."

She and Spencer ate at Son's, then traded cars. Willa was outside sweeping her porch when Jemma drove up. "Ain't no boxes here," Willa yelled. "Gweny done took 'em to the post office herself. Said it was no trouble for her 'cause she had Weese's truck today."

Jemma drew back. "Gweny? How did she pay for the postage?"

"I give her what I had from my secret money jar. I hope that was all right with you, sugar."

"I suppose so. Here, this should cover it." She gave Willa all the cash in her purse. "Boy, Gweny really is trying hard to get things rolling. I guess she wants that paycheck. Well, okay, tell her thanks for me. Uncle Art should get this first dozen next week, and then we'll see how they sell. Keep your fingers crossed."

"Don't be crossin' no fingers around this place. Only the good Lord makes things happen. Ain't nothin' to do with crossin' fingers. Shame on you, child. Maybe you need a good swat with this broom."

"Sorry, just kidding," Jemma said and blew Willa a kiss. "I'll talk to you later."

Chapter 22
Bitter Pills

Her very next piece was of Grandma Hardy, but Grandma wasn't quilting. She was sitting in a church pew, her trusty spit can in her lap. Spencer laughed when he saw it. They had celebrated his birthday early, the night before, in Amarillo. She had given him a cherrywood pencil box for his desk. Lester had made it, but she had designed it and grouted the Celtic knots around the sides all by herself. His favorite coconut crème cake was almost ready for him, too. She was sprinkling the last flakes on it when she heard a motorcycle coming down their lane. It had to be Leon. He was the only motorcycle owner she knew. She put the lid on the cake and opened the front door.

A leather-clad rider got off the motorcycle. Leon was dressing well to be drawing unemployment, and he was also looking extremely good in the leather pants. The rider took off the helmet and grinned.

"Spence?" Jemma's jaw dropped. "What are you doing with Leon's cycle?"

"Excuse me, baby, but *this* is not Leon's cycle. C'mon, I'll take you for a ride."

"You know I don't ride motorcycles. Whose is it?"

"It's my birthday present to myself. I thought I'd surprise you."

The countryside noises around them became suddenly louder as Jemma stared daggers at the black motorcycle. It might as well have been The Cleave grinning at her behind her husband.

"So, what do you think?" Spencer kept a safe distance, as if he didn't know what to expect.

She turned without a word and went inside. He followed her. "What's the matter, baby? Are you sick?" Ignoring him, she went to their bedroom and shut the door. She even locked it. "Jem, open up. Are you mad at me on my birthday?"

She was more than mad; she was livid. She was so furious, in fact, that she had retreated rather than attack.

He set his helmet on the floor and went through the mail to have something to do. This could be disastrous. He exhaled and sat on the couch. His leather pants felt kind of odd once he got off the cycle. He should've given her some warning, but he knew she would throw a fit. He had always wanted a cycle, and she had fervently voiced her opinion that they were too dangerous. This BMW was his dream. It wasn't like he had a macho desire for power; he just wanted this one thing. She would indulge him, hopefully.

"Jemma, come out and look at it. You don't have to ride it. Please. I know what you're thinking. We should have talked about it, but there was no hope in that idea. You would have vetoed my plans." He paced in front of the door. "Just come out and talk to me."

Nothing. He went outside to peek into the French doors of their bedroom, but they were locked, the blinds tightly drawn. He sat for a while on a deck chair, then went back to his cycle. It had some bug stains on it. He rubbed them off with a chamois cloth from the garage. He got on it and revved up the engine and took off for parts unknown, sans helmet. Maybe she would lighten up by the time he got back.

Jemma watched him disappear in a cloud of dust. How could he buy something like that behind her back? He knew how she felt about motorcycles. He'd even picked out that stupid leather stuff without her. He must have been thinking about the whole mess instead of working. Maybe his mind was on it even while they were together. Good grief, it was like he had a girlfriend.

She opened the door to the great room and saw the helmet. She gave it a solid, thundering kick, then got a Dr Pepper out of the fridge, staring at the helmet as it wobbled on the hardwood floor. She bit her lip and went back to their bedroom.

Spencer got it up to 90 on the Farm to Market. He totally forgot that the helmet was at home. Jemma would get over this. He had gotten the same feeling of freedom when he flew Hueys in training, before the reality of Vietnam. It was exhilarating — like he was the wind. She would come around. He slowed down considerably at the crest of the hill above Plum Creek. He pulled it into the garage and went in the house, whistling and feigning hope.

The sunset cast a warm glow on their home, but there was no sign of his sweet wife. She was still holed up in the bedroom. He salivated at the beautiful cake but made himself a sandwich and ate it on the deck, hoping she might come out. This wasn't a major thing. It was just a motorcycle, for Pete's sake. He fell asleep on the couch.

He knocked on their bedroom door the next morning. "C'mon, Jem, give me a break. You told me not to ever bring it up, so I didn't. It's really fun to ride."

Silence.

"I have a meeting in Amarillo this morning. May I at least take a shower and get dressed?"

Nothing.

"Are you okay in there?" It was worth a shot.

He sighed and walked toward the guest bathroom shower.

Jemma picked through Spencer's wardrobe and put a gray turtleneck, black slacks, socks, and clean underwear outside the door, then shut it, locked tight. The sweet scent of his aftershave brought tears to her eyes, but she blinked them away. He shouldn't have done this.

Spencer saw the pile of clothes in front of their bedroom door. She was alive. He got dressed, drank a glass of orange juice, and slapped some of Lizbeth's preserves on toast, again eyeing the cake in the glass holder. He ate on the deck again. The onset of autumn nipped at his face. Surely she would come out of that room by the time the cottonwoods turned. He moved to the French doors and peered inside. All he could see were the blinds. He wrote her a note, stuck it on the phone, and left.

Jemma waited several minutes after she heard the monster disappear over the hill. The house was quiet. She went into the guest bathroom just to be where he'd been. The towels were damp, and his footprints were on the plush rug. If he had a wreck on that thing, she would die. She roamed around the kitchen but wasn't really hungry. Maybe she should call him. She turned toward the phone and saw the note.

> Jemma, I love you, not the cycle.
> It's only a motor on wheels.
> You are my life.
> Spence

Rats. Why'd he have to write that? Now she'd have to call him. She climbed the stairs to the pouting room and sulked in their tiny Sainte-Chapelle.

"The Corvette is here, but Spencer isn't," Sandy said on the phone. "What did you do when you saw his new toy? I bet you flipped out."

"So he rode that thing to Amarillo?"

"Yeah, but you didn't answer my question. I'll bet a dollar he slept on the couch."

Jemma sniffed. "I assume you knew about this all along. Some friend you are."

"Hey, I've just known since he rode up on it yesterday afternoon. I sure wasn't going to be the one to break the news to you. I remember the Kelseys, too."

"How did he get to Amarillo to buy it? I suppose that's where he bought the thing."

"Leon."

"Blood brothers. Maybe Spence will grow a ponytail, too." She hung up the phone and painted for a few hours.

That afternoon she took her sketchbook and sat in his chair on the deck. Up until now, Spencer could always get her out of a pout. This time he hadn't even tried — except for the note. It wasn't so much that she hated motorcycles. It was that he had planned the whole deal without including her, and he had to have been considering it for a while.

What had Sandy called her? A possessive wife. She gave that some thought. At least the thing he'd bought was quiet, unlike Leon's. Quiet, though, wouldn't help if he were in an accident, and the way Spencer drove, he could be propelled through the air at a hundred miles per hour. She shuddered at that image, as well as those of Carol and Bill Kelsey bleeding to death on the road to Jericho, while a buck and two doe grazed serenely in the ditch. Jemma had watched from the car as Carol died in Alex's arms. Spencer Chase knew that story well.

The phone rang, startling her.

"Jemma, it's Leon."

"Oh. Hello."

"It's about Spencer. There's been some trouble near Amarillo."

Her body went limp. She braced herself on the counter and couldn't form anything close to a word. Nausea crept up her throat, and she tried to think of a scripture.

"Uh. You might want to get on up here."

She drew a breath. "Which hospital?"

"Naw, he's not in the hospital. He's at the Big Tex Truck Stop."

"What do you mean?"

"The state patrol yanked his license and impounded his bike. I'd bring him home on mine, but I'm starting a new job in an hour. We just happened to be at the same place at the same time."

"Leon, what are you telling me? Is Spence hurt?"

He laughed. "I guess his pocketbook is gonna hurt. He got clocked at 95 on the highway, and since it's his umpteenth speeding ticket in three years, there's a big price tag to pay. Listen, I gotta go."

"Wait, Leon. Why didn't Spencer call me himself?"

"A man's got his pride, I suppose."

She parked right under Big Tex's waving arm. Spencer was sitting in the window drinking coffee, and he didn't look up when she came inside. She slipped into the booth.

"Hey, babe, know any good lawyers?" she asked, shooting for a light tone. He avoided her eyes and chewed on his lip. She touched his hand. "I didn't know that you'd gotten so many tickets. Have you been keeping things from me?"

He exhaled. "I got one in California and a couple in Houston and New York; you know about the others. I just didn't want to worry you."

"Good excuse. I'll have to remember that one. You're a real menace to society, mister; let's go home."

The Suburban moved along the highway just under the speed limit. Jemma listened to the radio, and Spencer looked straight ahead, holding a large paper sack with both hands like a little boy on his first day of school.

"What's in the bag?" she asked after a long silence.

"My stuff."

"What stuff?"

"The leather clothes and boots."

"Did you wear them to the meeting?"

"No, and it looks like I won't be wearing them ever again."

"I don't know about that. You looked really hot in those pants."

"I should have told you about the tickets. I have a lead foot."

"Well, everybody in town knows that. I'm just glad that you got stopped rather than transported to the hospital or the morgue."

He reached across the seat and touched her shoulder. "Sorry about the cycle, baby. I know it got to you, and I handled that all wrong."

"Me, too," she whispered, then looked at him out of the corner of her eye. His face showed signs of weariness, like it did when he got his draft notice. This day the weariness had sprung from stress of his own making, coupled with the impending embarrassment of the consequences. She touched his cheek, and he immediately kissed the palm of her hand like a puppy starved for its mother.

He slipped his hand under her hair and let it rest at the nape of her neck, tracing his fingers over her skin for the duration of the ride home. The air between them sizzled as Spencer unlocked the front door.

"Spence, I should have . . ."

He pinned her against the river-rock wall and kissed her. She thought she would explode with affection for him. There were no more words, only love.

The morning brought the first frost of the season, but inside the Chase home, life was blissful and quite warm. The coconut crème cake was nothing but crumbs, devoured before sunrise.

Lester hadn't been so happy since his fourth wife, Paulette, had agreed to marry him. Living next door to two cultured ladies, both easy on the eyes, was like breath from heaven for an old fellow like him. Lizbeth watched him with interest. He was sweet on Helene, it was plain to see, and Helene enjoyed the attention. This was working out very well for them all. Helene had brought a few of her elegant belongings to Chillaton, and after a fresh paint job by Jemma, Lizbeth's home was taking on a whole new look. She awoke each morning with a sense of anticipation. It was almost like having Jemmabeth back.

"Lester, do help yourself to another scone. If we were in Devon, you could lavish them with clotted cream and strawberry jam," Helene said, wearing a starched white apron.

"These are delicious," Lizbeth noted. "I think they are an eloquent cousin to our biscuits."

Lester wiped crumbs off his moustache. "Now, if you want somethin' clotted, you need to give a tall glass of buttermilk a try. You crumble yourself up some corn bread in it, and you've got yourself a meal." He stifled a burp into one of Helene's linen napkins.

"How are things in the village, Lester?" Helene asked.

"Well, sir, things are hoppin'. Lots of folks are feelin' bad for Spencer. Drivin' fast don't mean he's a criminal or nothin'. Nobody would ever say a word against that boy. On the other hand, that sorry Flavil Capp's done got hisself thrown back in the hoosegow. He tried to break into The Judge's house, of all places. To top it all off, some pranksters got into Shy Tomlinson's truck and tore up his pumpkins. Throwed 'em on the ground and busted ever' last one of 'em."

Lizbeth shook her head. "Who would do such a cruel thing to Shy?"

"Young'uns got too much time on their hands. If they worked in the fields like we did, they'd be too tuckered out to get into mischief after dark," Lester said.

Helene lifted her teacup, then paused midway. "I do hope our Spencer shall be able to carry on after this nasty bit of humiliation."

Lester chewed on that thought. It hadn't occurred to him that Spencer might let this thing get the best of him.

"You could hire Lester to drive you around," Jemma said as they drove home from the proceedings. "At least it's been delayed until the end of December. Good thing the judge is going on vacation."

Spencer closed his eyes. "Yeah, but I still can't drive until he decides my fate. I can't believe how stupid I've been. You've married an idiot."

"Maybe this will force you to work at home with me. You said you would. I think you even promised me."

"It's embarrassing. You'd think I was still a teenager."

"You aren't listening to me at all. Now who's the one not turning their problems over to the Lord? Do you need to stop by your office?"

"I might as well get it over with. Sandy will never shut up about this."

Sandy started singing "He's in the Jailhouse Now" as soon as they walked in the door. "I wonder if we'll lose business over this," she asked, then giggled.

"Are there any calls I need to return?"

"Of course. There's a stack of notes on your desk, and Jemma, your uncle Arthur called, too."

Jemma called him immediately. "Hi, Uncle Art. Did you like the quilts?"

"Actually, that's the reason for my call, Jemmabeth. We've not received another thing from you, and quite enough shipping time has elapsed."

She bit her lip. "I suppose they could be lost," Jemma said, thinking of the women and their dutiful labor. "I'll call you back. Thanks, Uncle Art. Say hi to Do Dah for me."

Spencer was on the phone and Jemma needed to think. Rats. She should have mailed the quilts herself. She had let the women down, and now it was all going to flop. She paced Main Street, battling more than the gusty wind. A '57 Chevy pulled alongside her, and the pair inside emitted lengthy wolf whistles.

"Hey, good lookin', what kind of husband lets his wife walk all over town? Ain't he still got the 'Vette?" Wade Pratt asked.

Jemma exhaled. These two were all she needed in her plight.

"We miss you in the band. Now there ain't nothin' for the guys to look at," Dwayne Cummins added. "That's includin' us."

"Y'all take off. I'm busy right now. I need to think." Jemma pulled her hair back with a rubber band.

"Thinkin's my middle name." Wade gave a thumbs-up in complete confidence. Dwayne kept the car rolling along beside her while Wade continued. "My mama sent me to the store the other day to get some soap, and I was standin' there just lookin' at the wrapper. It said 99 percent pure. That started me to thinkin'. Pure what?"

Dwayne laughed. "Pure soap, you dummy."

"Not necessarily. The guv'ment could be controllin' our minds with some pure chemical."

Dwayne laughed again. "Shut up, Wade. You don't bathe enough to have your mind controlled by no chemicals. What's so important that you've gotta spend all this thinkin' on it, Jemmabeth? You gonna dump ol' Spence and take up with me?"

"I had some packages disappear in the mail." Jemma neared Spencer's office. "I should have mailed them myself, but I let someone else do it."

"Well, I can solve that one," Wade said. "Ask Paralee. She don't mind tellin' you about whatever has passed through her office. Rules or no rules."

Jemma stopped. Of course. She should have thought of that instead of worrying so much about not mailing them herself. "Thanks, guys!"

She went straight to the post office. Paralee, engrossed in *The Guiding Light,* glanced at her. "Hi, hon, I'll be right with you. It's almost time for a commercial." H.D., the cat, stirred, but didn't bother getting up either.

Jemma drummed her fingers on the counter. "It's about those boxes I sent to Uncle Art in Houston."

Paralee turned down the television and leaned across the counter. "I'm sure sorry about Spencer and all them tickets. I reckon he'll be walkin' for a while. He most likely got that from his daddy. Max used to tear around town like a maniac. Now what about them boxes, hon?"

"My uncle hasn't gotten them yet. Isn't there a way to trace them and see where they went?"

"I figger they went right where you sent 'em. That colored girl told me that you changed the address on 'em at the last minute."

"I what? I did no such thing. What address were they changed to?"

"Law, hon. I ain't supposed to tell stuff like that. It's unethical."

"Those were my boxes. I paid to have them mailed. If somebody changed the address on them, isn't that a crime?"

"That could depend on if they did it inside this building. I saw a story close to this very predicament on *Perry Mason.*"

"Please tell me. You could save the day, Paralee."

"You don't say." Paralee drew herself up. Her silver hair was still tucked behind her ears, the way she wore it to Jemma and Spencer's wedding, but the rest looked like the curlers had evaporated while leaving every hair still coiled in place. She raised her Joan Crawford eyebrows. "I'll just look up the record of that transaction." H.D. harrumphed as she shooed him off her ledger.

"Yesiree, Bob . . . here 'tis. Bonna June Lampkin, P.O. Box 42, Paducah, Texas. I don't suppose you need the zip, do you, hon?"

Jemma scribbled the address on a scrap of paper. "Thanks, Paralee. I owe you one." She was out the door before H.D. could blink.

Paralee made a soft noise at the back of her throat and checked her lipstick and hot pink rouge in the mirror. She drew her thumb and forefinger across the air in front of her. "Paralee Saves the Day," she said. "Nice headline."

"Willa!" Jemma barrelled into her house without knocking. "Have you seen Gweny or Weese around today?"

"Sugar, what's wrong? I seen 'em yesterday. Gweny was over to the Dew Drop buyin' Fritos and Twinkies. Said they was headed off to see kinfolk. I didn't ask where."

"Gweny sent those quilts someplace else. Uncle Art never got them."

"Now why on earth would that child do such a thing? What's gonna happen next?"

"I'll talk to Spencer. He'll know what to do."

Jemma started the Corvette and peeled out just like her husband. She rattled off the story to the office crew.

"Maybe she wants to undermine the business," Trent suggested.

"Or sell the quilts and keep the money herself," Sandy said.

Spencer rapped his knuckles on the desk. "This is a matter for the police. I'll call Sheriff Ezell."

"Are you sure you don't want to just *drive* down there?" Sandy snickered.

The sheriff arrived quickly, got all the information, and promised to call if he learned anything. Jemma could just picture him questioning all the women who had worked with Gweny. Maybe she should've handled this herself, with Leon's help. They'd made a good team before.

She waited at Lizbeth's for Spencer to get off work. They sat around the kitchenette as Lester tapped his foot, but with no windy tales on this evening. Helene kept them entertained with stories of her childhood in England. Chelsea and Vincent eyed one another through the window.

"Hot dog!" Lester said, interrupting Helene. "Bonna June. I know where I've heard that name before. She's the gal who was with Flavil Capp at his mama's funeral. I heard him call her Bonna June several times while the minister was talkin'."

Jemma kissed his cheek. "I'll call Sheriff Ezell right now. Lester, you've saved the day!"

Lester beamed. He hadn't saved the day in a good, long while.

"I'm buying a bicycle," Spencer announced as they snuggled up in front of the fireplace. "That way I can get to work without bothering you, and I'll get a good workout as well. I came up with this idea in the pouting room. I seem to spend a lot of time there these days."

Jemma looked him in the eye. "Are you going to wear that leather outfit on your bicycle?"

"Maybe. It's supposed to protect you from road burns."

"Why won't you work here, at home? That was our plan, big boy."

"I know. It's just that I have to go in to the office sometimes."

"Aw, you'll get so cold in the winter."

He moved her hair away from her face. "I love you, Jem."

She smiled and kissed him just as the phone rang.

Spencer sighed and answered. "Hi, Simone."

Jemma rolled her eyes. What now? Another magazine story to get the ladies stirred up at Nedra's? They were probably having a field day already with his license suspension.

"It's for you." Spencer held the phone out to her.

"Hello," she said, then covered her mouth until the conversation was complete. Whereupon she squealed in delight and landed on her husband, knocking the breath out of him.

"I take it that you have good news."

"Simone wants to me to meet her brother in New York City next month to discuss a show at his gallery in London! Can you believe it? He owns a gallery in London. I have to get a slide presentation ready for my portfolio."

"I told you that something good might come out of that magazine fiasco. The Lord takes care of us."

Her mind was already working on the details. She took a breath and put those thoughts aside. "If you lose your license for a year, it could be you getting justice for breaking the speed limit all the time."

"Like you said, it's better than a trip in

the ambulance. The Lord knows this is the only way to break my bad habit."

The phone was ringing when Spencer unlocked his office door. His chauffeur, Jemma, used her best secretarial tone as she answered.

"Chase and Lillygrace. May I help you?"

"Jemmabeth, Sheriff Ezell here. Could you come by my office within the hour? I need you to look at some photos."

"We'll be right there." They headed to the Connelly County jailhouse.

The sheriff laid several sheets of mugshots on his desk. "Look at these pictures, hon, and tell me if you recognize any of them."

It didn't take her long. "I sure do. This is Gweny Matthews and there's her brother, Weese Matthews. I don't recognize anybody else. You mean Gweny and Weese have been arrested? Did they find the quilts yet?"

The sheriff nodded and filled out a form for Jemma to sign. "I think we're on to somethin' bigger than quilt stealin', but I'm not at liberty to talk about it just yet. I'll be in touch."

"What do you think he meant by 'something bigger than quilt stealing'?" Jemma asked as they left.

"You got me. That Weese looked like a surly character. Didn't you tell me that he had a confrontation with you?"

"It wasn't bad. He believed that I was to blame for all his misery. Speaking of misery, Trina and Nick are running low on funds right now. Neither of them have a job yet."

"I'll get a check right out to them. I wonder if he's tried at the Golden Triangle Hospital in Amarillo? I'll mention it in my note. You and I need to go by the nursing home and make a final inspection of the living quarters for Philip and Carrie, then I have to get to work on other projects. Could you help me move some of my files out to the house?"

Jemma threw her arms around his neck. "I can't wait!"

Spencer took slides of her paintings with his fancy camera; then she wrote artist's comments for all twenty-five. She was ready for Simone and her brother. To see Spencer across the studio from her, his head bent industriously over blueprints and to hear his gentle voice on the phone with clients, warmed her heart. This was all she needed to be happy. To those nosy few who continued to inquire about "starting a family," she flashed a polite smile.

They had just started breakfast when the doorbell rang. Sheriff Ezell rubbed his hands together, then tipped his cowboy hat. "Mornin', folks. Hope I'm not disturbin' you, but I figgered you'd want to know about your quilts."

"Did you bring them?" Jemma asked. "Come on in."

The sheriff took off his hat. "Well, you probably aren't gonna see those quilts for a while. They're in the evidence room down in Childress, hon."

Jemma looked to Spencer for help.

"What was the official charge?" Spencer asked.

"Theft, burglary, destruction of property, and possession of stolen money. It appears that your quilts were used to transport over eight thousand dollars to Flavil Capp's girlfriend down in Paducah."

The Chases were dumbfounded.

"The girlfriend broke down and told the whole story. The sheriff down there said that the brother and sister duo never opened their traps. They arrested the whole bunch and Flavil's girlfriend started talkin' fast. 'Course they're all in jail now."

"How did they manage such a thing?" Spencer asked.

"Apparently, Flavil and the Matthews boy

burglarized several businesses a couple of years back and stole the money. Flavil got busted for somethin' else, and the Matthews kid was scared stiff and hid the money in old plastic bags from the dry cleaners. Then he snuck around and stuffed the plastic into the dirt around the edges of old Shy Tomlinson's truck garden. Shy never digs around the sides, you know. Anyway, the kid got arrested at the time, but there was no evidence. A judge in Amarillo sort of sent him off to Vietnam. When Flavil got out, they came up with this plan to sew the money in the quilt bindin's and send them to Flavil's girlfriend. Crazy, huh?"

Jemma shuddered. "What am I going to tell the women?"

"Tell 'em there was a criminal in their midst." Sheriff Ezell put on his hat. "Well, there it is. I'm sure sorry about keepin' the quilts for evidence, but we need to throw the book at these turkeys. I'll talk to the district attorney and see if he can do anything, but I'm afraid you'd best get your crew up and sewin' again. By the way, I think it's a good thing that you're doin' across the tracks. Farmin' is changin'. Everything's goin' big agribusiness with more machines and less people. Coloreds are gonna be hurtin' just like whites. Maybe then folks will feel more like we're all in this mess together."

"Why didn't they just take the boxes to Paducah themselves?" Jemma asked, still in shock.

"The girl said she thought that the postal service was a cinch as a hidin' place. 'Course they don't know Paralee Batson too well, either. She never misses a thing."

"Thanks for coming out," Spencer said, shaking the sheriff's hand. They watched the patrol car head down the lane.

Jemma plopped on the sofa. "Rats. All that work for nothing. Those ladies probably won't even be interested after this."

"You might be surprised, baby. They may want to overcome such a mean setback."

"I'd better call Uncle Art. He's going to give up on this project. Maybe the Lord doesn't like this idea, and that's why He let this happen."

"Have faith, Jem."

"I'm trying."

The Bethel Negro Church had a special prayer circle about the quilt trouble. Brother Cleo delivered a stern sermon about fool's gold and the real thing. He quoted from First Corinthians 3:13: "It shall be revealed by fire; and the fire shall try every man's work of what sort it is." Brother Cleo adapted the verse to Gweny, without mentioning her name. He admonished the congregation, the majority of whom had never seen gold of either kind, that when fool's gold is given the test of fire, it stinks and smokes, but when real gold is put to the test, it stands strong. Jemma had never heard him quite so peeved. It had to be because Gweny did the deed in the basement of the church and the whole story filled the front page for two issues of the *Chillaton Star.* After the prayer circle, Brother Cleo gave Jemma a sturdy hug and assured her that the Lord would prevail.

Willa took off her hat on the front steps and fanned herself. "I should've known that pickle-headed Weese was up to no good. I think my old heart was hopin' that he was headin' down a better road this time. Now he's in cahoots with his little sister to boot. I bit the bullet about that young'un so much that now I'm about ready for a new set of teeth."

Arthur requested, on the basis of the quilt she'd already sent, that they try to fill the order for twenty-four. His point was that he'd already had interest from their advance marketing campaign and could sell the quilts quickly. Jemma called a meeting of the quilters. Everybody knew about Gweny and the money.

"Ain't nobody gonna quilt any faster than we did the first time around. Now Gweny's gone, and she had the quickest needle," Bertie Shanks lamented.

"You gonna have to get us more help," Grandma Hardy scolded Jemma. "My old bones ain't workin' too well like it is."

"They'd work a whole lot better if you didn't have to take a spit every five minutes," Shiloh said, straight to her face.

"You hush. You ain't too big to whup, girl," Grandma Hardy shouted, then spat extra loud.

"Now everybody just hold it," Willa ordered. "I'm still in charge of this here business. Sure, we need help, but where are we gonna get it? We don't want Amarillo folks comin' down. Let 'em start their own business. We already got Red Mule and Pleasant drivin' over, and that's okay 'cause they go to church here. Who's got an idea?"

Not one hand went up.

"I have an idea," Jemma said quietly. All heads turned. "My grandmother is a quilter. She has volunteered to work here or at her home to help meet the deadline. I don't know how you feel about a white woman working with you, but she has offered. She will not take any money for herself, though. She wants you to know that."

Willa cleared her throat. "I have to speak up about this. Lizbeth Forrester is just about my best friend, and there's no finer woman on either side of them tracks. When she makes a quilt, it comes straight from her heart. I know this notion may not set well with some of you, but I'm all for it. The Lord knows that we need help to make up for Gweny's mess, and Miz Liz is just the ticket."

Someone coughed and Grandma Hardy made another audible deposit in her can.

Teeky Samson stood. "I say that if somebody's willin' and ain't hopin' for no money, we let 'em get with it. I spent too much time ridin' back and forth from Red Mule to let this drop."

"I'm for it," Bertie said.

Willa gave Jemma the nod. "Let's vote on it. All those in favor of takin' on help, no matter what the skin color, raise your hand."

"Just so long as they ain't interested in the purse," Grandma Hardy added.

The vote passed unanimously.

Word spread quickly about Flavil's misdeed and about the fate of the quilts. To Jemma's surprise, Brother Hightower rang their doorbell early one morning. Spencer had taken off on his new bicycle, and she wasn't even completely dressed. She threw on a pair of jeans to let him in.

"Mrs. Chase, how are you?" he asked, choosing to remain on the porch. His thin frame seemed even more fragile away from his pulpit. He had never looked like the picture of health anyway. He was what Papa called "pasty-faced."

"What brings you way out here? Is anything the matter in town?" Jemma asked, somewhat concerned.

"Oh, nothing like that." He fumbled for words. "I, ah, we, heard about the unfortunate business with your efforts across the tracks. The thing is that we, I, would like to help."

"I didn't know that Mrs. Hightower was a quilter. How nice of her."

"That's not exactly what I meant." He exhaled. "When I was a little boy, my grandmother taught me to quilt, knit, and embroider. I was an only child, you know, and she doted on me. I still enjoy all those activities. I've made several nice quilts over the years."

Jemma gulped. Not only had she misspoken, but she'd misjudged the reverend's talents, taking him for a pompous male chauvinist. "Brother Hightower, we'd be delighted to have your help. Gram is working already. Maybe you'd like to join her at the Bethel Church."

"I don't want to intrude, but I would like to help. Could you go with me, perhaps to ease the introductions?"

"Let me change clothes, and I'll meet you there in thirty minutes. Thank you so much." She watched him get into his car and drive away. She smiled. The Lord did work in mysterious ways, indeed.

The addition of Brother Hightower to the group proved to open a door for several members of the North and South Chillaton Quilting Clubs to assist as well. The initial discomfort was replaced by polite conversation, and then, gradually, to commingled laughter. Jemmabeth could not have been more delighted. This had to be God's plan. She stayed up half of one night painting the scene she'd witnessed for several days at the church. She left Brother Hightower out, though, so he wouldn't be a curious focal point in the painting. The message was revealed in the gentle portrayal of eyes that observed one another with fresh hope and cautious acceptance.

■ ■ ■

Jemma concentrated on typing her last artist's statement on Gram's kitchenette. Her old portable needed a new ribbon. She didn't even notice that she had company.

"Hey, girl, what are you doing?" her guest inquired.

"Trina! I'm so glad to see you. What's going on? Where's Nick?"

"He's in Amarillo for interviews at the hospitals. I'm here to quilt. Are you heading to the church soon?"

"Yeah, Helene is baking cookies for everybody. It's great to see you looking so happy."

"You too," Trina said. "I'll talk to you later. Wait, you aren't pregnant, are you?"

Jemma shook her head. "Just happy. How about you?"

"No way, but I'm happy all right. I decided not to worry about jobs as much as Nick does. Maybe he'll get this one in Amarillo. The Lord will bless us with something. Thanks a lot, girl, for the loan. Maybe we'll end up being y'all's maid and butler so we can pay you back."

"Get out of here and go quilt. I'll be over in a minute."

Jemma watched as Trina walked through

the hollyhock patch and up to the tracks. It would be a long time before she'd be able to rid herself completely of the shame of never knowing Trina and Willa all those years they had been separated by those tracks. That guilt might never go away.

They met the deadline, such as it was, set by Arthur. There were six big boxes, taken personally by the whole group, to the post office. Paralee doused her cigarette and recorded each one in her ledger. Jemma even took pictures for the *Star.*

"You put us over the hump, Trina. Thanks for your help," Jemma said as they sat in the empty church.

"I hope this works. If not, then you take some consolation in the fact that you gave it your all. Don't look at it like that basketball game you lost at state, okay?" Trina said. "This project has lifted everybody's spirits and opened hearts and minds."

Jemma reached for her hand. "You're gonna make me cry, but I think this will work. I have faith that the Lord wants it to." She exhaled. "Have you heard from Nick yet?"

"Nope. This is the first time anybody's asked him to come back, though. That has to mean something."

"How about you — any nibbles with your design portfolio?" Jemma asked.

"Aw, I might as well be trying to make it in the NBA. Fashion designers must be a starving lot."

"Have faith. That's what Spencer keeps telling me. Look how this little idea turned out. I just hope they sell all those quilts."

Trina smiled. "They will. What fun to see Gram's friends laughing and eating cookies with Mama's neighbors. Who would have thought it?"

"I know. Carrie and Philip move into the nursing home next week. It would be perfect if y'all moved to Amarillo. Things would just be too good. Have you spent much time with Helene?"

"No, but she's cooking supper for everybody tonight. Lester has his eye on her, doesn't he?" Trina asked.

"Yeah, but she's just a friend, I think," Jemma said.

"Hmm. I believe Lester hopes otherwise."

"A toast," Spencer announced. "To the newest member of the Golden Triangle Hospital."

If Nick had grinned any wider, his teeth would have fallen right out. "Thanks," he said, drinking his sweet tea. "It's been a lengthy haul."

"We're all proud of you, son," Joe said. "I can't wait to make an appointment. I've got a list a mile long of ailments."

"I won't be taking appointments," Nick clarified. "I'm part of the emergency room staff. You'll have to be in really bad shape to see me."

"Helene, the meal was delicious," Jemma told her. "I'll have to run an extra mile tomorrow to get rid of the calories."

"You look perfect," Spencer whispered in her ear. "Let's go home."

Lizbeth watched them and smiled. It had been such a peaceful night among family and friends. She only wished the rest of her family could be there because she could have no better feeling than to gather all her loved ones under the same roof.

Lester cleared his throat. "I thought me and Joe could entertain for a spell. It's been a while since we tuned up together."

"I like that idea," Helene said. "I'll just tidy up in here first."

"We'll take care of that, Helene." Jemma volunteered. "You go on and enjoy the show."

"Meet me in the pouting room in ten minutes," Spencer said in her ear. His breath tickled her neck, and she raised her shoulder, giving him the eye. He went right to work on the dishes.

"I'll help clean up, too," Trina said.

"No, that's okay." Jemma nodded in Spencer's direction. Trina got the hint and moved into the living room with the others.

"What are you doing?" Jemma asked, closing the creaky door in the pouting room at the appointed time.

Spencer pulled her to him in the dark. "During supper, I was thinking about the time when we were hiding in here and your parents came in the kitchen. Let's try that again."

"You're my kind of man." Jemma attacked him like they were alone in the house. "What do you think about that?" she asked, coming up for air.

"I think we'd better leave right now, or I'm not responsible for the outcome."

She giggled. "I'm not scared. Everybody's listening to the music, and besides, we're married now."

"Okay, woman, you asked for it."

She would never again look at the pouting room quite the same.

"Shy!" Jemma yelled across the street. "I want you to see a photo of your portrait. I'm on my way to New York right now to show it to a gallery owner."

"You don't say? I always wanted to see them skyscrapers. Take a long look at 'em for me, would you?" Shy grinned, showing a wide expanse of gums.

Jemma opened her portfolio on the hood of his truck. "There. What do you think?"

"Well, I'll be Uncle Johnny. That beats all I ever saw. You've got yourself a real knack, Jemmerbeth. Them folks in New York don't know what they're in for."

"Thanks, Shy. That was some surprise about those people hiding that money in your dirt."

"Yes ma'am, them newspapers are wantin' to take pictures already." He pushed his hat back and scratched his head. "It makes me look even more foolish, drivin' around with my garden and eight thousand dollars underneath it."

"Nobody thinks that, Shy. It just makes your truck a landmark, that's all. When I get back from this trip, Spencer and I want to take you out to supper or you could come to our house."

"Thank you, hon. I'll have to clean up real good to go back to your place. Did you tell Spencer I was sure impressed?"

"I did. I have to go now, but we'll be getting in touch with you soon."

■ ■ ■ ■

"This is pathetic," Spencer said. "I can't even drive my wife to the airport."

"Yeah, but if you were driving, I couldn't do this." She kissed him.

"None of that." Sandy adjusted the rear-view mirror. "I don't want any distractions in my chauffeuring duties."

"Get over it," Spencer replied and paid Jemma back.

"I thought you said you would never let me go off alone again."

"Sorry, Jem. I just have to get caught up. I didn't dream that Trent and I would be so busy this early in our career. I think this trip is quick enough so there won't be any trouble, especially with you-know-who."

"I think Helene had a talk with him."

"Really. It must have worked; at least we can hope so. Call me when you get there."

"I will. Don't let Sandy get to you on the way home. Bye, babe."

Sandy waited while he stood beside the car, waving at the plane as it rose into the clouds. Spencer Chase was the most handsome and the sweetest man she'd ever known. Her serious attention however, was on someone else — someone cute and sweet, too. Maybe he wasn't as perfect as Spence, but he was more than able to steal her heart away. She smiled at the thought of Trenton Lillygrace.

Chapter 23
Test by Fire

"Ah, Mrs. Chase," Simone said. "This is my brother, Jonathan Essex. Jon, this is Jemmabeth Chase."

Jonathan Essex stood eye to eye with Jemma. He wore a black turtleneck like the one Spencer had on when she kissed him good-bye at the airport. She offered her hand and he acquiesced to shake it, to her relief, rather than kiss it. He had dimples; that was the second thing she noticed. He also had a great smile and black hair, like Simone, and eyes like two perfect turquoise stones.

"My sister has been relentless in her efforts to get us together. I must say things look good thus far," he said, raising an approving brow toward Simone.

Jemma smiled politely. "I have my portfolio. Would you like to see the prints or the slides?"

"Right to business, I see," Jonathan

quipped. "Let's move down to Simone's viewing room and see what you have, shall we?"

"I'll leave you to it then," Simone said. "Do give Spencer my best." She turned to a cluster of assistants who were waiting for her in the hallway. At least she didn't call him *Spence* this time.

Jonathan pressed the button on the elevator. "So, you're from cowboy country? I've never been to Texas. We've shipped pieces to Houston, I believe. Do you live near there?"

"No. I live at the top of the state. It's an area we call The Panhandle."

"Quaint. Here we are. After you, Jemmabeth." He touched her waist as they walked down another corridor. "Is Chase your maiden name?"

"No, my maiden name was Forrester."

He stopped. "I saw your work in Paris. You were the Girard Fellow, were you not?"

"I was. How nice of you to remember."

He opened the door to a room with a large screen and seats much nicer than the Parnell. "A Girard Fellow. Now I truly am excited to see what you've brought. Please, sit anywhere." He loaded the slides into the projector, then dimmed the lights and turned his turquoise eyes on her.

The images of her work flashed before them. Jemma relived each brushstroke. Jonathan didn't speak until the final piece was on the screen. It was of Grandma Hardy in the church pew.

"Exquisite, darling, simple perfection. You have such a way with eyes. I assume you have heard that before, but I am very impressed. You must show at my gallery. Is this your complete portfolio, or is there more? Don't hide anything from me, because I want it all."

"I have a few other pieces in our private collection, but they will not be offered under any circumstances. I learned that lesson the hard way. What time frame are you considering? If I have a few months, I'll have more pieces. I'm a prolific painter."

He studied her face. "Of course you are, darling. I am on holiday next week in Greece; then we are booked solid until the spring. I might be able to shift things around a bit. What would you say to an April date? Our showings are six weeks in duration and the gallery retains fifty percent of the sales."

"Fifty percent? How do you determine the pricing?"

"You set your price, and we double it. Fair?"

"Sure, if you can get it."

"We can. I assure you. Your work is splendid. Don't be shy about pricing it because it will be irresistible to our clientele." He stood close enough to make her uncomfortable.

Neither spoke for a few seconds. Jemma frowned at the carpet. He massaged his chin.

"Where are you staying tonight?" he asked. "I could ring you up later, and we can meet for drinks to discuss things further. Shall I?"

"I've forgotten the name of the hotel, and I don't drink anyway. I don't even know the name of your gallery."

Jonathan was nonplussed. "You don't drink? Curious trait. My gallery is known as The Lex, short for The Lexington, on Regent Street. Do you know it?"

"No, but I'm sure my grandfather does. He is an art connoisseur."

"Oh, and what is his name?"

"Robert Lillygrace. He owns several newspapers in the Midwest."

"That name does sound familiar, and is he a non-drinker as well?"

Jemma giggled at that. "No, I think he is also a connoisseur of fine wines."

"Perhaps we could meet regardless of the

devil's nectar, then. Say, nine-ish?"

She flushed at those familiar words. "Why don't you give me your number and I'll call you?"

"I'm in and out, best let me do the calling. Surely you have your hotel name written somewhere, darling."

"It's The Madison."

"Ah. So you were toying with me earlier."

She blushed, full-blown. "I don't like to give out personal information."

"I see. I'd like to keep the slides for a while, if you don't mind."

"That's fine. I have two sets."

"Until later, then, Jemma." He gave her an admiring glance, then turned back to the slides.

She took a cab to The Madison, staring blankly out the window. She hadn't been attracted to any man since Spencer walked up to Gram's door that summer after Paul. She wasn't attracted to Jonathan, but something nagged at her. Mention of the *devil's nectar* brought up her beginnings with Paul, and she hadn't been able to really look this guy in the eye to see if he was honest. She paid the driver and checked in to her room. Spencer had booked it for her. He had stayed there on his last trip to New York.

She kneeled beside her bed and prayed

for an angel to follow her around on this trip. What did happen with Jonathan? Rats. It had to be the devil, or maybe it was the turtleneck like Spence's. Not a single wrestling idea had come up during this meeting with Jonathan, and something about his eyes had gotten to her, too. There was no need to meet with him anymore on this trip. She sat on the couch and stared at the phone.

She picked it up and dialed the long-distance operator. The maid answered. "Lillygrace residence."

"Hi, Margaret, it's Jemmabeth. Is my grandfather there?"

"Certainly, Mrs. Chase. One moment."

Robert Lillygrace picked up the phone. "Jemmabeth, where are you?"

"I'm in New York City at The Madison Hotel. How are you and Grandmother?"

"Fine, fine. How's Spencer?"

"He's great. I need to know something, Grandfather."

"Of course. How can I help?"

"Are you familiar with a gallery in London called The Lexington?"

"The Lex? Oh yes. It's a fine gallery. Why do you ask?"

She exhaled. "I may have a show there next spring."

"What marvelous news, Jemmabeth! Catherine is out at the moment, but she will be thrilled to hear about this."

They visited for a while, and then said their good-byes. Jemma was getting a stomachache anyway. She would have to answer if he called. It meant a show in London. This was silly. She was not attracted to him.

She got out her New Testament and read some scriptures. Maybe this was her test by fire. What was the deal with Jonathan calling her "darling"? She was nobody's darling but Spence's. Of course Paul called her darlin' with every other breath, and he had the same black hair and devil eyes. A therapist would most likely have a name for this.

She took a shower and put on her cowboy pajamas that her mom had sent. Spencer would call before he went to bed. This would be a touchy matter to share with him. Double rats. She bit her lip and turned on the television. A knock at the door made her jump.

"Who is it?" she shouted from the couch.

"Jonathan Essex. I thought you might like some company, darling."

"No. I'm waiting for my husband to call me, I'm not feeling well, and I'm ready for bed."

"Which of those would hamper my visit?"

"All of them."

"Too bad. I was hoping we could talk about your work."

"Thanks anyway, but I am really looking forward to the show."

"As am I, but I do feel rather foolish talking through the door like this."

She picked up her New Testament and walked to the door.

"Good night, Jonathan," she said, her eye wide open at the peephole.

"You have such lovely, golden eyes, Jemma. I don't know what to make of it, but I am very much attracted to you."

"Oh." She stepped back.

"I sensed that the feeling was mutual."

"Well, you must have misinterpreted something, because I'm very much in love with my husband."

"I see. Are you certain that we couldn't just chat for a while? Go over some things about the show?"

"Like I said, I'm not feeling too hot. You can call me when I get home, though. My number is on all the slides."

"Very well." He stood for a moment, mumbled, "Feel better, Mrs. Chase," and left.

She returned to the couch with an overwhelming desire to talk to Spence. As she reached for the phone, it rang. "Spence!" she squealed into the mouthpiece.

"No, dear, it's your Grandmother Lillygrace. I wanted to offer my congratulations on your London show. What a wonderful opportunity."

"Thank you, Grandmother. It's sweet of you to call."

"Does Alexandra know yet?"

"She knows that I'm in New York to talk about it."

"I won't keep you, Jemmabeth, but we are very excited and proud of you. We shall not miss it, and we'll make certain your mother doesn't either."

"I'm sure Daddy would love to come, too."

"Well, of course. We'll make a party of it. Sweet dreams, dear."

"Good night, Grandmother."

"One more thing, Jemma. I would keep my eye on that gallery owner, Jonathan something-or-other. He's a notorious ladies' man, very nice-looking and smooth. That's an established fact around London. The last time Robert and I visited The Rex, he tried to seduce me. A friend of ours told us that Jonathan has specially made contact lenses from Germany, and he wears a different colored pair every day. Now, that's the devil's doings if you ask me. Good night, dear."

Jemma hung up the phone and burst into laughter. The idea of Catherine Lillygrace being hit on by Jonathan was too much. She wondered what color his eyes had been on that night. When Spencer called, she told him everything. It took him a minute to get over it, but, after all, he had his chance to come with her. She wasn't keeping anything from him ever again. Unless, perhaps, she got a speeding ticket. Fair's fair.

Spencer pulled onto the county road right as the sun came up. Papa's old windmill stood silhouetted against the horizon. He was pedaling right along until he came up behind a combine moving at about two miles an hour. He passed the combine at the wrong spot. Its big wheels splashed pothole mud directly in his face and on his slacks.

"All English art dealers are out to get my wife," Spencer said into the wind as he rode his bike toward town. He wiped his face and pedaled faster. A school bus splashed more mud, and the kids in the back seats stuck their tongues out at him. It would be the pits if he lost his license for a whole year. It served him right, speeding and endangering lives.

At least he could be home more with her, and that part delighted him. What if someday a guy put a move on her and she liked it? No, that could never happen. Jemmabeth was true blue since Cowboy Paul. He and Paul were like characters in an old novel, both in love with the same woman. He hoped the day would come when he didn't worry about the cowboy and his past with Jem. She hadn't told him all the details of their relationship, but maybe that was for the best. If he knew them, he might not feel halfway sorry for the guy. Skinny Jack passed him, too, honking and laughing. The pits.

Lester and the ladies were enjoying midmorning coffee and conversation, but Lester had something on his mind. "Roy Bob Sisk told me he saw Spencer riding his bicycle into town early this morning. He said he looked like the old schoolteacher in that Judy Garland rainbow movie. Roy Bob swears that Spencer had been in a mud-wrestling match. I just don't think that boy should have to ride a bike like a young'un for a whole cotton-pickin' year."

"I suppose the law must be equal for

everyone," Helene said. "Perhaps the judge will be lenient. You know, in Germany, the autobahn has no speed limit. Drivers may go as fast as their cars will take them. My Nebs frightened the wits out of me every time we went there."

Lester smoothed his moustache. "Looks like the judge could take into consideration that Spencer was in that war and got shot down. It just don't seem right, but far be it from me to tell a judge what to do. Maybe if Judge McFarland was in charge, he'd have mercy on such a fine young man. One of them tickets Spencer got was in Los Angeleez. I didn't know they even had any laws in that town."

"Jemmabeth thinks this will change Spencer's bad habit of speeding. We surely don't want him to wind up having a wreck," Lizbeth said.

"Well, sir, the more I think about it, I should help that boy out." Lester tapped his foot relentlessly while the women exchanged glances.

Lizbeth proceeded with caution. "No one is stopping you, Lester, but we are curious as to what you have in mind."

"You'll see. I ain't tellin' until I get my thoughts collected."

"I admire a man who acts on his convictions. Bully for you, Lester." Helene raised her teacup in his direction.

Lizbeth raised her brow.

"So, did you miss me?" Jemma asked, sitting on Spencer's desk, blowing bubbles with her gum.

"Nah. I think it's good for us to be apart. It refreshes the senses," he answered, concentrating on his slide rule.

"Really? Which sense is that?" She poked at his leg with her foot. "Good grief, your pants look like you've been playing football in them."

He sighed. "I'm going to have to wear old clothes into town and change when I get here. These slacks are ruined."

"Which senses are refreshed when I leave?" She popped a big bubble.

"My common sense. I consistently send you off into the arms of other men. That has to change because it's driving me nuts."

She grinned. "Very good answer. I wasn't sure where you were going with that." She moved to his lap. "Are there any senses that need refreshing now that I'm home?"

He dropped his pencil and turned his full attention on his wife until Sandy knocked on the door.

"Hello in there. Anybody want to go with

us to Son's?" she asked.

Jemma and Spencer separated. "No ma'am, we're heading home right now." He smiled at his wife.

"Thanks anyway," Jemma said. "Ya'll have fun."

Sandy and Trent left. He had his arm around her.

Jemma watched them get in his car. "I think it's a done deal. What do you think?"

"I think I'll lock this door and drag you back into my office," Spencer said.

"No dragging required, mister."

Lester had his plan. He wrote it all out and got Paralee to type it up for him. She swore to secrecy and made him several carbon copies, too. The easy way would be to leave them around town at the barbershop and Nedra's, but he was going to do this thing right. He was going door-to-door and pledging folks to secrecy. He should be done by Christmas.

Carrie and Philip sat in The Judge's study. Carrie winked at her husband while The Judge rummaged through his desk. "I'm very pleased that you're going to be living in Chillaton. I want you to know that," The Judge said.

464

"Well, that's good to hear, Dad. What kind of father would you be if you weren't happy to have us here?" Carrie hadn't lost any of her sassiness since she'd left home. "It looks like you've lost weight. We need to get you some new slacks because those could fall down anytime, and what would happen in the courtroom then?"

The Judge looked up at such talk. Nobody spoke back to him like that. At least not in his chambers. "Yes, well, I have been cutting back on a few things. I hope we'll be seeing quite a lot of one another, so you might like to have an extra key to the house. Eleanor has one, but I know that there is one in here somewhere. Ah, here it is."

Philip took the key and examined it. "It's too bad that you were burglarized last month. Maybe it's time you invested in an upgraded security system. Not many people use skeleton keys anymore."

"I'm well aware of that, Philip. Fortunately, the thief didn't get far with the silver. He probably thought a more prosperous man than myself lived here."

"We've thought it over about your offer to move in here, sir, and . . ."

Carrie finished Philip's sentence for him. "We need our own place, Dad. It'll be important for Phil to be right at the nursing home to keep it running smoothly."

The Judge shifted his bulk in the chair. "I hardly think a two-minute drive would impede such a goal."

Carrie smiled. "We'll see. It might work out later. We may get tired of living and working at the same place."

"You're afraid I'll try to run the show around here, aren't you?"

Philip glanced at his wife. "It's nothing like that, sir. We're still sort of newlyweds, you know. We like being alone."

Carrie rallied. "I think your assessment is right on target, Dad. Let's be honest. You've lived here forever, and I was cooped up in this house for longer than I should have been. I love you, but I don't want to live here anymore. We'll see you a lot. It'll be okay."

The room was quiet; then The Judge pushed back from his chair. "I guess that settles that. I've given Eleanor the evening off. I'm hoping you'll join me at this new restaurant we have in town — Son's Money, I believe it's called."

Carrie laughed. "Correction — *Daddy's Money*. Are you sure you want to eat out? In my whole life, I don't remember ever eating out with you until our wedding reception."

"You may be surprised at your old dad, young lady. I'm out to show you two that there's life in this old boy yet. If Max can stop chasing skirts, I can change my ways, too. Max Chase and I are old poker buddies, Philip. Maybe you'd like to join us sometime."

The two men considered that unexpected offer for a moment. Carrie, not exactly sure what to make of this newfound friendliness in her father, maneuvered her walker between them and down the ramp to their van. She looked around at her father's grand old home. It was a sorry sight. Maybe together, the three of them could resuscitate it. After all, it had seen very little joy in the past twenty years. It was time for a change.

"Ver gonna haf to make ush a big cawendar, Shhpence."

"What did you say?"

She took the paintbrush out of her mouth and repeated it. "I can't keep up with your projects, and I feel like I'm the last one to know your schedule. Our life is all chopped up into puzzle pieces, so maybe a big planning calendar might help."

He nodded. "Part of it is that I have to depend on everybody else to get me around. You know what I need? A helicopter. I could fly us to every business meeting, with refueling stops, of course. This is a great idea, baby, because I can go places with you. What do you think?"

Jemma had stepped back from her painting to check it out. She looked at him like a scolding mother in church. "Oh great. You get your license taken away for going 90 miles an hour on a dumb motorcycle, then you tell me you want to park a helicopter outside our door so you can be a pilot again and worry me to death that you'll crash somewhere. Where would you park it in town? On the football field?"

"Listen, Jem, this is not all that crazy. If I had a chopper, we could quit messing around with airports and travel arrangements."

"How much does a helicopter cost anyway?"

"I don't know. A couple hundred thousand, maybe more."

She dropped her brush.

"Of course one that size wouldn't have a very wide flight range. Maybe three hours. We could get to Dallas."

"What for?"

"Okay. Forget that idea. I'm stuck with the bicycle and the kindness of friends and family. I need to just shut up and take my medicine."

"Good. No more transportation creativity. Get to work. Rats. I forgot to call Robby. His flight gets in at eight o'clock. We'll need to leave about six thirty. I'll set the timer on the oven."

"If I had a chopper, we could be there in twenty minutes."

"If you had a driver's license, you could pick him up yourself, and I could finish this piece."

"Speaking of licenses, they passed a new law, and Phil is going to have to pass a nursing home administrator's exam. Hopefully, we'll have the state inspection done about the same time." He watched her as she retouched an area on the canvas. The light that was so perfect for her work was also dancing in her hair. It bounced off cascades of dark auburn and gold, transforming her into a princess like those from the fairy-tale books Harriet had read him when he was a little boy.

She wiped some paint from her hand onto her jeans and turned to him. "What did you say?" Her pouty lips spread into a big smile.

"I said that I love you, Jemmabeth Alexandra Chase. Step into my office, and I'll explain my project dates to you." She walked across the room and kissed him.

■ ■ ■ ■

Lizbeth sat in the porch swing, moving it slightly. The air was full of early winter, and she was beginning her mental Christmas list. How much fun it was to share her home with Helene. Everything was lighter and happier, especially during Robby's visit. He had kept them laughing and hopping with his ideas. Robby was the image of her Luke. Lester loved that boy, as did Spencer. Spence was going to be a special father someday. Her constant prayer was that the Lord's plan could include her granddaughter bearing a child, if and when He was ready.

She clutched her sweater around her and considered the day ahead. Turkey and all the trimmings for thirteen people — fourteen if Judge McFarland decided to join them. Everything was easy, though. That was another bonus that came with Helene. She was a gourmet cook, but not pushy in the kitchen. She couldn't be; there wasn't enough room. All that was left to be done was bringing in the box of Helene's beautiful china dishes from Lester's shed. It would be a pleasure just to wash them. She stretched her arms and went inside. Only the presence of all her own menfolk could have made this Thanksgiving Day more than it promised to be.

Robby had taken over Plum Creek. For a twelve-year-old, he could certainly rule the roost, but it was a hilarious monarchy, partially due to the fact that his voice was changing. He had also lost his Texas accent, which made him seem somewhat like a different kid to them.

All was bright and shiny fun until Spencer rode his bike into town and Jemma was alone with Robby. She painted while he tried his hand at sketching on Spence's big table. She caught him staring at her, but then he shifted his gaze to the window.

"Jem, I need to ask you something."

"That's what I do best — answer hard questions." It sounded good at the time.

"Is the Bible against smoking?" he mumbled.

Oh great, a growing-up question. Rats. "Do you mean smoking a ham or a turkey?"

"I mean cigarettes."

"I think the Lord wants us to use the brains He gave us and take care of ourselves." Good one.

"Yeah, I know all that, but does it say in there somewhere not to smoke?"

She bit her lip. What happened to the cute

little brother who wanted to buy a monkey? She could ruin his life with her answer. If she were walking right with God, He might drop a scripture into her brain right now. She stalled. "You tell me what's going on; then I'll tell you if I know what the Lord had to say about it."

Robby lowered his head. "When I get home, some of the guys are going to go to Kenny Hall's basement and smoke a pack of his big brother's cigarettes. I told them God wouldn't like it, but they said prove it."

The only scripture that popped into her head was the one about gold. She had no idea how to use it. "In the first book of Corinthians it says that everything we do will be tested by fire to see if what we did was good. So that means if you smoke, you stink, and if you stink, God's not happy." She kept her eyes right on his to add some credibility, hoping the Lord would approve of this translation to help out a woman trying to do the right thing.

"Cool. You're sure that's what it says?"

"I said that's what it means." She blew out her breath and picked up her paintbrush.

"Jem, how do you think a cigarette tastes?"

"I wouldn't know, Robby, but I guess it

would taste like smoke."

"What do you think a real gold nugget tastes like?" he asked, playing with the chain on his gold cross necklace.

She gave that some thought. "Probably all metal tastes bitter, but nobody cares what it tastes like. We like it because it's beautiful."

"Typical girl answer. I care what it tastes like. I bet the real thing tastes sweeter than fool's gold. Ricky Bates brought some fool's gold to church camp, and we busted it with a hammer. That was cool. I even tasted it."

"Do Daddy and Mom know about this smoking party?"

"No, and if they find out, I'll know who told them."

"You're getting a little smarty pants with me, sir."

"I'll be thirteen on my birthday." Robby shrugged and turned his attention back to his drafting project. "Right now, I'm still called a tweenager."

Jemma returned to her painting, grateful that she didn't have a tweenager to figure out on a daily basis.

Robby returned to his drawings for Shorty's jar. Even Shorty would probably notice a decided difference in the quality and the subject matter — race cars.

■ ■ ■ ■

Lizbeth invited them to stop by for lunch on the way to the airport.

"Do you ever shut up, Robby?" Jemma asked as they reached the city limits. "If I didn't love you so much, I think I would put tape over your mouth at least once a day."

"I only speak pearls of wisdom," he said, straight-faced.

Spencer grinned. "Well, that's a matter of opinion. If you talk this much at Gram's house, Lester won't be able to get a word in sideways."

"I'll let the old boy talk. He's one of my heroes. He's got style."

Jemma smiled as she turned into their driveway. Lester would love to know that last bit of information. True to his word, Robby only talked half the time, swapping antics and moneymaking schemes with Lester. Everyone laughed and looked forward to Christmas vacation when they could all be together again. Jemma watched her brother; he was no longer the mischievous wart who teased her by reading her diary or the stinker who sold tickets to his friends to watch her sunbathe. Someday soon, he wouldn't consider the taste of gold anymore, but he would buy it for some special girl because it was beautiful. Rats.

Chapter 24
The Kindest Thing

Shy had Christmas lights strung on his blue spruce. Jemma waved at him as she waited for Spencer. The idea hit her hard. She ran into his office.

"I'm nearly done, baby. I promise," he said with a pencil tucked behind his ear and his attention on a blueprint.

"I have an idea."

"I don't think the quilting ladies can fill any more orders. Aren't they working overtime as it is?"

"This is not about quilts. It's about teeth. I want to get Shy some teeth."

Spencer stopped working and grinned at her. "You just kill me, Jem. Let's do it."

"I'll talk to him first. That's probably a wise move, but surely he'll like the idea," she said, then was out the door before he could agree.

Jemma caught up with Shy as he was leaving the hardware store and shocked him with her plan.

He swallowed to get shed of the big lump in his throat. "I ain't sure what to say, Jemmerbeth. I don't rightly know how to turn down such a offer, though. What would I do with a full set of choppers? I might have to change my eatin' habits."

"Then I can do it? Thank you, Shy. I'll get everything set up and let you know."

Shy was stumped. He sat in his truck considering the possibilities of having teeth. Imagine her thinking of such a thing. He looked in his rearview mirror and moved his lips apart. It would be nice to eat corn on the cob again and maybe some storebought peanut brittle like he'd seen at the five-and-dime. It'd be a fine thing, too, if one of the front ones was gold. Might improve the taste of his cooking somewhat. That child sure was a lot like her grandpa. It was Cam Forrester that gave him the money for his tools to get started in the fix-it business. If Spencer and Jemmerbeth ever needed anything fixed, he'd do it for free until the day he passed, that was for certain sure.

Willa and Joe held hands as they walked across the tracks to Lizbeth's house. Each carried a grocery sack with pans of Willa's cobbler in them. Joe stopped just as they got to the alley. "Lovey, I don't know why the Lord has blessed me like He has, but I want to tell you how much you mean to me. I think about my ol' lonesome life sometimes, and it gives me the shivers to think that you were sittin' right here in Chillaton all them times I drove my rig through here. I just wish we could've been together all them years."

She patted his arm. "Could be the Lord knew that I'd have to touch Sam's grave marker across the ocean before I could let him go and tuck them memories away in a corner of this ol' heart. Now I got all this room for lovin' you, Joe Cross. Bend down here and give me a kiss. No disrespect to Trina's daddy, but you're the best kisser I ever laid a lip on." They set the sacks on the frozen ground and spent a few extra minutes behind Lizbeth's garage before joining the Christmas festivities that lit up her house with food, laughter, music, and love.

Spencer and Trent spent hours at their office with Arthur. There were numerous details to wrap up before construction began in January. Sandy was there every time they were, taking notes and smiling at

Trent. When they joined everyone else at Lizbeth's, he introduced her to his dad and his Lillygrace grandparents as his girlfriend. Sandy was not exactly what Robert and Catherine had in mind for their grandson.

"Do you have plans for furthering your education, dear?" Catherine asked.

"I'm thinking of taking some classes at Amarillo Junior College to learn more about computers. The guys want me to bone up on that stuff."

"Oh, I see, and what does your father do?"

"He owns Household Supply. They sell furniture, flooring, and appliances."

"A businessman. That's good," Robert said. "Are you and our Trenton 'serious,' as they say?"

Sandy actually blushed, something Jemma had never seen her do. "You'll have to ask your grandson about that," she said and excused herself to say hello to Carrie.

"Jemma, come and sit by me. We need to talk," Julia said. "The quilts went like hotcakes and honey during the holidays. My idea now is to add some baby quilts and wedding ring patterns. Those will sell during the spring. Of course, babies come all year round, so that should become a staple. How are your business partners holding up?"

"Amazingly well. They had a meeting last week to talk about expanding to a real location. You know Spence and I bought some land just down the tracks. They even named their business — *Stitchers*. There was some hot debate about the name, but I like it. To me, it's a metaphor for stitching hope back into their neighborhood. Corny, huh?"

"Not at all. How's Spencer taking this speeding ticket business? Lizbeth told me that he could lose his license for a year. That has to hurt a busy man like him."

"It does hurt, but he's willing to take it. His court date is next week. He's so sweet. I'll never get used to being his wife, Do Dah. Sometimes I feel like I'm going to pop with happiness."

Julia patted her hand and looked across the room at Arthur. He puffed on his pipe and laughed at a joke that Max Chase was telling. She knew about popping with happiness; it could last a long, long time.

"Lester, where have you been? Joe's been itching to get started. Willa's been leading the Christmas carols a cappella," Lizbeth scolded.

"I had me some business to take care of, but I'm set to entertain now. If I could just have a cup of coffee to warm up and maybe a piece of your pecan pie, Miz Liz."

Lizbeth cut him a healthy piece and set a steaming cup of coffee in front of him, then put her hands on her hips and gave him a good stare. "What's going on? I know you too well. Out with it."

Lester's eyes darted up at her. Her lips were puckered.

"I'd like to keep it kindly quiet, Miz Liz. If you'll step out to the porch with me, I'll let you in on it."

Lizbeth stepped briskly to the screened-in porch ahead of him.

"Well, sir, it's about my idea to help Spencer out when he goes before the judge in Amarillo," Lester said. "I reckon I've been in every house in Chillaton since September. I feel like one of them traveling salesmen."

"Lester, what have you done?"

He drew a sheet of paper out of his jacket and offered it to her. "If you're of a mind to sign this, Miz Liz, you'll be number 2,035 to sign a petition that I'm sending to the judge before he makes up his mind about Spencer's license."

Lizbeth read the petition then scanned the signatures until her glasses fogged over. She put her arms around him, without asking. He stood perfectly still and held his breath. She pulled away and wiped her cheek. "You are a dear, dear man, Lester Timms. Get me a pen."

"How on earth did you keep a whole town quiet about something like that?" Jemma asked, blowing her nose. "I can't believe that nobody has said a word to us. Nedra and Paralee must be about to explode."

"Folks got a lot of respect for Spencer. I didn't hear nothin' bad from nobody except Skinny Jack and his pa. I didn't even ask them to sign, but they was at Pinky's house when I stopped by. I did get a nip on the leg from Pop Whatley's mutt. Bernie Miller put out a page for me at the Dew Drop Inn, too."

"You are certainly to be commended, Lester," Helene said. "This project exemplifies the American spirit."

"Well, sir, if I'd had me a son, I couldn't have done any better than that boy. Things ain't always been good for him, even if he does come from money. Gettin' chased by a few pooch hounds and having to eat some odd vittles for manners' sake was nothin' if it'll help him out."

Spencer sat at his desk. It felt about ten times too big for him. Lester and Jemma had left only minutes earlier, bringing the petitions by before Lester mailed them, and it had hit him hard. Spencer could only manage to hang on to Lester with a tearful, long embrace. Everyone in the office was crying.

It was the kindest thing anybody had done in recent Chillaton memory. It wasn't like Spencer had a deadly disease and needed a kidney or that sort of thing, but he was the grandson of a state senator and the son of a reformed skirt chaser and a recovering alcoholic. He'd gone to war without pulling strings, and he'd brought his business back to his hometown. He was their golden boy, and folks were happy to do what they could. Now it was up to some bigshot judge.

The ribbon cutting for The Kenneth Rippetoe House was on a freezing cold Saturday morning. The license from the state board had come in the mail the day before, but they were still waiting to hear if Philip passed his administrator's exam. They had the ceremony inside. Jemma recited the Emily Dickinson poem that she'd read over the P.A. system when she was in junior high and Kenneth was in elementary school. She only choked up once, at the part about not living in vain. It was engraved on marble plaques, too, in the garden and above the doorway.

They served chocolate cake, Kenneth's favorite. Jemma had eaten his mother's version only weeks before she and her son were killed in a tornado that ripped their old trailer house in two. Now his dream could begin, though, and Philip was determined to make this the best home for the elderly in the state. Spencer and Jemma had done their part by donating this spacious, gleaming facility.

The day of reckoning was upon Spencer.

"Good luck, son," Lester said. "We all know your speedin' days are behind you, and to my way of thinkin', California should've kept them tickets in Los Angeleez."

"Thank you, Lester, for everything. I still don't know what else to say."

"It was my pleasure. I just hope it helps a little."

They got to the courthouse an hour early. Spencer was quiet as Jemma held his hand in the hallway. The doors opened and all the accused filed in. Spencer's name was one of the first on the list.

"Spencer Morgan Chase, how do you plead?"

He cleared his throat. "Guilty, sir."

"Mr. Chase, I have before me one of the

most unusual situations I've encountered in my term. Are you aware that the bulk of the citizens of Chillaton have signed a petition to ask the court to reduce the terms of the forfeiture of your license?"

"Yes, sir, I am."

"I also received a very touching letter from a Mr. Timms explaining that you had no knowledge of this petition being circulated."

"That's correct, sir." He sounded more like a soldier now.

The judge leafed through the petition, then looked at Spencer over the top of his glasses. Jemma wondered if that was a requirement for being a judge. Carrie's father had given Jemma a similar look right before he fired her.

"So you were missing in action, Mr. Chase. Where was that?"

"Just south of the DMZ, sir."

The judge nodded. "Mr. Chase, I'm going to have to ask you to forfeit your license for one year, as required by law." Jemma flinched, but Spencer stood arrow-straight. "However, I'm going to suspend six months of that forfeiture. You will also be given credit for the four months you've been in compliance. That means you have two months left from this date before your license will be reinstated."

Spencer nodded. "Thank you, sir."

"Don't let me see you in here again, son."

"Sir, you won't."

Jemma grinned at him and he grinned back, squeezing her hand. They went to eat at Cattlemen's restaurant atop the Golden Spread building.

"I owe it all to Lester," Spencer said. "Bless his heart. What a good man he is, sort of like Papa."

"That's true, but you'd better not get another ticket."

"Can you imagine? Never again. I'm a changed man."

"That's what Flavil Capp said, too." She clicked her tongue, then smiled.

Helene had kept her red MG roadster in Lester's garage, but lately, she'd been taking it to the post office and out for spins around the county. Lizbeth wasn't nearly as prone to riding in the cold air like Lester was. He loved bundling up and zipping along the Farm to Market Road with the Englishwoman. He liked everything about her and wished that she'd let him bring her mail to her like Lizbeth did.

Jemma had fired up the heater in the car house once again so she could paint on those days that Spencer had to be at his office. She had added six more pieces to her portfolio for the London show. Jonathan Essex communicated only through his secretary, but everything was on schedule for April. The show would open on her birthday.

Helene knocked on the car house door. "Care for a break, dear?" she asked, nodding at Jemma's progress.

"What do you have in mind?"

"I was thinking of driving out to the river. We shan't be but a few minutes. I want to snap a few wintry photographs."

"Sure. Just let me clean up."

"I'll be in the car."

Jemma liked to watch Helene operate. She had such perfect posture and composure, but her eyes twinkled in such a way that Jemma knew she was a corker in her youth.

Jemma directed Helene to a place she and Spencer knew very well. It was their special stargazing spot. Helene took several photos with her old-fashioned camera.

"Dear, would you please look in the glove compartment and bring me another roll of film?" she called out from the little cliff that overlooked the Salt Fork of the Red River.

Jemma opened it and found the film. She

also found something else. A letter from Paul.

After a week passed, Jemma still didn't know what to do about her discovery. It wasn't clear if this was something to worry Spencer about or not, but she couldn't let it go. Rats. This could be another test of fire like in Corinthians, but she had to ask Helene.

So they met at Daddy's Money.

Helene's hearing aid screeched as she adjusted it. "How nice to have lunch with you, dear. I do like the country ambiance at this restaurant."

"Yes ma'am. It's country all right." Jemma stirred her Dr Pepper with a straw. "Helene, I need to know why you have a letter from Paul in your car."

It was the first time Jemma had ever seen Helene rattled.

"Oh my. I suppose I should have told you about my correspondence with him."

"Maybe so."

"You see, dearest, I went to Paul before I moved here and pleaded with him to stop harassing you. He touched my heart, that's all I can say. Truly. I agreed to let him know, now and again, how you are getting on. I consider it to be no more than a small kindness on my part, but I must have left one of his responses in the MG. I am so sorry."

"So he writes you back. I can't believe that."

"Yes, dear, he does. Such a pitiful fellow and so passionate about you."

"Don't you feel weird doing this? I mean, I appreciate your point of view, but it just seems like you're on his side or something."

"No, no. Not at all, Jemma. I think Paul is a man who needs a mother figure, of sorts, and I'm just trying to help him see his life in a different way. You and Spencer are like family to me. Paul is but an incomplete man."

Jemma lowered her eyes. She had never heard it put quite in those terms. "That's not my problem, though."

"Most assuredly not. Would you care to read the letter? I don't mind."

She would be like the fool's gold in Brother Cleo's sermon if she said yes, plus she'd have to tell Spencer. That wouldn't be good. "No, thank you," she said, but her spirits were dampened by Helene's choice of words.

Helene drove back to Lizbeth's. Jemma returned to the car house, but Helene remained in the MG and opened the glove compartment. She read it again.

February 1, 1972

Dear Helene,

Thanks for your letter. I'm glad you are enjoying living with Mrs. Forrester. She seemed like a real sweet lady. I've been busy here. My father has turned more of his caseload over to me. I think he'll retire soon.

I read in the Dallas paper that Jem will be having a show in London this spring. I know she's always wanted one, and I'm sure it will be a hit. What is she painting now? I'd like to add more of her work to my collection, but it seems to make her even madder at me when I do.

I'm thinking of buying another place with more room for horses, and maybe invest in some cattle. The airport authority for the new Dallas airport is buying up everything around here. My own family sold a prime section to them, and I represent several of the other land owners myself, so, you can see that the airport is certainly helping my bank account. This area is going to boom when they get that thing built.

I hope Jemma is well and happy.

Maybe I'll run over to London when she has her show, but I won't bother her. I'd just like to see her face and maybe hear her laugh. Thanks for all your advice.

                        Best wishes,
                        Paul

Helene sighed. She had nothing but good intentions with this postal relationship. However, it certainly was not worth the look she'd seen on Jemma's face at lunch, nor the worry that she herself was enduring over his potential attendance at the London show.

"Happy Valentine's Day, baby," Spencer said, bringing her breakfast in bed.

Jemma sat up, giggling at her husband and his red swimming shorts and angel wings. "Where on earth did you get those?"

"I grew them just for you."

"Did you stop at one of those tacky shops in Amarillo?"

"No way. Sandy borrowed them from her niece. She was an angel in the Christmas pageant." He sat on the bed beside her and flapped his wings with a little yarn pulley.

She laughed and set the breakfast aside. "Well, Cupid, what else can you do?"

"I thought you'd never ask."

■ ■ ■ ■

Willa had been thinking for weeks about the best way to approach Helene about her salvation. If she was going to live in Chillaton, she should be in church, and not just in the pew, but also in the Lord's fold. Lizbeth agreed, but she was a more patient woman than Willa.

"Miz Helene, I might as well not beat around the bush about it. The time has come for you to choose the Lord," Willa said, sitting across the kitchenette one morning.

"I know, Willa. I have that on my agenda."

"On your what? The Lord don't show up on no agenda. You could get yourself killed drivin' around the county, then where would your *agenda* be, then? Hush puppies. Nobody never said such a thing around here."

"Perhaps I used the wrong term. I realize I have some decisions to make in that area, but I'd like to speak with a minister first."

"Brother Cleo will speak with you. He'll be here tomorrow."

"That would be nice, but I prefer to talk with Reverend Hightower."

Willa turned to Lizbeth, whose startled

look spoke for them both, but Willa couldn't keep quiet. "Well, I never. Who knew that on top of bein' unchurched, you was one of them racists? I'd best be goin', Miz Liz, before I say somethin' I can't take back."

Helene laughed out loud. "Heavens, Willa, it has nothing to do whatsoever with Brother Cleo being a black man. He's a fine orator and completely worthy to be my spiritual counselor. I'm surprised you would think such a thing. The whole of it is that I have this ghastly fear of drowning, and I know your church submerses new recruits. I want to see if this Reverend Hightower follows the same policy."

The room was quiet when she finished. Then Willa let loose with one of her belly laughs, and Lizbeth followed. "Whew, you had me gettin' hot there for a minute," Willa said and gave Helene a bear hug.

On the first day of spring, Helene Baldwin Neblitt was accepted into the Chillaton Presbyterian Church, the church of Spencer's grandfather. Her infant baptism sufficed in their eyes, and a righteous celebration was held at Spencer and Jemmabeth's. Trina and Nick drove down from Amarillo to eat cobbler and homemade ice cream on the deck. Plum Creek babbled along as they visited.

"I need to talk business before you go to London," Trina said. "Do you think anybody in Stitchers could make some dresses for me?"

"They're good with straight seams on the machines, but I'm not sure any of them are ready for dressmaking. Maybe after a year or so. Why?"

"A boutique in Amarillo likes my designs and is willing to let me put some on consignment. If they sell, I may need some help."

"That's great! You should talk to Sandy. She makes almost all of her own clothes, and she won the state Sew It with Wool contest in high school. Show me the designs you're going to use."

"Only if you give me a preview of your London show."

"I have photos, but the paintings are gone. We shipped them two weeks ago."

"Is Spence going with you?"

"Yup. He wants to check out the guy who put some moves on my grandmother Lillygrace and me. It's going to be a blast."

They were dancing to "Only the Lonely" when Twila called to ask if they could watch Sweetybeth while she and Buddy went to the movies. Jemma would have graciously declined, but Spencer said they would be happy to help out. He told Jemma that it would be fun to play Mommy and Daddy for the evening.

He was not quite as enthusiastic thirty minutes later as Sweetybeth screamed her lungs out. Her reddish hair and complexion made her look like an angry rosebud, and the two of them scrambled through the mountain of stuff that came with her to try and figure out how to make her happy. Nothing worked. Jemma changed her diaper, offered a warm bottle of milk, sang, and rocked her. She wailed on. Spencer played his guitar, made silly noises and faces, all to no avail.

As a last resort, they packed everything up and drove around in the Corvette. It worked; she fell asleep with her pacifier hanging limply from the corner of her mouth.

They circled The Parnell until Buddy B and Twila came out, laughing and holding hands. Spencer honked at them and woke up Sweetybeth, who sucked cheerfully on her pacifier as though nothing else had happened.

"Oh my precious, you look just like your daddy," Twila said as she took her from

Jemma. "She's cutting teeth, but you'd never know it. Yes, yes, honeybunches, how's my Sweetybeth?" she cooed to her daughter. "Did you hear the news? Missy got a contract to be a Breck Shampoo Girl. Somebody from that company saw her on the Miss Texas pageant. She'll be in magazine ads this summer. Mr. Blake has a big poster about it in the lobby of The Parnell."

Jemma sighed. "Good for her. She's very proud of her hair, and it's beautiful."

There was a hush as the rest of the group absorbed that comment.

"Look at that — our Sweetybeth's grinning at you two. Now you've done it. She's gonna want to spend every Saturday night with y'all," Buddy B said.

Spencer and Jemma exchanged alarmed glances. "We need to get home. We'll see y'all around," Spencer said and revved up the Corvette like he was going to peel out. He didn't, but it crossed his mind.

"Spence, do you think Shorty Knox knows that it was you who gave him a television?" Jemma asked as they enjoyed the quiet drive home.

"What on earth brought that up?"

"Shorty has a smile like Sweetybeth. I just want him to know, that's all. Maybe he thinks we never thanked him for saving my paintings from the tornado. Do you think he's made that association?"

"He knows, Jem. I taped a photo of some of the paintings to the TV screen. He made the association, I'm sure of it."

She reached for his hand. He and Shorty were both heroes to her. One slightly more than the other.

Chapter 25
Heartfelt Visions

The Suburban was packed and ready for Lester and the ladies to drop them off at the airport for their flight to London. Trina had made four new outfits for Jemma and had completely revamped her wardrobe after a shopping spree in Amarillo. Now there was even a special section of Jemma's closet reserved for visits to the Chase castle. She picked through it for the third time.

Spencer slipped his arms around her waist and waited. "Remember, these all have Trina's stamp of approval. You just close your eyes and grab something. It'll be perfect because it'll be on you."

She closed her eyes and put one hand on his and the other she held blindly out and took a hanger off the rack.

"Now, that wasn't difficult, was it?" He pulled his turtleneck over his head.

"That's easy for you to say. All you have to do is choose between turtleneck colors."

She gave him The Look that he loved.

"Don't start something that we don't have time for, Mrs. Chase."

"Zip me up, will you?" She held her hair up and turned her back to him.

"Oh no you don't. You can reach that zipper all by yourself. I'll go back the car out."

"Rats," she muttered. It was no use to buy time. She might as well get it over with. Maybe Rebecca would be in another good mood tonight.

"Hello, you two sweethearts," Harriet said as she answered the door. "Don't you look pretty, Jemma, my girl."

Rebecca greeted them in the study. "We're having your favorite, tonight, Spencer — chateaubriand, hearts of artichoke and tomato salad, and cheese soufflé. Hello, Jemmabeth." Rebecca was one of those Texans who had trained herself to say *tomahto.*

Max gave Jemma a wink. She wanted to say something like, "How funny, we just had that last night," but she didn't. Spencer nudged her toward his mother. Jemma bent down to Rebecca's chair and gave her a peck on the cheek.

"So you lovebirds are flying the coop tomorrow, huh?" Max asked.

"You bet," Spencer said. "We've waited a long time for London. Jem has added several new pieces to the show that the gallery hasn't seen yet, and they are outstanding."

"We really should have Jemma do our portrait, Max. We keep putting it off and I don't know why." Rebecca set her glass of V-8 juice on the coffee table. "I'm sure you will enjoy London this time of the year. I know we will."

Jemma's eyes widened as she turned to Spencer.

"What do you mean by that, Mother?" he asked.

"I mean that your father and I are going over for the show." Rebecca drew herself up in triumphant glory for taking them totally off guard.

Max stood and took his wife's hand. "Some shocker, huh? Becky cooked this idea up all by herself, but I have to say I'm looking forward to it. Let's eat, folks."

"When are you leaving?" Spencer asked.

"Day after tomorrow, of course; we don't want to miss the grand opening." Rebecca nodded sweetly at Jemma, whose eyes were the size of a plump artichoke heart.

Supper was surprisingly pleasant. Rebecca talked to Jemma more than she'd ever bothered before. Jemma figured that some therapist had earned his pay to turn her around like this.

"Jemmabeth, I'd like you to see the art that we inherited from Spencer's grandparents," Rebecca said. "Come with me, please."

Jemma shrugged at Spencer, then followed her mother-in-law up the stairs.

Max put his hand on Spencer's shoulder. "Don't worry, son. We won't be barging in on Jemma's spotlight. I know how much this show means to her."

"That's fine, Dad. I'm just surprised that Mother wants to attend."

"Your mother's a decent woman. If there's any fault to be laid concerning her personality, well, that probably rests squarely with me. At least that's what I've been told."

Spencer put his arms around his father. "I love you, Dad, and I respect you for saying that."

Max couldn't speak but sniffed and blew his nose. "I almost had us a whopper of a land deal last week. It's probably just as well that I got outbid. We would've looked like Panhandle land barons or something."

"What deal was that?"

"Spence, you need to get out of that office

more. Old Marvin Jacks put the Lazy J up for bids right after Christmas. Some cowboy lawyer from Dallas made the winning offer. He got himself one good chunk of dirt, too. That place is spread out over three counties. 'Course it'll take a good while to iron out all the details. Marv's a tough man to deal with when it comes to a dollar . . . what's wrong, son? You look like you just saw a ghost."

Spencer puffed out his cheeks and exhaled. "I sure hope not, Dad, believe me." He sat on the couch and stared at the floor while Max talked about the price of cattle.

Lester loaded the batch of critter coffins in his pickup for the delivery trip to Amarillo. He'd made a fair amount of money on this adventure, but nothing to brag about. He'd kept good books on the business, too. Right down to the postal stamps. The government was charging way too much for stamps these days. If a feller had to buy more than a couple, he could ruin a good quarter doing it. Besides, he'd never figured on this being such a solemn business. After all, the deceased was only critters. Now he understood why the Boxwright Brothers had them sour faces. Maybe the time had come for him to make fewer coffins and more hope chests.

He could make a special one for Helene. That thought put a grin on Lester's face. He took his time detailing it and presented it to her with a big red bow on top, just as Lizbeth entered the room.

"Why, Lester, this is lovely. Whatever is it?" Helene asked.

"Folks around here call it a hope chest. Young ladies come hence to puttin' things aside in it, hopin' for a husband. You know, table linens and what not. I thought you might like to have one to keep your fancy English things in. No offense about the husband part."

"No offense taken, Lester. I shall treasure it. Jemma had one when she lived with me in Wicklow."

"Cam made it for her when she was about to turn sixteen. I watched him do it."

Lizbeth raised a brow at the conversation and eyed Helene, then Lester. "Lester," she asked, "have you heard anything about a community retirement party for Dr. Huntley?"

"No ma'am. All I heard is that he's gonna keep his office open until they find a replacement. Seems to me nobody wants to throw a party for him if he's not retirin' just yet. The funeral parlor is changin' hands, though. I don't suppose them sourpuss Boxwright Brothers will be gettin' no retirement party." Lester chuckled.

Lizbeth smiled somewhat. "So many families have gone through their doors in grief."

"Well, sir, I recall one time when a family went through them doors as mad as all get-out."

Helene was always ready for a yarn. "Do tell, Lester."

"The Boxwright Brothers had all them kids, a dozen between 'em, and the whole batch was as wild as jackrabbits, too. The girls weren't so bad, but them boys was always a whiff away from the hoosegow. The only car they had between 'em was an old Packard hearse. Well, sir, them boys was well taken with the young ladies and never went out with the same one twice in a row. Seeing as how there was so many of 'em, they come hence to fussing over the hearse. The oldest of the cousins, Byron and Basil, was all set for a double date. In the meantime, their daddies was all set, too, but for widow Selma Henderson's service. Selma must've been over a hundred years old when she passed on. They had her loaded up and in the hearse for the trip to the church the next mornin'. Well, sir, that night, them two boys took off in it without askin' or lookin' in the back, neither. The Meachum twins was waiting on 'em over to Goshen way, so that old Packard was flyin' along the county road when they smacked right into the Salt Fork bridge. The back door of the Packard flew open and Selma slid out and down to the water. Them brothers had sealed her up good and tight because it never come open. The cousins got banged up bad, but Selma's coffin floated in the Salt Fork all the way down to Pleasant. Her folks come into the Parlor with a shotgun and pointed it right at them boys' daddies. It took the sheriff, a new coffin, and a complimentary chapel service includin' floral displays to persuade them to lay down their double barrel. I figger Byron and Basil didn't hear much in the way of compliments from their daddies for a spell. I heard that them boys went into the insurance business down near Bowie."

"You have a plethora of oral history, Lester. Someone must transcribe these anecdotes for posterity," Helen said.

He hadn't understood a thing she'd said, but he tapped his foot and smiled. He did admire an educated woman.

There was no time for making inquires about the sale of the ranch, and Spencer didn't dare ask Lester as they drove to

Amarillo. It had taken all his concentration to keep this anxiety to himself. Paul wasn't playing fair. If he really had bought the Lazy J, the only option for Spencer was to take his precious wife and move as far away as they could.

The expanses of green burst into view as they emerged from the thick cover of clouds. Pieces of London loomed up like one of Spence's miniature shopping mall models back on the conference table in Chillaton. For reasons she'd never dwelt upon, London had been the place most elusive to Jemma's artistic connection. She'd shown in Paris, New York, Florence, Dallas, and now this beautiful city was about to welcome her, she hoped, like Gram's flowers in the springtime. She reached for Spencer's hand and held on for the landing.

At The Lex, Jemma stood next to a chic banner, "Visions from the Heart — Works by The Artist, Jemmabeth Chase" while Spencer took her picture. She had an irrepressible urge to take the banner home with her.

"Ah, Mr. Chase." Jonathan Essex bowed slightly and forged a smile. "It's a pleasure to meet you, I'm sure. My sister tells me you are an up-and-coming architect. How nice to have two artists in the family. Although I suppose artistic temperaments could ignite more readily."

Spencer shrugged. "That might be the case in some relationships, but with us, the only thing ignited is passion." He kissed Jemma's hand, then looked squarely into Jonathan's violet eyes.

Jemma thought she would melt with joy over that comment as the three of them toured the gallery. She differed with only a few placement choices, but overall, the exhibition was perfect.

A skinny young gallery manager named Fiona followed them and took notes. "If you don't mind me saying so, I have an odd feeling as though the subjects are somehow acquainted with me, but, of course, I've never been to Texas. It's the eyes. They are quite unique. Where did you train in order to capture such intensity?"

"In a cotton patch with a stack of *National Geographic* magazines." Jemma grinned at the memory.

"Lovely," Fiona said and wrote that in her notebook.

Trina had made Jemma a royal blue silk dress with a short jacket for opening night.

Her hair was swept up and fastened with a bejeweled clip that Spencer had given her for Christmas. The prime minister and his wife were scheduled for a private showing, without Jemma's prior knowledge, requiring that Jonathan accompany her for an hour. Her parents, her grandparents, and her in-laws waited in the reception area. Jemma, however, kept an eye on Spence because she sensed that he had something on his mind.

Spencer watched her float from piece to piece in animated conversation. She loved to talk about her work and no audience fazed her. She was just as composed with celebrities as she was with Shy Tomlinson. He couldn't have Paul diffusing that radiance. It was hard enough watching Jonathan place his hand at her waist as they moved around the gallery. She shook hands with the dignitaries, then turned her eyes on her husband. His heart jumped up at that. When the doors opened to the general public, she was able to be with him again.

They made small talk with interested patrons and she was pulled aside for more photographs and the press questions that she disdained. "Who influenced your work? Is there one piece that represents your style more than others? Do you have a particular modern artist whose work you admire? What's it like to be from a small village in Texas and show your work to world leaders? What inspiration would you offer to young artists? How do you explain your artistic gift? Your work depicts the common man. How do you explain its popularity?"

The last question caught her ear. "Our world goes by too fast, and the human spirit often gets trampled. As an artist, I feel that whatever gifts I may have should connect audiences to those small moments in life that they might otherwise miss. There is no such thing as a common man or woman in my opinion. Each of us is uncommon, and I hope one of my pieces will open a heart to a different perspective or attitude. That would validate my efforts."

Spencer and the rest of their family hung on her every word.

Jim exhaled and surveyed the crowd. His baby girl had made all this happen. She had gone through countless pencils, paper, crayons, and paint sets to get to this point. He had scolded her many times for not doing her chores or her homework and choosing, instead, to create art. Now she was reaping the rewards.

He moved through the gathering to tell her that. "You make your old daddy proud, baby girl. Look at this place. It's incredible. I only wish Papa could be here. This is too much for an old country boy like me to handle."

She giggled. "I'm so glad you came. Lots of these people just want to be seen at a show. You know that I paint because I have to, because it is given to me by the Lord. If people want to spend thousands of dollars or pounds on it, who am I to stop them?"

Jim lowered his voice. "Thank you, Jem, for sending your mom and me to visit Matt and Luke's graves. I don't know how that'll play out, but I think it'll be good for me."

"I hope so, Daddy. Gram did it, and I know she's glad. We'll be praying for you. I have to find Spence now. Love you."

She rushed off, leaving Jim behind. He sighed and brushed his cheek with his hand. *The world goes by too fast.* He had heard that all his life, but now he realized that it was true. Even his little girl had noticed.

Rebecca Chase was right at home with the Lillygraces, but Max hung out with Spencer. "When did you know that Jemma was this good, son?"

"You know I've loved her art since the first

grade, but then I've loved her all that time, too; I'm biased."

"She nails everybody she paints. It's almost spooky. I wish that slick crook she wrestled to the floor would show up. I'd like to give him a taste of my fist again. Do you think he knows about tonight?"

"I'm sure he does. Dad, do you know the lawyer's name who bought the Lazy J?"

"All I know is what I've told you. I didn't think you'd be interested, or else we could've put our money together and outbid him."

They were interrupted by The Artist.

"What do you think? Crazy, huh?" She kissed them both. "Come on, you two. Let's get some fancy little sandwiches." She hooked her arms in theirs, and they walked to the reception area. "Guess which painting Mr. Prime Minister bought?" She popped a canapé in her mouth.

"Just so it's not of me," Spencer said.

"Nope. I wouldn't have sold him those. He bought *The Sermon and the Can,* the one of Grandma Hardy sitting in the pew with her chewing tobacco can. Isn't that hilarious? He said that was his favorite."

"Did you get to shake his hand, Spence?" Max asked.

"Only when my wife introduced me."

Jemma grabbed a handful of mini-sandwiches. "Shy's getting his teeth today, and I can't wait to see him when we get back. Let's go catch up with Mom and Daddy. You come, too, Max."

Across the crowd at the gallery, Alex thought she saw him, but dismissed the idea. Then again, how many men in the world could look like that? She excused herself from Jim and her parents and made her way across the room. There he was. Her first reaction was to tell her daughter, but she changed her mind and moved up next to him as he studied the show's catalog.

"Are you a collector?" she asked, heart pounding.

Paul jumped at the sight of her. "Just this artist."

His eyes were jade green. Despite everything she knew about him, he remained exquisitely handsome. He didn't have on the cowboy hat like he did that day in the Wicklow post office parking lot, but he was wearing boots and English Leather.

"You look familiar to me," she said.

"I was thinking the same thing about you," he replied, studying her face.

"Are you Paul Turner?"

"Are you Jemma's mother?"

"We've never met. I'm Alexandra Forrester." She extended her hand.

He blinked and took it. "You look like her," he said, his voice barely audible. "Your voices are the same . . . I guess you know all about us."

"I do. Are you in London just to see my daughter? She's married, you know."

"Yes ma'am, I know. Please don't say anything to her. It's easy for people to misjudge my intentions, but nobody understands how I feel about her. If I hadn't messed up, you'd be looking at your son-in-law right now."

Alex smiled. "My son-in-law is just over there with his wife. I do have some idea of how you must hurt, Paul, but that doesn't mean you should take advantage of her."

"I can assure you that won't happen. I was only hoping to buy a new piece of her art and maybe catch a glimpse of her, but I guess meeting you comes close. I'll take off. Maybe, if you think it's right someday, you could tell her that we met. She's never out of my mind, ma'am; I'm sorry." Paul put his hand out, and she took it without thinking. He lifted her fingers to his lips, and then was gone.

Alex stared after him, her hand suspended in midair.

"What do you think, Mom?" Jemma asked as Alex rejoined them.

She exhaled before answering. "I think you are a remarkable young woman, Jemma-beth, and you've made all the right choices in your life. I'm so proud of you."

A frown crossed Jemma's brow, but then she smiled. She took her mother's hand — the very one — and they began their own tour of the show.

Paul sat in his rental car. Her mother had thrown him for a loop. She didn't have those honey-colored eyes, but everything else was there. It gave him great peace to kiss the hand of the woman who gave her birth. He hadn't told Alex that, before she found him, he'd been watching Jemma for an hour from another crowded corner of the gallery. He had heard her talking with the press and laughing between her husband and another man. That would have to do him for a while.

He thumbed absently through her exhibition catalog, *Visions from the Heart.* He still wanted her heart, even though it was denied him. For now, he'd have to settle for seeing life through her eyes. He should have paid more attention to her work when there was a chance that she loved him. He traced around her photo on the back page. He'd never shed a tear over any woman other than his mother, until he lost Jemmabeth.

He turned to the page with the painting he had just purchased, *Jemmalou's*. It had surely come straight from her heart because he had read her artist's statement, but then he knew already how she felt about her Papa. It was almost spiritual the way she captured the cotton fields in the hawk's eye. He had been so much in love with her that he'd never realized the depth of her talent that summer in Wicklow. The piece tore at him, but it would also be a great comfort when he moved it into his new weekend ranch house on the Lazy J. He hoped to get a glimpse of her more often now that he owned a place in her hometown.

Alex saw no point in telling anybody, at least not in London. She and Jim knew that Spencer had a surprise for Jemma's birthday, and she wasn't about to let Paul spoil it. She realized that he'd kissed her hand out of respect, and she did feel sorry for the guy, but the Lord had steered her daughter back to Spencer, answering everybody's prayers and shutting the door on Paul. He would just have to buck up. After all, he was a gentleman cowboy. He must know something about riding off into the sunset.

∎ ∎ ∎ ∎

The Lillygraces had booked a celebration table at The Ritz Hotel in honor of the birthday girl. It was a slight upgrade from Daddy's Money. After everyone had said their good nights, Jemma and Spencer took a cab to their hotel, kissing shamelessly in the backseat. By the time they got to their room, she had forgotten it was her birthday.

He hadn't. Spencer unlocked the door, and she stepped in. The entire room was stuffed with baskets of roses, delphiniums, and lilies. Resting on her pillow was a flat package wrapped in gold paper and tied with purple ribbon. She gave him The Look he loved as she unwrapped it, looking a bit perplexed at its contents. "Great photo," she said. "I remember this little castle; it's the one at Kilton. What are you telling me? Did you sneak around and plan a trip to Scotland?"

"Could be."

She pulled him down on the bed with her, nose to nose. "Thank you so much, Spence. It'll be fun to get away for a while. Where are we staying?"

"We can stay in the castle if you like, m'lady."

She sat up, her elegant hairdo coming undone. Spencer took out the clip and her hair fell around her shoulders.

"Okay," she said. "Now what exactly are you talking about? If this is a camping trip, I'll have to go shopping and get some clothes. Everything I brought is uptown stuff. What? Why are you looking at me like that?"

"Turn the frame over."

She crawled over him and retrieved the gift from the lamp table. On the back was an envelope. She opened it to find several legal documents, and, after reading the first paragraph, she flipped to the last page, then dropped the papers on the floor, staring at him. "Spencer Morgan Chase, have you bought that castle?" she shrieked.

"Happy birthday, Jem."

She fell on him, pretending to faint. "How do you think of these things?"

"I think of thee," he said and lavished her with birthday affection.

Chapter 26
Gracious Gold

Julia and Arthur had surprised them with their attendance and purchase of the painting of Shy Tomlinson, whom Do Dah had known all her life. British celebrities and strangers toured the show. After two more evenings at The Lex, the younger Chase couple took the night train to Scotland. "The Hottest Artist in Town," as the *Times* had called her, now slept soundly as the train rocked along, but Spencer lay awake watching as the lights of villages sprang out of the darkness.

The last thing on earth he wanted was for Paul to move to Connelly County, if indeed Paul was the buyer. In his heart, Spencer knew that was the case. He also knew he couldn't take Jemma and flee the situation. No, they would have to stick it out — "like it or lump it," as Max would say. Spencer couldn't control Paul's life, but he would have to have a heart-to-heart talk with the man. Surely it was not still a contest between them for her love because he was certain where Jemma's affections permanently lay. It had to be that Paul needed to be near her, to catch a sense of her presence. He understood that, but he could never again allow him close enough to see if her hair held the fragrance of flowers. That privilege belonged only to her husband. God's Great Plan, as Jemma called it, had to be unfolding, somehow, in this quandary.

"I'm never going back to Texas," she said, taking in the view after their long hike. Rugged hills encircled Loch Tarron, and the tiny fishing village of Kilton nestled along the curve of its harbor. "My great-grandparents were born in this village. I belong here."

"We have a major project ahead of us if you really want to move into our castle," Spencer told her.

Jemma inhaled. "I don't care. Even if we never have any furniture in it, we can come here and sit. Everything just looks good enough to eat. See, even the clouds look like perfectly baked meringue."

"Let me show you something." Spencer took her hand.

They climbed the crest of the craggy cliff that overlooked the castle and loch. He wrapped his arms around her waist, and they turned in a slow circle. The ancient Highland mountains gave way to the sea and the Isle of Skye beyond. The moon spilled into the mist of the loch, and the darkening horizon brimmed with clouds laced in shades of orange and gold.

"I could stay here forever with you," he murmured.

Jemma smiled up at him. "Aye, I keep it in mind, you Englishman."

As the mist moved into the hills, it shifted to a soft rain, forcing them to seek shelter under the tangled branches of an old rhododendron. Spencer spread his jacket on the ground as they waited for it to pass. She lay her head on his shoulder. "Spence, I've been thinking about those verses from Numbers that Brother Cleo said over us. God has been so gracious to us. Sometimes I do feel His face shining down."

A bird moved among the rhododendron, sharing its evening song.

"Thank you, Jem, for loving me."

"I'm the one who owes all the thank-yous in this relationship, let's not forget that. Hey, was something bothering you in London? You seemed a little different."

He avoided her eyes. "It was probably business. I guess I have some of that in the back of my mind."

"Business, huh? Spence, please say that our life will always be full of surprises and of this feeling that I can't put into words when I wake up beside you."

"I know that feeling. It's called joy. I can promise you that our life will always be full of love, Jem, and the rest is a given."

"The rest includes sad times, though."

"That's because we're not in heaven yet."

"This comes close, babe. Who else buys his wife a castle in Scotland? Only you. You are my Candy Man, my hero, and the sweetest husband in the world."

"C'mon, I just happen to have enough money to buy castles. It's not very big anyway, and how do you know who's the sweetest husband in the world?"

"I know things." She kissed the little scar on his chin and couldn't stop. The bird sang again, its eyes darting down at the rhododendron.

The rain settled back into a mist without their notice. Jemma sat up and ran her fingers through her hair.

"Let's see what our castle is like in the dark." Spencer pulled a leaf from her tresses.

She shivered as they edged down the trail. "What happened to springtime in the Highlands?"

"Beats me, but this is like a fairy tale, hen."

"Hen? That's not very romantic."

"I read that when a lad likes a Scottish lass, he calls her 'hen,' and I happen to like every bit of you. Since we are land owners here, I thought I should start practicing the language of the land."

"Well, did ya now?" she asked in her best accent and cradled his face in her hands. "I do adore you, Mr. Chase."

He forgot about cowboys and ranches and kissed her palms as the faint sounds of a fiddle drifted across the loch from their hotel. He drew her close, and they moved to the music. The tide rippled in near the castle, lending its own gentle rhythm to the crisp night air. They lingered for a while, whispering and giggling while the mist rose off the loch and settled around the castle.

She clasped the warmth of his hand. "May the Lord bless and keep thee, my husband."

"May the Lord make His face shine upon thee, and be gracious unto thee, Jem." He rested his head against hers. "Now I'm in the mood for some more of that fiddle music. Let's go."

"Spence, I can't even see the trail."

"Looks like we'll be walking in faith, then." Spencer took her hand and they inched along the path, talking quietly about other things.

Their hushed conversation blended into the mist as it suddenly slipped away to reveal the hillside. Far above, the full Scottish moon, with its golden, smiling face, graciously brightened all that lay before them.

ABOUT THE AUTHOR

Sharon McAnear is the author of five novels in the Jemma Series and three books in the Stars in My Crown Series. Find Me a Man Club in Portland partners her penchant for humor, strong characters, and snappy dialogue with Wells' irresistible story of Internet dating.

Sharon McAnear lives in Colorado with her periodically dramatic family. She is currently plotting her next novel and perhaps sneaking added inspiration from her vast collection of Far Side cartoons.

Learn more at: www.sharonmcanear.com

The employees of Thorndike Press hope you have enjoyed this Large Print book. All our Thorndike, Wheeler, and Kennebec Large Print titles are designed for easy reading, and all our books are made to last. Other Thorndike Press Large Print books are available at your library, through selected bookstores, or directly from us.

For information about titles, please call:
 (800) 223-1244

or visit our Web site at:
 http://gale.cengage.com/thorndike

To share your comments, please write:
Publisher
Thorndike Press
10 Water St., Suite 310
Waterville, ME 04901